NINJIRATES

Magia's Destruction

by

Tarrence Bryant Jr.

To all who read this book, I hope I have crafted a story worthy of an investment of your imagination.

And for Grandpa, who has already invested everything I could ask for and the biggest fan and Motivator, I might as well add you as an author, too.

Acknowledgments

I want to thank first my mother and father for even entertaining the idea of me becoming an author and buying me all those books to feed my desire for stories so I can craft my own. I also wanted to thank my friend Jonathan, who I wouldn't have had this story to even begin with if he hadn't played Legos with me when we were younger; I'm still sorry we couldn't write this book together, though. I want to thank all of the people who read my work, which includes Yvonne Durant, Kendra Cacevedo, Belinda Williams, and Valerie Henderson, who gave their honest opinions because the source of my motivation was most definitely everyone who said that I had a good story to tell. I also wanted to thank my unpaid editor, Olivia, thank you for spending your precious summer free time to focus on my work when I knew you had your own work and school to deal with. Thank you for your instant support. Last but not least, I want to give the most thanks to my grandfather because I need another longer book to detail how much you have helped me over my writing journey. There isn't anything else that I could ever ask for than the input, time, and thought you have invested in me. Those Saturdays at McDonald's are better than a college-level course with the best writers in the world.

Contents

Prologue

A tall, robbed figure sat on the top of a lonely hill. The cold morning sun shone on his back, drying off the layer of crisp frost that lay like dust. Small flurries fell, announcing the coming of winter, the start of a larger storm, but the man sat unmoved by the weather. The small flakes of ice fell, sticking to his beard and speckling his forehead. Eyes closed, he took a deep breath and spoke to emptiness. His voice was both loud and quiet at the same time. It was a voice that spoke with experience, age, and wisdom. He seemed to have chosen each word and rehearsed one thousand times before. "It's time," he spoke.

Frost and snowflakes started to swarm on a spot to his left. They grew in frequency and intensity until there was what seemed like a miniature blizzard six feet tall. Suddenly, it stopped, and stray fluffs of ice drifted away from an extremely detailed statue of a man. The sitting wizard was undisturbed. AS the ice sculpture started to melt, it dissolved with such intensity that it started to steam and boil, but it never shrank. Instead, it became more lifelike until the statue was completely gone, and in its place stood the man who was sculpted.

He stumbled forward with momentum and shook his head and arms as if waking up from a daze. "Whew," he gasped, rubbing his face, "You'd think that after all of these years, I would get used to it..."

The first man got up and took his hand. "Diadus, it's been a while."

Diadus gave a smile that seemed friendly but insincere. He offered a firm handshake and remarked, slightly sarcastically, "You're looking older, Parquen." He spoke with an accent that seemed to be faded, like bronze that had sat in a forgotten tomb.

"Looking this old is just another illusion, Diadus." Parquen turned to face the cliffside again and, ever serious, asked, "I'm guessing you want to know why I called you?"

Diadus replied, "Naturally. You could have chosen a better time, though. I was running from a band of pirates and ninjas. They were no problem. It's just that I had a precious artifact with me…"

He reached behind him, and in his hand appeared a picture of Diadus, Parquen, and their master, who had no name.

Parquen stared at the picture, a blank look on his face.

Diadus, with a bit of anger, walked in front of Parquen and replied, "Five hundred years, and you still don't care?" He put the photo back in his pocket and turned back to the cliffside to continue, "Are we really going to give away this gift?"

"Burden," Parquen replied quickly, almost as if he were expecting this question.

"I'm not up for discussing this right now. Is your apprentice ready?"

"He's ready."

"Good," Diadus turned to Parquen and finished, "Bring your apprentice to my school, and we'll complete the cycle." He then turned and started to head back down the mountain but stopped, turned, and asked Parquen, "Do you ever think of our master?"

Parquen never broke his gaze from beyond the mountain, even as a single tear dripped slowly down his face.

Diadus turned and walked away, not waiting for an answer.

Part One: Dimidium

Chapter 1

Balast awoke to the sound of thunder and lightning outside his room. He lived in Castellum Grex, the most prestigious school in all of Magia and Balast's workplace. Lightning was uncommon in the town of Obsecro, even when it was rainy. Balast pulled back his silk sheets and jumped out of his bed in confusion. There were no clouds in the sky, and yet he heard the crackling sound of pure electric energy. He looked around his room. It wasn't the biggest room on the school campus, barely bigger than the broom closet, but it was exactly how he wanted it. It was barren but clean, with only one coat hanger for his magic cloak. He walked over to the door, only two feet away, and grabbed his coat off of its hanger. He had just put it on when he smelled burning wood.

He adjusted his cloak, tightening the sash that went around his waist. He lightly smacked his ivory-colored face to wake himself up and rubbed a hand through his black, spiked hair.

He faced his door, folded his arms, sighed, and called out, "I'll give you a chance to walk away before you get hurt."

Then the door exploded towards him, and a child who looked no more than seventeen years old barreled towards him, vibrant blue sparks flying off him. Balast recoiled from the explosion, blocked the boy's fist, and grabbed him by the neck. The boy thrashed and shot electricity all around the room, hitting Balast in many places. He stood unaffected. Throwing the boy out of the room, he bent over and checked the smoldering remains of his door. He then proceeded to put on his leather sandals and reconstructed the door from charred ashes to its original wooden oak planks. With a wave of his hands, the pieces of the charred door rewound in time; the door became brand new as the pieces floated back into their original places and rehinged it to its marble frame. He grumbled about it under his breath, muttering something about teenagers and his beauty sleep. He stepped out of his room into a huge corridor.

The ceiling stretched to hundreds of feet above them, and there was at least one chandelier every five feet. Very glamorous, though not to his liking. He closed the reconstructed door. When he turned, he found the random teenager barreling at him again. This time, Balast sidestepped and tripped him. He grabbed him from his hair and pulled him up from the floor to look him in the eyes.

"Now," he started to lecture the boy, walking down the hallway and out of the corridor into the courtyard, "What would give you the idea to interrupt my sleep and break my precious oak door that may have cost more than your life?"

His assailant was too busy squirming around in his grasp to answer. Finally, he stopped and looked into Balast's obsidian-black eyes. In a despairing voice, he asked: "Why can't you just *die??*"

Balast was slightly taken aback. After half a beat, he snapped out of it and replied: "You're not the first person to ask that one, kid."

Now, in the middle of the courtyard, he paused at the central fountain, which was pumping out gallons of water in its artistic patterns as it stood. Balast looked up at the full moon and wondered if he would ever have an uninterrupted sleep again. After a moment or two, he turned and threw the boy into the fountain, and all of the electricity in his charged body was released into an explosion of water vapor and loud pops.

The next morning, there was a commotion on the campus. Balast slept till midday, waking up to the chatter of curious students.

"Who was the attacker?"

"Will you find him?'

"I'll fight him for you!"

"Was he strong?"

"Did you recognize his face?"

"Are you OK?"

Balast spoke over the crowd, "Ok, everyone, calm down. I just want to say that he interrupted my sleep, and he paid the price…" An avalanche of questions came after his statement and was soon hushed when the headmaster and a few of the school guards, dressed in standard bronze, parted the crowd.

"Ah!" Balast exclaimed. "It's headmaster Corin!" He walked over to him and put his arm around the short, slightly pudgy man as he asked, "What brings you to my humble abode?"

"We need to talk," he then looked around and whispered, "Privately."

Balast nodded and faced the children, "Ok, students, get back to your classes. I'll comment more on the events of last night this afternoon."

His statement was met by another cascade of questions, and one student exclaimed: "But Headmaster Balast, it's already noon!"

Balast looked around, turning in a full circle, before replying with a devious smile, "No, it's not…" He snapped his fingers, and the sun went backward in the sky. Time rewound exactly four hours and thirty minutes. The students all cheered at the impressive display, but the headmaster had different opinions.

"Balast, come with me." Headmaster Corin beckoned. He and his guards then proceeded to walk out of the grand hallway while Balast waved off the students' other questions.

Once they entered the headmaster's grand office, Balast faced about twenty angered teachers and an extra confrontational Headmaster.

Balast closed the door quietly and said, after a moment, "Are you planning to attack me?" He looked at every person in the eye.

The headmaster spoke up, "Balast, I am afraid we are going to have to ask you to leave Castellum Grex."

Balast looked genuinely surprised. "What?"

"Well," the headmaster started to explain, "We," he gestured around him to the group of teachers of various degrees, "all agreed that since over the past few weeks, you have been attacked about ten times, not including threats upon your life, or the threats of raids, we cannot continue to endanger the students and lose our prestigious reputation as the finest magical arts school in all of Magia."

A look of understanding came over Balast's face, which changed into a look of humor. He replied, "Yeah, I guess my exploits have been consequential…" he then walked to the middle of the room, shook the hand of headmaster Corin and said, "Thank you for telling me. I know I have been kind of a bother to this school ever since my master started it…" He walked towards the door but stopped before he went out. "Oh, also, I can leave all my currency here because I will be going to build my school somewhere else. I trust you will use it to fund exactly one hundred thousand students' tuition." He snapped his finger, and the room filled with gold. From jewelry to coins, the room was filled with precious metal.

"The majority couldn't fit in this room, so it's outside in the courtyard." Then he turned and left the headmaster's office with a smile. One of the teachers by the window fainted when he looked out of it. The courtyard was also filled with gold, almost as high as six or seven feet in the air.

"Balast…" the headmaster said, shaking his head, "…that man is too powerful for his own good."

There was a grand party in the town the night before Balast left. He didn't want to attend because of all the hard work the villagers would do just to celebrate his passing. This was also the exact reason he had to attend: A paradox.

That afternoon, he found himself sitting at the head of a very large table, right in the middle of a grand temple that he had constructed for the town's governing body. From the ceiling hung dozens of egg-shaped lanterns, glowing with a warm yellow light. The fifty-foot table was decorated with table heads, each with a small sculpture of the person who sat before it. Balast's was made of a gold-like substance. There was an immense amount of food, from roast pigs to small plates of tiny waterfowl. Others sat at smaller tables, eating, drinking, and laughing. There were at least a thousand people in that room alone, all of them doing something for the banquet or for him. *I never deserved any of this.* Balast thought.

When everything settled down, Balast stood up and yelled over the crowd, silencing them. He raised his cup of wine and said, "A Toast for the good people of this town!" Everyone cheered, toasted, and had a great night.

Balast was the last one to leave the grand hall. He tipped the groundskeeper handsomely right after he locked the doors. Then Balast walked around the town, looking at the buildings he helped build like he was double-checking the integrity of their structures. He remembered all the things he had done for it and the people with an odd sense of dissatisfaction. He looked up, seeing the sky reflecting his mood as the clouds turned dark and a drizzle started. He tipped his wizard hat down as he continued on the main road, heading out of the town as the sun started to dip below the horizon. He was on the outskirts of the sleepy town when he heard a cry of pain. And cries of pain could not be ignored. He activated a camouflage spell, went invisible instantly, and hurried into a dark alleyway where he heard the sounds of a small fight. He crept around the corner of two large brick buildings and found three boys scuffling about, punching and slapping each other senselessly. It seemed to be an unfair fight, though. As Balast observed further, he saw that the two bigger boys were beating the smaller one down. The fight eventually de-escalated into the two larger boys kicking the smaller one on the ground. They then shrank to about the same size as the smaller boy, and Balast realized they were using magical enhancements to gain an upper hand in the small skirmish.

"Body Augmentation Magic…" Balast whispered to himself. "So sloppy."

The two boys laughed at the third and said, "That's what you get for failing the master." Then, they scurried away and disappeared into the darkness.

The boy that was left behind slowly picked himself up and started walking towards the entrance of the alley where Balast was standing.

He then undid the invisibility spell, "Have you learned your lesson?" The boy jumped backward and almost injured himself even more.

"Who are you!"

Balast took a step out of the alleyway into the moonlit street, and the boy got up and ran. He didn't get far because of his injuries. But when Balast teleported in front of him, he immediately dropped to his knees. "Sir, please don't kill me. I can be your servant, your slave, or…or…" he looked up, and Balast couldn't look him straight in the eye. The boy had a large gash on his face, and it was bleeding down into his eyes. One eye was half shut because of a huge bruise, and his nose was bleeding profusely. Balast saw none of the horrible injuries that he had gained, but instead, he saw a kindred spirit. He saw the pain of living life on the streets, and he saw a replica of himself. He glimpsed a type of raw pain that could not be known by any regular person, and he couldn't hold back a lone tear falling down the side of his cheek. As he came back to reality, Balast composed himself and replied to the boy.

"No child," he touched the boy on the forehead and the boy fell to the ground unconscious.

Balast was a few miles from Obsecro when the boy awoke from his slumber. Balast was carrying the boy on his back in an almost ragdoll-ish way. The boy's arms were wrapped around Balast's neck, and his feet were only a few inches from the ground. Balast noticed the boy's eyes were open and greeted him.

"Finally…" he said with annoyance, "that healing spell might as well have given your body enhancements as well for how long it took." he looked around the windy grassland and saw a large boulder that had been carved into a dome-like shape. It looked like someone had created it specifically for travelers.

He walked over to the rock and sat the boy against the inside wall. Still sleepy, the boy curled into a ball against it. Balast sat on the opposite side looking at the boy with kind eyes.

He's 16 years old, height: 5,11…

"I know Vox…" Balast said seemingly to no one. He turned his head to see a white wolf cloaked in a magical blue mist.

"You know I have the same perspective skills you do. Also, why do you choose now to present yourself?" Balast said with annoyance.

"Is it because of the boy?" Balast said as the figure came and sat beside him. He then heard the ethereal voice again,

It's not the boy… Vox said. *You are using too much magic again.* Balast sighed and turned back towards the boy, who was slowly waking up. He looked around and saw Balast talking to thin air.

"Are you ok… sir?" he said warily.

Balast looked at him, then Vox, and he laughed. "Ah, yes, I'm fine. I just forgot to show you, my magical companion…" he looked at Vox and nodded his head towards the boy, "Go, let him see you.." Vox stood up and trotted over to the boy and bit him squarely in the face. The boy couldn't see what bit him, but he sure felt it. He recoiled onto the back wall, screaming with pain and shock. Balast came over and touched the boy on his shoulder.

"Calm Down! Calm Down…" he then moved his hand over the boy's face and used a sedation spell so the boy wouldn't feel as much pain. The boy slowly stopped squirming and settled down on the floor, breathing evenly. Then he sat back up and saw a supernatural wolf that was almost as large as a lion staring at him. He was a little surprised, but he would have been running if it hadn't been for the sedation spell Balast had put on him.

"Wow…" he said as he walked towards the creature. Vox looked unamused as the boy patted his head.

"That's Vox, my magical manager," Balast said. "This guy lets me know when I expel too much magic." Then the boy snapped out of the sedation spell and realized he was petting a giant magical wolf. He jumped back and put his hands up, expecting a fight. Balast then pointed his finger at the middle of the small enclave they were in, and a fire sprouted from the rocks. The boy flinched but didn't put his hands down. Balast started, "Now I want to ask you a few questions."

The boy took a wary step backward, still cautious.

Balast chuckled, "Relax, kid. If I wanted you to be dead, I could have left you where I found you." The boy sat back against the cave wall, blinking a bit then staring at the magical beast intensely.

"I suppose you want to know why I attacked you?" The boy said.

Balast stared at him, thinking. Observing. "Why the sharp attitude? You were begging for your life when I found you in the alley."

The boy looked around sheepishly and replied, "I thought you were one of them."

"The boys that attacked you?" Balast questioned.

The boy backed up and said, "Yeah, they did," the boy said, looking toward the dirt, tears forming on the cusp of his eyes but then he snapped back toward Balast, "but I don't see why I should tell you anything. I don't know you!"

Balast stood up and began: "Well then…" He turned his back to the boy and walked into the rain. "We can talk on the road. I'll start…"

Chapter 2

As things churned in the great cauldron of time and space, somewhere in the Intervallum seas was a moderately sized ship. On this ship were about three or four dozen pirates who were about to meet their match and seal their fate.

"Boys, I'm telling you, this is a completely foolproof operation!"

Gutbane stood up from his chair, which was so large that it may as well have been called a throne and started walking around the cabin. The walls shook with each landing of his immense feet. Some say that he was the descendant of giants, or that he wasn't human at all. Where there weren't tattoos on his bare chest and back, there were scars, which were worn just as proudly.

His voice made specks of dust fall from the roof of his old, rickety cabin, and he wasn't even shouting. He turned toward the front of his cabin, which was located right under the helm of the mahogany wood ship. "The man who lives on Dragon Tooth Island is a fossil. Most people say that he doesn't even move anymore. He lives in a mansion, and any fool that lives in a palace like that by himself has to be a guardian of some loot." He paused and turned, looking toward the back of his cabin to size up his nervous and slightly excited crew.

"Listen, boys, we've slaughtered entire villages for some booty. This is one old, defenseless man. He ain't going to do nothing."

One man, who very closely resembled a lobster with beady eyes and large forearms, spoke up: "Aye, Cap'n! And, well, we ain't worried about the oldie. It's just--"

"Just... what, Redback?"

"Well, the coin said--"

Gutbane slammed his hand on the table, breaking it into fine splinters. "I don't care WHAT the coin said about 'a mighty warrior' or 'the coming of justice,' I am GUTBANE, bloody murder, Gutbane the SCOURGE, my name is FEARED, this old man doesn't stand a chance."

All the people in the cabin were silent, completely stricken with fear.

"Now have someone rebuild that table. We'll be there shortly."

He exited the cabin and looked over his ship. It was a large ship, too big to be a sailboat and too small to be a freighter. A speedy vessel, the ideal one for a pirate and for an outlaw. Gutbane looked up at the port side flight of spiral stairs that led to the helm of the ship and stared off the boat to look at the open ocean. His mind wandered to the prophecy.

"Ahoy Cap'n!" He was hailed by his first mate, Rat Boots. He was a skinny fellow and a dangerously curious one too. He was skilled in storytelling and urban legends and that was about the extent of his usefulness on the ship.

"Whatchu thinkn bout' cap'n?" Rat Boots asked.

Gutbane looked at him with disgust and then found a reason to talk to him. He leaned on the railing of the ship and asked, "Refresh my mind on what the coin said, hmm?"

"Of course, sir!" Rat Boots said as he rummaged through his pockets, pulling out various items. Eventually, he found what he was looking for: a gold coin no more than three inches across. Words were etched along its sides, looking as though they had been carved in there for years. He cleared his throat and began to read with his high-pitched voice:

"The Destruction shall sail to an island small;

And though the leader speaks

He does not know all.

The Elder shall win

And the younger shall fall,

And the victor shall lose the golden hall.

For years, the one who loses shall prosper

And the winner will roam free.

They will both meet again,

But not as an enemy.

The victor, for better or worst,

Will be washed in the coming tide.

But he shall not die alone;

And the warriors will fight side by side."

Rat Boots coughed. "Well, it's unclear, cap'n, but ya oughta win the mansion, that being that the victor loses the hall. Unless, of course, you are older than him, then that means that--"

"Rats, Shut up."

"Yes, Cap'n."

"Land HoOooOOO!!," came the breaking voice of the lookout.

"There it is boys. Look at that mansion," Gutbane chuckled roguishly, trying to disguise the wonder beneath his off-handish attitude.

There on a small island stood something that could only be called spectacular. It was a mansion that boasted of the owner's wealth and power, one that was telling the world itself that it was owned by the richest person alive. The parts of the building that were not carved out of marble seemed to be made of pure gold. It not only covered most of the island but stretched out onto the sea, where the foaming green waves caused a strange contrast to the shining fortress. On the shore stood a bent old man, watching the incoming vessel, looking unafraid and even slightly relieved that this band of marauders was approaching.

The ship hit the island with a muffled thump, and moments later, the air was filled with the sound of pirates unsheathing weapons, punctuated by hoots and yells. Over the raucous sound, Gutbane yelled down to the man from the stern.

"Ho there, dinosaur! We've come here to do the favor of finding someone to take ownership of that castle you have! Would be a shame if you had no soul to give it to once you passed."

The man looked up to him and smiled. "What is your name?"

"I AM GUTBANE THE SCOURGE, TERROR OF THE 13 SEAS, AND LEADER OF THE--"

"Wow, that's a long title; I think I'll just call you a fool and we can get by with that."

"Unfortunately for you, that will be the last that you…"

"...Say?"

Gutbane sputtered, red with rage. "NO-- you--." He shouted and with one swift motion ripped the anchor off of his own ship, swinging it like a mace on a chain. "I am going to enjoy watching you--"

"I think not." Before his very eyes, the old, hunched person transformed into a middle-aged man, with dark unmoving brown hair. He had piercing grey eyes and a face like stone: cold and hard.

"Now I'm going to give you a choice, fool. You can stay here, in this house; nobody gets hurt, and you never leave." he clapped his hands together, and instantly a sword appeared in them. "Or we can do this the hard way." Gutbane overlooked the summoning magic of the wizard's sword and looked at him with pity.

"And here I thought ye were an old man…" he then wrapped the anchor's thick chain around his fist. Roaring with fury, he dove from the front of the ship, which rocked from the force of his takeoff. He landed on a crater of dust and shouted to the lone figure:

"EVEN YOU SLIMY WIZARDS SHALL KNOW TO FEAR ME!!" He swung the anchor around, and it made contact with the wizard, making a dull thud. The wizard crumbled and fell on top of Gutbane's anchor.

However, as he looked closer, the wizard's body shook, quivered, and then turned into a pile of sand.

Gutbane stepped back in surprise, looking at his hand in disbelief.

"There's no way it's that easy…"

He sensed movement behind him, turning around his eyes scanned the beach angerly. The wizard was sitting down on a chair that wasn't there before, with a smug grin on his face. "Correct. Now we can negotia--"

He was cut short by a roar from Gutbane as his anchor slammed down onto the Wizard and broke his chair in half. Except, the wizard wasn't there anymore. Only a pile of sand.

"Tch. Really, you *are* slow."

The wizard was on his left now, hand on his hips. Gutbane was at his face, yelling so loud that he turned into a statue of sand instantly. "STOP THIS SORCERY AND FIGHT ME YOU COWARD!"

He felt a strong hand, inhumanely strong, grip his shoulder. The pain made him wince and nearly buckle. Nearly.

"Nobody. Ever. Has dared to call me a coward and lived to say anything else. Lucky for you, I don't want anyone to die today." The voice grumbled, surely that of the wizard's.

Pain racking half of his body, Gutbane gave a battle cry and grabbed the arm. He swung the man over his body and down onto the sand in front of him. Then, he quickly spun the gargantuan anchor over his head in a figure-8 and slammed it down onto the sand over and over and over again. The man rolled, dodging each and every blow.

Gutbane heaved the anchor up again, but he jerked to a stop. Crouching, the wizard had somehow managed to get both of his hands clasped on the anchor. He seemed to be pushing his hands together, *through* the neck of the weapon. Before Gutbane could yank it away, the wizard's hands made contact, and Gutbane was driven back in a gigantic golden explosion.

He awoke seconds later on a sand drift, the ringing in his ears sounding like a swarm of bees. He scrambled up the small mound, trying to get away from the wizard, who was stalking towards him. Hundreds of shiny coins fell from the sky, pelting him on his head and shoulders. He looked around and pocketed a few of the golden coins.

"Does your greed extend that far?" the wizard said as he walked toward where Gutbane lay. Gutbane quickly stood up and drew a small pistol out of his back pocket. The wizard was there before he even had a chance to aim it. He knocked the small gun out of his hand, grabbed Gutbane's shirt, and pulled the massive man up to his face. The wizard's skin was the color of the sand that was all over Gutbane, which felt like tiny ants burrowing into his skin. His eyes were dark grey, freezing cold yet intensely hot. His hair was the same color, despite all the dodging around in the sand after Gutbane tried to inflict damage to him. Out of nowhere, the sky darkened, and the sun turned back into the sky. The sun cast dark shadows over the face of the wizard, making him seem even more like a thing of legend. For an instant, Gutbane felt something: Fear.

The wizard drew back his fist and said, "My name is Inferneous. It's been nice meeting you."

Gutbane blacked out from pain that blossomed like a tiny explosion on his face.

Chapter 3

It wasn't the best day when I met my master and became an apprentice. In fact, it was the worst day of my life.

I grew up in a small countryside area called Razing Plains. It was nice living there. I had two little brothers, a hard-working father, and a loving mother. My dreams were filled with the thoughts of becoming an astronomer. My life was a fairytale. The only real thing that made me anywhere near annoyed with my life was the walk to my school.

My father owned a few windmills so naturally, we lived in one. We were the only family in the middle of the plains with a few windmills here and there. I had to walk at least two miles to school every day. That equated to a lot of time not spent with my family. I left in the early morning and came home at suppertime. My family understood that to become an astronomer I had to have an education. As I ate dinner with my family every night, I told them about the things I had learned and the things I had done while at school. I always hoped my parents were proud of me. I played with my brothers afterward in the plains because there was none out there but us, the wind, and the stars. It was everything a boy could want. Until one day...

It was exactly 3:00 in the morning when I woke up. I knew because I had a very keen sense of time. Even in a windowless room, I could tell the exact time the sun set. This uncanny ability of mine came into use when I had to go to school every morning.

I hopped out of my straw-filled bed and walked around my room. It was small and very empty, just how I liked it. I could hear the gears of the windmill turning. It wasn't loud, but it was enough to notice if you were paying attention. I then looked out my little window and saw endless stretches of grassland, the delicate light of the rising sun enveloping it with illumined hues. I couldn't enjoy the sunrise for too long though, because I needed to get to school. I grabbed my books from under my bed and brushed off the dust that had accumulated on them. Then I moved my bed to the other side of the room to reveal a small trap door that led to the entrance of the windmill that doubled as a living room and kitchen for my whole family. I heard the soft snores of them as I stepped out of our house into the cool morning.

It was just any normal two-mile walk to school, through the winding path up the hills that led to the small brick schoolhouse that rested overlooking the whole town. It was a nice little town. From this distance, I could still even hear the chatter of everyone's everyday life. Only, this time, the chatter was different. Louder. Higher. I walked to the school building, pushing open the ancient, heavy oak doors, expecting to be greeted by my friends. Instead, the whole place was empty. I wasn't early. In fact, I was exactly on time. But not a soul was inside. The thirty or so desks would usually be filled by now, but they were barren and collecting dust.

I walked back to the front, and I closed the door so the wind wouldn't sweep all the spare papers lying around away. Then the whole place started to rumble. The walls looked like they were closing in. I can still remember the scream I gave at that sight. I still have no idea how, but the walls had somehow become as thin as paper and were all falling down on top of me. I closed my eyes and covered my head, as I was pelted by… cards. I opened my eyes, and it was as dark as it was with them closed. I can't remember what I did next, mostly because of the terror I was feeling when I discovered I couldn't run. I couldn't even hear myself breathing.

Somehow, I made it back to the outskirts of my city when I could see clearly. It was like I had actually just opened my eyes. Maybe my eyes were closed the whole time. What I saw, though, I will never forget. The whole town lay in ruins. People were, well, let's just say that I found out why that 'chatter' I heard was so off. The first thing I thought about was my family. I turned and ran as hard as I could back through the rolling hills, now burning with ablaze pieces of wood that were scattered about them… My house… the quaint little out-of-the-way windmill that could have been ignored, was caved in, still smoldering.

Sometime after I could pull myself away, eyes still stinging from tears and from the billowing smoke, I saw shadows. It doesn't sound as terrifying as it actually was, but what I saw was living, twitching shadows. They didn't even move towards me at first. They just floated there, twitching and spasming like dying fish, staring at me with their heads that had no eyes. Soon enough, a few *of them noticed me and just floated to me like there was some sort of wind pushing them. I put my arms around me and crouched to the ground, just embracing whatever was going to come next, and that's when I noticed… Light. The shadows were turning into a bright golden light, so bright that I had to cover my eyes. When I opened them, there stood a man, about seven feet tall, with a rough-looking beard. I'll never forget what he said to me:*

"Healing isn't Linear, don't be afraid to show emotion."

I just broke down then and there. I could barely even process what was going on; I fell to the ground, legs given out as my brain focused on trying to understand the gravity of the situation. I'm surprised that I didn't go completely insane then and there. After I had cried until I was thirsty, I stood up and the man said some other stuff, about how his name was Parquen, how he needed an apprentice, and how this whole town had been destroyed by Malums, an ancient unspeakable evil. He told me how I could get my revenge, how I had the strength and clearly needed somewhere to go. I met another guy who had the same amount of skill as me, if not more, who had also been taken as an apprentice by Parquen's friend.

Then, you know how it goes, I was given an incredibly long life, along with this guy Inferneous, who became my best friend. Then after years of getting along, there was an incident… We haven't talked since.

…

"…And that's my story, kid." Balast said, wiping the rain from his hair, "Now can you tell me your name?"

The boy walking alongside him raised his head, "Right. First, why did you two have a falling out? Did he steal your girlfriend…?"

"What? No, I--"

"*You* stole his girlfriend??"

"I'll tell you about it if you tell me your name," said Balast with a sigh of frustration.

The teenager thought about it for a moment and then responded:" Fine. It's Zach. A terribly original name, almost like I was a character in a poorly written book. Now, why did you two split?"

"Zach?"

"What?"

"No, that's *actually* your name?"

"Just tell me what happened!"

"Hey, remember I'm the wizard here and I technically don't have to tell you anything...." Balast got up and looked at the sky and saw that the rain wasn't going to let up. He stopped and looked around. He saw nothing but fields and mountains.

"Zack, run up the road, come back, and tell me what you see."

Zack ran up to the ridge of the next hill and yelled back to Balast, "There's nothing for miles!" Balast looked back at where they came from and there was nothing but fields of grass too.

"You better get some sleep because this rain is not going to stop until morning." Balast then waved his hand and a blanket and pillow appeared out of thin air and landed in front of Zack. He then started floating in the air sideways and said, "Goodnight."

Zack was a little amazed that Balast could just sleep on air, but the shock soon faded after he wrapped himself in the blanket and went to sleep.

Chapter 4

The sky was furious, blindingly dark shade of red. The sun did not shine through the thick smoke that rose from the city. A city that shook and pulsed as if there was some monstrous behemoth trying to break free from it. A little boy of only six years looked around as his district burned around him. As he turned his head toward ominous whispering from a corner that seemed darker than normal, a hideous monster appeared... Six eyes, two jaws with needle-like fangs, and the body type of a snake. A Malum.

It lunged at the boy, twitching and screeching when a burst of flame caught it in mid-leap. The monster writhed and crumpled into an inky black husk, dripping midnight-black liquid as it released an unearthly howl. The boy covered his eyes from the blinding light, shaking all over. When it faded there was a man, standing with one hand in the air, and the other holding a sword. He was wearing a brown scarlet-tailed cloak and an average-looking scabbard. He put his hand down and ran over to the boy kneeling and saying to him softly but steadily, "Hi, my name is Inferneous. I'm going to need you to close your eyes and count to ten alright?"

The boy nodded, with his lower lip quivering and tears leaving streaks on his soot-covered face. Inferneous picked him up and ran back to where he was standing. He turned and looked behind him, where five Malums materialized out of the walls of shadows that bordered either side.

"Nine." the boy whispered.

He turned the next corner and found that the monsters had trapped him in a four-way intersection.

"Eight"

He set the boy down and started speaking spells and flinging fireballs at the nearby monsters.

"Seven"

He picked up the boy again and started running through the gap the Malums had left after being injured.

"Six"

He was almost through them when one grabbed his leg, and he fell. He shot a fire spell at it, and it shriveled, sizzling. He whipped his sword out of its scabbard, and it ignited with a brilliant yellow flame. He swung at approaching Malums, slicing through enemies as a hot knife slices through butter.

He started running again when he panicked. The counting. He turned and saw one of the Malums handling the boy in his arms. Inferneous immediately grabbed the boy out of its hands and blasted it in its face with a fireball, but when his hand brushed the boy's hand, his whole world stopped. *No, not again…* The boy was already dead. A tear rolled down his cheek as he stood there for a moment, cradling him in his arms. He set the boy down and whispered a long spell that incinerated the Malum enclosing him, heating the air until it snapped with a molten flame. The body of the boy was turned to dust and was blown away by an unseen wind. He whispered a teleportation spell as the boy disappeared from his hands. Then Inferneous was gone.

Across the city, the crushing of gravel announced Inferneous' presence as he approached a lone figure, unmoved by the world outside him. The lone figure was whispering a lengthy incantation.

"We must strike now, Balast." Inferneous said, walking up to where Balast sat, no longer muttering his spell.

"Balast, the only way these people can be safe is if we strike first-"

Balast started, ignoring Inferneous' remark. "I've tried to close off this hellhole, but there is no spell strong enough. I need help evacuating the people."

"We almost cleared half the city. That should be enough for most of them to be safe while we attack their leader.

Balast stood and turned to him saying, "But, what if the Malums go to the other half of the city?"

"What if they never stop, Balast?"

"It doesn't matter!" Balast yelled, "I have *seen* what these things can do, Inferneous; they are not safe!"

"And you think I *haven't*?!"

A shockwave went through the ground as a tower toppled in the distance. The tremor caused the crack in the ground in front of them to grow even larger. Inferneous walked toward the giant fault, talking as he walked.

"*None of us* are safe until these things are destroyed, no matter how far we run."

"*Run?!*" Balast shouted, "You think I'm doing this to save my own skin?! There are *families* there, Inferneous. They can't defend themselves, but we can." He grabbed Inferneous' shoulder.

Inferneous spun and smacked Balast's hand off rather forcefully. Heatedly he responded, "Don't touch an angry wizard, or that may be the last thing you do."

"You really think you can quote my master?" Spat Balast.

"You only wish you could," said Inferneous with a grimace on his face, almost as if it hurt to say it. "I just watched a little boy die." Inferneous looked at Balast, "He could have been saved if we were strong enough to fight back."

"I have watched many die, many who could have been saved if they had been given *time,* Inferneous." He drew his sword and deflected a beam of searing heat thrown by Inferneous. Balast clenched his hands into fists, and his body glowed a purple radiance. Inferneous readied into a fighting stance and the air around him grew hot. Both bodies tensed, ready to attack, but before they could do anything the ground started to quake.

The buildings around them shook and the small trees creaked and groaned. It was an unnatural kind of shaking, one that seemed to even break the foundations of their minds. The rift edge they now stood on began to break and crumble, forming a monstrous hole.

Both wizards snapped out of their fighting mindset and scrambled into action. Intense dark smoke began to pour out of the hole, forming into unnatural, twitching shadows.

"The People!!" Balast stumbled over a piece of fallen rubble while disintegrating a clump of shadows. He was running to the edge of the city shouting: "INFERNEOUS!! The people!!!"

Inferneous didn't hear him. Couldn't hear him. He was covered by shadows, which were pulsing and emitting unearthly howls as they were being sliced and slashed as Inferneous summoned a flaming sword. He reached out in front of him and an explosion erupted where he gestured, propelling a ton of bricks down onto another group of shadows, crushing them into a thin grey smoke. His sword and sliced through another and the pieces fell to the ground, causing the severed shadows to wither and dissipate into the air. He then got up and faced the enormous condense of shadows in front of them.

Then, "It" came. Rising from the rift in the earth like smoke rises from a burning pyre. A whale-sized thing of darkness. It had huge, muscled arms and wielded a crude-looking sword that was as dark as the air that surrounded it. The sky pulsed with energy as it gave an ear-shattering roar.

"It's a Demonium. An Innominatus Demonium." Inferneous said with fear.

The monster stared at him, but its attention was turned to the caravan of people that Balast was leading from the city. It walked towards them, monstrous footfalls from unknown feet shaking the ground and breaking nearby structures. Inferneous took off after it, wincing in pain from a wound on his leg.

Balast saw it last and wasn't able to react fast enough. The monster's massive tentacle slammed into a nearby building, and Inferneous sliced it seconds later, and it fell to the ground, squirming. Balast locked eyes with Inferneous as he fell to the ground, a concerning cut on his forehead and multiple wounds on his arms and legs.

"Balast. Balast! Wake Up! We need to get to cover!"

Balast looked at him then shook his head warily. Inferneous looked at him then sheathed his flaming sword and threw Balast over his shoulder. He ran up the street and into a small inn that had a large hole in the front. He set Balast up on the wall and kept checking behind him to see if the thing was following him. He looked back and heard Balast whispering something, but he didn't listen. Looking back outside the hole they came in from he saw the flickering shadow of the Innominatus Demonium heading for the civilian ships that were still being loaded by the city's army.

"Balast, I'm going to buy us some time." Inferneous then walked back out the hole they came through and started gathering his magical energy. *I'll transform this beast into something harmless…* he thought.

He then ran straight to the beast. With his spell literally in his hand, he used his Enhancement magic, felt the sinews in his legs strengthen and tighten, then launched himself into the beast with his right hand forward. He was inches away from the beast when, from the corner of his eye, Balast appeared at his side with his left hand forward. Around his hand was an invisible energy that made his hand shimmer back and forth, as if it were moving back and forth in time. Balast and Inferneous collided and then tumbled into the beast. There was a blinding light and the last thing Inferneous felt was a burning pain in his right hand…

Then he woke up.

"What a nightmare." Inferneous whispered to himself. He rose and stepped out of the cabin. Inferneous looked up from the Mahogany deck of his ship or, more accurately, the ship he commandeered from the band of pirates who raided his island. He looked at the stars, then looked at his scarred arm and noticed that in his hand lay a peculiar coin shimmering with what must have been a magical nature. He had gotten the coin from one of the crewmates called Rat Boots.

"Time to try this out." He got up in a cross-legged position and examined the coin. *I don't feel any magic coming from it…* he thought. He then flipped the coin into the air and almost fell from the power that radiated from the coin in the air. When it landed in his hand, he dropped it due to the heat released from the coin because of the magic expelled from it. It landed on the deck and settled on heads. *That means I get my wish.* He thought. He asked into the air.

"Am I headed in the right direction?" The coin sat in its metal silence, which disappointed Inferneous.

Rat Boots (his real name was Leonard, but he liked the nickname) shuffled up from the crew quarters, replying groggily: "Your answer will be on the rim of the coin."

Inferneous turned and addressed him, "Thank you Rat Boots." He turned and picked up the coin and said without looking at him. "You can go back to your quarters."

The scrawny kid yawned and returned as Inferneous read the inscription on the coin:

'Regret lies

On the road not taken.

The path you lead

Will make it unbroken.'

He turned and looked out at the open sea. The water splashed as some type of dolphin dove back in. "That's rather…" he said as he sat back down. "Rat Boots!"

A few seconds later, Rat Boots responded from below and answered, "Yes sir?"

"The coin gave me the wrong answer!"

"You have to be very specific about it sir!"

Inferneous made a face at the coin as he flipped it up into the air again. Right before the coin hit the ground, Rat Boots yelled out from below deck,

"Also, make sure it lands on heads! If it lands on tails, it disappears!"

Inferneous went wide-eyed and stared at the coin… it landed on heads again. He breathed a sigh of relief, picked up the coin, and asked,

"Am I going to the right *location?*" he looked at the side of the coin and it said,

"There's no place like home.

Unless that place

Is where others roam."

Chapter 5

The old boat creaked and groaned as it bumped into the rickety dock. Inferneous looked out the window of the captain's quarters, surveying the place where they landed. *It looked,* he thought, *like the greyest, seasidey-est' town I have ever seen.*

The shore was a thin strip of smooth gravel. The houses all looked like they had seen better days. And worse days. They seemed like the people though, hardy, grizzled, and tired. Most of them you could see where the building materials had collapsed and failed. There were holes in every house from loose stones. The houses nearest to the beach had a thin layer of white on the walls facing the ocean, showing the salt that had built up from the ocean spray. The whole scene was blanketed by a thick, soupy, layer of fog.

Inferneous sighed. *Home sweet home,* he thought, and got up out of the gaudy chair that Gutbane used to sit in. Before stepping through the door, he snapped his fingers, and the chair went up in flames. When the fire died down a few seconds later, the chair was nothing more than ashes. *Good riddance...* he thought as he walked out the doorway and down the flight of stairs on the starboard side of the ship. Rat Boots was already on the dock, marveling at being on dry land again. He had a backpack almost larger than him on his back and was carrying it with no difficulty. Inferneous walked down the dock just and asked Rat Boots,

"Are you ok with that bag? It is literally twice your size and probably triple your weight..."

It's completely fine sir." Rat Boots replied immediately. "I have suffered more than you can imagine under Gutbane." he looked down at his shoes, eyes darting and shimmering with an orange hue, obviously reviewing a bad batch of past memories.

Inferneous looked at the boy and put his hand on top of his head. "Those days are over, kid."

Rat Boots looked up at him, blinking tears out of his eyes. Inferneous then continued forward into the portside town of Reditus.

The fog became so dense that they had to walk slowly to keep from tumbling off the weathered docks and into the frigid water below. After walking for nearly fifteen minutes, they entered a makeshift town that was full of makeshift shops and makeshift houses. They were walking on when Inferneous' stomach started to rumble. He was about to suggest that they find a place to eat when Rat Boots started talking.

"Hey yeah, so you want to find somewhere where we can eat somethin? Dried kelp, y'know, sticks to the roof of the mouth and makes my tongue taste all rubbery."

"Sure, yeah alright." Inferneous turned a corner and seemingly out of nowhere, there was an entrance to a warm-looking tavern called *The Windowless Soul*. The tavern seemed to add an orange hue to the street through the windows in the front of the tavern, making this the first instance of a color other than black, blue, or grey.

"Look kid, there isn't the best crowd in this town, so just try to keep the odd comments to yourself, okay?"

"Yeah sure, I know how to look out for myself," Rat Boots replied, sniffing indignantly.

They were about to step through the doors when Inferneous paused. Rat Boots asked: "What is it?"

They waited in silence for a minute or so when Inferneous shrugged. "Usually someone comes flying out--" He was interrupted by the shatter of glass as a stocky, scarred man broke through the leftmost window. Inferneous grinned. "*There* we go."

He pushed open the double doors and stepped through. There was a vast contrast from the cold, shrouded outside. In the tavern were about twenty or so people, chattering, bartering, and arguing. There were the occasional brawl as certain arguments were "discussed." Inferneous walked cooly to the counter, dodging a poorly aimed projectile here or there, with Rat Boots trailing behind him.

The man behind the counter was quite an unexpected character. He was a rather average-looking man, with a pleasant face and a large, curly mustache. He looked like he hadn't seen one day of work in his life, even though he was middle-aged, and his hands looked as soft as the expensive velvet suit that he wore. He was polishing a large grandfather clock when Inferneous walked up.

"Be with you in a second, traveler."

"No time for friends, then?"

The man spun around at the sound of Inferneous' voice, a wide grin on his face. "Inferneous! Why I'll be! The last time I saw you must've been about thirty years!" He pulled Inferneous into a hug over the counter.

Inferneous returned the hug rather awkwardly. "Seems like you've made a living for yourself since the last time I saw you, Grahmn."

The man laughed, stepping back. "Well yeah, that's a story... for another time." He gave a small chuckle as if remembering an old joke. "Well, what have you been doing with yourself these past years?"

"Ah y'know, built a mansion, sold the mansion. Bought a boat, er, stole a boat."

Grahmn released another laugh, patting Inferneous on the shoulder. Rat Boots had already sat down next to a large, beefy man with sausage-like fingers and a nasty-looking scar on one arm. Grahmn cleared his throat, "So what can I do for you two?"

"First off: do you still have that fizzy, sorta semi-sweet brew that your great-great-great-grandfather used to make? I haven't been able to find it anywhere else."

"Let me check..." Grahmn went rummaging underneath the counter, and Inferneous kept talking.

"Second, I was looking for some new attire. As you can see," he gestured to himself, even though Grahmn was still under the counter, "I am in desperate need of at least decent if not fashionable clothing, I suppose.

"Third, I had heard rumors about a certain group of uncharacteristic individuals that have been causing the town some, I dunno… 'trouble'?"

Grahmn returned with a glass flask that contained a light-pink, sizzling liquid. He pulled out two tall, thin, glass cups and started filling them with the rosy, popping fluid. "So, you heard." His voice dropped to a whisper, and he leaned closer. "In all honesty, Inferneous, they aren't the real trouble."

Inferneous took the glass from him and took a sip. "Ahh. Good stuff." he gestured with his hand, telling Grahmn to continue.

"Well, it goes like this. About 10 or so years ago, all of us in this town decided to form a small militia of sorts. Y'see, we've had trouble with bandits, marauders, ninjas, and such. One kid in particular, his name is like…Mace or something like that. He takes control of this situation. He hired some mercenaries too but… Look, Inferneous, the kid has potential, but being honest…

"Anyways, the group couldn't do much, but that didn't matter for the first, I dunno, seven or so years. Most of the time, pirates avoided the town because they heard that we have actual arms now. So recently, this one nasty group came in. We figure our boys can take em, but *our guys* end up destroying a quarter of our land. Now everything is up in the air. Honestly, I'm surprised you two didn't get mugged on your way here.

"The boys formed a group of their own with some ridiculous names. Now they try to take on pirates at least once a week. Usually, they end up destroying more property than enemies." Grahmn shrugged, "This town has been through worse, Inferneous. We just need *our soldiers* to stop fightin'."

Inferneous leaned forward and set his empty cup down on the counter. "I think I can help with your problem, Grahmn. Actually, I think your problem can help *me* more than you know."

Grahmn let out a laugh. "Well then, I'll toast to that!" He picked up the other glass of the peach-colored substance and drank it in one gulp. In an instant, his eyes changed to a pale pink color that seemed almost the same shade as his drink. He blinked twice, in an attempt to reenter the gate of reality and gazed down at his empty glass.

Suddenly, his head snapped in the direction of the man sitting next to Rat Boots, rage on his face. Inferneous chuckled and got off of his stool, pulling Rat Boots with him. Grahmn grabbed the man by the collar of his shirt and pulled him towards his face. He somehow lifted the man over the counter and off of his feet, even though the man was a foot taller than him and outweighed him by at least 200 pounds. "YOU BRAGGART! YOU STOLE MY DRINK, DIDN'T YOU!?!"

The man shook his head viciously, on the brink of tears. "N-no sir, I-I can get you a new one, I--"

"LIAR!" Grahmn shouted, spittle flying on the poor man's face. With one mighty growl, Grahmn lifted him up and threw him towards the one unbroken window of the tavern, which shattered, frame and all, as the sailor broke through it. Grahmn stood where he was before, chest and shoulders heaving with heavy breaths.

His face flushed instantly, and his eyes became his normal shade of hazel. His breathing became normal, and he straightened his tie, saying, "Ah gosh, somebody broke that window too then? Odd, I never actually catch the person who destroys those things…"

Inferneous shook, jaws clenched, battling the tide of laughter that obviously wanted to escape. Rat Boots looked at Grahmn, confused. Then he looked at Inferneous, the expression on his face more confused than it had been when looking at Grahmn.

"Well, thanks for your hospitality, Grahmn. We'll be on our way then. Oh, by the way, where do you think I can find this militia?" Inferneous said, walking toward the door.

"They usually hang around the entrance to the town to kinda check everyone entering and exiting but be careful if you're going over there. The buildings have taken a good beating from the amount of fighting." Inferneous nodded and headed toward the door.

"Thanks for the information Grahm. I'll see you around."

"Ok then, Inferneous! Don't be a stranger!" Grahmn said, a cheerful smile on his face as he waved goodbye.

As they walked out the door into the night, the man who was thrown out of the window went limping back into the bar, cut up and bruised.

Rat Boots watched him going in, now totally confused. "Why did he just go back…?"

Inferneous shrugged. "Can't find his drinks anywhere else."

"And that huge freakout? What the heck was that about…?"

"Well, that's just his cross to bear, but he doesn't actually know about it, and everyone is too scared to bring it up. It deters bad crowds from his place, so I suppose you should just let sleeping dogs lie." Inferneous looked down at the broken glass beneath their feet and then looked at Rat Boots, thinking.

"He might appreciate an apprentice, though…" Inferneous said, still staring at Rat Boots. Then he shrugged, and they continued to walk into the night.

Little did they know, a scout was watching them from afar. Behind the building across from *The Windowless Soul* was a short black-haired man donning a white tiger mask. He stared at Inferneous and Rat Boots as they walked to the nearest hotel. He chuckled under his breath as he ran away towards one of the boats at the island's dock. He knocked on the boat two times and then waited. A minute later two figures stepped out of the shadows behind him. One had a larger and more fearsome tiger mask on, while the other wore a green and white dragon mask. The one with the tiger mask had a hulking build and looked like he could snap the scout in half. The one with the dragon mask on was a woman with a thin frame. The scout turned around and kneeled and bowed his head to the ground at the sight of the woman with the dragon mask.

The scout spoke.

"Master, I have found the one you seek. The Flame weaver Inferneous."

The woman looked at him and asked in a demanding tone, "And where is he staying?"

The scout bowed again and continued, "They are staying at the Fog Masters Inn."

She then looked at him with satisfaction. "Good work, Bryan. You have served your purpose well."

"Thank you, master-" he was interrupted by an arm choking him from behind as the man with the tiger mask slowly suffocated him until everything went black.

Chapter 6

Inferneous woke in the dead of night with a blossoming pain in his right hand. Turning his head he saw that his hand was engulfed in flames. He sighed and shook it to put it out, but it only made the fire grow bigger. Now fully awake, he groaned, got out of bed, and started to search for something to put it out, holding his arm above his head so that he wouldn't catch anything else on fire.

He was in the Fog Masters Inn, on the second floor. The room that Rat Boots had bought them was said to be the best room they had, even better than the manager's bedroom.

They must have low standards, Inferneous thought as he looked around the room.

It was built out of old dry boards (like the rest of the inn). They creaked at the slightest movement, whether a gust of wind or a stray mouse. On the left side of the room was Inferneous' bed, next to a huge wardrobe that contained a few left-behind rags from the previous resident. On the far wall were the heads of their beds. There rested a dirt-covered window, which gave a large view of the town, when the fog wasn't covering it all. On the right side of the room, Rat Boots was sleeping soundly in his bed. Inferneous smiled after remembering he said that it was, "the most luxurious room I've ever seen!"

I guess it's not that bad... he thought.

Then he remembered that his hand was on fire.

He moved carefully to the bathroom, floorboards squealing in protest with each careful step. He entered the small bathroom and viewed it with disdain, mentally taking back his thoughts. It smelled terrible and the only things inside were a hole in the wood for a toilet, a bucket filled with water with a moldy rag on the side, and a mirror facing the entrance. He lowered his hand into the water bucket that acted as a sink, sighing in relief as it evaporated in a cloud of steam. Looking up at the mirror, he saw a shadow move from behind him, disappearing in the darkness.

Now fully awake, Inferneous glanced around at the steam that had gathered around him. He grabbed a handful of it and seemed to mold it into a ball. He stepped out of the washroom, a ball of steam in his hand. Suddenly he dropped to the splits, as two daggers whipped through the air and pinned themselves on the wall above him, right where his head had previously been. He jumped up and flung his ball of water vapor at his unseen attacker. His attack was met by a light "oof!" as the ball of steam broke, releasing its gas with a hissing noise. His attacker went off running and vaulted out of the open window. The room quickly filled with the foggy substance, until it became hard for Inferneous to see a foot in front of himself. He leaped over his bed and landed at the foot of Rat Boots's, crouching.

"Hey, we gotta go," he said to Rat Boots, his voice urgent.

Rat Boots mumbled something that sounded like 'omelet package' and sat up when Inferneous tapped him again. Inferneous knocked him back down and then said: "Meet me outside." And took off running to catch their assailant.

He took a running leap out of his window, seeming to forget that they were on the second story of a building. He hit the ground and rolled with his fall, the bottom of his shoes scraping against the rocks as he stopped at the end of the hotel's long gravel walk. He scanned his surroundings and only saw a few beggars and drunkards walking around aimlessly. The assassin had departed in the darkness of the early morning.

Rat Boots came running out of the entrance. He had both of his legs shoved into one leg of his pants, so he was tripping while he rushed to assist Inferneous. Inferneous gave a sigh of frustration and tore his eyes from the horizon, patting Rat Boots on the shoulder. "That guy's not coming back. We might as well get some rest before sunrise. I think it's going to be a long day."

The next day Inferneous woke up early in the morning. He heard a commotion outside. He walked downstairs and saw outside the window there were people running away from the pier.

Rat Boots came down the stairs behind Inferneous, bags packed and ready to go. He asked worriedly, "What's happening?"

Inferneous was about to answer when the roof collapsed beside him. He dodged just in time to avoid the debris. He got up and wiped the dust off his face, ready to attack. Just as he was about to lunge, a face popped out of the wooden rubble, followed by a head and shoulders. Its owner was a man with dark caramel skin. He had golden fiery eyes and shining golden hair, covered in a fine layer of dust. He had a broad pirate's cutlass in hand and was wearing a heavy-looking chest plate. He didn't look fazed that he fell through the roof as he got up and looked around. He gave a goofy grin that made it seem like falling through a layer of wood beams was enjoyable. He climbed out of the rubble and looked out the window. "Hey you," he said, turning then pointing at Inferneous, "Which inn am I in?"

Rat Boots ran to the soldier in distress, "Sir, y-you just came through the ceiling!"

He looked Rat Boots in the eye and asked again: "Which inn am I in?"

Rat Boots took a step back and broke eye contact, responding, "The Fog Master, or summin' like that..."

The fighter gave a laugh. He paused for a moment, looked out the window, and laughed again. "*Wow,* he threw me *far.*"

Up until this point, Inferneous had been silent, staring at the newcomer with his hand on his chin. Thinking. Calculating.

"I've thrown farther." Inferneous instinctively said. He then looked at the stranger's armor and weapon and recognized that it wasn't normal for a regular citizen to have armor that shone as brightly as the stranger's.

"Hey, are you a part of the militia?"

The stranger became serious once more and turned to look Inferneous in the eye. "The name's Jayce... Fog Master."

Inferneous stared back into his eyes. This had become a contest. Neither one dared break eye contact. The blond-haired man squared his shoulders and clenched his jaw. Inferneous smiled. After another moment, Jayce backed off, and Inferneous chuckled, shaking his head. "I applaud your effort," he said sarcastically.

The soldier gave a sigh of frustration and started to walk away. "Whatever. You should know that I have important business right now. *Very* important… Stuff. Yeah." He put his arm on the doorway, turning back to Inferneous and Rat Boots. He took a breath, as if to deliver a comment but exhaled instead. Then he turned and walked away with a nod of farewell.

Inferneous rubbed his chin so hard Rat Boots could almost see the sparks between his forefinger and thumb. Inferneous strode toward the door in mild haste. "Come on, Rat Boots," he said as he walked onto the gravel road in front of the Inn. "I think I've found my apprentice!"

Rat Boots trailed behind him as he strode towards the sounds of shouting and the sound of steel clashing together. "Wait, I thought I was your apprentice…" Rat Boots said, with a tone of disappointment in his voice.

Inferneous chuckled. "Well kid, you would make a good apprentice, but not to me. The life I lead is too full of danger for someone like you. I don't mean to offend, but you would do better at something slightly more mellow."

He put a small piece of parchment paper in his hands and said, "Turns out I was right, Grahmn is looking for an apprentice, and you check all the boxes."

Rat Boots unfolded it and stared at the paper for a moment. He looked up, saying, "Yeah, that does make sense." Inferneous was scratching the back of his neck, awkwardly.

"So… anyway. Let's go see what's happening over there." He gestured to the street where the sounds of battle were coming from. The ring of metal and the distinct smell of sweat and blood.

Rat Boots rubbed his nose with the back of his hand and composed himself. "Yeah yeah, sure let's do that."

Inferneous was halfway up the hilly slope of the town when a building with green paint and in the wide windows different types of clothes displayed with their prices written on a folded piece of paper on the floor in front of them. As Inferneous calmly walked forward to examine the building, it exploded, showering him with a hail of timber and tiny pieces of stone. He jumped back and waved his hand upwards, causing fire to erupt around himself, protecting him from the debris. Suddenly, a large chunk of cobblestones hurtled past him. He breathed out in anger and the firewall disappeared as he waved his right hand, firing small balls of fire in the debris. The chunks exploded into smaller pieces, embedding themselves in the walls of the buildings around them. When the dust settled, Inferneous dusted off his shirt and waved back at Rat Boots

"Alright, I'll see you around."

He nodded and stepped away, with a wave of his hand. *It's better this way...* He thought, trying to reassure himself. Before he could make the crest of the hill, Rat Boots grabbed his arm. "Thank you, Inferneous."

Inferneous smiled and said, "You're welcome." Another large explosion drew his attention, "You should go back to The Windowless Soul. Things are getting wild."

Inferneous ran over the hill, almost tripping on some of the debris as he gawked over the mess of destruction. Buildings that had been torn apart, giant cracked in the ground like some beast had clawed into the ground, and a few bodies scattered here and there.

Inferneous turned to the building that had its first and second floors on display. The whole front wall of the building was torn down and splayed in front of itself to the point you could see through it into the plaza behind it. He stepped into the building and watched his step as he crept through the shattered remains. There he saw a large skirmish taking place. He nodded in affirmation, thinking, *so this is what Grahmn was talking about.*

There were about a dozen or so young-looking fighters dressed in makeshift armor. They each held a thin golden-bronze rod in their hands, with a round spearhead on the end of each. Every once in a while, one of the fighters would point their weapon at one of their opposers, and the tip would launch a brilliant orange projectile. More often than not, they would miss, and the energy bomb would hit something, exploding with a loud bang.

Their enemies were dressed in black garb, which looked like those of an assassin. Each wore a painted mask that represented an animal more or less fictional. They were good fighters by the looks of it and either fought with a long, razor-sharp dagger or with nothing at all.

The mercenaries (or what Grahmn called "militia") were fighting one ninja per person and hurting the nearby buildings more than their enemies. At the center of the fighting was the young man who had crashed through Inferneous' inn earlier on. He was fighting a man twice his size, who had a heavy-looking quarterstaff. He wore a distorted rhinoceros mask that Inferneous could have sworn he had seen before. Jayce was attacking and defending with surprising skill, acting completely nonchalant about the incoming assault. The man with the rhino mask swung his quarters staff and Jayce backed up out of the man's reach. Stepping left, pivoting his right foot, and twisting his waist to land a blow to the ribs of the man with the rhino mask. He smiled, putting one hand in his pocket and turned his head towards Inferneous, who had just stepped into the clearing.

"Had a feeling you would stop by, Fog Weaver," he remarked, looking bored. His right arm was still defended against the man with the Rhinoceros mask, and he was starting to push the offensive. He looked back at his attacker as if remembering that he was fighting. Turning back to Inferneous, and putting his index finger up, he said, "One second."

But his attacker had lost attention. All of the fighters had. Instead of fighting their opponents, all had turned their attention to Inferneous. Blocked the next attack from Jayce, who backed up from Inferneous, recognizing him immediately. The man with the rhino mask saw Jayce's concern and struck, swinging his staff upwards, smacking the battleaxe out of Jayce's hand. He swung it around again, and it connected with the metal chest plate Jayce wore. Jayce fell to the ground, rolling on the ground. He took the momentum and planted his feet to help him stand back up, putting his hands up and breathing heavily, but he still had a glint of adrenaline in his eye. He looked at the huge man with the Rhino mask on and stepped forward, ready to attack again, when his eyes flitted back to Inferneous, causing him to trip and as he fell the man with the rhino mask grabbed Jayce by the neck and held him up in the air. Jayce squirmed and yelled, "Put me down and fight me!"

He continued struggling until he heard Inferneous say, "Put him down," the man with the rhino mask did what Inferneous said and backed away from Jayce. Inferneous stepped down into the small ravine the Ninja's and Mercenaries had carved into the land with their magical abilities. He patted Jayce on the shoulder and said, "Great fighting, *Captain.*"

Jayce shoved Inferneous' arm aside. "What are you doing here?" he looked around and saw that everyone had stopped fighting and had separated into two groups. On the right of Inferneous and Jayce were the rugged mercenaries that Jayce had brought and on the other side were the Ninjas.

"Take your mercenaries and go get a drink. These people are here for me."

Jayce huffed and stepped back with the other men as he watched Inferneous saunter up to the man who he had fought. "From the animal on your mask I know you're not the leader, so state your purpose."

The man knelt on one knee, and head bowed. He said, "My master challenges you to a battle on Fog Mountain at midnight tonight."

Inferneous put his hand on his chin and smiled. *Just what I've been looking for...* he thought excitedly. He waved his hand and said, "Alright, begone with you."

The man with the rhino mask on stood and bowed deeply to Inferneous then stepped back into the group of Ninjas. One particular ninja, with a splintered Jackle mask, waved his arms and started calmly moving his hands in a circular motion until a black circle appeared between both of his hands. He turned the circle, and the Ninjas started to give off a cloud of black smoke. It disappeared after a few seconds, leaving only rubble in their place.

Inferneous turned and put his hands together. "Well, that means that everything is going swimmingly! Drinks on me!" he said to the group of skeptical mercenaries.

They all stood for a moment, grisly silent. Eventually a soldier who was just a few years younger than Jayce raised his hand. Inferneous looked at him and said, "Yes, young man with the battle axe."

"How did you tell them off? And uh…Who are you again?" he said, putting his hand on his battle axe. The group was getting restless and were handling their weapons and grumbling and saying all kinds of things like they were preparing for a battle.

"Who's this guy ta' tell us,"

"He looks barely older than Jayce,"

"He's got to have some weight if he told the ninja's off…"

Inferneous looked at Jayce and said, "You better get your men under control, or this town may not have anyone to protect it anymore."

Jayce turned and yelled into the crowd. "Shut UP! Do you not see that he just single-handedly drove off our enemy?" The men calmed down after he properly yelled at them. Jayce turned back to Inferneous. "Anyways, thanks for helping us, I guess… can you tell us your name… please?" he added with a slight pause.

Inferneous looked up at the fog-covered mountain and said, "My name is Inferneous, Weaver of Flame." He looked at the group, expecting expressions of shock and awe, but got nothing but blank stares. "And I used certain 'Persuasive techniques' to drive them off."

Jayce started regardless, "Well, let's go get some drinks at the Windowless Soul before we all get some rest to fight another day!" The men behind him cheered and started walking back through the damaged building that Inferneous came through.

Before Jayce could follow the rest of the men, Inferneous stopped him. "I want to offer a proposition," he said, looking the young man up and down. "I want you to be my apprentice."

Jayce looked at him in confusion. "No," he said, shaking his head.

"Why?"

"I can't leave my men behind. I've been through too much with them to leave suddenly."

Inferneous smiled, "Who said you would leave them?"

Jayce scratched his head and said, "Well, I saw you come in on your ship today with only a boy, so I thought that you didn't need a crew." Jayce then folded his arms, "Plus, I don't really know who you are and any man who can call off a platoon of High Shadow Ninja's without the proper mask and with shady 'Persuasive techniques' can't be a nice company."

Inferneous gave a sudden laugh. "Well, you sure are observant!" He walked through the hole in the building and turned to look up at the massive volcano called "Fog Mountain."

"I want you to come with me to face the High Shadow Ninja leader. I want to show you what you will be inheriting as my apprentice." He turned and walked in the opposite direction of the mountain and headed for *Windowless Soul.*

A few hours later, the mercenaries were all drunk and the three had been at least three people thrown out of the windows, but no one kept count. Inferneous sat at a table with the young man with the battle axe, Jayce, and a few other people. Inferneous was staring at the ring of his mug. It was his third one and he didn't even feel a bit delirious. The conversation was a bubble of unintelligible chatter of drunken sailors and soldiers until someone shouted out Inferneous' name. He slowly looked at the young man with the battle axe and saw that he was probably the drunkest one at the table. He was a well-built young man with brown hair, brown eyes, and a freckle here and there. His accent spoke of his homeland in the southern part of the continent and his clothing confirmed it. He was wearing a heavy leather coat and reddish metal knight pants.

"My name is Morrowsine, Holdren Morrowsine." he held out a limp hand to Inferneous. "What's yur name?"

Inferneous chose not to shake Holdren's hand and replied, "I told you, Inferneous, Fog Master and Weaver of Flame."

Holdren with his flushed cheeks, gave a smile. "Ok, Holdren, how did you get those fancy titles, hmm?"

Inferneous shook his head at the very drunk man. "My name is Inferneous and it's a bit of a story. Plus, you're drunk, you won't remember any of this."

Holdren slammed his hand down on the table gaining the attention of everyone that sat around it saying, "Every man has a bit of a story, Holdren! I'm only asking for yours!"

Inferneous gave in and leaned back into his chair. "Well then, I grew up here."

"Yeah?" Holdren said, taking another swig of beer.

"I was a strong child." Inferneous continued. "I actually helped build this town when my father decided to invest in the local bar…" he gestured around them. "I loved fighting, and he loved drinking, so this was the best place for me and him after my mother died." He paused and it seemed like the world paused with him. "I mean it was something. My father funded the business while the original owner was running it. Eventually he grew old, and he wanted me to take over the bar in the place of the original owner who was also very old. My friend Grahmn over there," he pointed towards Grahmn, who was talking to a man at the bar and cleaning a dish. "He was my best friend at the time and his father was the original owner. I thought it unfair to take a business from a family and he had already been taught how to run the bar by his father, so I decided to leave the ownership to them. My father was a bit disappointed, but he grew to love Grahmn like a second son. After I made sure things were settled here, I left and fought in an arena. I was mildly good, but I couldn't even defeat the fifth-biggest fighter. I grew frustrated and I ran into my master, Diadus."

The room fell to a hush. Every man in the room, drunk or not, was quiet. Holdren looked at Jayce, completely sober. Jayce then looked at Inferneous with a worried face and asked, "Did you say Diadus?"

"Ok, I know that my master wasn't a popular man before people tried to assassinate him but-"

"Tried? Tried to?" exclaimed a man from far back. "My great-grandfather was on that mission with his father, and he only escaped with one arm intact! The people who survived went insane from how powerful he was. My father would beat me if I even spoke his name! Plus, that was too many years ago to count! He is dead!!" The rest of the bar cheered at the man's speech and resumed the drunken bar aura.

"I know my master was a bad guy before…" Inferneous looked around then lowered his voice. "But before he taught me, I didn't think it was this bad…but anyways, my master taught me how to fight properly and I beat the grand Champion a year later." he smiled and got up from the table. "I have to go defeat a High Shadow Ninja leader right now…plus I would rather not talk about the rest."

He patted Jayce on the shoulder, signaling him to follow but Jayce waved his hand and said, "I'll catch up with you." Inferneous shrugged, "Ok," he said, walking out of the bar door. He started walking down the road when Jayce came out and ran up to Inferneous. "I'll go with you because I don't want these 'High Night Ninjas or whatever they're called to come back." Inferneous smiled. "Glad you decided to come."

They walked for a good bit, walking past the entrance of the town, which was still terribly destroyed. The hilly plains, which glowed slightly blue as the moon, were illuminated from the slightly damp grasses making the ruins look more like shadows against the sky. They walked on a dirt path until the dirt turned into gravel, indicating they were at the base of *fog mountain.* Jayce spoke, "So, how do you know these High Shadow Ninja's and why does the leader want to challenge you to a duel?"

"Well, I used to be a part of them a long time ago. Back when they really first started." Inferneous responded, eyes glazing over as he stopped to look back at the way they came, as if looking back on his past. "Must have been a good 60 years ago at this point."

Jayce turned to look at Inferneous and as they continued to climb the steep mountain, he saw Inferneous' true age for a second. Inferneous' seemingly flawless skin flickered in an odd way, like it wasn't real and as Inferncous looked at him in the eyes, there was a sparkle of wisdom that betrayed the illusion of his youth.

"How old are you really? An apprentice of Diadus would have to be older than anyone I've known before."

Inferneous chuckled. "Well, I've lost count. I could recount my age by experiences I've had, but the rest of my story isn't something to brag about really. I am just a traveler and a wizard who has been blessed with a life longer than he deserves. Jayce saw Infereneous' face drooped as he thought about the past.

"That's probably not true…" Jayce said, climbing until he saw the crest of the mountain.

The whole top of the fog mountain was flat rock. A dark obsidian ground blanketed with a blue misty fog that was illuminated by the bare moon. Inferneous sighed at its beauty taking off his shoes as they reached the top.

"Ok, this is where your journey ends," Inferneous said to Jayce while taking off his satin flowing red silk cloak and sword and setting them on the ground. Jayce looked confused, "Why are you setting your weapons down? I thought this was going to be fight…?"

Inferneous smiled, "The concept of a 'Real fight' has been lost in the development of weapons, the only people who have kept to the best ways of fighting are the High Shadow Ninja's. Plus, they love one-on-one fights." Inferneous turned to Jayce and said sternly, "You are not to interfere in the fight no matter what. For your own safety."

He then stepped into the mist, and it cleared immediately as if it was running from him. It revealed about twenty or thirty High Shadow Ninja on the other side of the flat space. They were all kneeling, facing Inferneous and Jayce and in the middle of them was a black painted wagon that had black drapes, decorative red wooden pillars, and a black dragon crest on the top.

"Oh, that is not the person I was expecting," Inferneous said.

Jayce looked confused as a woman dressed in a black training uniform and a dragon mask walked out of the drapes. She walked until she was a little farther than five feet from Inferneous and said, "Fog Master." and bowed. Inferneous bowed back saying, "Erica Gutbane."

Jayce stepped back in shock. "Wait, WHAT?"

Inferneous looked back at Jayce with a smile of pleasure from his shock, and then he put a finger to his lips.

"I don't appreciate your lack of formality, Inferneous." Erica said, rising from her bow.

"Well, how am I supposed to keep track of the multitude of names you've had over the past decade? Straight Shadow, Dragon Behind the Moon, Bane of the Sun…there's so many I can only remember the most ridiculous ones." Inferneous gestured to the High Shadow Ninja's behind her "What are they here for? Hopefully not to violate any rules that your clan created for this duel…" Erica's face was hidden behind the dragon mask, but Inferneous could tell she was angry. He could feel the vibrations of her heavy footsteps and could see the mist of her flow behind her as her breathing increased. She stopped and spoke,

"They are a safeguard against any trespassers that might sabotage the integrity of this duel."

Inferneous looked behind him and back at Erica and said, "Well, that must not be me and my friends because they wouldn't dare interfere or even climb this mountain…." Inferneous put his hand to his chin and smiled, "You must have made more enemies. Probably ten-fold more than when I met you-"

"I am rather insulted by your words." She stepped forward, spread her feet, assuming a solid stance, then put her hands up, ready to fight. Inferneous smiled and shook his head, muttering under his breath, "Always getting to the point, you are."

They both stepped forward under the darkness of the clouds until the back of their hands touched. Inferneous stared down at Erica, who stared back at his now magical glowing eyes, and she flinched as if reacting to a thought. She then closed her eyes and breathed, trying to gain her composure, but when she opened her eyes, she saw that Inferneous was smiling. A bad feeling set in Erica's gut as she witnessed the smile, it wasn't murderous exactly, just excited.

The clouds parted and as soon as the moonlight hit the obsidian surface the whole top of the mountain began to glow with a light orange tint and for a second Jayce could see below the ground into the mountain and saw lava and fire bubbling beneath the surface slamming against the cap that was the obsidian. He would have enjoyed it more if Inferneous and Erica hadn't started their fight.

Erica, in a vain attempt, swept Inferneous' front leg with her back leg, planted it in front of her, and then raised her other leg to come down onto Inferneous' face, but Inferneous wasn't there. Her kick landed in thin air to stomp on the obsidian with a thump. Her eyes went wide as she looked up to see a flaming fist coming at her face. She reacted appropriately, dodging to the right, onto the side of Inferneous' exposed torso, but she was incorrect in thinking he wouldn't respond two times faster. A blow from Inferneous' left hand caught her in the stomach. She managed to block with her forearm, but in truth, it didn't matter. She lost all the air in her lungs after the punch and Inferneous wasn't fazed. Instead, as she looked up to try and regain some oxygen, Inferneous remarked, "I'll only use my arms for offense this time." He then raised his right hand and slammed it into her face, shattering the mask and sending her rolling back to her men.

Jayce only saw Erica crumple then roll back to her men. The blows Inferneous threw were only bright flashes of light that left burn marks on the shattered pieces of her mask on the ground. Jayce opened his mouth in shock as he saw Erica slowly standing, raising her hand to the ninjas who rushed to help her. As they backed off she turned back toward Inferneous and Jayce saw her face. Her cheek was a deep blue but that was the only color that was apparent on her face besides the hazel brown of her eyes and the blood dripping from her busted lip. Her face was palely thin and sickly, but her hair was still tightly woven into a bun and she still looked like she was trying to keep appearances.

"Wow, it looks like I was right." Inferneous said, stepping forward to Erica. "Tell me you concede."

Erica then jumped into the air, spun, and landed a back kick to Inferneous' face, knocking him back a few feet. He immediately closed the distance before Erica could properly land and slammed Erica into the ground with another wide right hook. Jayce watched in silence as she tried to stand and Inferneous pushed her over and said,

"I'll give you one more chance. Swallow your pride; don't forget what happened between us and the institution you are holding up right now."

"DO IT!" Erica yelled, "Kill me and solidify my place among the greats!" Jayce saw that from the ground she smiled in an insane way, but tears streamed down her face as she faced the kneeling Inferneous. Inferneous frowned and shook his head. He then raised his fist and it glowed bright as it set aflame.

"I tried, don't say I didn't." He reared back and was about to end Erica when he heard a set of footsteps running behind him. He dropped to the ground a second before a battleaxe could slice his head off. He rolled away and jumped up to see Jayce grabbing Erica's hand and pulling her to her feet.

"I told you not to-" Inferneous stopped when he heard the commotion of multiple drunk mercenaries climbing the mountain behind Jayce. Jayce turned around to see the whole of his mercenary group climbing the mountain. He heard Inferneous sigh in exasperation, anger, and a hint of something else he couldn't really tell. The mercenaries took one look at them and all gathered behind Erica and Jayce, drawing their weapons facing Inferneous.

Erica looked around and her gaze landed on Holdren who stepped between them and asked, "You two alright?" she nodded and wiped the blood from her lip and yelled out, "Inferneous, let's duel! With all of our men combined, this should be a proper challenge for you, right?"

Inferneous looked around him in disbelief. Ninjas and Mercenaries standing side by side at every angle, aiming all sorts of weapons at him. Remembering that they were fighting earlier that day was uncanny. No dialogue had been uttered between them. They all just united against someone they believed was evil. Most of them were just following the leaders they trusted. He then looked at the odd duo of Erica and Jayce stepping forward to lead the group, and then he nodded and smiled.

"Yeah! We don't like quiet nights anyways." Holdren said, putting his arm around a ninja-like they had been friends.

"And to think you were all fighting each other earlier today," Inferneous said, his face contorting into a frown, trying to hide a wicked smile. Jayce and Erica exchanged glances.

"I think she understands that she was overwhelmed by you. Me and my guys don't discriminate against who we fight with, but we don't like unfair matchups." said Jayce.

"You have passed the test Jayce and Erica." Inferneous said, smiling even wider. Everyone was quiet and still bearing their weapons toward Inferneous as he continued, "I have a proposal for you and Erica. I want both of you to be my apprentices and I want both of your crews to join us so we can become legends of the high seas."

Erica's brow furrowed. "You want us to become your apprentices and our crew to become pirates?"

Inferneous rubbed his chin. "No," he started as he snapped his fingers and said, "You already are!"

Jayce looked around him and realized they weren't on top of the mountain anymore. They were all on a boat a mile out to sea.

"Now, I can either defeat you all in battle in which there will be only two survivors." he pointed to Erica and Jayce. "Or you all can become a part of a greater experience."

The ninjas and mercenaries alike started to back off of Inferneous and sheath their weapons. Only Erica and Jayce remained opposing Inferneous. "You think you can just intimidate us into doing your will?" Erica questioned, looking to see if Jayce was with her. Jayce was hesitant but he stood his ground against Inferneous. Erica unprovoked swung at Inferneous. He dodged and slapped her, and she fell to the floor unconscious. As his back was turned, Jayce took the initiative to surprise Inferneous from behind but all he saw was a glowing orange fist before he was knocked unconscious.

Chapter 7

The morning sun was just awakening over the rain-drenched earth when Balast shook Zack awake. "Hey, kid, we should start walking. We've still got a ways to go."

Zack grumbled, muttered something incoherent, and rolled back over, ignoring Balast's request.

Balast gave a sigh of frustration. Then, waving his arms around in a circular motion, sat down with his legs crossed and his hands over his head. He held his eyes closed, and slowly, the wet grass around him started to dry up. All of the water was emptied from the wet soil around them like a sponge being squeezed, and the droplets from blades of grass were gathering together, forming large goblets of water. This all gathered into a large, rippling ball of water. It spun in a clockwise direction fast enough for small droplets to fly off but not enough to really take away from the mass. Balast moved it with his hands until it was floating about five feet above Zack's sleeping body.

"Okay, last chance to get up."

"Or what? You'll drag me there?"

Balast let the water drop onto Zack. He shrieked as the cold liquid burst over him like a waterfall. Sputtering, he exclaimed, "Well what?! That?! *Why?!*"

Balast, gathering his sleeping materials, started walking down the road. "Don't worry, you'll dry along the way."

A few days later, they arrived at the town. It was a place that, Balast thought, was nice at a point. The brick and metal buildings now had fallen into disrepair, and the road was reduced to a broken, pothole-filled mess. The buildings looked much worse with holes, rotted wood, and broken windows on almost every home. Besides that, there were poor, homeless people on the streets in plain sight and groups of mercenaries and thugs lurked around looking for trouble. He gave a sigh of contentment and, rubbing his hands, said, "This is the place."

Zack looked at him in shock. "*This* place?! Look, this is where I came from. People here want to kill you. *Dangerous* people." He cleared his throat while looking at his feet. "And I suppose they want to kill me too."

"Exactly," said Balast, putting his hand on Zack's shoulder. And without another word, he walked into the town. The road they went down led to the business sector of the town, which wasn't different from the entrance. On one side there were stone and mortar buildings that all really looked similar. It was very loud because shopkeepers were yelling out their items in the hope of getting someone who wasn't poor to buy them.

"Balast, we have to get out of here… we could be ambushed at any minute! I don't think there is an innocent person here." he said pulling on Balast's sleeve, "What are we doing here anyways? Where do you think you're going?"

"We are here to build my school," Balast said, looking for something among the stalls.

"Well, can't you build your school somewhere else? This town is full of scumbags and thieves!" cried Zack.

Balast took his focus off his search and looked Zack in the eye. "Now listen Zack, I'm going to teach you a lesson," he looked around and saw a homeless man on the street and a soup vendor a few feet away from him. He walked up to the homeless man and touched him on the shoulder. The homeless man had torn rags on, had dirt all over his face, and shaggy, uncut hair. He flinched back when Balast touched him on the shoulder. "Excuse me sir," he said.

In a grisly voice, the homeless man said, "What do you want?"

"I was wondering if you would be interested in a job position." the homeless man looked at him in confusion and then despair.

"I don't think you want me to work for you. There are people who will kill me and you just because we showed our faces."

Balast smiled. You could tell he hadn't done so in a long time because it was crooked and unsure. His face contorted in a way that made it look like he was more trying not to grimace by upturning the corners of his mouth than genuinely trying to smile.

"That's alright sir. I have the power to fix that." Balast hand started to glow orange. He pushed on the man's nose, and it shrunk to half the size it originally was. Then he touched over his eyes and his eyes changed to a sparkling blue from muddy brown. Balast then summoned a mirror and showed the man. He was shocked and amazed. "Now," Balast stood up and said, "Follow me." he started walking towards a soup vendor with Zack and the homeless man.

"Excuse me sir," he said.

The vendor stopped yelling, "Hot Soup!" and looked at Balast. His face showed years of selling soup and doing it single-handedly. "Do you want some soup, kid?"

"No sir, I just wanted to let you know that my friend here would like to work for you if you could provide at least one meal a day and seeing as you look understaffed, this might be of benefit to you."

The vendor looked at Balast and asked, "The small one or the big one?" he said, looking at Zack and the homeless man.

"This man right here sir."

He motioned for the homeless man to come closer. He walked slowly up to the counter of the stall right next to Balast. The vendor looked skeptical but then his face softened. The homeless man's new face reminded him of his son who went off to war.

"Fine," he opened the small gate on the side of the stall and let the homeless man in. "There's a bed in the back you can sleep in. I'll have you working first thing in the morning."

The homeless man turned to Balast and gave a confused and surprised face. "R-Really?"

Balast nodded his head. "Now friend, tell me your name lest I fail to see you again." he put his hand out to shake.

The homeless man grabbed it tightly and said, "My name is Jack, Jack Septem." he said with a still slightly awed face.

"Well Jack, have a good day." he nodded his head to signal Zack to follow him as he walked away from the soup vendors' outlet.

"You see Zack? Even though it may seem like only evil is present at the moment, Good is always there if you search and Magic can help you find it."

The two walked along the straight of the road until they came across a decent-sized shop with a sign that said "Carpenter" on it. They entered through two large swinging doors and found a lavishly made interior with a rare type of wood called Lifeweed.

"Oh my…" Balast said, looking at the walls. Even though they were glowing with blue pulsing lines with purple wood filling the cracks, he wasn't surprised about the awesome light display.

"Zack, be careful not to touch the walls. The plants they are made out of are life-sucking monstrosities that only grow upon the dead things in nature. The person who made these walls is not to be messed with."

They walked up towards the counter that was also made of the same wood as the walls. Zack walked up to the counter, set his hand on the counter, and screamed, "Balast, I can't move my hand; it burns!"

Balast tried to take the boy's hand off the desk, but Zack's complexion, growing paler by the second. Balast could see the bones in his hands, and he acted without thinking. He slammed his hand on the counter and the walls, and the counter glowed with a blue hue. The door and windows exploded out onto the street. Zack removed his hand from the counter and regained the blood in his face and his hand.

Balast put his hand on Zack's shoulder asking, "Are you ok?"

Zack looked scared for his life, but he nodded as he rubbed his hand. Balast took his hand off the counter and the walls glowed purple now, but the pulses were weaker than before.

"What in Diadus's name is going on out here?!" A short man with a thick, wiry pointed beard came out from the door behind the counter, stared at Balast for a second, and retreated back where he came from. There was noise of whispering and it sounded like two people were talking, more like arguing, in hushed tones. The arguing ceased a moment later and the small caramel-colored man came back to the counter. His small body looked like wood, knobbly and brown. The pale tone on his face added to his complexion. "Can I help you, sir?" he placed his hand on the counter, not suffering from the effects of the wood.

Balast reached out his hand to shake, "My name is Balast and I'm looking for someone to build my school…" the carpenter stared at Balast's hand for a moment before shaking it.

"My name is Gareth, Gareth Heldmoore and if your mind has ever crossed the idea of Lifeweed, you should know my profession and my talents." Balast grimaced hard and froze when he touched the carpenter's hand. *It seems like the second I step out of my comfort zone they find me…* he thought. It had been a few awkward seconds of Balast staring at Gareth when Zack pinched Balast's arm to wake him up. The sharp pain brought Balast back from the depths of his memories and he retracted his hand back to his side.

"Yes, I know that you are very skilled in collecting Death Roses and other dangerous objects, but I am here for your talent in carpentry." He looked at his hand and realized that it was dirty. He wiped his hand on his pant leg, but the dirt didn't come off. He looked back up at Gareth and continued, "How much exactly will it cost to buy forty acres of land and for you to build about five three-story buildings and a pit arena?"

Gareth laughed. "You are a funny man. I would love to build a masterpiece of a city, but the time and strength are beyond me."

Balast raised his eyebrow, "So, you would do it for free if you got the chance?"

Gareth looked at him and frowned. "This isn't a world where you can just conjure things like that. Plus, I would still do it for a price. Now tell me what you need so I can tell you one."

Balast sighed. "I am being serious. Name your price."

Gareth's eyes closed. "Six million gold," he said firmly.

Zack's jaw dropped and he looked to Balast, "Does that kind of money even exist?"

"Such an amount does exist, but I am a little short of your price Gareth. I will return to you in a month. I suggest you prepare the materials."

Balast turned and walked out of the store with Zack at his side. As soon as they exited the shop, Balast grabbed Zack by the arm and pulled him into a narrow alley.

"Hey!" Zack exclaimed, shoving Balast's hand off his arm. "Could you at least warn me when-" he stopped talking when he looked at Balast. Balast's usual face of contempt had twisted to something that gave Zack goosebumps and made the hair on the back of his neck stand straight. "Balast, I don't know if I did anything wrong…" Balast raised a finger and Zack jumped.

"Listen, Zack," Balast started, "What we just experienced in that shop was something I don't want you or anyone else involved in, but I'm afraid that it's already infested this town. I need to know if you want to come with me. I took you from Obsecro thinking that it would be enough to give you a new start in life, but if you follow me, it may be the end." He looked out the alleyway to make sure no one had noticed them and turned to Zack. "I need you to make a decision…"

Zack weighed his options. Leave this town and fend for himself or have one of the most powerful wizards ever at his beck and call? "I'll stay with you. How bad could it get anyway?"

Balast sighed and his face returned to normal. "You are going to regret that saying. Now," they both stepped out of the alleyway and Balast continued, "What is the name of this town? The sign at the town entrance was so damaged I couldn't read the name."

"Tywardreath, a rough translation is "Town of Dying Breath." The people that built this town were known to have short lifespans, so they kinda had a gloomy outlook on life." Balast eyes lit up a tiny bit and he said, "I think I have an idea how to make six million gold."

It had been a week and Zack still didn't know what was going on. He had a leather vest, pants, a cloak just like Balast's, and a brown oversized wizard's hat. He was standing in front of a purple tent with a sign that said "Life Extensions" with an arrow pointing toward the entrance to the tent. The tent was set up in the market with dozens of other vendors selling all kinds of things. People came and went through the streets, mostly not paying any mind to him but he wasn't aware because he was quite nervous that the wrong people could come down the wrong corner at the wrong time any minute. He set the sign down on the ground and ran inside the tent.

"Ok, can you explain to me what I am doing out there looking like a fool with this stupid hat on?" Balast was sitting at a small glass table that was levitating all by itself. He had his arms crossed over the table with his head between them, seemingly trying to sleep, and was sitting on a barrel they found in one of the alleyways.

"Have more respect for elders. You almost ruined my spell." he put his head back down and continued to sleep. Zack wiped his face with frustration and a little bit confusion. "What spell are you talking about?" he didn't get a reply and as he walked outside again, the busy street was empty. Zack looked around, baffled. He ran back into the tent and exclaimed, "Balast, everyone's gone!" Balast woke up again and said, "Calm down and go back outside. You just entered my pocket space." Balast put down his head and went back to sleep.

Zack looked around in confusion and walked back outside to the bustling town that he came from. He became even more confused, but he picked up the sign and started waving it around, hoping his flailing motion would attract someone's attention. Balast came out an hour later and saw Zack beside the tent, fast asleep with the oversized hat over his eyes. He shook Zack awake and shouted,

"Zack, where's the sign?"

Zack groggily replied, "What sign?" Balast rolled his eyes and wiped his face. "How in magic's name did you lose track of a wooden sign…?"

Zack sat up and started picking at the weeds at his feet saying, "People around here will steal almost anything. You should know this. You're like two hundred years old, right?"

Balast shook his head. He looked around at the crowd passing by. Mostly human, but there was a good amount of magical beings in the crowd. Balast's eyes glowed a light blue as he used a spell to view the crowd in a different way. He soon found what he was looking for.

"Sir! Sir!" he called to a little blue man who had pointy ears and no pupils. He only had a mossy tunic on and a wooden basket on his back. He froze in place as he saw Balast and Zack running towards him. "Sir, if I am correct, you are a Blizzard Goblin, right?"

The goblin looked dismayed and replied, "Yes…"

Balast continued, "Then I understand that your race has an extremely short lifespan…"

The goblin sighed, "Look, I've been ripped off by a few different 'magicians' who say they could expand my lifespan before, so thanks, but no thanks…"

Balast flicked the goblin on the forehead and Zack could see the consciousness fly out of the small creature. The goblin started floating slightly above the ground and Balast turned and started walking back toward the tent while the goblin followed him. Zack was alarmed but followed reluctantly into the purple tent.

Zack whispered, distressed, "Ok, I wasn't aware that we were straight-up kidnapping people but as long as I get a fair cut, I'm fine with it."

Balast turned to Zack and shook his head. He sat behind the glass table and grabbed one of the Blizzard Goblin's hands. A bright blue flash blinded Zack before the goblin woke up.

"Congratulations sir! Your life has been prolonged by seventy years!" the Blizzard Goblin smiled, jumped, and cried for joy and said, "Thank you sir! I'll make sure to tell all my friends and family about you!" he ran out of the tent, skipping on his way.

Zack looked at Balast, "Should I go catch him?"

Balast stood and put a hand on the boy's shoulder, "No, you have been in too many manhunts for your age. As you heard, I extended his life by seventy years and Blizzard Goblins only live twenty. He was exactly nineteen years old, so I saved his life."

Zack looked at him and said, "Umm…are we working a charity then? I'm not good at helping people."

Balast sighed, "We are going to earn money by extending people's lives, Zack. Especially beings who don't have very long lifespans."

Zack's mouth dropped open. "You can do that? I wouldn't mind having a few more years at the end of the rope…"

Balast looked him in the eye and said, "No."

Zack was offended "Why Not? You said that traveling with you could be the end of my lifespan. Why not extend it?"

"That logic doesn't make sense, plus you don't have a goal in life. A few extra years of life would be torture down the line."

"What do you mean by I don't have a goal in life? I have plenty of goals!"

"No, you don't," Balast said, putting a firm hand on his shoulder, "You have been orphaned and that makes you ambitionless. The importance of parents and a healthy community fills your soul with desires that make you want to live life. You…"

Balast glance at him while sitting back down at the table, "You have grown up around the wrong men and women. You also have grown up to have a cold lie buried in your heart that says, 'Only I matter' because that was the truth in the gutters of this town."

Balast paused when he realized Zack was crying but continued with an even harsher voice, "I explained your whole life, didn't I? Suck it up. It only gets worse." Without concern Balast went back to sleep, while Zack ran out of the tent into the cold day.

Balast woke with a yawn and stretch. "Alright, the pocket spaces are ready. Has anyone shown interest toward the tent?" he said to the open air.

He looked around in the darkness of the tent until his eyes adjusted to it. There was no one there. "By magic...Where has that boy gone?"

Balast stood and walked out of the tent to see the barren streets. Everything was silent. His eyes tried to adjust to the further darkness of the town, but human vision could only go so far, so he would have to resort to magical means. Balast shook his head and whispered a light incantation that made his eyes glow with white light, allowing him to see in the dark. He walked the length of the road until he saw a group of men laughing and drinking. He was quite a bit away but there was no light with them, and it was pitch black out, so they shouldn't have been able to see each other. Balast took a closer look and saw that on each of the men's necks rested a black vein that led from under their clothing straight to their eyes.

A Malum fusion? Balast thought, confused at the notion that some ordinary men could fuse with a low-level Malum. It would usually require a massive amount of Lifeweed exposure to even begin the process.

I wonder how bad their infections are... Balast thought as he crouched down behind a stall. The men stopped drinking and laughing when a light appeared opposite them. It was two young boys, and in the middle, Zack was struggling to free himself from their grasp.

"Here's the failure." the first boy stated. "To think he would come back after such a pathetic loss." Balast rolled his eyes as he realized that these were the same boys that beat up Zack in the alleyway, he found him in. They were twins with such striking similar features that they appeared to be one individual. The only way Balast could tell who was who they were by their scars. The one on the right had a scar that sliced through his right eye and the one on the left donned a scar through his left eye.

They were named aptly on this defining characteristic by the men, "Righty and Leftie, what excellent work again. You boys are surely going to getn' a good word to the boss for this."

The first man stood and walked toward Zack. He wore all black leather with shining silver armor pads on his shoulders, thick furred pants, and heavy metal boots with a large silver axe at his side. He was bald and had teeth that jutted out from his bottom jaw, indicating he was not only human but maybe half orc or troll. He spoke in a guttural tone, "So, why have you come back to this rotten pit of a town boy? Must be somtin' special if you failed an important mission." he put his face close to Zack's and Zack pinched his own nose.

"I haven't killed him because he was too powerful for me! Did you and the boss think that I could defeat him with only one? Have you ever eaten anything other than fish and onions?" Zack said sarcastically. The half-orc grabbed the top of Zack's head, and his hand almost encompassed his face and neck as he shook it around.

"You better be careful boy. Don't you remember my name? I used to give you yur job straight from the boss."

Zack fanned in front of his nose. "Sorry, I think your breath is giving me amnesia."

The orc shoved his face to the ground, which sent dust flying into the air. "You better start remembren' or else you might end up dead or even worse, unprotected in the gutters."

Zack muttered, "I hate you Spuma." The half-orc smiled and raised Zack's head to his face. "Now that you know yur place, what have you brought me?"

Zack shook his head to the best of his ability. "Nothing, I just came back looking for another job."

"That couldn't be true. You know the rules! The only way you get ta' see my face is by bringn' me something of value. Now what is it?" Zack was defiantly silent.

Righty threw a wooden sign that Zack had been carrying earlier that day.

Zack sighed and shook his head. "Of course it was you."

Righty slapped Zack on the side of his head. "That'll teach you to lie again-"

"Ey!" Spuma boomed as he thumped Righty in the chest, sending all of the air out of his lungs.

"Don't be mean te yur companions! That's my job," he punched Zack. Zack fell to the ground, coughing hard from the pain.

Leftie and Rightie stood him up again, and this time Spuma grabbed him by the throat. "Tell me where the wizard is so I can kill em' myself, then maybe you can grovel at my feet, just like you did before."

Zack struggled to breathe, but with a fire in his eye, he managed to squeeze out, "No." Spuma squeezed harder, making Zack feel the pulse of his own blood rushing to his head. Suddenly, Spuma's eyes rolled back, and he fell to the ground unconscious. In his place stood Balast. Zack stood up quickly as Righty and Leftie stepped back and dropped the lanterns in shock, shattering them.

The other two men at the table were already out cold and slumped headfirst into their drinks lying on the table.

Balast grabbed Zack's shoulder and nodded. "Your bravery and selflessness have proven you worthy. Such great traits deserve to be guided to a worthy purpose." He looked past Zack to Righty and Leftie running back down the alleyway where they came from. He smiled and said, "Would you look at that...looks like your friends have run away."

"Really? I couldn't tell because we are almost in complete darkness," quipped Zack with a weak smirk.

Balast laughed and summoned a ball of light into his hand. Zack was bleeding from his lip and his nose was running with blood, but he smiled and said, "Thank you." with more tears in his eyes.

"Don't you start crying again. I should be the one crying, looking at your face right now." They both laughed as they headed back to the small purple tent set up in the middle of the road.

Chapter 8

When the sun rose the next day, Balast was shuffling around the purple tent hurriedly. He shook Zack and said,' Wake up! The customers are here!"

Zack sat up sleepily and rubbed his face. There was still a bruise on the side of his face from last night but most of it had healed because of Balast's healing spells. "What customers?" he grumbled.

"Remember yesterday when I enchanted that blizzard goblin?" Zack groggily nodded his head. "I was expecting a few weeks until we got a good stream of customers, but it looks like my spell was more attractive than I thought. I would say we have our work cut out for us today."

Zack rubbed his eyes, slowly sitting up, "So what, we're dealing with a small mob?"

Balast chuckled, "More like a riot." He opened up the tent flap, revealing a horde of beings, most of them humanoid. Zack could identify many species like the one that Balast helped the other day. Not only the goblins but humans, halflings, and beasts of all kinds were lining up in front of the tent. The crowd of beings crowded the streets, overflowing into the narrow alleyways. They clung to the rooftops and chimneys, dotting structures as far as he could see.

Zack blinked, wondering if this could still be a dream. He rubbed his eyes in disbelief, shaking his head in wonder, "Balast, how are we going to accommodate all these people? This tent is only big enough for the two of us!"

Balast sat down on the small chair behind the glass table and smirked. "Don't worry Zack. Remember when you exited the tent and found yourself in an empty plaza? The same thing is going to happen to all these people, except they will all encounter me."

Zack shook his head, "How…?"

Balast chuckled again, folding back his sleeves, "The back of your brain might itch for a second here…" He then pressed his palms to the sides of Zack's forehead, and all in an instant, he saw a flash of blue, and his world became black.

He woke up a second later in a dream. *Or at least, it feels like a dream,* Zack thought.

Perfect, you did better than I thought! Came a familiar voice.

Balast?

Welcome to my head, said Balast, *surprised?*

Zack was taken aback for a moment. *I mean… yeah. I thought it would be* way *emptier in here.*

Ouch. He said with mock indignance. *Well, if you want to see more…*

Then, with an audible woosh, Zack was standing in front of a purple tent. It looked, by all means, like the purple tent that they had stayed in, aside from the fact that there was an identical tent about ten feet away from that one. In fact, there were at least a dozen tents up and down the street.

Zack was speechless. Balast, seemingly able to sense this, explained it to him: *I have created multiples of what I like to call "side rooms". The tents are, more or less, like a doorway to those rooms. Nothing much, really.*

Zack's mouth opened and closed in shock. *This is amazing Balast. I've never seen such a thing before…*

Zack could sense Balast grinning. *Yes. Magic is pretty new to the world, and there are many other things that I will teach you as my apprentice. The best part is that there are clones of me in each one, making deals, receiving money, and making contracts with the customers.*

Wow. So, when does my training start? He opened his eyes and was back in the original tent.

"You have already started. Every simple task I have given you has been a part of the training… even the ones I haven't given you. You were tasked with my assassination, and you came hurling lightning. How exactly did you do that?"

Zack sat down and sighed. "I was given a flower. It was a glowing purple-ish and they told me to eat it. I did and it tasted terrible."

Balast nodded thoughtfully. "A death rose plucked right off some Lifeweed. Must have been full of life energy too. This explains a lot..." Balast rubbed his chin and then asked, "Do you remember where you got this flower from?"

Zack shook his head. "They blindfolded us and then we were in a very dark room. The flower was the only thing lighting the room."

Balast gave a *hrmph* noise, his eyes staring off into space, looking deep in thought. After a few moments of silence, he stood up abruptly and rummaged through his rucksack, talking while he searched. "That flower comes from the plant that we saw in the carpenter's shop. That plant - weed, actually - absorbs life, as you saw firsthand. No pun intended. The flowers that grow on it are fueled by that life and eventually glow from it." He stopped, pulled out a short silver rod, inspected it for a moment, and dropped it back into the bag. He continued, "When glowing, they are extremely potent in magical spells, potions, and whatnot. In your case, it was used for enhancing magical abilities. Ah, here we go," he pulled out a golden rod about as long as his forearm.

Balast held it up to his eye, seeming to measure for straightness. It looks slightly wider than a pencil, covered in a thin layer of glassy material. The gold underneath the glass was shining brilliantly, seeming to flicker with supernatural radiance.

Zack stared at the rod as Balast inspected it. Then seeming to remember a question, he asked, "*Enhances* magical abilities? You mean to say I already had the abilities before?"

Balast looked away from the item and looked Zack in his eyes, "Yes. The death rose acted like a steroid, boosting your magical abilities and allowing you to control them. I had heard of something like this being done before, but I had also heard that it was *extremely* dangerous. Whoever... or *what*ever did this to you knew exactly what they were doing."

Both of them were silent for a few moments before Zack spoke up: "So what's the stick for?"

"This *stick* is used for channeling magic," Balast scoffed indignantly, "specifically the electric magic that you use. With it, you can harness and control your abilities until you won't have to use it anymore."

"So, it's a wand?"

Balast grinned, "More like magical training wheels."

He handed the relatively thick metal rod to Zack. The second the boy touched it; he felt a surge of adrenaline through his arm. An arc of electricity sparked and popped at the top of the rod. "Whoa!" he said, dropping the rod. It stopped sparking as soon as it left his hand.

"Looks like you truly do have an affinity to lightning magic. Eating a death rose just enhances any magic, but it looks like it brought out yours immediately." Balast picked up the rod and handed it back to Zack. "Keep the rod in your hand and try to form something out of it as your first task. I have to focus on all these deals my clones are making."

Balast stepped out of the tent, blinking to adjust his eyes to the midday light. He noticed that the lines of people had mostly gone down but were still very large. He skirted by a group of people and stepped into one of the tents. There was a bent old man sitting in a stool, and directly across from him sat an exact replica of Balast. The clone glanced upward at Balast as he entered but then went back to talking to the man.

"What can I do for you today sir?" He asked in a voice exactly like Balast's, if not slightly monotonous.

The man sighed deeply, "As you can probably tell, I'm reaching the end of my years, and I had heard rumors of a man who could extend one's time," he said in a weak, dry voice, "As I can tell, the rumors were true. I've always wanted to go on a quest with my son, but I've never found the time to do it. Now that my time is up, I realize how much I needed to do that both for him and for myself."

Balast's clone was silent for a moment, staring at the man. Then, in that same voice said, "This request sounds reasonable… I will give you five years." He then grabbed the man's right hand, and a warm blue light filled the room.

The man smiled widely, shaking the hand of Balast's copy that he still held, "Thank you sir, I am indebted to you! Thank you!"

Balast watched the man leave and sighed. *Another fulfilled dream.* He was silent for a moment, then realized that he didn't pay. Balast smiled. *Probably no ill intentions behind it. I'm glad they had a goal in life to the very end and that we helped them achieve it.*

He strode up to the clone, who was sitting on the stool as before and touched its shoulder, and a slight blue flash renewed the magical energy in it. He was about to teleport to another clone when a familiar face walked through the purple veil.

"I was wondering where you were going to get the money to fund the project you came to me about." Gareth said, folding his arms. He couldn't see the real Balast, so he was addressing the clone instead.

The clone, only meant to make deals about life extensions, repeated the line Balast had set. "Please tell me your Name and age," the clone said, smiling.

Gareth replied, "I'm not here for your magic, I came here to tell you that your materials are ready."

The clone opened its mouth to repeat the same line as before, but Balast merged with the clone and apologized, "Sorry, that was a clone. Anyways, you are agreeing to construct my school?"

Gareth disregarded his statement and continued, "I see that you have attracted quite a crowd here. I don't think this many people would be here if this was a hoax…"

"So, you came to see that your money was insured? No problem. I expected this kind of caution from an expert craftsman like you. Follow me."

A golden portal appeared to their right and Balast walked through it. Gareth was hesitant but stepped through to see mounds and mounds of gold all around him. His mouth opened wide as he turned around to see even more gold for miles and miles.

"Gareth," Balast handed him a brown leather bag. "This bag will supply you with your pay." Gareth fondled the bag and was about to turn it over when Balast stopped him urgently, sighing in relief.

"Don't turn the bag upside down unless you want all of your pay immediately. Just reach into the bag whenever you need coins, and the bag will stop supplying gold when your debt is paid."

Gareth nodded. "Well, magic certainly is useful. When are we going to start building?" Gareth exited through the portal Balast conjured and saw a large open field with a forest of at least a hundred acres around it. Balast stepped through the portal and said, "Now."

Gareth shook his head, "I can't, I don't have my-"

"Tools and Materials?" Balast said as he gestured to a large pile of materials like stacks of dark oak wood, carpentry tools, and even food in neat rows with a large line of people behind it.

"Who are all these people?" Gareth asked, mouth open with shock.

"All of these people are people from the town who came to my shop, and they all have a contract with me to work for you. Some of these people are even carpenters and architects, just like you," replied Balast.

He opened another portal and before stepping through it, he asked, "Do you need anything else before I go?"

Gareth opened and closed his mouth a couple of times before answering, "I-I don't think so."

"Good. I'll be back in a few hours to see how the first designs are going."

Zack stood watching the last tent shimmer away, the potency of Balast's magical abilities yet confounding his mind. He was turning to leave as Balast stepped out of the disappearing tent. Balast rubbed his hands together, "Excellent, that was the last of them. Now onto the next order of business."

Zack exhaled, "Can we rest for a moment? This glow stick really takes a lot of effort to work," he said, holding up his wand.

"It's an ancient, magic-channeling wand, and you're calling it 'glow stick'?" said Balast with an arched eyebrow.

"Well yeah," Zack scoffed like it was obvious, "It was either that or 'the lightning rod'."

Balast let out a breath, admitting defeat. "Whatever. We can rest now for a few hours; this next part can wait until midnight."

Balast knew midnight had struck by a sharp itch at the back of his hand that he scratched immediately by patting Zack on the back, motioning him to stand up and walk.

"So, where exactly are we headed?" Zack asked quietly as they walked the dark streets.

Balast continued walking, not looking at him as he spoke, "Those friends of yours, the big ugly one and the twins, I'm interested in meeting their connections. I'm sure I don't need to tell you this, but they're involved in some seriously shady business.

"Spuma? What gave that away?" Zack said darkly.

Balast continued walking for a moment before he began talking again, "That flower you ate, the death rose, can also be used to make dark and deadly mutations. There are abominations - Malums - which I will introduce you to later... unless they introduce themselves first, which is a possibility. The death rose makes beings vulnerable to being infected by these Malums. I'm pretty sure that Spuma and the twins are deeply involved with transporting, harvesting, or distributing the roses," he paused for a moment, his feet making soft sounds as he stepped on the damp cobblestone, "or all three of those possibilities."

"So, where exactly are we headed?" asked Zack again.

"Nowhere, we're already here." Balast stopped walking and turned sharply.

Zack followed his gaze to a wall that had pieces of brick that were crumbling off as they stood there. As they stepped closer, Zack could see that the bottom row of bricks wasn't aligned with the ground, so you could see underneath which a light shone a dim, unnatural pink. "Yeah, no." Zack said turning around. Balast grabbed him by the shoulder and turned him back toward the wall. Balast waved his hand, and he balled it into a fist and pulled back like he was readying for a punch. The stones started to glow red and as Balast pulled his hand back, the bricks detached from each other and shot outwards towards them. Nothing hit them except the cold darkness of the new passageway that Balast had uncovered. As Balast stepped in, he looked around to find the pink light revealing itself was seemingly gone.

"We must locate the people who are giving random criminals powerful magic abilities and most likely making a profit too." Balast said, continuing the conversation.

They stepped into the sewer and Zack covered his nose from the stink and tried to step only on the dry spots. As they ventured deeper Balast noticed that the walls and roof were getting more and more structured.

"Looks like we stumbled into underground catacombs. I wonder how long these go." Balast said, summoning a ball of light to illuminate what was otherwise a gaping maw of darkness, save for the faint glow of pink coming from ahead of them.

Balast slowed down his speed and dropped to a crouch, and Zack mimicked his movements. Balast made the light in his hand dim as they crept closer to the corner that gave off the pink radiance.

"Ok, Zack, things might get a little bit dicey up here, so I'm going to teach you a simple spell that you probably aren't ready for yet. Do you have your wand with you?"

Zack stuck his hand into his deep pockets and produced the wand. "What now," he whispered.

"Right. All you need to do is point it at something and jab the wand, except *don't* actually 'jab' it. Simply mentally envision you are making said motion. You have to imagine that the wand will destroy something in order for it to work most effectively."

"Wait wha--"

Balast stood up and threw the orb of light around the corner, causing it to explode into a blinding light. Zack let out a shrill noise that seemed a hybrid between a squawk and a shout as he ran around the corner, his wand held in front of him. The light died down, and Balast exhaled loudly. "There's nobody here…" he looked around and saw that most of the crates were new but there were stray petals of dead roses. "These are fairly new, must have cleared out a lot yesterday."

Zack relaxed, "Good, because I would hate to vaporize anyone with a spell I don't even know yet."

"You wouldn't. You don't have that much control yet." Balast said, moving around some boxes, searching for anything revealing.

The pink light was brightest in this room. As they both looked around their surroundings, they could see that it was coming from pink flowers that covered the ceiling in such great numbers. The light was radiating from each flower so brightly that bunches of them were almost bright enough to light the catacombs where Zack and Balast came from. The only reason they didn't was because the room was tucked away into a corner. The back of the catacomb was blocked off by a solid wall of unmined rock which had wooden crates stacked to the ceiling. The ceiling had a good amount of dirt covering it, enabling the flowers to take root and light the space from above. Compared to the width of the other catacombs, this space was huge, with thick grey-green vines coiled up and down the walls like dead veins upon a strangled corpse. Around the lair were medium-sized worktables with tools still on them. There were ladders that reached up to the ceiling, and they leaned haphazardly against the vines.

"Looks like I was right about the roses," said Balast with a grimace. "They aren't fully charged yet, which is good, but we need to find what they were feeding them with."

He looked around the hall and stopped on a large pile of vines that gathered in the corner. Motioning Zack to look towards it, he walked slowly, grabbing a large knife from one of the counters. "Remember how I told you I would introduce you to Malums?"

Zack took a cautious step forward, peering into the corner, "Yeah, unless they…"

"...introduced themselves," finished Balast. He grabbed Zack's shoulder and pulled him under a table with a few jars on top. He dispersed his light source after signaling Zack to be quiet with his finger. He touched Zack again and he felt a slight shiver in his body and suddenly everything was clear as day. He could see everything in the dark and was fascinated. He looked back at Balast and was shaken by what he saw: Balast was shaking.

Zack's breaths came a bit unevenly and a bead of sweat came from his forehead. He swallowed hard seeing Balast in this state. He only grew more scared as he saw Balast's eyes slowly scanning the darkness frantically from under the table. He felt his chest tighten more and more as he looked at Balast, so he looked around, trying to spot what Balast was looking for. He didn't see anything in the darkness even with magical help, so he looked closer at the crates. He looked to his right, and in the crate next to him, he saw a jar with a name written on it. It read 'Gareth.' Zack thought it might be useful, so he reached out and grabbed it.

Balast, seeing no immediate danger, calmed himself and pushed Zack and himself from under the table. Looking around once more he started running back the way they came. Zack followed hurriedly behind him but asked, "Why are we running?!?!"

"This was a trap, Zack, we need to leave!"

Suddenly the room shook with unnatural howls, and gross shapes stepped out of the darkness. A mass of tentacles and eyes dripping with black slime. He threw the knife at a large eyeball, and it punctured the eye before returning to his hand.

"The doorway, Zack, the tunnel!" He yelled.

Zack needed no further urging. He ran as hard as he could toward the doorway as the tentacles started reaching his feet. He made it about halfway through when his coat was caught on the corner of a table, causing him to fall with a yelp. A Malum descended upon him before he hit the ground, and he fumbled for his wand as the shadowy beast pounced. The Malum rolled over him and some of its tentacles hardened, stabbing the ground near his head. One tentacle was headed straight for his head.

Then, before it landed, a brilliant arc of lightning burst from his rod, evaporating the Malum. The bolt of electricity danced around the room, destroying several more monsters before it returned to his wand.

Zack was stunned but stood up immediately, turning to look back to Balast. The wizard was surrounded by a host of Malums, but at his back stood a glowing blue copy of himself. Both Balast's were slashing and stabbing at the monsters with their knives, eliminating threat after threat.

He looked toward Zack, who was by the door. "Zack!" He yelled, "I need you to shoot that wand at me!"

"At you??" Zack yelled back, perplexed.

"Don't argue, obey!"

Taking a deep breath, Zack pointed the rod at Balast, and from it came another blinding lightning bolt before hitting Balast. However, it turned and hit his replica. The replica exploded in a brilliant flash, evaporating every Malum within a yard of it. As soon as his copy blew apart, Balast sprinted toward the makeshift entrance, and Zack followed.

Then, without a word, Balast spread his fingers and pushed his hand forward. A tentacle reached out toward him just as the rocks Balast had magically removed started to slowly float back to their original positions. Balast wove his way through the bricks and as he reached the other side, he pushed his hand forward and the bricks accelerated and fused themselves to the wall, cutting the Malums off from the outside world.

Balast and Zack stared at the reformed wall, their eyes darting around anxiously for any signs of a breakthrough. The howls died down and they let out a simultaneous sigh.

"So, those were Malums?" Zack looked to Balast. Zack was shaking a bit more now and his eyes were still glued to the wall.

"Are you okay?' Balast asked, looking over Zack.

"Yeah, I'm ok. Are you?"

Balast turned and started walking away saying, "Of course."

Zack followed warily, seeing Balast lean from one foot to the other, his head twitching at every sound that made its way to his ears.

"Oh, wait! Before we go, I found something on the ground in there…" he gave Balast the piece of glass that said, "Gareth" on it.

Balast nodded slowly.

"This makes a lot of sense. Looks like we are going to have to talk with Gareth tomorrow."

Chapter 9

The next day Balast woke up before the sun rose. He wiped his brow, feeling the cold sweat that dampened his bed.

Nightmares… he thought, shaking his head.

The sight of a Malum had shaken him more than he thought it would. It had been some time since he had seen and fought a Malum the sight of one made him revisit unfriendly memories. In his nightmare, he saw the faces of all the people whom he had failed and even the one person who had failed him.

Inferneous is fine. Move on. He thought to himself, pushing down the worry and simultaneously the fear of his enemies.

He stepped out of the tent he had set up on the site of construction breathing in the fresh morning mist. It had a smell of fresh pine and dirt from the forest. Looking to the horizon, he could see the trees covered with fog in the distance, making for a picture of serenity that Balast wished he could replicate inside his head. As he exited his tent onto the grassy area in front of the construction site of the first building, he looked over it to see what they had done since he and Zack had gotten back. The area had been cleared of grass and wooden boards and logs outlined the base of the building, making a neat rectangular shape. Realizing there were more people up at this time than he might have thought, he slowly turned invisible as one of the workers approached him because he was not one to engage in conversation in the morning time.

The majority of beings up were the people planning out the construction of the base of the first building. They were all huddled under a leather tarp held up by sticks, each of them gazing down at a table with drawings, numbers, and measurements. There were almost ten in all there and Balast distinctly remembered twenty contracts being made.

He came out of his invisibility and addressed the carpenters, "Where are the other ten of you?"

Most of the carpenters were a bit startled by the sudden appearance of Balast, with the exception being Gareth. He just turned to Balast and said, "They all said that they had family business to attend to."

Balast grunted. "Okkkayy… when did they say they were going to return?" Gareth shrugged his shoulders. Balast shook his head. "Well, do you ten have the construction details under control?" Most of them shook their heads.

This is amazing… Balast thought sarcastically.

"What do you need?"

"We need an accurate count of all our materials." Gareth said, leaning against the wooden table. "There is a massive amount of resources but this project is bigger than we thought, and we need to be sure that everything is here." Balast waved his hand, and a piece of paper appeared on the table. Gareth picked it up and showed it to the others.

"That's the whole count of what I've contracted people to bring to this site, is it enough?" Balast asked.

The parchment was passed around and Gareth nodded. "Thank you."

"No need," Balast said walking away, "You are building my school anyhow."

He turned invisible again as he stepped back but didn't walk away. The carpenters continued to do their job, conversing adamantly about the construction of the school. Balast looked at them and his gaze landed on Gareth. He remembered the piece of glass that Zack had shown him yesterday and decided to follow Gareth around for the morning.

Gareth didn't seem unusual when Balast first met him. Besides the Lifeweed incident, nothing particularly strange had happened around him. It was pretty common among carpenters to have something made out of life weed in their shops, as it was hard to come by and dangerous to handle, it was a ritual among their craft to prove they would dedicate their lives to carpentry.

But where and how would he get enough life weed to cover his walls with it? There aren't any mountains around for miles and it would take at least twenty men to harvest all of it…

With a sudden shock, Balast realized the life weed had been living, it was glowing brightly in the center. Balast knew that Lifeweed at the peak of its blossom, which means it had consumed enough magic or lives, would be safe to handle and ready to consume.

Just like in the catacombs thought Balast grimly.

In that one instant of thought, Gareth had turned into a partly constructed hallway, outside of Balast's visibility. Balast turned the corner, to find that Gareth was nowhere to be found.

Strange…

Putting the workers behind him he walked back into the tent to find Zack just waking up.

"Oh good, just in time. Get up quickly, we start your physical training today. Get up and start with a light jog around the building site four times."

Zack's mouth dropped open. "Four times!? That's at least three miles!"

"Yes, quite gracious of me." Balast said, grabbing Zacks wand.

It shimmered a light green as he handed it to Zack.

"Carry this with you and swing it around like a sword."

Zack almost fell over when the rod dropped in his hands.

"What did you do to it?" Zack asked, standing and attempting to lift it up, only to abruptly drop it instead. The rod sank into the ground, stirring up the dust.

"I made it heavier of course. You need to build at least a bit of muscle if you want to properly perform magic. Balast picked up the rod and tossed it around from hand to hand with ease, then set it gently in Zack's hand.

"Now go. I'll be timing you."

Zack sighed and dragged himself out of the tent, running toward the outline of the base of the first building. Balast watched him stumble away until he was out of sight.

He chuckled to himself, "I hope he does better than me."

He turned back inside the tent, sat on the ground, closed his eyes, and breathed evenly. To anyone viewing him, it would look quite disturbing to see a wizard floating in the air, seemingly unconscious. In Balast's mind the slightly damp atmosphere disappeared around him as he started to levitate about a foot above the ground.

He opened his eyes and found himself floating in a starry black void overlooking Magia. He pushed his hand toward Magia, and he zoomed into the clouds. He seemingly flew through the clouds, dipping in and out of the sunlight as he dove into the deepest oceans and into mountain caves. He emerged out of a cave and saw a town flourishing with people in a busy seaside market. He weaved between trades and deals of all kinds and smelled the freshly baked bread and sea salt. It was all wonderful, too wonderful. He looked off the pier and saw a black, swirling mass.

"What is-"

Suddenly, Balast was blasted backwards as the whole town was instantly turned into a burning inferno. The black mass was upon the town and there were casualties everywhere. Fire burned in every corner and dark forms of monsters walked the streets in search of survivors.

Balast shook his head at the destruction as he walked the main road. He stopped when he saw a man holding a small boy in the middle of the street, surrounded by monsters. He ran towards them but stopped when he saw the man's face. It was him but younger. The child in his hands was Zack, his mouth open in a scream of anguish as blood trickled from a gaping wound in his chest.

The younger Balast looked at the older Balast and asked, "Does it end?"

All the monsters then turned and gazed at older Balast, whispering without moving their mouths, repeating what younger Balast had said. "Does it end?"

Thousands of horrible voices echoed in his head. Balast reached his hands outwards and as he pulled them towards his chest, the images blurred past him, dissipating into echoes. He opened his eyes to see the familiar drapes of the purple tent. Covered in sweat he stood up and stepped outside into a cool evening.

I can't escape them. He thought, looking around for some relief from the terrifying vision he just had. He saw the workers walking away from the building site. It looked like the general frame of the building was done.

Zack came huffing and dragging his feet behind Balast. He grabbed Balast's arm and collapsed, trying to keep himself upright. Balast picked the boy up and carried him into the tent. He set him on the ground and put a blanket over him as he fell into a deep sleep from the marathon he had just finished.

"You did better than me Zack, you didn't run away." *Now I have to do the same.* He thought, exiting the tent and going invisible once more.

Half an hour later Balast became visible once again as he looked upon the rocks at the wall that he had removed to enter the catacombs and raised his hand. An explosion blasted all the rocks inward and Balast braced himself. No guttural howls sounded in the darkness of the cave as he stood outside in the moonlight. The cave was on the backside of a small mill in an alleyway that a hay cart could fit through but not much else. Balast was skeptical whether he should approach or summon the beast or beasts out, so he decided on the latter and summoned a ball of light and threw it into the cave. It landed onto the ground in the inky darkness, only conveying depth by the light bouncing off the damp ground. He approached cautiously and picked the ball of light off the floor to behold a Malum carcass. The original smell of the cave was nothing compared to its present stench. Balast gagged. Not even the flies dared to land and feast on the disgusting pile.

Something killed it before I got here., he thought. Balast looked around it and noticed footprints in the dirt surrounding the monster. He followed them and saw that they stopped right at the Malum. There were scuffed marks of boots showing a bit of a struggle but not nearly enough for a regular fight between a Malum and a human. He also noticed droplets of the congealed black blood from the beast leading into the darkness.

It was no ordinary person…, he thought as he looked at the corpse closer. It looks like the heart of the beast had been ripped out viciously. The folds of the Malum's viscous skin with its blood protruded outwards to show in the open air a black and purple streak. What was even more intriguing was that there were black cloth and blood on the end of the Malum's spear-like claws. Balast snapped out of his thoughts as he took a breath and the carcass smell got to him again, making him gag once.

I have to burn this. He thought as he walked out of the entrance. Orange lights appeared over his hand as he drew an orange circle with his right hand and he covered his nose as he pointed towards the malum bodies. Beams of molten lava shot from the circle burning the ground and malum in tandem. He shuddered in disgust, turned around, moving both hands apart, as he stepped outside of the catacomb entrance. The rocks started to float, moving back to their original positions, blocking the entrance. Sparks of red magic popped from the wall then faded as the rock wall was blocking the entrance once more. Balast heard the hissing of Malum flesh as he returned.

Since there is another entrance or an exit the smell of a burnt monster should be recognizable anywhere. I'll be able to track where the other entrance is by the smell. He walked out of the alleyway and looked up to the moon and sighed in relief. *I'm glad I didn't face harm this day,* he thought as he walked back to the tent. He laid down and before he fell asleep, he reminded himself, … *but I cannot ignore the fact that there are definitely dangerous times ahead and I do need to address them accordingly.*

The next day, Gareth was nowhere to be found. Stranger still, the ten men who had been missing the day before also had not shown. Balast walked up to a group of workers who were engaging in some argument about the blueprints.

"You," said Balast, pointing at a tall, lanky man with a mop of brown hair on his head, "have you seen Gareth around?"

The man looked uncomfortable but stepped out of the argument and talked to Balast, "Yeah, uh, Gareth said that you said that he was done here. You had some sort of an argument about something or something like that?

That's what he says you said. He said that you would come looking for him, so he didn't say where he was going and told all of us not to ask."

Balast stalled for a minute and furrowed his eyebrows asking, "What?"

The man tried to start again when another man who looked just like the first put his hand on the first man's chest and stopped him, "Tavin gets a little confused sometimes," he put out a hand, "My name is Tevin, Tavin is my younger twin brother. We are the head of the demolition and build crew." Balast shook his hand and asked, "Can you explain what happened clearer?"

"Yes, it seemed that you got into an argument with Gareth? He said not to look for him. The remaining ten planners didn't come and he said he quits."

"What?! How- I didn't get into an argument with him," Balast started when he realized that there were significantly fewer workers here than yesterday too.

"Where are the rest of your men?"

"Don't know. They didn't even show up."

"Doesn't anyone know where they went?" Balast asked.

"Well yeah, I mean, Gareth was the one who said they were gone so he should know. Except now he isn't here and all..." Tevin muttered.

"Ok then. Tevin, Tavin," Balast pointed to both of them, "You and the rest of the workers have the day off. I want you all to go home or someplace else, but nobody goes home alone, got that? Stick together, and if anyone is missing, I want you to try to find out where they went."

The brothers nodded in unison and as they were turning to tell the others, Balast stopped them, "Wait, which way did Gareth go?"

Tavin pointed towards the woods, "He went into the woods, weirdly enough. I don't know why he would do that, what with the rumors of bandits and..."

"And?"

"And monsters." Tevin finished for his brother, "There have been a few people who haven't returned from those woods in the past year so people should know not to go in there." Balast turned towards the woods and whispered an incantation, closed and covered his eyes, and then opened them. As his eyes glowed light purple, he saw footprints leading all the way into the dark forest.

"This day just keeps getting better." he said, walking back to the purple tent. "Zack! Wake up, we are going into the forest. Bring your wand with you."

Zack groggily sat up from the ground and he hurriedly picked up the wand, the wizard's cloak they had bought off a street vendor, and headed out the tent flap after Balast, who was running toward the dark forest behind Tywardreath. Once they reached the line of trees, Balast stopped Zack.

"If anything happens to me you run or fight as hard as you can. Don't hold back on your magic. I would rather have you run than do anything stupid though." Zack nodded. Before Balast entered, he turned and said, "Also remember you are stronger now," he pointed at the wand Zack was holding and Zack realized that he wasn't struggling to carry the wand at all.

"Use this power wisely."

Zack nodded again and said, "Let's go."

The forest was densely packed with trees occupying almost every inch of the ground, enveloping the ground in darkness that was near pitch black in the spaces that were not lit by the sparse holes in the canopy. Balast could see clearly where he was going because he could see the glowing purple footprints of Gareth through the trees with his magic. Zack on the other hand was stumbling through the forest, tripping on roots, and stumbling his way through the darkness. While they journeyed deeper and deeper and deeper into the forest, the number of holes in the canopy diminished leaving them in darkness.

"Balast! I can't see, a little help?"

A pair of purple eyes turned to Zack and he jumped when a hand covered his eyes.

"Calm down. You won't survive a Malum attack if you keep reacting like that." Balast said, removing his hand from Zack's face. Zack blinked and he could now see everything clearly.

"Wow, is this what you see every day?" Zack said, standing up.

"Only when I need to. There are multiple different spells to make you see certain things but it's hard to maintain the focus of keeping a spell active forever."

Balast continued to walk forward then slunk behind a tree and motioned Zack to do the same. Zack came behind him and peered in front of the tree to see what Balast had seen. It was an open space, almost crater-like.

Gareth was standing in the middle of about thirty rough-shaven people and beasts. Spuma was in the mix with them. They all had weapons and armor, donning them thickly.

Balast's jaw clenched as he could see black veins running down the sides of their necks, signaling they had a part of a Malum inside of each of them. On top of that, at their feet were the missing ten contractors and workers.

"Well, this is much more organized than I thought." Balast said as he surveyed their surroundings. Balast then stepped from behind the tree and dropped down into the middle of the crater saying loudly, "So!" He walked up to Gareth and put his right hand on his left shoulder, "Why would a respectable man and carpenter associate with Malums and thieves?"

A black arm emerged from Gareth's turned back and gripped Balast's shoulder as Gareth turned to face him. Balast eyes went wide. Gareth's face was completely covered in black sludge and eyeballs that were triangular in shape. Gareth's left hand rose and slammed down on Balast's shoulder causing him to fall to his knees. There was a loud scream and another large man with scaly skin dropped into the crater, dropping Zack with him. The man grabbed Zack's arms and pinned them to his sides, making him face Balast.

In a deep, gritty, and almost bubbly tone, the Malum that had taken over Gareth spoke, "I am a soldier of the Malum King and I have taken over the one you call 'Gareth'."

The being shoved Balast to the ground and four other arms sprouted out of Gareth's back, slamming into the ground around him. "I have a choice for you. Since you know about the business I have been dealing with here and you saw the remains of my superior, I require you to leave this town and never speak of it again."

"You killed another Malum? How did you manage to survive the daytime?" Balast exclaimed.

"Many things are possible with an easily manipulated host." The monster raised one of its limbs and it lengthened and shaped into a sharp sword. It pointed it at Balast, saying, "Now, make your decision. I'm sure you don't want to repeat your past mistakes."

It swung around and pointed the sharp limb at one of the contractors who shrieked in response. Balast's face hardened and his teeth gritted as he sat up.

"Repeat past mistakes?" he spread his arms wide and purple symbols appeared across the crater's bottom.

"There aren't enough people here to be able to recreate what happened, let me fix that!" The runes glowed brightly, blinding everyone as Balast snapped his fingers. As the runes shine faded, he could smell the Malum's burning flesh. His vision cleared as he saw the Malums standing in front of him, running to the shade of the buildings covering half the main plaza of Tywardreath. People walking through were pushed aside by the Malum soldiers and some screamed in shock at the Malum in front of Balast. It shouted out to the soldiers, "Don't let anyone in the plaza leave!" The guards nodded and let go of the original hostages to quickly block the four entrances at the front, back, and sides of them.

"You're outnumbered, even if your men try to kill everyone, these people won't give up without a fight." the Malum turned to him and gave a gurgle that almost sounded like a laugh.

"Are you sure? Most of the people here have come to me for one reason or another." Balast gave a confused look and saw around him, people were not showing signs of extreme fear like a crowd that had never seen a Malum before. Some were avoiding their eyes as if they were ashamed of themselves, while others just watched with turned up noses. There were a few in the crowd that did have wide eyes in fear, but most were standing still or trying to make themselves invisible by standing to the side, getting away from the center of the plaza.

"Your magic cannot reverse the suffering I have inflicted upon these people, and it cannot heal this world. But since you chose not to accept my offer, I shall kill you!"

The Malum grabbed Balast by the throat and raised him up a few feet in the air while cackling. Balast formed a ball of light in his hand and pointed it at the Malum while trying to remove its grasp.

"Do it! Fire upon me and the villagers die!"

The Malum's soldiers pulled out their weapons and faced the people around them, ready to attack. The ball of light dissipated in his hand as he saw the frightened people's faces.

"LISTEN!" Balast yelled loudly. The cries of people died down. "You are wrong about magic. It may be relatively new to this world, but it can heal it. Even if it may seem destructive, it's meant to be used for good."

Balast looked behind the Malum at Zack's terrified eyes, closed his own, and said, "There are already people who have the potential to prove me right."

The Malum hissed as the rest of its limbs sharpened into daggers and shot towards Balast. Before he was impaled by them, a loud shriek sounded behind the Malum as Zack ran towards it. His eyes glowed blue as he gripped his wand and a large jagged sword erupted from the tip. It was blue and made completely out of electricity and cut through the Malum like butter. The arms of the Malum dropped to the ground as stray lightning bolts radiated off of Zack. He turned around at the stunned Malum and things seemed to go in slow motion as Zack sliced open its chest to reveal a glowing purple heart. He yelled as he plunged his sword straight into the Malum core. The creature let out an ear-piercing screech and fell to the ground, unmoving. Balast dropped to the ground, landing on his feet. Zack stood over the monster, staring at it as electricity sparked around him, breathing hard. The Malum soldiers fell to the ground holding their heads shaking until they too went still.

There was silence and then cheers erupted out of the crowd. All the people in the plaza cheered and flooded around him. As the lightning sword retreated back into the wand and the magical lightning subsided. A large man lifted Zack on his shoulder so everyone could see him. Balast stood to see the smiling and relieved faces of the villagers and the wide grin on Zack's face. Balast couldn't help but smile and laugh as he was surrounded by people celebrating Zack.

It must feel good Balast thought, nodding his head. *It must feel very good to be loved for the first time.*

Chapter 10

As the villagers took Zack away, celebrating him more, Balast inspected the bodies of the Malum soldiers and the fallen Malum. He raised his hand and they all levitated off the ground and followed him as he was walking out of the plaza. The sun was setting behind the forest, bathing the town in a brilliant, golden light. Balast was enjoying the view when a foul stench assaulted him. He went to cover his nose from it but stopped as he recognized the smell. Despite the rising headache and upset stomach caused by the smell, he didn't shy away from it. Instead, he followed it through town all the way back to where he began.

"This makes sense in hindsight." He said aloud as he pushed the door open and held it open for the floating bodies of the Malum and Malum soldiers.

Once they all floated inside, he closed and locked the doors despite the windows being blown out from the situation he and Zack had been in a few days earlier. He walked behind the counter and followed a small hallway to the right that was also lined with Lifeweed.

The hallway led to a small courtyard that had tools of carpentry scattered around it. The courtyard walls were composed of the four stone walls of the surrounding buildings, united by an open space between them. The roofs of the buildings matched together perfectly to match a square of sunlight in the middle of it. The most outstanding thing was the massive hole in the middle of the yard. As Balast walked around it, he noticed pieces of broken stone and other rubble between tools.

This is where the first Malum must have burst through from under the catacombs... Balast thought, jumping into the hole. The bodies floated downward with him as he walked along the catacombs when the stench of burnt Malum hit his nose again.

"Ah, we are here," he grunted as he walked toward a smoldering pile of foul-smelling acid and black goo.

He kicked dirt over it and the stench and smoking died down a bit. He turned to the floating bodies lined up on the wall and turned his hand to make the bodies face him standing up. As soon as they were he put his hands together and rubbed them until a bit of yellow electricity crackled between his fingertips. He stopped and walked towards the Malum and put both his hands on its head. The Malum gasped awake, screaming in cursed agony. It convulsed then its head rested downwards.

"Welcome back for the time being," Balast said, noticing the beast looking around in confusion. Its attention settled on Balast as it spoke,

"Mortal, you have no idea what pain I shall inflict-"

"You misunderstand the situation you are in." Balast interrupted.

The Malum was taken aback.

"You...!" it screamed and lunged at him, creating five spear-like tentacles aiming at Balast's head. It kept attacking him, spearing limbs flying back and forth, slashing the ceiling and walls around them, but none touched Balast. He stood there, not moving as the spears tried to stab him in vain. The Malum grew weary and stopped slashing to be amazed by Balast's unharmed figure.

"I want to know where you came from," Balast said calmly, walking toward the creature. It backed away and then stepped forward again to attack him. The spears went at him again, but they did not come back. It screamed more, pain shooting through its body as the spears lashed harder around Balast. Balast waved his hand and a shimmering barrier of light surrounded him, pulsing outwards, shattering the spears in half. Balast frowned as the tentacles shriveled against the light of the barrier shining and as the spears detached from the limbs. He stepped on the monster's midsection and pushed it to the ground. The purple heart that Zack had cut through was only damaged slightly, but Balast's foot was causing it to crack under its pressure.

"I asked where you hail from, beast?" he hissed under his breath, leaning forward his face inches from the black flesh of the monster.

The beast's many eyes dilated and looked in all directions as it yelled out, "From Avius Island of the Simul Sea!!"

Balast leaned more unto the heart and cracks splintered from the center outwards on it. The Malum breathed heavily and fast as it gurgled in silent torture. Balast nodded.

"It is truly funny how Malums are silent after telling truths. I swear ever since you scum learned our language that I haven't met one mute Malum." he leaned forward, putting more weight onto the heart as he whispered,

"Don't think that any one of your kind could kill me. Now go. Leave and never sight a living thing again."

The Malum scuffled back and ran down the tunnel as fast as it could.

"Actually," Balast snapped his fingers and time rewound itself until the Malum's heart was under his foot again. "You don't deserve a second chance."

He slammed his foot down onto the Malum's heart and the Malum's screams shook the walls as it disintegrated into black vapor and mist.

Zack was walking back to the building site with at least three baskets full of trinkets and food with the biggest smile no magic could ever produce. Things were falling off the edges of the baskets, leaving a good trail of wealth in his wake. Zack noticed this and made sure to trek himself through the poorest parts of the town, leaving things for the slum children to pick up and keep for themselves. People walking by would recognize him and cheer and clap or add something to the top of his baskets as he passed them down the cobblestone street. He thanked some of them and tried to bow in a heroic manner, but most of the time, he was just trying not to hurt his jaw from smiling too wide.

He spilled all the remaining items onto the floor of the purple tent and gazed at it all. From freshly baked bread to small rubies and high-quality daggers, he had a taste of the finest things the town had to offer. He sat down in the middle of it all and ate everything he could while counting the money he was given or examining the quality of the small weapons that had been gifted to him. He then lay on the floor and fell fast asleep.

He woke early the next day and saw that the workers were just arriving and gave them all the rest of his food that he hadn't eaten. They all seemed happy and smiled as they worked after having eaten their fill. Zack hung around the building and started helping the builders do their jobs and he gained a quick liking by them. At midday, Zack sat down resting from working and a thought occurred to him.

"Hey guys," Zack yelled to the contractors in the now walled-off building, "Where is Balast?"

They looked at each other and shrugged.

"We haven't seen him since yesterday. He was in the crowd and then he wasn't."

Zack shook his head and thought *Jeez, you think you would cherish someone who saved your life more.*

He turned toward Tywardreath and saw Balast walking beside a limping, bandaged-up Gareth. Zack ran toward him with a smile on his face and hugged him. The air was squeezed out of Balast as Zack hugged him and he gave a raised eyebrow in response.

After the hug had gone, Balast asked, "Haven't you got enough affection at those parties the villagers threw you?"

Zack smiled and rubbed his nose, "I'm just glad to see you haven't died of old age."

"Time has nothing on me, Zack. Remember that as you help Gareth get back to the build."

Zack looked Gareth up and down saying, "Don't you think he should take a break after being possessed by a Malum?"

"He insisted." Balast said when Zack realized that part of his face was bandaged so tight, he couldn't speak.

"Ah." Zack said, turning around to help Gareth limp along toward the building site. The day went by in a blur for Zack and the workers as they worked and ate snacks throughout the day.

Balast, on the other hand, was contemplating the future. He was sitting in the tent when he decided to peer out into the world again using the Double Space spell. He opened his eyes overlooking Magia, raised his arms toward his chest, and pushed his hands forward. The world expanded as his vision narrowed into a large expanse of blue between two land masses.

Over the Simil Sea with his consciousness floating above the water, he looked around. For miles there was nothing but a vast expanse of teal ocean water. He moved his hand left and right moving himself across the entire ocean. The odd thing was, he saw no island. He stopped searching, nodded to himself, and thought, *Must be magically hidden-* he was interrupted when in front of him a barely visible specter of a gray-haired man appeared.

Balast shook his head, thinking *It must be another bad illusion. He wouldn't be-*

Forty years. A voice echoed in Ballast's head. *That is a good chunk of time, even for people like us.*

No stop. I don't... I just don't... Balast thought back at the specter. *I don't care what you are doing searching the same place as me...just make sure I don't see you again.*

Does your guilt burn that hot? the specter thought to Balast.

The blurry shadow sharpened a bit more to accentuate the figure's fiery golden eyes staring right at him.

Does your consciousness not move and change like every other being?

Balast's specter turned to the other specter as he said, *Maybe that's just the side effects of this bonded curse we have.* He turned around to face the open ocean, raised his hands, and thought harshly to the other specter. *Heed my warning.*

The other specter dissipated from Balast's view as he pushed his hands out to open his eyes back to the reality of the purple tent. He felt a cool breeze run through the tent and noticed a warmth by his side. It was a tiny bright orange flame that was hovering very close to the sleeping body of Zack. The flame had a fierce heat almost like that of a normal fire, but it didn't burn anything, not even the ground beneath it.

Balast was enraged. He put his hands around the fire and was about to put it out when Zack shivered and pulled the cheap magician's cloak over his body as much as he could. Balast's anger melted before his eyes, and he unhanded the small magical fire. He glared at it angrily, thinking, *Looks like the Angelus blessing is bending fate to its will again. I wonder what chaos it will bring upon us...* He laid down next to the fire facing the sleeping Zack and fell fast asleep to the endless chatter of his worried thoughts.

The next morning, Balast shook Zack awake as the purple tent curled up into a ball and disappeared by itself.

"Wake up Zack, we are going now. I don't want to deal with everyone's questions."

Zack stood up, rubbed his eyes, and bent backwards, stretching his back and arms out. He rubbed his eyes again and then opened them wide saying, "Wait, what? Where are we going?"

"I said I didn't want to be bothered with questions, so be quiet unless you want to be unconscious most of the trip."

Zack took the time to reflect on past events silently to try and put out the fears of Balast's anger. As they walked past the construction site, Zack saw another larger grey tent was set up beside it. Balast parted the flaps of the grey tent and entered the small space. In the center there was a large square table with papers of all shapes and sizes covered with building details. As they approached the table, Balast reached into a small, tiny leather bag and pulled out a peculiar object. He pulled out a book made of stone. The book was of a smooth white stone and as he set it down on the main contractor's table, it opened magically to blank stone pages.

Zack touched the book and felt its grooves and edges, marveling at its beauty. He tried to pick it up, but he couldn't even squeeze his fingers under the book. It was seemingly one with the table, and it wouldn't move an inch.

"Stop messing with it! We are leaving!" Balast yelled, stamping his foot on the ground and staring at Zack. He turned and started walking toward Tywardreath at a brisk pace.

Zack hurried behind him but stayed silent, sensing Balast's anger. *The heck is wrong with him?* Zack thought, fiddling with his metal rod.

They walked through the quiet town noticing drunkards and others still partying from the defeat of the Malum. To Balast's relief, none of them noticed them walking by when they reached their destination: Gareth's shop. As they entered, Zack stared at the walls in disgust. The life weed had rotted out of the bindings and was sticking out, leaving holes for the wind to blow through. The whole place looked like it had been ransacked by bandits, but even more powerful than Zack's disgust of the dead plants was his curiosity.

"Why are we here?" Zack asked as they walked to the back.

Balast ignored him and continued to walk behind the counter and through the hallway to the small courtyard. He immediately walked straight into the hole in the ground leading to the catacombs.

"Wait!" Zack exclaimed, hesitating before jumping down himself. He looked around the cavern and noticed it was no average cave. There were intricate glyphs on the walls that in the dark seemed to glow dark purple and white. Zack walked toward the part of the cave with more glyphs and started winding down through multiple tunnels. Zack was pretty confident that he would find Balast until he couldn't.

The tunnels got darker and darker at each turn and Zack started to feel nauseous. He stumbled and almost fell at one point and when he looked up he couldn't see anything ahead of him. The cold crept into him as he continued to walk, like the room was starting to freeze. He rubbed his hands together as he started to shiver and he could see his breath billowing in front of him. He turned around, hesitantly looking back to see how far he had come, but all he saw was the jagged turn of the tunnel. As breathing grew harder, he scrutinized the walls behind him. As he turned back around, his stomach lurched and his head spun. He fell to his knees then laid on the ground and stopped moving as a wave of dizziness hit him. The ground felt like wet ice, the cold penetrating his clothing as if he had been doused in water already. As his limbs stiffened and his fingers went numb, memories started to flash across his vision. His father leaving him at the orphanage, the years sleeping on the streets, getting beaten by the other children, and even his brief moment of happiness with Balast. His tears froze as they rolled down his cheek. His thoughts spiraled downwards the more he lay there thinking, *I'm going to die here. In the dark. Alone. No one needs me. I saved them once now what was I going to do, save them a second time? The villagers should have known it was a fluke....*

Balast's voice snapped him awake. "What are you doing?"

Zack looked around and he was still standing at the bottom of the wide hole just outside of the sunshine, holding his wand to his forehead with both hands. Zack put his hands down and opened his mouth but no words came out. He paused and then replied, "Nothing."

Balast gave him an annoyed look and walked forward into the glyphed caverns. Zack followed warily behind him. The tunnel stretched for what seemed like miles to Zack because every time he lost sight of Balast a splitting headache would set upon him until he caught up. It was torture for Zack until he yelled out to Balast to stop.

"What is it now?" he said, retracing his steps to a hunched-over Zack.

"What did I do to deserve this? Is this another test because I can't take it anymore!"

Balast gave a look of confusion, "What-"

"I don't know why you're so mad at me but just please slow down or stop for a minute. My head is hurting from staring at all of these walls."

Balast sighed, "I'm not mad at you." he looked at the walls and shook his head. "There is a person we are inevitably going to run into and he and I have an unfavorable past together..." Balast was now leaning on the wall and looking through the cracks of the glyphs etched on the wall. He saw swirls of a dark purple and white substance flowing in between them, flowing ever so slightly toward where he was heading. He stuck his finger in a big enough crevice and the substance disappeared.

Zack stood by him and watched the entire process and did the same. But when Zack's finger touched the substance, it began to crawl up his finger with an arcane, almost graceful gradualness. Zack quickly pulled away his finger and tried to shake the substance off but it kept spreading. Balast grabbed his hand, squeezed Zack's finger and it was healed instantly. The substance burned off, melting onto the floor.

"Wow." Zack said, rubbing his finger. "I don't think we're safe here..."

Balast shook his head. "I don't think you are safe here." He turned and continued to walk down the dark corridors and caves saying, "Don't touch the walls anymore, we aren't going to be here long."

"How do you know that?" Zack asked as he followed him turning the corner only to be blinded by a shining purple and white portal.

Balast was examining around it and nodded his approval. "This is a creation of the Malum I defe…" Balast stumbled over his words as he turned to Zack's curious face, "I mean the Malum you defeated. This is going to take us to where the Malum came from, which should be somewhere in the ocean on an island, hopefully."

"What do you mean hopefully?"

Balast grabbed his arm and let go and he started to float.

"What the heck is this?!?!"

"It's a precaution," a blue bubble appeared around Zack as Balast continued, "This portal is made of the same substance inside the wall and you may not survive the trip through without protection."

Balast stepped up to the portal and waved his hand around. The glowing goo shied away from him, stretching the sides of the portal. "Well, before we try this out, you should know we may have to fight someone…or something…if we get through, so be prepared."

Zack nodded, taking a deep breath before Balast stepped into the portal with Zack floating in behind him. The dark magic dissipated around Balast, making it easy for him to walk forward but inside the bubble, Zack was having a hard time. When they entered, the bubble started collapsing. Sharp spikes from the dark magic inside the portal tried to pierce the bubble. Zack moved constantly to try and avoid being stabbed by the spikes.

"The bubble's breaking Balast!"

Balast looked back and then broke into a sprint, trying to get to the end. Step after step, the bubble collapsed inward more and more.

Suddenly, they were both lying on the ground in a brightly lit forest. They both groaned and sat up.

"Wow, and I thought you were a talented wizard." Zack said, checking out the multiple cuts he had on his body.

Balast waved his arms and the cuts healed as he said, "I am the most talented wizard, but I haven't spent a lot of time researching protection Magic, so I'm not proficient in it."

A snap of a twig alerted Balast that something was nearby and as he put his hand on Zack, they both turned invisible. He covered Zack's mouth as trees collapsed. In front of them a procession of Malums stormed across the landscape. Rushing tentacles, wings, and what looked like limbs flashed by their eyes and tore down the forest. There were almost a thousand of them. Once they passed, Balast uncovered Zack's mouth and followed them. Zack just followed, shaking in shock. At the top of the hill Balast climbed he saw a black, caste-like structure in the distance with shadows enveloping every inch of its twisted structure. He shook his head.

"This is not good," he said quietly, rubbing his eyes.

Then Zack exclaimed, "Hey, Balast, there are people behind us." Balast turned around and came face to face with the only person he despised.

"Inferneous."

"Balast," Inferneous said, walking up to him. Zack could tell that things were going to get a lot crazier.

Part Two: Solidum

Chapter 11

Jayce woke to the pungent smell of rotten wood and salty sea air. He rubbed his head, getting off the straw that he was lying on and surveyed what looked like a small dungeon in the hull of a ship. The bars were a black iron, and the wood was so old that you could pull it apart yourself. Erica was sitting across from him, and she sighed when he looked around. His eyes settled on Erica, and she rolled her eyes.

"Why put us in the same cell?" Jayce questioned.

Erica stood and clenched her fist. "I don't understand how thick some people are," she muttered, turning toward the small window and looking out at the teal seawater to calm her anger.

Jayce took the time to examine her for the first time since they had met and immediately started fighting together. She was garbed in black cloth with red ties around her waist, arms, and legs. Her broken dragon mask was also tied to her waist, serving as a piercing reminder to Jayce as to why they were here. He got up and tried to look out the small window with Erica, but she pushed him down to the floor.

"Ay! What was that for?"

Erica chuckled, "You don't get to observe the beauty of the sea. You interrupted an important duel between our captor and I."

Jayce put his hand out to her in defense, "He was going to kill you!"

Erica scoffed, "I wish." she said, then slumped down to the floor. "We know each other too well to kill each other so cold-heartedly." She slammed her foot on the bars of the cage in rage, "As if I could kill him…"

The bars gave way and fell, peeling away some of the rotted wood on the ceiling and bits of the floor, leaving a wide gap. Erica stood nonchalantly and walked out of the cell and up the ladder to the main deck. Jayce scrambled to get on his feet and reluctantly followed her. When their heads surfaced from the hole that led to the main deck, they saw a functioning crew of northern pirates and High Shadow Ninja. Erica's mouth dropped open in shock while Jayce nodded his head with a smile on his face. Each of their crew was working as a perfect team together, keeping the ship sailing for an undetermined destination.

"Oh good, you guys decided to come out," said a voice behind them. It was Inferneous. They both looked him up and down as he walked down the side stairs to the helm of the ship. He was wearing a maroon-red vest with golden buttons and black leather pants that looked almost slick because of their dark hue. Quite stunning from the decaying rags he was wearing before. "So, do you guys want a round two or are you willing to be a part of the team?"

Erica scoffed, "I'd rather die. Who do you think you are?" she said, backing up to the clear space of the ship. She stopped a few feet before the mast, noticing the crowd of her own men working the ship.

"You haven't been in the High Shadow Ninja clan for years now. Their loyalty is unwavering!" She folded her arms with a smile and pointed to one of the ninjas who donned a turtle mask and was pulling a rope, "Lower Rank, attack Inferneous!"

Lower Rank ignored her and continued to pull on the rope with two other ninjas.

Her smile faded as she yelled louder now, "ATTACK INFERNEOUS!"

The ninja stopped pulling on the rope, seemingly nervous and then turned to Inferneous, "Per- permission to attack you, sir?" he said, stuttering.

Inferneous gave a slight smirk. "Permission denied. Attack your former leader here." Inferneous ordered the ninja.

The ninja immediately faced Erica and sank into a fighting stance, holding his shaking hand in front of his face. Erica was in disbelief. She looked around noticing all the other crewmates had stopped doing their jobs and were gazing at the two of them. The boat, which was rocking slightly from sailing the seas, was now still.

She turned to Inferneous in rage, "You have used magic to influence them!" she swung at him and he caught her fist again.

Inferneous smiled and said, "Now soldier." Before Erica could question his words, she crumpled to the ground, revealing a still shaking ninja behind her. From the bruise on her neck, the ninja had chopped her into unconsciousness. Jayce covered his mouth in amusement, "That was awesome."

"Agreed." Inferneous said smiling. "Take a rest in the cabins," he said, patting the still-shaking ninja on the back. As soon as everyone had resumed their work Inferneous addressed Jayce, "I want you to be my apprentice."

"Why?"

"Because you seem like a very capable young man," Inferneous said, beckoning him to walk up to the wheel of the ship.

"That isn't a real reason for me to abandon my hometown and my crew. Plus, I had to stop you from trying to kill Erica Gutbane before her father caught wind of it."

Inferneous turned to Jayce, smiling.

"You really are determined to help people. Didn't you hear us say that I defeated Gutbane? That's the whole reason she invited me to a duel!" he chuckled and shook his head, "Plus, I've known Erica her whole life. I know her like the back of my own hand."

Jayce shook his head, "That's not possible! Gutbane has been known to destroy legions of ships with his crew! Who are you?" Inferneous looked at him with a look of skepticism, furrowing his eyebrows and turning his head to the side. In confusion, he said quietly,

"You don't know who I am?" His hand slipped off the helm, and he stared at the open ocean.

I guess I didn't make that big of an impact before the incident... He walked down to the main deck and clapped his hands. All the ninjas and mercenaries stopped working the ship and turned to face him.

"Do you all of you know who I am?" There were murmurs between the mercenaries but the ninja all stayed silent, giving Inferneous the information he needed.

"Ok then. I haven't made my mark on the world clear enough. They should know who I am." he waved his hand and yelled, "We are going to change that!"

He backflipped high into the air and landed back where the helm was and yelled out orders with a smile on his face, "Set a course for the nearest island! Hoist the anchor and pull out the rum! We are going to be known far across all the lands…" he ripped off his shirt and fire appeared in his hand, swirling and dancing vividly. "We are going to rob every single pirate and return their loot to wherever they stole it from. We will rid the world of the monsters that plague it, and we'll be known as the-" Inferneous paused and looked down. "The-" he stuttered again. "Huh, anyone got any ideas for a team name?"

All of the crew shook their heads.

"We'll figure it out as we go along."

Inferneous turned a wheel and they set off on the teal-blue seas of Magia. The crew grumbled and heaved as they took shifts working the ship day and night. It had been at least three days before Inferneous called Jayce, Holdren, and Erica to the captain's quarters. The smell of rotting wood, gunpowder, and sea salt greeted the three of them as they stepped through the door. Inferneous was lying on the wooden table in the middle of the room with dancing flames above him. He smiled and brushed his hands through the bright display and smiled. Erica coughed loudly signaling their presence. Inferneous waved his other hand and the flames dissipated as he sat up and crossed his legs on the table.

"Oh hey." he said smiling again. There were a few seconds of silence between the four before Inferneous asked, "Did I call you here?"

Erica sat down in the wooden chair next to the table and covered her eyes, whispering, "I can't take this.."

Holdren held his breath so he wouldn't laugh out loud while Jayce smiled and shook his head responding, "Yes, you yelled for us, saying you had something important to tell us?"

"Oh yeah!" Inferneous said, slapping his forehead. "Do you know where we are going?"

Holdren burst out laughing now, holding his stomach. Erica stood and walked towards the door. Jayce grabbed her arm and she shoved him against the wall,

"Don't," she said, pointing her finger at his face.

"Erica, if you don't control your rage, I'm going to put you in the dungeon again," Inferneous said, standing up.

"Please! Do that! I'd rather be unconscious than deal with your decisive idiocy!" she yelled, raising her arms.

"Idiocy? I only asked if you could show me where we are going…"

"There's no way…" Erica said, walking towards him, grabbing him by the shoulders and continuing, "That you have been sailing a ship and not have known where you were going. There isn't a way. Especially given who you are."

"Then how about you three drive the ship then, hmm?" Inferneous grabbed her hands and removed them from his shoulders. "I'm trying to be a nice captain by allowing myself to be advised by people I've defeated, but I guess you people want to be thrown overboard-"

Inferneous was interrupted by Holdren unfolding a large map and slapping it down on the table behind Inferneous.

"We are in the middle of the Simul Sea. We are five nautical miles from the nearest land and we have been going in a figure eight for the past three days."

All three looked at him with looks of surprise.

"I was the map keeper and pathfinder for my family. I love keeping track of where we are going and I thought it was intentional that we were working out the ship crew." he rubbed his hands together and pulled out a compass and set it on the table. "I've also got a magic compass that tells the holder where they should be going."

They all were silent for a minute until Erica grabbed the map off the table and scanned over it.

"It's accurate." she said, setting it back down. "So, what do you mean by where we are supposed to go?"

Holdren stopped rubbing his hands and picked up the compass, looking at it. "Usually, it points to where you want to go, but in times of confusion or when you don't know where to go, it points somewhere."

Erica grabbed the compass out of Holdren's hand and examined it, "What the heck is this?" she said, turning the compass around.

It didn't look like any compass she had seen in her life. It looked more like a thick golden coin with two swords pointing away from each other, marking the north and south hands for the compass drawn on top of it. It looked more like a collectible than anything. Erica was about to hand it back to him saying, "You're crazy-" when the swords started to move. It stopped pointing south-east, but both swords started to point in that direction.

"Wow…" Erica said, moving side to side and watching with awe as the swords continued to point in the direction they had landed on. She looked up and realized the swords were pointing back at Holdren. She tossed it to him and asked, "Is it specifically tuned to you or something?"

"No. I don't think so." He looked down at the compass and noticed both swords pointed north-west, back at Erica. "Huh." he said, shaking it to see if it would change.

"Hand it to me. I want to see where I want to go." Inferneous said, extending his hand. Holdren put the compass in Inferneous' hand, and Inferneous' eyes went wide.

"Wha-" he stared at the compass, and his eyes dilated until they couldn't see the whites of his eyes. He stood there with his eyes and mouth hanging open. There was complete silence until Jayce put his hand on his shoulder. "Are you-" he was interrupted by the large breath Inferneous took as his eyes returned to normal. He grasped Jayce's arm and breathed heavily.

"Ok, I know what to do. Sorry if I blanked out on you guys. This is one of my master's creations, and it has a paralytic spell on it. I just deconstructed it, but I was already frozen."

He dropped the compass on the table. Upon impact, a bright flash came from it, blinding all of them. When they could see again, there were two broadswords on the table. They both glowed a fiery orange. The coin now had a regular compass on it.

"By the Angels' wings, that is awesome!" Inferneous picked up the swords and examined them. "There is a lot of magical power coming from these swords. It's a familiar energy, though…" he paused for a minute, and then his eyes lit up, "This aura is from Parquen! The genius inventor and magical librarian!"

Inferneous' smile faded when his thoughts fell on Balast. *How long has it been?*

Inferneous looked to Holdren, Erica, and then Jayce, "What is the worst disaster in recent history?"

Jayce looked to Holdren, and Holdren started, "Ahh, maybe the fires of Yorsika? The tragedy of the hundred islands?" he guessed.

Erica scoffed, "Idiot. The death tolls on those disasters aren't even close to what happened at the fall and massacre of the Aureus empire."

Inferneous' right arm lit on fire as soon as the sentence left Erica's mouth. They all jerked back in surprise as the flames burned away his right sleeve, revealing a zigzagging dark black scar up the length of his arm. Inferneous whispered quietly, "Yes. That's the one. How long ago did that happen?"

"Forty or fifty years ago-" the flames burned brighter and hotter, interrupting Erica as she shielded herself from them. Inferneous waved his left hand over his arm and the flames leaped off of it and into his hand. He closed it into a fist, and the flames dissipated.

"Set a course for the nearest harbor. We need a new ship and supplies. Erica," he looked towards her and she stood straight. "You are the helmmaster. Holdren will be our pathfinder, and Jayce will be the crew's advisor." he opened the door they first came from and gestured out with his scarred arm, "I have something to attend to. Please keep the ship in order and inform me when we are docked."

Jayce, Erica and Holdren walked out of the door and stood in silence for a minute after Infereneous closed the door.

"What happened?" Holdren asked.

Jayce rubbed the back of his neck. "I don't think I want to know, honestly. Maybe it has something to do with that Aureus accident-"

"More like phenomena. No one knows what happened there because no one survived. Don't you two know your history?" Erica interrupted.

Jayce shook his head, "I never went to school. I learned how to read and write when a kind mercenary taught me and my crew."

Erica looked to Holdren, and he shrugged, "I thought it was boring." she sighed and walked to the helm, saying, "Get to work. The faster we get to land, the faster we get to leave that madman's grasp."

Five days later, one of the mercenaries yelled out, "Land Ho!" Erica could have smiled or even laughed with joy. She had been through situations of varying stress on her mind, but nothing was more suffocating than being on a ship out at sea with a full crew of men. Her High Shadow Ninja counterparts were bearable on a daily basis and became useful in battle. But Jayce's mercenaries, when deprived of battle, sought their own plight in fighting amongst themselves. She heard cheers from the crew as she pulled into the dock, and the men dropped the anchor.

"Finally…" she muttered under her breath. She looked at the deck and saw a few of the High Shadow Ninjas glancing at her while tidying the ship.

They continued to gaze at her as they worked as if they were waiting for something.

It looks like Infereneous' influence has waned over the past few days. Perhaps my men have regained their senses and are waiting for the command to overthrow the ship,… she thought, smirking.

Once they were docked, Erica walked down the plank and onto solid ground breathing in the earthy scent of land. Her right-hand man, the ninja with the rhino mask, stood beside her as the whole of the High Shadow Ninjas filed in behind them. Jayce knocked on the door of the captain's quarters, and Inferneous opened them with a solemn face. Jayce remained silent, but Inferneous could sense his burning curiosity. Jayce stared at Inferneous, his teeth grit as he tried to work out a proper question in his head.

"Don't worry, I'm fine. Bad memories fade, and scars heal." He looked away and rubbed his arm, "Eventually."

"I was actually wondering why you brought us back to the mainland. Didn't you kind of kidnap us all?" asked Jayce.

"I guess I did, didn't I-" Inferneous said before he turned and faced a group of angry High Shadow Ninjas. They were all facing the boat with Erica at the front, and the only thing separating them was the plank.

"It was a mistake making me captain of the ship and my own crew. I think my steering them in the proper direction reminded them of who was really in charge." Erica said, pointing a thin needle like dagger at Inferneous.

Inferneous rolled his eyes. "Do you really think that's inspiring? Dragging your men under the High Shadow Ninja name? You know how many enemies your master and his masters before him have made with mad goals and ideals-"

Erica removed her dragon mask in anger, "You have no right to disrespect the people who taught you their way of life. You had no reason-" she stopped and wiped her eyes. "You should be apologizing for what you did."

The mercenaries had gathered behind Inferneous and Jayce, readying their weapons for a fight. Inferneous shook his head.

We won't get much farther like this. he thought.

He smiled widely and said, "Alright! Since my behavior has been seen as unacceptable, I suggest a compromise," he beckoned Jayce, Holdren, Erica, and Rhino Mask and huddled them in the middle of the gangplank.

"I'll take everyone out to dinner to settle our differences, but for now, I'll need you not to attack each other."

Inferneous looked at Jayce and then Erica, who was smiling uncomfortably wide. Jayce stuck out his hand toward her, and Erica grabbed it. Jayce grimaced as she squeezed his hand to the point that his hand was turning bright red. He smiled and still shook it as Holdren and Rhino Mask shook hands, too. Inferneous nodded his head, "Now into town! We have to find lodging and a proper place to eat!."

As all of them walked through town, the stares of the residents held the common air with distrust and pessimism. However, none in the group took notice. They were radiating equally more of the same energy towards one another instead. Mercenaries and High Shadow Ninjas walked side by side, scowling at each other with Inferneous, Erica, Jayce, Holdren, and Rhino Mask. The whole group occupied the width of the main road so most people had a reason to instantly loathe them.

The town was built on the base of a mountain, so as they traveled down the main road they gained a new perspective on the town as the sun started to set. Jayce, sweating and panting from the long walk, looked behind him and gasped as he saw the horizon and almost the whole of the town lit by the setting sun.

He tapped Inferneous on the shoulder and asked, "How far are we going? The men and I are tired."

Inferneous turned to him and then looked at the rest of the company. The mercenaries were huffing and breathing hard as they struggled to take another step. The High Shadow Ninjas who had monkey masks on looked winded, but the ones with tiger masks. Along with Erica and Rhino, Mask weren't fazed.

Inferneous patted Jayce on the back with a smile. "We are almost there; you'll be fine." Erica chimed in, "I'm glad we actually had a destination; I saw at least twenty bars and restaurants on our way here. Plus, I was getting bored."

Inferneous laughed, "We'll have to go the way me and my master took when we took this journey."

He walked forward and exclaimed, "Oh, looks like we are here! It's closer than I remember."

As they cleared the small ridge, they all saw a large wooden and run-down building carved into the side of the mountain. There was overgrown grass and weeds everywhere in the front yard. There were no lights inside, and the door fell off when Inferneous opened it. "It's just like I remember," he said as he walked into the rotting building.

Inside, there was a large stone table with dozens of chairs on each side. There were also various items lying around, like a fishing rod, an anchor, a battle axe, and various mirrors. Inferneous drug his hand over the table and took the seat at the very head, exclaiming, "Alight! Everyone hurry and sit down!"

Everyone hesitantly gathered themselves and sat down. Each person would have sat with their own perspective group if they had the time to but they hurried and sat wherever there was a seat. Inferneous was at the head of the table, with Jayce and Erica at his left and right, respectively, with Holdren and Rhino Mask sitting next to them. As soon as everyone was settled, silence wrapped its gentle arms around the room. No bird nor insect made a noise. The creaking of rotted wood filled their ears until Inferneous spoke.

"I am one of the most unwilling people alive today. I am also one of the two people who have the most control of magic in the entire world. I don't have to do anything anyone says or follow directions because I'm just that powerful. The thing is," he stood up, putting his hands on the table in front of him. "I hate being alone. I've done amazing things all by myself, but none of them have made it to a legendary status. I could destroy everything if I wanted to, but even in that, I wouldn't be happy." He took a breath and felt the cool wind blow through the door. "I've been searching for a team. A team that would go through everything with me and people I could call a proper family. People who were well disciplined and skilled," he gestured to Erica, "people who were wild and courageous," he gestured over to Jayce, "the people that would change the world with me. Even in the smallest of ways, I dreamed of doing something worthwhile. Something everyone would know and remember." A strong breeze blew through the cabin, cold at first, but as it continued it got warmer and warmer. Inferneous then stood and clapped his hands together, flames sparking out of his hands. He then opened his arms and fire swept across the table. As the flames settled the crew all looked agape as delicacies of all kinds appeared on the table included with silverware of the finest quality. Pitchers filled with the finest juices and wine with candles lining the table and lighting the room.

Inferneous lifted the golden cup, lifted a glass pitcher to fill it with a golden orange juice, lifted it high and gazed toward the setting sun outside.

Both Jayce and Erica were in awe as they laid eyes upon the moment Inferneous had created. They could see that he wasn't just gazing at the beautiful scene overlooking the town at sunset, but at something much grander. Inferneous' eyes burned and burst with a golden flame. It would have been the most dazzling thing in the area if the sunset hadn't lit up the room with a glittering masterpiece. Everything was shining, and the rays of light bounced off almost everything from the fisherman's hook to the stone table. Everyone but Inferneous was awed and amazed at the natural light show.

Inferneous continued to stare into the distance. He set down the cup and sat down, continuing. "This place is a remnant of my past adventures and I would love to be off on another adventure now, but I know that isn't everyone's idea of a good life. You are free to leave if you want to. I wish you the best in your future." he stopped, leaned back, and grabbed a chicken leg, finally starting to eat after the speech.

Jayce then stood up, clapping and saying, "I'll always be here for you. No other adventure calls me. And for my men…?!?!" he turned and raised his arm in their direction, and an uproar of cheers erupted from their full stomachs and dirty beards. "Looks like they're with me." he sat back down, starting to eat too.

Erica and her ninja were silent, but Inferneous could tell most of it was on Erica's shoulders. The ninjas seemed to shift toward Erica discreetly. With a flick of their hands or a small step toward Erica, they conveyed their need for orders. Some of the ninjas with monkey masks on had taken a few bites of their food but were scolded by their peers as they all watched Erica's every move.

She stood and the tension strained as everyone perked to listen to what she would say, but instead, she turned and left the building. Half the ninja rose to accompany her but she raised her hand and said, "Gain your strength." and then she exited the building. Some of the ninjas looked around, wondering what to do, but most stacked their plates with food and started to devour it.

Inferneous was intrigued by Erica's behavior, but his intrigue was ripped from thoughts on Erica by the faces of the ninjas who had removed their masks to eat. Most of the ninja seemingly lost control and started to devour their food with no thought of the masks. Mostly, monkey masks fell to the floor, revealing damaged, bruised and even deformed faces of young adults to children.

Inferneous had to stop eating and focus on not staring at some of them. As he sat up from eating a delicious soup, he wiped his mouth to hide his awe. He didn't know how to feel when he saw them and when he looked around he realized that he was the only one really surprised. The ninjas who kept their masks on were watching the others eat with unflinching postures.

He leaned over to Jayce and whispered, "It's no longer an option. They have to join us. I can't let her lead these people anymore."

Jayce nodded, "I heard about a rumor that the clan was dying but this is terrible."

He nodded his head and Inferneous waved his hand towards the door, "So do something. She's around your age."

Jayce shook his head, "No I-I I can't-"' he looked towards the door and saw Holdren leaning against the post looking out of it. They couldn't tell but he was staring in Erica's direction. She had her mask off and had her arms folded with one arm holding her chin as if she was analyzing the cityscape in front of her. Holdren approached her and she sighed when he was an arm's reach away from her.

"Were you born in a rankless society? You should not approach one of such high status. Especially when she has been separated from her peers."

"Oh, there it is." he stepped back, "I knew you were one to look down on those who were below you...but you have been lenient. What stopped you from yelling at me when we were in the captain's quarters?"

Erica scoffed, "Adequate observation. My frustration with Inferneous was the larger problem, plus you became useful in the end."

She turned towards him and he saw that her eyes were red, a bit swollen. He also realized that she was very pale and her skin was peeling a bit.

"Oh," he said in surprise.

"Say anything about my mental state, and I'll kill you," she said, putting her mask back on.

"So, the real reason you are here is to convince me to stay, right? Make your appeal." she put her hands behind her back and held her head high waiting for his response.

Holdren shook his head, "I don't care if you stay. Just let me come with you."

Erica stood still for a moment, trying to act unfazed. "Continue."

Holdren shrugged to her command. "There isn't anything else to say. I've been an advisor to Jayce for a bit and I think he's grown into his leadership position. Either he will become a living legend, or he'll die with loyal friends and a makeshift family. You, on the other hand…" he glanced back into the building and looked back at her, "you are making everyone the captain of a sinking ship."

"How so?"

Holdren shrugged.

Erica uncrossed her arms, pointing a needle-like blade at him, "If you are going to insult me like this, at least explain the phrase that led to your death."

Holdren backed up a bit, putting his hands up, "I truly don't know, that's why I shrugged. The only thing I could tell is that most of your soldiers are untrained and are just following you around. It looks like you are carting around villagers…" he stopped slowly backing up, and his eyes widened as he realized, "You are, aren't you?"

Erica shook with rage and screamed as she threw the weapon at him. It embedded itself in his shoulder and he recoiled in pain. Erica tore her dragon mask off her face and threw it against the mountain rock and it shattered into pieces on the grass. As Holdren removed the weapon, he didn't feel pain. Instead, he only felt sorrow as he saw Erica fall to the ground, tearing at the grass at her feet. Her sobs were silent, but her strokes were powerful. Her sobs racked her body with each torn weed. When only clumps of dirt remained for her to claw at, she slammed the ground in one last wave of anguish.

Holdren stepped over to Erica, though he was bleeding slightly from the wound she, but his eyes refused to waver from her. "Are you ok?"

Through her tears, she whispered, "I tried. I tried to keep them safe. I knew that my dream and their survival were polar opposites, but-," she shook her head, "but I'm just a disgrace to everyone who's looked upon me."

Holdren grabbed both of her hands and lifted them so she was looking into his eyes, "You have been incredibly strong to bring them all the way here alive. With the number of enemies that your reputation has and by how well you fought us when we ran into you, you have been amazing. Don't tell yourself lies."

He pulled out his compass, and the compass rose and pointed toward her again. "I'm here to help you. Even though I could travel with you, we are all better off with a powerful ally like Inferneous. For the sake of the villagers, please set aside your grudges with him."

She stood and wiped her eyes and nodded.

He smiled and then fell to his knees. Blood was trailing from his shoulder down to his feet, and his face was pale.

Erica held him up as he apologized, "Sorry, I just felt like someone hit me in the back of the head right there."

Erica tried to prop him up as he struggled against her, but she threatened, "Put your arm around me or else I'll leave you here to die."

He did so, shaking his head and apologizing some more as they walked back into the building.

Chapter 12

The room had dimmed as the sun set below the sea level, so Inferneous lit little balls of magic fire that floated around the room to light the table and dinner participants as night came upon them.

"When are we going back down the mountain?" Jayce asked Inferneous, looking at the rising full moon through a hole in the roof.

"Well, first, we have to get a ship that isn't falling apart if you didn't notice," he poured himself some more wine from a clay jar on the table, and Jayce grabbed it out of his hand, "Pardon me, I don't want our local power source to go on a drunken spree."

He tipped his head back as he drank the whole mug in one go. Inferneous rolled his eyes as Jayce continued, "Ok, so how much is a ship around here?" he said between hiccups.

"Let me see," he stuck his hand in his pocket and pulled out a small sack. He first put his hand inside, then continued to put his arm inside the very small pouch, which had no physical way of fitting anything bigger than a few gold coins. "Why don't you just stick your head in there?"

Inferneous pulled his arm out and put the bag over his head and over his shoulders, still searching for something inside. Jayce just rolled his eyes. Inferneous pulled his head out, and in his mouth, he had three triangular gold coins. He spit them out on the table and, with a disappointed face, put the bag in his pocket.

"Looks like it costs three coins less now." he sat back and shook his head, "I usually keep my stash stocked full, but it looks like I'm dry now unless someone extends the portal." He remained silent as his thoughts fell upon the person who created the bag. "It doesn't matter how we get the ship, really. We just need to get a better one so we won't sink in the middle of a voyage." Inferneous muttered.

He snapped out of his thoughts when he saw Jayce on the table snoring loudly. Most of the others, Ninjas and Pirates, were in the corners sleeping. Inferneous' fire orbs were warming those who slept and provided light and warmth for those who were still awake. The ones who couldn't sleep and those who remained sober were speaking to each other quietly at the table.

"Looks like our crews have chosen this place as a hostel." a deep voice said from Inferneous' left.

A man with a hard jawline, stubble and a short dark brown mustache leaned forward. His long hair swished forward, covering his scarred cheeks that moved weirdly as he spoke.

His voice was crisp and deep as he said, "Didn't think I'd look this way?"

Inferneous blinked and sat back. Looking down, he saw the Rhino mask tied to his belt swinging back and forth as he moved. Inferneous covered his opened mouth in awe, but then he stopped as he looked at the man's features, faintly recognizing something.

"What is your name, and how old are you?" Inferneous asked.

"My name is Rhinda. I'm Forty-nine. Surprised?" he smiled, "Do you want me to put my mask back on?"

He lifted the gray rhino mask to his face, and Inferneous swiped it from him.

"What is your lineage?" he said, placing his hand on the table, looking at him intently but was interrupted by Erica and Holdren stumbling into the room.

Erica half dragged Holdren and sat him down at the table. One of the people at the table with a tiger mask stepped to his side and checked his pulse in a calm manner.

"His pulse is lower than it should be, but his injury isn't life-threatening." She said as she pushed aside his metal chest plate, pushing his shoulder with two fingers.

"OW OW!" Replied Holdren.

"He's responsive, so he'll definitely be fine if we wrap it…" The female ninja looked at Erica.

Erica nodded, "Do it."

The tiger-masked ninja ripped off Holdren's left arm sleeve and tied it around his left shoulder, earning a grunt from Holdren.

"He'll be fine. It would be best for him to rest for a good two weeks, but we definitely don't have that kind of time." She returned to her seat and dipped her finger into the mug and swirled her finger in it. The water started to glow a faint pale blue, lighting her mask up a bit. It started. She then took the mug and splashed it onto him.

Holdren woke with a start. "Wha- what happened?" he said, looking around.

Jayce looked at Erica judgingly, and she replied, "I made a deal with him. My soldiers and I will travel with you in exchange for education in martial arts tactics and magic."

Jayce and Inferneous blinked in response.

Holdren wiped his face and looked at Erica, confused. "Did you…?"

She looked down at him with a taunting smile. "I could always take my soldiers and leave…"

Holdren looked at her and then looked at the civilians. He sighed and nodded, muttering, "Just like we agreed."

"Sounds wonderful," Inferneous spoke while yawning. "I'm going to go to sleep, and I suggest you all do the same." He turned and faced the back of his chair, lying sideways as he finished saying, "We have a lot to do tomorrow."

The next morning, Erica woke up to the smell of the ocean breeze. She turned over and ruffled the white linen sheets making the wooden frame of the bed creak. She rubbed the linen between her fingers and sat up quickly. This type of luxury was foreign to her. She removed the sheets and placed her feet on the wooden floor, wincing as her bare feet absorbed the cold. As she took in her surroundings, she noticed she felt lighter than usual.

She patted her black, slightly tattered gi down and exclaimed, "Where are my weapons?"

She looked around again and immediately opened the lavish wood closet in front of her. Inside were a few spare changes of clothes that looked like they were generically picked for a woman, along with all of her weapons arranged neatly on the bottom of the closet. She picked a few up, her eyes narrowing as it dawned on her that someone had removed them from the folds of her gi.

"Ax, needles, shuriken, kunai, psi…it's all here…thankfully," she muttered, refitting them in the folds of her gi. She closed the cabinets, and then she heard a shout and more shouts from the door to her right. She opened it slowly to see a wooden balcony overlooking a large stone courtyard. On the courtyard were at least twenty people in formation performing what looked to be punching drills with each other. She walked the length of the railing until she descended into the courtyard by a wooden flight of stairs.

The people were all in lines of four and she saw that they all had a monkey mask except one. He was in front, separated from the rest, and it looked like he was leading them. It was Holdren, and he was sweating a bit as he focused on punching the air in front of him. Erica circled them until Holdren spoke up, "Alright, that will be enough training for today. Good Job, everyone, get some rest." he continued punching at the air as the others walked behind him to what Erica presumed was the main lobby of the hostel.

They avoided Erica by a good distance and sent glances her way as she stared at Holdren with a mixture of amusement and fury. He paid her no attention and continued punching into the air, sweating a little more with each thrust. She walked in the line of his punch, and he sighed and rose from his stance to look down at her at his full height.

"Yes?" he asked.

A slap echoed off the stone walls of the courtyard as Erica conveyed her displeasure through violence and verbal abuse.

"I would have thought a man like yourself would have manners enough to ask for my permission before removing my weapons."

Rubbing his cheek, his face held a smile. "And you thought right." He removed his hand from his cheek and looked at it, seeing a red stain of blood. "Ask the ninja that healed me. I consulted her on what you would like most."

He looked back at Erica, and she stepped back, losing her stoic composure as her eyes widened in fear. She quickly turned around but failed and fell backwards but was caught by the waist by Holdren. He helped her get to a steady position and then she pushed him away, walking briskly into the hotel lobby, leaving Holdren confused.

Erica was confused as well. She was half walking, half stumbling into the small bar and dining hall, and she searched the crowd frantically. She started when she saw two tables with three tiger-masked individuals sitting around each table. She recognized one by the red stripes on the forehead of the mask, marking the medical tiger. She stumbled over, and as the tiger masks realized it was her, they all stood rigid from their seats. Erica ignored all but the medical tiger mask as she grabbed the ninja by the arm into a dressing room.

"What's wrong with me?" Erica asked her.

The tiger mask squinted her eyes at Erica, looking her up and down. She took Erica's hands in hers and shook her head. "You are having a panic attack."

Erica shook her head and sat down on a stool in the corner of the small space, taking her shaking hands from the tiger mask's hands. She sat there and stared at the wooden floor in silence for a minute before she felt a hand on her shoulder.

"Erica, look at me."

Erica jerked her head up and started, "How dare you refer to my real na-"

She was silenced by the piercing blue eyes of an elderly elven woman staring back at her.

"Erica, my name is Drathni. I've served under you for years now, and I've overseen your physical and mental health rise and wane, but this is the first time I've seen you afraid since you were a child."

Erica sat down once again, staring at Drathni with a shocked look on her face.

"I've never seen your face before," Erica whispered.

"Neither I yours until the recent string of events and it's bringing new revelations to me every day. One of which was revealed to me right now."

She grabbed Erica's shaking hand and held it at Erica's eye level. "When you faced Inferneous in battle, you never wavered. Even after you lost, you remained stoic. So, I have to believe that there is something else that has driven you to such fear." Erica held up her other hand and saw it shake unsteadily.

"It was Holdren."

"His kindness scared you, didn't it?" Drathni said, shaking her head. "Makes sense for a girl raised by power-hungry men."

"But it wasn't just his actions. He's been kind to me since the beginning. Wh-what…" she exhaled, not able to finish her sentence in confusion.

There was a knock on the door, and Drathni put her mask back on while whispering to Erica, "You'll be fine. Breathe and take your time in here."

She opened the door and faced Jayce standing next to Holdren. Holdren had a piece of cloth he held to his face that had splotches of blood on it, but he didn't seem bothered.

"Is she ok?" Jayce asked tentatively as Drathni closed the door quickly behind her.

"She is as well as she can be. She asked not to be disturbed." Drathni explained.

"Alright, well, when she comes out, tell her to come over to the table across the hall to discuss what we are going to do next."

Drathni nodded and stood rigid in front of the door, staring forward. Jayce looked at Holdren, concerned, and Holdren shrugged. They walked back through the hall and sat down at a large round table with a brown sack in the middle and Inferneous with five to ten cups of beverages around him. Holdren and Jayce pulled out chairs, and Holdren reached for one of the cups to have his hand gently heated by a flicker of flame. He pulled his hand back quickly and looked closer and realized that between the cups were little fire beings apparently guarding each cup.

Holdren glanced at Inferneous and smiled. "Nervous drinker?"

Inferneous with his hands on his forehead with his head down perked up, and smiled, shaking his head. "I can't find a good drink, so I just ordered everything they had, and I'm having my little sprites heat and mix them to create something palpable."

One of the beasts barked at him, and he took the cup it was sitting on and took a swig.

He nodded, "It's got a nice fruity flavor but needs more alcohol."

The little flame stared at him intensely as he spoke and barked when he put the cup back down. He watched them dunk themselves in and out of the cups and sometimes pour different cups together until one barked again, and he tried another.

Seeing the whole thing happen was highly amusing for Holdren and Jayce, but they snapped out of it when Inferneous said, "We can't buy another boat.."

Holdren's small smile disappeared, and his face scrunched a bit as he asked, "What do you mean we can't buy another boat?"

Inferneous pulled open the sack in the middle of the table and showed it had around twenty to thirty gold triangles inside.

"When we took apart the boat we could only get so much from the broken and rotted wood that that ship was."

Jayce leaned back in his chair, frowning in thought. "So where can we get a ship? Could we possibly rent one?"

"We'll have to question the motives of anyone willing to rent a ship to forty people, the majority of which includes the High Shadow Ninja clan," Holdren replied.

"Yeah, they do have a very bad reputation. Plus, the request itself is absurd in itself. Forty people is enough for a functioning crew." Inferneous added, drinking another cup, "you guys can drink some of the cups. I'm sure you will like some of them." He waved his hand over the tiny flame beings, and they all dissipated into his hand with only sparks left.

"Is that a magic spell you like to do often?" Jayce asked, pointing his finger at the table.

"No, actually. It just happens naturally. My flame magic has always been a kinda of a sentient being on its own. I know only two spells that actually use flame magic, and the rest just react."

Inferneous paused as a familiar lithe figure pulled up a chair and grabbed a cup, almost spilling the contents on her black gi.

Before Erica could drink, Inferneous put his hand over the top of the cup and guided it back to the table to push it away from her.

"Shouldn't drink angry, bud."

He slapped his hands together and started, "Anyways, I think we should just travel inland and start construction of our own boat from materials we gather ourselves."

Holdren coughed as he almost inhaled his drink and coughed some more to inquisitive his next point, "That's ridiculous. Do you know how long it takes to do that? Do you even know how many people it takes to do that? Why would you even say such a thing?"

"Shut your mouth and give actual answers!" Erica said, grabbing one of the drinks again.

Inferneous quickly slammed his hand down on Erica's cup before it even left the table, and it was so loud that the semi-bustling bar went quiet. Erica, Holdren, and Inferneous were locked in a triangle death stare across their table but were interrupted by the wooden door entrance opening and a sweaty man falling into the bar. Everyone stopped looking at Inferneous,

Erica, and Holdren and turned to glance at the man stumbling in through the door. The man's clothes were ripped, and he had black smudges on his torn white shirt and brown leggings. He looked around desperately and yelled in a hoarse voice,

"Does anyone want a ship?!?!"

Murmurs went across the tables.

The death stare was broken as Jayce stood, raised his hand, and said, "Yeah, over here!"

Inferneous, Erica and Holdren all looked at him in confusion. He smiled back at them like a puppy that had just caught a ball. The man stumbled toward them and slammed his hands on the table, knocking all the drinks over. Inferneous and the others scooted their chairs back so the alcohol rained on the floor instead of their laps.

"Please just take this boat away from me. My whole crew," tears started to flow from the man's eyes to the table as he continued to speak, "We were doing our usual supply runs when we were attacked by wraiths!" he swung his head around crazily, yelling, "Wraiths! Wraiths on the ocean! Can you-"

Holdren stood, wrapped his arm around the guy's neck and mouth, silencing while he spoke, "Well, sounds like a hearty tale! Let's speak of your travels while you show us this ship of yours!"

He half led, half dragged the man out the door as he finished. The rest followed him out hastily, shrugging off the odd glances from the rest of the crowd. Inferneous winced at the brightness of the day as they stood in the road, looking down the hill at the pier.

Holdren unfurled the man from his arm and pointed to the docks, asking, "Point out your ship."

The man hesitated and then his arm outstretched to point at the largest ship at the dock. It had three masts and two layers and looked like it could fit the whole town inside for a voyage.

Holdren shook his head, "Be serious if you actually want to sell this ship you are talking about."

"That is the ship! I swear! Go down and see it for yourself but please lend me food and water for at least a week so I can start my journey away from this place and back to my family!"

Holdren raised an eyebrow and looked to the rest. Inferneous smiled and shrugged back. Erica shook her head as Jayce was awed at the enormous ship.

"I guess you have a deal then," Holdren sighed, handing him a bag of golden triangles. The man grabbed the triangles, put them to his forehead, thanked him, and ran away. Jayce immediately took off down the street to go and board the ship.

Holdren brushed past him to stand next to Inferneous, asking, "How in the world did a ship fall out of the sky and into our hands like that?"

Inferneous smiled and said, "You'll learn that luck is a necessary part of a great adventure like ours."

Erica started back into the bar, saying, "I'll gather the others."

Inferneous then tapped Holdren on the shoulder and nodded towards Erica, "You should probably go with her so no one gets hurt. I'll go check out the ship with Jayce."

Holdren smiled and turned to leave, saying, "Might as well be magic!" Inferneous laughed a hearty laugh, then set forward to check out what their amazing luck had brought them.

Chapter 13

Inferneous stared at the seaside sunset, pondering over the teal ocean over a darker purple sky as he flipped around Holdren's magic compass between his fingers. The compass pointed towards the distance, and it swayed back and forth as if the swords magically encased inside wished to escape. Just holding the magical item and feeling his master's magic was therapeutic in a way. He could feel the energy flowing out of the object like silk flowing through his hands. He could still remember the hulking muscle of his master against the moonlight, his skin glistening with sweat and with a fiery crimson glow. He looked to his side and saw Balast sweating and panting hard. His legs were shaking from the strenuous activity they had just finished. He remembered the immense pain he felt from the training and sighed fondly.

I wonder if Balast feels the same way… Inferneous thought, flipping the compass like a coin in his hands.

Holdren snatched the compass out of the air and asked Inferneous, "Do you know where we are going yet? The men are anxious to get going."

Inferneous swung his legs off the railing of the ship, knocked his heels on the wood on the other side and nodded. "Yeah, we are going to go to Obsecro. Castillus Grex is where the civilians will learn how to defend themselves and somehow shed their affiliation with the basically non-existent-" he looked around to make sure Erica wasn't in earshot, "the non-existent High Shadow Ninja clan. Honestly, it's better this way."

"What? Are the civilians learning magic? Or the end of the High Shadow Ninjas?"

"Well, both, of course. Did I ever tell you guys what the High Shadow Ninja clan was known for before they dwindled?"

Jayce shook his head.

Inferneous looked down at the ocean as if he was looking at the past directly and reading out what he saw, "They were known for being great assassins and ninjas, of course, but what was secretly known by all that opposed them is that they held the key to the only type of magic neither Balast nor I could ever perform."

Jayce's eyebrows furrowed, "Something more powerful than both of you?"

Inferneous raised his hand, and a ball of black flame appeared in his hand and as it did so, the black scar that ran up his forearm pulsed an evil purple.

"This is how I chose you as my apprentice."

He held his hand toward Jayce and the flame died, and the pulsing slowed. Inferneous, for the first time since Jayce had met him, started to look pale and maybe even a little afraid, like his arm was going to rip right off of him. He pulled his arm back. He held his right hand with his left and he calmed when the flame was gone.

"That was binding magic. The only magic that we can't use."

Jayce wiped the back of his neck and asked, "So, how do you know how to use it?"

Inferneous shook his head, "I didn't use it just now; that was the effects of it."

He swung his legs back into the boat and, looked Jayce up and down and said, "We start your training tomorrow. You'll definitely become a great wizard under my surveillance." He smiled a hopeful smile.

Jayce smiled back, nodding.

They were interrupted by Holdren calling out, "Inferneous! Do you know where we are going yet? We need to get moving before we have to pay a docking fee, and that will be all the money we have because of this big boat."

Inferneous walked over to the table under the first mast and explained their route.

"So, we are going to drop them off at a school?" Erica asked with her usual annoyed attitude. "How are we going to pay for all of their tuition? Is the school going to even accept them for who they once affiliated with? Why don't you detail these things out!?!?"

Inferneous held up a hand to stop Erica and responded, "It's my friend's master's school. He is basically an heir to the land if anything, and he teaches there. He should be able to afford a few new students and if not," he touched the compass and the swords fell out in a flash, "we have these. They can teleport the user anywhere they desire."

Inferneous grabbed them, and in a teal flash, he teleported behind Holdren. Holdren stepped back in shock and awe. Inferneous smiled widely, pleased he surprised him.

"Ok, so they can teleport you anywhere. Are you going to rob a bank with them?"

"No. I have an extensive collection of priceless gold items and other monetary collectibles on the island I was on."

"Why don't we go there first, then?" Erica smirked coyly.

Inferneous shook his head. "I've spent so much time there that any one of you would have gone insane by yourselves, so I would like to steer clear of that island for a while."

Erica scoffed and leaned against the mast as Holdren turned the map on the table every which way.

He stopped and nodded, saying, "Alright, I can plot a route for us. Alright, get ready to set sail!!" he yelled out as the crew began running around the boat to find their positions.

The boat pulled away from the dock just as the sun started to set against the teal waves, turning the sky into a wondrous green hue. It was fully nighttime when they couldn't see the harbor on the distant horizon. Even though the cold waters were dark, the ship was lit with a myriad of lanterns accompanied by Inferneous' magic, which now manifested as dogs of fire roaming around the ship. Holdren noticed most of the crew began to get tired and were falling asleep at their jobs; he walked over to Inferneous who was playing cards with Erica, Jayce, and Rhinda. From the look of it, Erica was winning because she wasn't making faces or yelling at anyone.

"I can't make any use of this hand," Rhinda said, splaying out his multicolored cards on the table.

"Me either," Inferneous said, folding too.

Erica turned to Jayce and smiled, a vein showing itself on his forehead as she gritted her teeth.

"I don't have the guts to bluff into that smile," he said warily and threw his hand onto the table.

Erica shook her head and laughed, "It really speaks to how pure you all are when you can't lie to yourself for personal gain in a simple card game."

She revealed her hand, and it was nothing, unlike the rest of their hands. In fact, it was worse.

"And it definitely speaks to mine about how good I am at it."

Erica's smile faded as she finished her sentence and looked up to see Holdren watching them. "How's the route, Compass?" she said.

Holdren shook his head at the weird nickname "Compass" she had given him.

"Well, it would get better if the crew got some rest. Did any of you explore the rest of the ship?"

"I tried, but I couldn't find a hatch or door that led down there," Jayce said, reshuffling the deck.

"What do you mean you couldn't find one? Literally, every ship has one."

Jayce shrugged his shoulders. "Would you rather me break a hole in the ship?"

"Ok, how about I search for it?" Inferneous said, standing out of his chair. "It's probably been hidden with a magical seal or something."

"I'll help you search. I know some low level search spells that could possibly find it." Rhinda also said, standing.

"Alright, you search the front, and I'll search the back."

They both searched for a while scanning every wooden panel and board, pulsing most of the ship with faint magical energy. Inferneous started to feel a bit tired after a while and sat back down at the table with his chin in his hand, thinking.

Rhinda sat down next to him and asked, "Find anything?"

Inferneous sighed loudly and reached toward his drink on the table and accidentally tipped the alcohol over, and it spilled over the table.

"Ah!" he said, standing up so none got on his clothes.

"Well, looks like there really isn't a lower deck of this ship," Rhinda said as he started to shuffle the deck of cards when he messed up and the breeze took away some of his cards.

"What in the–" he said as he tried to grab the cards.

Erica was furrowing her eyebrow as she looked at Rhinda with a look of surprise.

"You never mess up your shuffles…"

Rhinda glanced at her over the table as he picked up a card and said, "And Inferneous never spills his alcohol. We're all human here."

She looked confused, half satisfied by his response but half curious. She was going to shrug it off when Jayce, who was childishly tipping his chair back onto the mast, fell to the floor as his chair slid away from him.

"No, something is going on right here." She picked up Jayce's chair, then Inferneous' cup, and helped Rhinda pick up the rest of the cards by putting them all on the table together. She then proceeded to throw Rhinda's cards into the air, knock Inferneous' cup over and kick Jayce's chair over. She stood there for a minute as Holdren and the others stared in confusion.

"Are you mad or something-"

"LOOK!" she said, interrupting Jayce and pointing down at the mess. Inferneous looked down and realized that all the objects had fallen in a single direction. And now that Inferneous was paying attention to it, he also noticed the spilled contents of his drink were pooling around a barrel at the base of the stairs that led to the helm. Rhinda walked over and moved the barrel aside to reveal nothing but alcohol-stained wood. The alcohol was swirling in a pool where the barrel was, and Inferneous dipped his finger inside it and tasted it.

"It's bittersweet," he mumbled with a concerned look on his face.

Jayce kneeled and dipped his finger in it to the mini whirlpool. He nodded, surprised, "Looks like that mead you were drinking decided it wanted to sweeten up."

"Or it just wanted a taste of dark magic," Inferneous said, slamming his hand in the alcohol.

The splashed water droplets floated into the air, circled Inferneous, and dropped back onto the wooden planks, which caved in on themselves. Without hesitation, Inferneous dropped into the dark corridor underneath. The rest of them looked down into the hole, and Inferneous looked back up at them and asked, "Ok, who's coming down with me?"

"I will," Jayce and Rhinda both said together.

They both looked at each other and smiled.

"Let me get my weapons," Jayce said, running away to retrieve his gear.

Rhinda put his feet over the edge and fell into the corridor with a deep thump. He brushed off his jet-black gi and looked in both directions of the corridor. They were so dark he could barely see either way. Jayce soon joined them and asked eagerly,

"Which way are we going?" He looked excitedly in both directions looking, ready to run a good mile.

"Why are you so excited about this? And why did you bring your weapons?"

Jayce flaunted his broadsword and shield, asking, "Why not?"

"Because your training starts now," Inferneous said, snapping his fingers and Jayce's weapons ripped themselves out of his hands and floated back out the hole.

"I'll tell you the wonders of magic as we explore these dark halls."

"Before you go, just be sure to come back as soon as you find suitable and warm spaces. The crew are going to freeze to death out here." Holdren said, basically yelling down the hole.

"For sure! We'll be back!" Jayce said, putting a thumbs up as they walked forward down the hall.

"It's a maze in here," Jayce whispered as they walked the length of the ship in hallways, ladders, and doorways.

They sat down to take a break in one of the hallways, and Jayce slid to the floor. Inferneous strolled past him, and a lick of magical flame came off of Inferneous' leg to settle next to Jayce. Jayce looked down to see the flame and it leaped onto his lap, making him sit up raising his hands. As he continued to look at the flame, it began to twist and morph until the snout of a dog was visible, and suddenly, the flame petted one of the fire dogs that had spawned next to Inferneous when it got too dark to see.

As Inferneous and Rhinda also sat down Jayce asked, "How long has it been since we entered?"

Inferneous looked over at him and smiled, "It's been at least an hour walking up and down these corridors. You know what that means?"

Jayce smiled back, "I think it means something exciting is going to happen."

Inferneous nodded, "This definitely was created by using special magic. Must have been the work of an early graduate mage because magical spaces are supposed to end at the mage's discretion..."

There was a creak at the end of the hallway, and Inferneous and Jayce both turned towards it.

"Didn't the guy say all of the crewmates died because of some monster?"

They heard a creak from the other side of the hallway, and Rhinda turned to face whatever was there. He was greeted by only darkness. Inferneous' fire dog continued to walk forward without them. As it continued on, they all saw with horror two spindly hands grab the dog's neck and with a whimper, the dog's light was snuffed out, leaving them in complete darkness.

"Rhinda, Jayce, stay back-to-back. At the same time, I want both of you to take a deep breath and close your eyes."

Inferneous paused as he did the same, "Now, as crazy as it sounds, I want you to look without opening your eyes. Try and sense the magical presence around you. This is your first lesson in magic."

As Jayce did as he was told, he couldn't see anything, but slowly, he noticed the faint outline of the wall in front of him.

"Ok, ok, Oooo-kay," he said, smiling.

For Rhinda, he could see the hallway even clearer. Almost as well as if it was exposed to sunlight. The halls lit dimly like a hole had been punctured through the hull, but he knew no light was illuminating anything where they were. He moved from left to right, seeing how the light moved with him, allowing the light to pierce the darkness in front of him. He looked down at his hand, and he realized, seeing his hand glowed dimly, that the light that was enabling him to see was the magic flowing inside of him.

"This technique is going to be very useful in the future." He looked behind him and saw Inferneous, who was glowing a bright golden hue, showing his magical power. Rhinda quickly looked away, the brightness exuding from Inferneous seeming to fill every corner of his vision. Rhinda said to Inferneous, opening his eyes.

"Don't move," Inferneous snapped, his fiery eyes locked on the looming, spindly figure of a corpse with dried, dead skin and bones protruding from it. It looked down blankly at Jayce with empty eye sockets. Inferneous, staring mortified, looked at its ragged and torn clothes and noticed an emblem of the letter *C* encompassing the letter *G* embroidered in faded gold. *It's a student of Castillus Grex!* He thought, analyzing the situation.

"Did you see something? What is it?" Jayce asked fervently. The corpse started to animate, and it half submerged itself into the wall as if dipping into a pool, backing up and looking Jayce in the face.

"It's a wraith," Inferneous whispered slowly, putting his shoulder on Jayce.

A warm feeling came over Jayce as he asked calmly, "What's a wraith?"

The wraith shifted once more, twitching its bony fingers closer to Jayce.

"It's a magic user whose soul got corrupted by Binding magic. It's a reanimated ghost of the user's powers but cannot speak. It's very interesting to you…" he stopped when the Wraith started staring at him. Its gaze flitted back to Jayce, and as it reached out to touch him, Inferneous acted on instinct and shattered the wall it was phasing through. Everything went silent as the hole in the wall exploded outwards, not into the ocean, but into an inky abyss. It was followed by a great suction force where Jayce and Rhinda would have fallen to their deaths if Inferneous had not anchored his feet into the wood and grabbed their collars tightly. Jayce and Rhinda's feet left the wooden floor as they started to be pulled toward the blackness in front of them. There was a loud screeching as the abyss started to materialize wood and doors into another hallway conjoined to the one they first entered. Walls of wood faded into existence from the dark and replaced the broken ones as Inferneous pulled Jayce and Rhinda back from the edge. They fell to the floor, gasping for air and coughing as Inferneous stepped out of the foot holds he had stomped in the wood. Rhinda gasped and asked, "What just happened was followed by a great suction force where Jayce and Rhinda would have fallen to their deaths if Inferneous had not anchored his feet into the wood and grabbed their collars tightly. Jayce and Rhinda's feet left the wooden floor as they started to be pulled toward the blackness in front of them. There was a loud screeching as the abyss started to materialize wood and doors into another hallway conjoined to the one they first entered. Walls of wood faded into existence from the dark and replaced the broken ones as Inferneous pulled Jayce and Rhinda back from the edge. They fell to the floor, gasping for air and coughing as Inferneous stepped out of the foot holds he had stomped in the wood. Rhinda gasped and asked, "What just happened?"

"I broke it's incantation."

Inferneous stared at the wall and saw a line of dark purple stains leading down the hallway. He put his finger to one spot on the wall and licked his fingers, grimacing in disgust.

"It's so bitter."

He turned back to look at the shocked Jayce and Rhinda, who were still a bit shaken. Rhinda was still breathing hard, placing both hands on his knees, trying to gain more air while Jayce stared at the new wall, wide-eyed and not moving.

Inferneous sighed and crouched down next to Jayce, who was still holding his throat and was shaking on the floor. He put his hand on him and patted his back.

"It's alright. I know the void is a very scary thing, but I will get us out of here. Trust me. I won't let you die."

Jayce looked up at Inferneous, still pale from fear and nodded as he started getting the color back in his face and hands.

"What about me? Did I make a mistake coming down here?" Rhinda squeezing his fist tight.

Inferneous scoffed, "This thing isn't strong enough to defeat you. You will be fine. Don't doubt yourself, Rhinda; you are more special than either of us may know."

"You don't have to butter him up," Jayce said, standing, shaking his hands, and moving around to try and gain warmth.

Inferneous laughed, "I'm not."

He turned and started following the trail of what they assumed was the wraith's blood. They walked for a few minutes until they came to a door at the end of the hall.

Inferneous gripped the door handle and put his arm out, saying, "Back up. Might be a trap."

Jayce and Rhinda did as told and Inferneous opened the door and stepped in. What he found on the other side was a large room. The room could fit at least two full-length cargo ships with room for people to board. It still had all wooden floors, but as Inferneous looked down, he could see through the crack's eyes staring back at him.

"Prepare your mind, boys. This is where you finish off the wraith."

Jayce opened his mouth but not fast enough for Rhinda to say, "You?"

"Yes, you." Inferneous pointed to both of them.

"What do you mean 'you'? We almost died a few minutes ago because you got rid of it!" Rhinda retorted, stepping into the room.

"That was partially my fault. When I punched the wall, I literally broke the wraith's spell and the walls, which means that the space that the wraith has harbored this…" he waved his hands around, motioning for the place they were in, "…it got in somehow and tried to suck us all into it. I can't be concise because I really don't understand either."

They all walked forward into the room, and then there was a loud groan of wood, and the door they came from imploded on itself in a flash of black and purple swirls, leaving just a seamless wood wall. *I hope I remember those healing spells.* Inferneous thought, smiling at Jayce and Rhinda nervously. There was another groan, and the middle of the room fell into itself. A corpse that was split in half by the waist rose up out of the abyss, and the wood filled back in from the void. Jayce and Rhinda stared in awe at the wraith as it was wreathed in purple and black smoke.

"Alright, guys. Go get him!" Inferneous said, raising his hands to Jayce and Rhinda.

"With no weapons?!?!?" Jayce yelled out as the wraith started to approach rapidly, flying towards the group. Inferneous sat on the ground and nodded.

"You guys can do it. Think of this as your first assessment."

Jayce and Rhinda shook their heads as they shot in opposite directions to avoid the creature. Rhinda ground his teeth as the wraith separated into two parts with the head, body, and arms heading for Jayce and the legs and waist heading for him. The legs separated, destroying the waist, straightened, and increased in speed, heading straight for his head. He barely dodged it, but as it flew past him, the other leg headed for his chest. He was agile enough to turn sideways to dodge, but the claw-like toes cut a gash through his gi and, subsequently, his skin. Blood dribbled down his right arm as he continued to dodge the legs.

Jayce was doing much of the same. He landed two solid punches to the head when he could, but it seemed like nothing was fazing the wraith as it clawed at him with an abysmal hunger. When he got tired, he ran away from the wraith and as he passed Inferneous, who was cross-legged and meditating, it stopped and hesitated before going around him to pursue Jayce once again. Jayce caught on and slid behind Inferneous to hide from the wraith. It stopped in front of Inferneous, and its face contorted in ungodly ways, swaying from side to side, seemingly trying to avoid Inferneous and get its prey. As the monster swayed away from him, its neck turned around with the snap of a spinal cord that was no longer needed to keep the form animated.

"That's kinda cheating, but I'll give you points for spatial awareness," Inferneous said before standing and walking away. Jayce stuck close to him, watching the top half of the wraith trail close behind them.

"What's cheating in the battle against evil, huh?" Jayce said sarcastically, "You said you wouldn't let us die here, so when are you going to destroy that thing?" he said, glancing back at the reanimated corpse.

"Once you land a hit on it."

Jayce rolled his eyes, "I know you have been meditating, but I've been slapping this thing in the face every chance I can, and it's done nothing."

Inferneous smirked at him and put his hand on Jayce's chest.

"Then use your head." he shoved Jayce backwards and jumped backwards so far that he was at least twenty feet away before he hit the ground. Jayce grimaced as he turned and ducked a lethal swipe to the head from the Wraith. He smacked it in the head a few more times while bobbing and weaving from its attacks, but to no avail. In the midst of it he failed to dodge a blow and instead blocked it with his arm and was sent flying across the wooden arena. He coughed and sputtered as he tried to regain his posture, but the wraith had hit him harder than he had been hit before. He tasted iron as he saw the wraith approaching him, growing closer every second.

He tightened up and thought, *You know what? I'm done.*

He then opened up and prepared himself to meet the wraith in an offensive stance. The wraith came at him and put its claws out to strike his chest, but when the moment came, Jayce wasn't there. For Jayce, his emotions had gotten the best of him, and he was enraged at the situation. In his anger, the fight was like slow motion; he easily wove out of the path of the wraith's swipe and delivered his fist to the wraith's forehead and took it to the wooden floor. The wood cracked under the pressure, but Jayce kept pushing until it bent and broke under the force. He jumped back quickly, expecting to be sucked into the void, but that didn't happen. The wraith was thoroughly stunned now, and Jayce smiled at the result of his frustration. He wiped the side of his mouth, which blood had trickled out from and noticed that his hand was glowing a bright red. He turned and examined the hand he had just dealt the blow with and heard a shout from Inferneous. He looked over to him, and he had a thumbs up, signaling he did well.

Inferneous smiled as Jayce gave him a thumbs up back with a glowing red hand. He grunted as he stood from where he was sitting and jumped over to Rhinda, who had both arms pinned down to the floor. Rhinda was struggling a bit but he wasn't injured much when Inferneous said, "I'll take the arms from you. You can definitely defeat the wraith now with the ability you told me about earlier.

Rhinda nodded, remembering their conversation over some drinks,

"So what can you do? What's your technique with the high shadow ninja clan?" Inferneous had said when he first sat down next to him.

"Well, it's called The Rhino's Point. I can magically make anything dull, slippery, or sharp slice through any object."

"Wow! I guess that's why you have a rhino mask?" Inferneous said, smiling and pointing towards the mask on his hip.

"Yeah, I guess so," Rhinda said, taking a swig of his drink, "Although I'm really soft, nothing much like a rhino."

Inferneous shook his head. "No, you're definitely not soft. Don't take much life advice from the clan. They have forgotten what true strength is." He turned to Rhinda, looked him up and down and said, "You are an excellent example of true strength."

Rhinda snapped out of his memory as he was dashing forward. Jayce still trading blows with the wraith's upper half. Jayce dodge rolled to the side just as Rhinda rammed the wraith away with his shoulder.

He helped Jayce up, smacking him on the forehead, saying, "He said use your head, not your fists."

Jayce looked confused but didn't have time to say anything more before the wraith lunged at him again. Jayce shook his head and put his hands behind his back as he tried to combat the wraith with his head. He wasn't getting any traction until Rhinda came back and tackled the wraith to the ground.

Through the wraith hissing, Rhinda screamed, "Now!"

Jayce ran to the other side, grabbed the wraith's head, jumped into the air and headbutted the wraith. There was a green flash as the wraith's head split open and started to shred into pieces like unwanted paper. All that was left was its fading hisses and screams. Rhinda stood up and dusted his gi off and checked his scratches and bruises. Both men huffed and puffed as they caught their breath, but once they did, they looked at each other, shook their heads and laughed.

Inferneous laughed along as he joined them where they were. When they stopped, Inferneous praised them.

"Nice going, boys, this place should disintegrate in three, two..." he was cut off by the gut-dropping feeling of the floor disappearing under them. They floated in a void for a few seconds before they stood in a small corridor that led to a well-stocked storage room and bunk beds. They all took a minute before breathing again, but they smiled as they turned around and found a ladder back up to the main deck.

As they ascended they were relieved to smell the sweet air of the teal sea and once again felt the rocking of the boat as it was sailing.

It was a cloudy day, which saddened Jayce because he was excited to feel the warmth of the sun again. They observed the deck and saw everyone working as a crew still sailing the boat, but they all stopped when they saw the men emerge from the hatch.

Erica greeted them first, "Oh, you guys are back." she said in an unsurprising yet expected sadness. "Have fun dealing with the monster?"

Jayce and Rhinda collapsed on the deck from exhaustion as Inferneous asked, "So you knew there was a monster?" he smiled and applauded. "Well played. Did you forcefully interrogate the poor man who handed us this boat so you could learn where it was?"

"Of course I did. So how bad was it that you had to take two days to defeat it?"

"Two days?" Inferneous questioned, and then it dawned on him, "Time moved faster in there. It was only like forty-five minutes for us."

Erica rolled her eyes and looked down at Jayce and Rhinda on the ground.

"Well, you must have had them take care of the monster then." she squinted her eyes and turned away with a dismissive, "Must have not been very powerful."

Later that evening, there was food and a small magical fire burning as the crew celebrated their return. Holdren, Jayce, and Rhinda were laughing with the mercenaries and tiger masks about their battle as the civilians ate food and played a bit of music with the instruments they had found in the cargo hold.

Inferneous and Erica watched them all from the helm in a comforting silence between them. It was broken when Inferneous said,

"You aren't really a liar, though."

Erica rolled her eyes and looked in the opposite direction. She did remember what she had said before they had left after their card game and she didn't regret it.

"You are just distrustful and strategic. Anyone brought up by a clan of assassins would be the same way."

"Ok, I'm sorry for letting you on by not telling you about the monster," she said, still not facing his direction.

She stared down at the main deck and her eyes eventually wandered to Holdren laughing along with the rest of the men and shook her head, grimacing at how she acted at the port.

"I'm just trying to help you gain a better picture of yourself so you can be a woman Holdren might court."

Erica clenched the wooden railing and smiled cynically at Inferneous,

"So, how was the ink monster, hm? From the way he described it, it sounded like-"

"Malum…A Malum!?!?" Inferneous held his head as he realized his grave mistake.

Binding magic… A wraith… Pocket Dimensions…

Inferneous' mouth dropped open, and he jumped from the helm and raised his hands as he did so. The magical fire spread around the rim of the boat just as he saw what he had just predicted would happen.

A civilian child on the ship was holding up an inky black blob with tendrils on every side of it and picking it up curiously. All Inferneous could hear was silence as he screamed with anguish for the child to put it down, but it was not to be. The inky blackness twitched and, in seconds, grew twenty times in size and consumed the child whole. The ship was a mess in an instant with civilians screaming and everyone else bearing weapons trying to fend off the whipping tentacles of the beast now breaking apart the third mast and consuming it.

As chaos ensued, Inferneous stood with the image of the child burned in his memory. He might as well have been stabbed and bleeding out. His mouth fell open as his flames burned out around him. Falling to his knees, he held his hand out, trying to use his magic, but no flame extended from his hand. The only thing that woke him was Jayce tackling him out of the way of the Malum's tentacle. Inferneous looked up and saw Jayce's determined, already bloodstained and bruised face and heard him say, pointing to Inferneous in the chest, "I won't let you die." Jayce then grabbed Inferneous' arm and made him stand.

Still staring him in the eye, Jayce said, "Get it together, soldier."

Jayce then turned back and issued orders in a demanding, almost angry voice, "Focus on the tentacles! Don't let them destroy the other masts! Get the civilians to the other side of the ship! Drag the injured back as well! This is just another enemy; don't cower now!"

Inferneous grew scorchingly angry as he snapped out of his shock and pushed past Jayce. He moved his hands in odd motions and did a number of hand signs in front of the Malum and then slammed his fist into the wood of the deck, and the Malum was magically thrown into the air, lifting a massive weight off the ship. Inferneous then stepped back, raising his left leg and drawing his elbow back like he was throwing a ball. He stepped forward and fire engulfed his arms as he threw the Malum into the sky ahead of them. The mass was so big it looked like it was going in slow motion, but when it reached far enough away, the waters below them glowed a bright orange and gold and lit up as bright as day as a giant whale made of golden fire reared its head out of the water and consumed the Malum midair.

As it sank back into the ocean, the area around them gradually darkened, leaving only the crescent moon above as a silver source of illumination. The boat was robed in a mourning silence for the moment, and then Inferneous lit a small fire in the palm of his hand, and Jayce could see the eased face of his master was not there for a minute. It was instead the face of a man who regretted his whole life, a man whose face could not bear the facade of his strength, a man whose face reflected that of a parent who had lost their only child.

Inferneous turned and set down the flame, and it spread onto the wood of the ship, and as it consumed the wood, it did not burn it up. As it reached every person, it healed injuries, bruises, and deep cuts, lapping up blood and sealing wounds with the flickering light it emitted. A collective sigh went around as the crew released their tension from the battle. Then, the fire settled into a bonfire again. Inferneous stood and walked towards the helm. Jayce put his hand on Inferneous' shoulder, but Inferneous shoved it off.

He approached Holdren who had just found his compass in a splotch of black goo, and said, "I trust you to take the ship in the correct direction."

Holdren nodded as Inferneous walked past him and opened the door to the captain's quarters. He walked in, and no one saw him until three weeks later when a mercenary in the crow's nest shouted out, "Land Ho!"

Chapter 14

Balast had just walked to the ridge to survey the land, knowing that the portal he and Zack went through could have dropped them anywhere. His face dropped when he saw a large party of people trekking their way towards him from the beach with a large ship docked poorly behind them. A few minutes later a gap of around forty years had been closed as Inferneous and Balast stood face to face again.

In the span of thirty seconds, Balast and Inferneous stared at each other and every human emotion was conveyed. The biggest in Balast's eyes were anger and confusion, while Inferneous was more joy and confusion. Inferneous opened his arms wide and approached Balast with a smile, intending to hug him, but Balast grimaced as he flexed his wrist and a powerful blast of wind made Inferneous step back a bit.

"So, what-" Balast started raising his hand and looking past Inferneous at the twenty-plus people who were observing their surroundings. He stopped and shook his head, murmuring, "Never mind."

"How's life been?" Inferneous asked rather awkwardly, putting his arms down, putting his hands in his pockets and looking down at the grassy hill.

"It's been terrible, and it just got worse," he pointed to the dark castle over the hilly island. "That is not a good sign. Actually, you know what's a worse sign?" he said, turning back to Inferneous.

Inferneous opened his mouth to speak, but Balast interjected, "You and I meeting is the worst sign. Plus, bringing a whole town with you is never a good idea!"

Inferneous looked back and saw a child running around under one of the villagers, and he fully turned around, yelling, "Who let the child come?!?! I told you all civilians and children stay on the ship!!"

Holdren came behind him and tapped his shoulder saying, "I got it." and then ran back to handle the situation.

Inferneous turned back to Balast and wiped his face, saying, "Your right as always. Nice to see you again, friend."

He reached out a hand to shake, but Balast slapped his hand away, saying, "Leave. There are too many Malums on this island for humans like them to just walk around and survive." Balast finished and beckoned Zack to walk with him as he started to trek towards the black castle in the distance.

"Hey! Don't talk to Inferneous that way; you should know better!" Jayce said, stepping in front of Inferneous. This is going to be a great lesson for him. Inferneous thought, preparing for what was about to happen.

Balast turned back and asked, "Is that one yours?"

Inferneous nodded, pushing Jayce a little bit farther in front of him.

"Jayce, is it?" Balast said, walking up to him. Jayce was two inches taller than Balast and Inferneous so Balast had to tilt his head the slightest degree to look him in the eyes.

"Your mother should have taught you to treat your friends nicer," Jayce said matching Balast's stare.

Balast eyes widened when he finished his sentence, and before he could do anything, Inferneous reached up to Jayce, grabbed his neck and pulled him down to his knees.

"Apologize," Inferneous said, pushing Jayce's head down,

"What? Why he–" Jayce started, but Inferneous cut him off as he squeezed harder on Jayce's neck, choking the air out of him. "I said apologize!"

A few seconds later, a weak "I'm sorry." whispered out of Jayce's mouth.

Balast shook his head, scowling and continued toward the black castle slightly faster than he did before. As he got a bit farther away Inferneous lifted Jayce back to his feet and asked, "You ok? Did I hurt you too much?"

Jayce rubbed the back of his neck, asking, "Why did you do that? Man, that hurt."

Inferneous put his hand on his shoulder, and Jayce felt warm all over, and the pain on the back of his neck faded away.

"Balast watched his family die in a fire."

Jayce got whiplash from how fast he turned to look at Inferneous. He covered his open mouth in awe, and Inferneous continued, "I wouldn't have liked him to put you in one of his pocket dimensions where thousands of years pass in a single second. I've seen him put people in there and they don't ever come out alright." Inferneous patted Jayce's back and started to follow Balast as Jayce stood there, shocked at what could have happened to him.

"These people are crazy." Erica whispered under her breath walking past Jayce following Inferneous.

Balast was numb from the rage. He acknowledged that by tearing and re-mending his cloak as he briskly walked towards the castle in the distance. *His apprentice is bold. I'll give him that...* Balast thought. He looked over to Zack, walking beside him with his hands behind his head, whistling no particular song. He didn't seem bothered by anything, really. In fact, he seemed excited.

"What are you so happy for?" Balast asked him, mending his coat one more time before leaving it be.

"I'm happy to see another living soul that can see you like I do. You're a mean old hound, biting at anyone's ankles." he smiled a taunting smile.

Balast rolled his eyes.

A few minutes passed before Zack asked an intriguing question, "You haven't really made peace with the death of your family, have you?"

Balast looked at the boy in a way that questioned what the boy had in mind, but Zack's face was all curiosity instead of the usual smug look.

"I guess I haven't," Balast said bluntly.

Zack shook his head, "Well, I guess watching people who loved you leave is better than watching the people who never loved you abandon you."

There was silence for a few seconds until Balast gave in, "Ok, how did you become an orphan? Or, more importantly, how did you meet those Malum-infected thugs?"

Zack sighed, saying, "I was at a low point. Well, if you can get any lower than digging in the trash for food. It was just a way to get more food and survive. Not many dreams touched my consciousness after the betrayal of my own blood."

Balast grimaced, looking forward.

"Anyways, I just thought you were a bit harsh on that guy for someone you grew up with."

Balast shook his head, "You wouldn't understand." he said, walking faster as he wove through the trees.

Zack shrugged and matched his pace until he looked back and realized that the other crew had caught up. He slowed down to meet them and introduced himself, "Hey, I'm Zack nice to meet you."

Inferneous met his outstretched hand and gripped it firmly, saying, "Inferneous, nice to meet you. How has it been being the apprentice of my friend Balast?"

Zack sighed and smiled coyly, "It's been better than his mood, for sure."

Inferneous nodded his head, slightly smiling. He pulled Jayce over and introduced him, "This is my apprentice, Jayce."

Jayce had to bend down a little to shake Zack's hand, and as he did so, he replied, "Nice to meet you. If it's alright, how old are you?"

"Seventeen, you?"

"Nineteen, thanks." Jayce let go of his hand and patted him on the shoulder, saying, "I guess I'll be a kind of older brother for you."

"No thanks," Zack said, removing Jayce's hand.

"Defeated your first Malum yet?" Jayce asked, looking up at him. Jayce opened his mouth and looked to Inferneous, who questioned, "You defeated a Malum…?" he looked Zack up and down and shook his head, "No, you could only slightly damage it."

Zack was offended by the remark, "I did! You can even ask your mean-spirited friend over there." Zack gestured to Balast, who was slowly fading into the distance as he exclaimed, "I took it upon myself to destroy the beast and save the townspeople! They cheered and feasted afterwards, and I got so many gifts that I sadly left back at the building site of the school…" he hung his head thinking about the presents and food he had gotten from the people as his stomach rumbled.

"Wait, where are we going exactly?" Holdren said, interrupting Zack's sorrow. He ran ahead and broke the tree line to be welcomed by a massive pitch-black castle. The castle was a strange outlier to its surroundings, which was a beach that stretched into a tree line that eventually ran into a rocky mountain ridge.

The castle was so pitch black that when they all looked at it, everyone except Balast and Inferneous had to avert their eyes. As they did, stifled cries came from them.

"What in Magia is that?" Erica hissed as she shielded her eyes with her hand.

Inferneous stared at it and shook his head. "A Malum creation, for sure."

He turned around and saw Zack and Jayce staring dead at the castle. They both had a grim look on their face and visibly looked more tired as they continued staring at it.

"What are you two doing? Avert your eyes!" Inferneous exclaimed,

"Why? This is what we are up against; we aren't going to cower from it," Jayce said as his nose started to drip blood onto the sand.

"What he said," Zack commented as his eyes fluttered and he passed out.

Inferneous caught him and lightly socked Jayce in the gut, making him break his gaze. He placed his hand on Zacks's forehead, and after a few minutes of Inferneous healing him with magic, he woke up with a start.

"Wow. I thought I was a bit stronger than that," Zack said, sitting up. He looked around, and eventually, his eyes settled on the castle but he didn't feel any strain when seeing it.

"Did you magic the problem away?" Zack asked, rubbing his eyes and looking at the castle again. This time he spotted Balast at the top of the stairs at the front gate of the castle.

"Look who is trying to get in." Zack pointed out to Inferneous Balast who was crouching and bending over, examining the door.

Inferneous sighed and checked on the other members of the group, and one by one put his hand over their eyes and magically shielded them from the castle's magic. Then as they all adjusted, he ran over to Balast, checking out the door.

"What is it?" Inferneous asked, looking the gate up and down. Looking through the bars, all he could see was the pitch black of the void but nothing else.

"It's none of your business," Balast retorted, randomly punching the gate. It reverberated and eerily groaned as Balast wrapped his fist, gritting his teeth from the pain.

Inferneous laughed at him and placed his hand on the gate, which caused his hand to be repelled by the magical spell on the gate. He held his hand winced in pain as Balast choked on his laughter.

"Yeah, it's got a pretty powerful shock and burn spell on it," Balast said, shaking his head. "We can break it, but the thing is, there are at least three to four thousand Malums inside."

Inferneous got whiplash from how fast he looked at Balast.

"Four thousand!?!?" Inferneous exclaimed.

Balast looked at him and nodded slightly. Balast walked to the side of the gate and pointed to a silver plaque that read "Mors Omnium."

"Death to All," Inferneous said aloud.

Balast shrugged, "Must have been a while since you've studied your Malum dialect. The actual translation is 'THE Death to All.'"

Inferneous rolled his eyes. "The real question is how do we get in without having four thousand Malums rushing out?"

"Why do you want to get in?" Balast questioned,

"Why do you want to get in?" Inferneous asked, "There has been no communication between us since we got here. You'd imagine after a good forty years you would like to see your old friend again-"

"Old friend? More like an old fool."

"I'm just trying to figure out how we got here. Could you please just—"

"I was following the trail of a Malum, ok? I was at an Obsecro, and they had a light Malum infestation. That boy Zack I saved from that infestation, and so I trained him and he showed results by immobilizing a Malum for a minute. I grew suspicious because I had never seen Malums that far east before so I took care of the Malum and followed its portal here." Balast finished his rant and looked at Inferneous, asking, annoyed, "Is that good?" he rolled his eyes and turned toward the gate.

"Yes," Inferneous said, turning toward the gate too. "I was on my island when,"

"Stop. I don't want to hear how you got here. I just need you to help me break this spell so I can investigate more."

Inferneous was taken aback. He sighed and shook his head as Balast continued,

"On the count of three, just magically charge the bars. One, Two, Three!"

They both grabbed the gate, and a flash of purple, teal and orange sparks flew out of the double collision. The gate then collapsed inward on itself, the bars then disintegrated and flew away in the wind. They both coughed and waved the dust out of their faces. As they were about to step into the castle, Zack grabbed Balast's coat, pulling him back.

"Wait! Did you forget about us?"

They both stopped and looked back seeing the whole group was already halfway up the stairs following them. Balast looked towards Inferneous while Inferneous rubbed the back of his neck.

"Umm, ok..." he started, "Jayce, Rhinda, and Erica can come. Holdren, keep the fort down out here. Hide if you hear anything." He pointed at each person he named and Holdren gave a thumbs up.

Before they all went in, Erica made sure to gather the tiger masks while saying to the group,

"Do what he says, although if it's human, you can engage it." They all nodded. As Erica started ascending the stairs, Holdren grabbed her hand and stopped her. She turned to face him, ripping her hand out of his. He backed up a bit, raising his hands, "Sorry," he started. "I just wanted to ask if there was anything wrong between us before you go in there. Just in case something happens to us out here or, more likely, to you in there. Erica was confused.

"Besides you violating every rank code in the High Shadow Ninja, there isn't anything you would think was wrong." Holdren nodded, "I guess that's good. Just making sure I'm not assassinated before Jayce comes back out."

"Don't worry, I would only kill you myself." She said walking up the stairs.

"I hope that was a joke!" he yelled and chuckled to himself as she walked away.

"Everyone ready?" Inferneous asked to check if all the people he called were with him. "Ok, let's go."

Beyond the gate was just a large arched hallway where they could only see the black tiled walls to either side of them as they traveled through it. The ceiling was nowhere to be found as an inky darkness replaced it. Inferneous lit the hallway with a sparrow made of flames, and as they continued, it flitted above all of them, lighting the hallway for a few feet in front of them, but that was all. As they continued in, there was no visibility beyond the light of Inferneous' magic. Not even where they entered had light anymore. The hallway was fairly narrow and very cold, which made the group stick together even more as they continued. They had been walking for a bit before Erica spoke,

"Alright I'm sure we would have arrived on the other side of the planet by now. Something needs to change before we all freeze to death." Balast sighed as he stopped, making the whole group take a break, except Inferneous. They leaned against the walls and slid to the cold floor, massaging their feet and legs. Balast, seeing them tired, shook his head and with a smile, he said, "You guys are young and agile; you shouldn't be taking breaks now. I haven't broken a sweat yet. I actually found the silence quite calming."

"Well, unlike you ancient fools, we don't have the magical power to animate our decaying corpses," Erica said, groaning and stretching her legs. "Besides the castle definitely was not large enough to have a hallway as long as this through the middle of it." Inferneous looked to Balast with worry in his eyes, knowing Erica was right. Balast rolled his eyes at Inferneous. Inferneous took a few steps forward, and Balast followed him until they were more than an earshot away from the rest of the group.

"She's right. When we were on our ship, there was a wraith that made the cargo space of the ship a pocket dimension. We might be in the same sort of situation-" Balast eyes widened at Inferneous' words, "A wraith? There's no way…" Balast looked off into the darkness in front of him and then shook his head, returning back to the current topic, "We have to keep walking." he said, starting to bite his fingernails. Inferneous was about to ask why but then noticed Balast was shifting from one foot to the other, and there was the slightest bit of perspiration on his brow. From how long Inferneous had known Balast and from his knowledge of how careful Balast was, he knew that multiple things had already gone wrong.

"How bad of a situation are we in?" Inferneous asked with a lowered voice. Balast shook his head, scratched his head in worry and said,

"On top of being stuck inside of a Malum void dimension and having no way out…they're in the walls." Inferneous raised his eyebrow.

"How many?" Inferneous asked even quieter.

"Almost a good thousand if I'm not too paranoid." Inferneous turned, hearing that, turned around, putting both hands on the wall and closed his eyes, trying to see what Balast was talking about.

"I can't see them," he said after not getting anything from his search. "You won't see them. You have to use your scar." Inferneous pulled his sleeve up and realized the scar on his right hand was glowing a bright purple. He closed his eyes once again and focused on it, and when he opened his eyes again, he gasped in horror, seeing writhing masses of Malums behind the black tiles. Horns, claws, maws, tentacles, and talons all scraped and slithered behind the walls, creating a deafening sound in Inferneous' ears. He was about to scream when Balast covered his mouth and said, "Don't let them know, don't let them…" he stopped when to the right of them behind the wall, four eyes with red pupils stared back at them. They made contact with Balast and Inferneous, and a claw came out of the ink and tapped on the wall.

"What was that?" Jayce asked, looking over at Inferneous and Balast. The Malum's eyes snapped to Jayce and then dragged its claw across the inside of the wall, creating a deafening screeching sound. To their horror, the black mass behind the Malum spawned more eyes in their direction, and they all started to press onto the walls. Balast yelled out, "Get up and Run!" and once the words left his mouth, the walls behind Jayce started to collapse, and an inky mass started to grab him. Inferneous sliced upwards with his hand, and fire emerged from the ground and severed the tentacles, freeing Jayce.

He stumbled forward to stop where Balast and the others were standing to look back and see that the hall behind them was collapsing into itself, bringing with it a black viscous liquid. He was snapped out of the horrifying scene by Balast's hand grabbing the back of his neck and shoving him forward.

"I said run, fool!!" he said and then turned around and raised both hands up, pushing them forward. As he did so a wall of ice grew out of the ground and cracked and splintered as the wave of liquid death pursued them. They all started to run down the hallway as it collapsed behind them. As they were running, there was an ungodly sound of what was the mixed howl of a wolf, the braying of a donkey, and the roar of a lion mixed together that echoed down the halls. Balast covered his left eye with his left hand, revealing a giant purple scar down his forearm and then looked to his left. Inside the black ink mass of Malums, a bigger Malum swam through them. Right before it broke through the wall to try and devour him, he flicked his right arm to the other wall, and a yellow portal appeared. Inferneous, catching on, jumped into it, leading the rest to follow. Balast made it in, too, but they couldn't rest because they all fell into another hallway, except this one had dark green tiles. There was a moment where they all breathed hard from running, and in that time, Balast looked to Inferneous and said, "A Le Lupus Asinus. We have to keep moving before—" he was cut off by the wall in front of them bursting with a black liquid.

"Move! MOVE!" Inferneous said, running in Balast's direction while behind him, the walls started to crumble and collapse. As they all continued to run, Balast put his hand to his eye again and realized that the bigger Malum was running beside them. He threw a portal to the ground in front of the group and they all fell in as the Malum broke in through both sides of the wall. As the group stood disoriented, the portal remained open, and a large Malum squeezed through before it closed. Immediately, Inferneous and Balast engaged the beast, and in blue and teal sparks, they held the monster at bay. It came to a short standstill where the beast, which had four huge massive paws and a skull made out of human bones, was pressing on both of them with its massive weight with one paw on each. When the others recovered, the first to attack were Rhinda and Jayce, who immediately attacked the joints of the paws, pressing Inferneous and Balast. The Malum recoiled and then released Inferneous and Balast from their weight. Then Zack and Erica ran forward with their weapons and tore at its underbelly, ripping whatever was keeping the Malum animated. The fallen Malum writhed around for a bit before laying still. Zack fell to the ground, shaking and taking uneasy breaths, recovering from what they all had just gone through. He wiped his cheek, which had a bit of black Malum blood on it and put his hands over his face, covering his eyes from the corpse in front of him. Erica stumbled away from the Malum and slid down to a seated position by one of the walls while sheathing her short sword and putting it back in the folds of her robes. Rhinda and Jayce just stared uneasily at the Malum, out of breath. Inferneous startled Jayce when he touched his shoulder, saying, "Are you ok?" from Jayce's reaction, Inferneous assumed he wasn't mentally, but physically he looked fine. He looked over to Rhinda and saw no cuts, bruises, or missing limbs, so he just left him be. As Inferneous went to check with Erica, Jayce snapped out of his daze, seeing Zack on the floor with his knees covering his face. He slowly walked up to him, crouched down so his face was his height and asked, "You, ok?" Zack raised his head and revealed a tear-streaked face, shaking his head. He smiled cynically and said, "We are going to die here." Jayce's gaze hardened, and he stood, pulling up Zack to stand up and said, "No, we aren't. That is what I can tell you." He then walked over to Inferneous and Balast, talking in whispered tones and started, "What is the plan to get out of here?"

Balast looked up in surprise, "Get out? We haven't done anything yet. We haven't even found out how this place got here." He looked down at Zack, and Zack turned away from his gaze, a bit embarrassed.

"We aren't going to be able to fight another one of those things. That," Jayce pointed a thumb at the Le Lupis Asinus and continued, "was not something we could handle by ourselves and being here is already putting a weird pressure on our minds. I feel like every thought I have could leave me paralyzed in a daydream, which would quickly turn into a nightmare if the Malums got to us."

"Well, those usually come in packs of six…" Balast said, pointing to the Malum, "I was just waiting for the rest to show up, but it looks like its brothers don't want to show." Balast looked around, putting his arm to his eye looking around. He was half relieved and half disappointed to see no Malums beyond the walls. Instead, he found that he could see along the void plane different separate rooms. They all differed in shape and size and some even had floating lights in them.

At that thought, Balast asked, "Wait, it should be pitch black in here. Malums love the dark best, so why is there light?"

He looked up and saw on the ceiling of the rocky room a fiery red rune that glowed softly but nowhere near enough to light the whole room. Balast jumped and became weightless, and he floated to the rune, examining it.

"What kind is it?" Inferneous asked, yelling up to Balast.

Balast shook his head, "It's an adaptation rune. It's for humans, too." he floated back down towards the ground and said,

"This is all very interesting. He waved two fingers and pointed them towards a wall and a portal opened up where he pointed. He waved his hand and said, "Ok, let's go find those other Malums."

"No!!" Erica stood in front of the portal Balast created with anger etched on her face.

"I demand you explain why we are here and what in the fourteen seas is happening!!"

Balast looked back to Inferneous and asked, "I didn't know you had a fiery taste in women, Inferneous." Inferneous closed his eyes and shook his head as Erica stood in shock from the insult.

"She's not my—" Inferneous stepped in front of Balast before Erica's fist could reach him. He grabbed her arm and held it away from Balast, saying to Erica, "He'll be less merciful than I. Plus, he didn't mean anything by that last statement." Inferneous glared at Balast, who smiled with an amused glint in his eyes. Erica shook off Inferneous' grip and massaged her wrist.

"Fine then." she said angrily, calming down, "But I still need to know what we are doing here in this death trap. Unlike you, monsters we can't deal with abyssal horrors on a daily, less multiple times in an afternoon." she looked at Balast and Inferneous with concerned malice and Inferneous responded,

"Yes, I realized that," he glanced at Zack, then to Balast and asked, "What are we doing here?"

"Were you not here on your own accord!?!?" Balast exclaimed, wondering why everyone was looking to him for answers. "Why do I have to answer all your questions? It's not like…" he gave up with a sigh.

"Just explain your thought process so we can make a plan to get through this place with everyone alive. Balast scratched his forehead and started, "Well, I left Castillus Grex, and when I arrived at Obsecro, I was planning to start my school, but to my surprise, there was a Malum infestation there, so I took care of that, but there had never been a Malum that far west because of the plains. So, I searched the town and found the portal the Malum made, and I arrived here. I was greeted by a raging horde of Malums and unpleasantly surprised by you and your crew," he pointed to Inferneous, "but I followed the Malums and found this," he looked around in confusion, "Place whatever it is."

"So, the fool doesn't even know what he's doing either. You both are imbeciles." Erica remarked, sitting cross-legged on the ground.

"No, I just don't know what this place is. My intention was to find out how and why there is a hidden island with a Malum stronghold." He looked at Inferneous and asked, "How did you get here?"

"A magic compass, but this isn't where we wanted to go. Actually," he thought back to right after he defeated the Malum on their ship and realized Holdren had picked up his compass out of a pile of Malum blood. In his mind he remembered vividly the dial was flicking back and forth erratically, probably between Castillus Grex and where they were now.

"The compass got corrupted by Malum's blood. Long story short, there was a Malum aboard our ship, and I had to take care of it. The Malum probably had connections here." Balast nodded, taking in the information. "Then we need to destroy this place. Whatever this is, it has to do with Malums, and that means it has to be destroyed."

"Ok, so what is the plan to do that?" Rhinda chimed in as he walked over to them. "Well, we are going to have to do something, actually many things, that are extremely dangerous." Balast stepped to Inferneous and whispered something into his ear. Inferneous' eyes grew wide, but then, as Balast continued to whisper, his gaze settled into a hardened determination and then into a grisly smile.

"Don't get too excited about potential death," Balast said to Inferneous as he walked toward the far wall where Balast's portal was still open. He then said, "Ok, so the plan is all of the people who aren't extremely capable are going to go through this portal." Balast shook his head, "Well, since we might die, I might as well explain to all of you what we are going to do." He turned toward all of them, took a deep breath and said, "We are going to summon every Malum into this room and kill all of them." Erica stood in disbelief, saying, "This is not the time to be joking or suicidal. How are we going to get out if you fools die?"

"When we summon all of the Malums into this room, the structure will reframe itself to protect them, and it will rearrange itself so that some parts will be exposed to the outside. That portal leads to one of the rooms that will be exposed to the outside." All of them except Inferneous looked at him like he was out of his mind, which he was for the moment.

"Don't worry if we don't make it out. Jayce and Zack will get our power, and Erica won't have to deal with us!"

"What do you mean by 'will get our powers'?" Jayce asked,

"Well since you have been named as our apprentice, we will pass our powers down to you. It's a bit complicated, but you'll figure it out." he patted him on the shoulder and pushed him into the portal before he could object. As Rhinda and Erica entered the portal, Zack approached Balast and put out his hand,

"Thank you." he said, putting his head down, "I enjoyed my time with you." he was shaking because of the tears slipping down his face. Balast grasped his hand hard and raised Zack's face, saying, "Have a bit of hope. There will be someone else out there, if not those other people in Inferneous' crew, that will care for you like a family." Zack was shocked at that last statement, and as he passed through the portal, that was all that was on his mind.

Before the portal closed, Inferneous said, "It's going to be a bit of a rough ride, so cover your heads and get ready. And if we don't survive, please stay together. There are so many dangerous things out there that would take each of you out on your own, but together, it couldn't possibly pull you apart." He smiled, and the portal shrunk in size until it disappeared from existence.

There was silence as they all stared for a minute at where the portal was as if it would reappear, but nothing happened. Jayce looked around the cave-like structure and said, "All right, get in the tight corners under the ledges just in case the rocks start."

A loud snap in the air made everyone cover their ears from the pain. The room started to shake and shift violently, causing the walls to break and crackle as they bent in odd directions. Erica and Rhinda reacted quickly, moving to the corners of the room and avoiding rocks, while Jayce and Zack moved along the walls under the ledges. They all waited in the shaking room before another loud snap sounded, and the far side of the room broke apart and disintegrated. They all were pushed against the back wall as it moved forward and launched them all with debris from the room out into the blue, sunny sky. They were launched so high that Jayce had a chance to look around as they were falling to their deaths. He saw Rhinda and Erica among a few rocks, and they made eye contact while trying to glide towards each other.

They succeeded and held each other close together when Jayce looked to his right and saw Zack flailing, trying to get himself upright. Jayce broke away from the group and glided towards Zack, grabbing his wrist to steady him. They all looked down to see that the tiger masks had created a fiery portal that they could see that led to the ocean, but just before they hit the ground, a rock split Erica and Rhinda away from Zack and Jayce. As Erica and Rhinda dove into the ocean, Zack and Jayce braced themselves for impact, but before they hit the ground, Zack's eyes lit with a green hue, and he extended out both hands, and a bright green surface appeared in front of them. It hit the ground before them and shattered, slowing their landing as the magic propelled them both upwards a bit. They then fell to the ground again and rolled into the soft sand, unmoving.

Jayce woke up clutching the sand as he slowly sat up. He clutched his side as a trickle of blood came down his nose. The salty taste really shocked him as he stood and whipped it away. He turned around and saw Zack lying faced towards a rock, and he guessed the worst, running over to him. He turned him over slowly and sighed with relief as Zack coughed. He had a few bruises on his face, but when Jayce looked down, he saw the deep purple of Zack's wrists and knew he needed to get some help immediately. He picked him up, grunting as he did so, and looked around. His legs faltered a bit, but he managed to stagger a bit forward when he saw the tiger masks helping Erica out of the ocean.

"Over here! Help!" He could see the tiger masks look to Erica for confirmation, and she nodded, sitting down in the sand. They rushed over, and one took Zack from Jayce's arm, and the other looked him up and down, raising his arms and pushing his face to each side.

"How are you feeling?" the tiger mask who was examining asked Jayce.

He snapped out of his tired haze and said, "I'm fine, just a bit bruised, and I think my nose is a bit broken." The tiger mask nodded and grabbed his nose, feeling around it, then pushed it back into place, making Jayce recoil in pain.

"OH, oh…!" Jayce yelled in pain. The tiger mask didn't say anything as he turned to the Drathni, who was holding Zack in her arms like a baby. She raised his arms, and his hands flopped around oddly, making her come to a conclusion. "His wrists are broken," she told the other tiger mask, "Let's get him to the ship so we can find materials for a pair of casts." She stood and looked at Jayce, saying, "Come on, you probably aren't as fine as you seem." She turned to walk towards the ship when suddenly Jayce felt like his soul was being ripped out of his body. He opened his mouth to scream, but the feeling had already ended. Instead of screaming, he looked up at the castle he had been launched out of to see that it was swirling with dark energy. It pulled the dark energy in and then exploded outward with more boulders, rocks, stones, and, most horrifyingly, Malum carcasses. Everyone who saw it winced and stood their ground as the concussive force from the explosion challenged their balance, but most held firm. When it was over, the sky was filled with all kinds of debris, and Jayce was in awe looking at it. He snapped out of it when Drathni grabbed his arm as she started to run, dodging debris from the castle along with parts, if not whole, Malum carcasses. They made it to the tree line and saw the others on the beach already under the cover of the trees. Jayce heard murmurs from the crew members as they waited out the gruesome rain,

"What is that?"

"How did that happen?"

"Where is Inferneous?"

That last question scared Jayce. He then began to look out in the debris for Inferneous and Balast, hopefully alive. When the debris stopped falling from the sky, they all emerged from the canopy's protection and started to make a pathway to the ocean through the debris. Jayce was not one of them. Instead, he made his way through the debris to where the base of the castle was still intact. He pushed aside a few Malum corpses holding his nose because of the stench and climbed over some boulders when he eventually reached the staircase of the base. He hurried up the stairs in worry, and he was shocked and also impressed to see Balast and Inferneous sitting on a shared base to a castle. It was a wide area, but they were sitting in the middle of a big black spot that looked to be the base of the explosion. Jayce walked forward, and the closer he got, the more he saw how beat up they were. Balast had a large gash on his forehead that was bleeding profusely, and his clothes had all kinds of tears and holes, but he still had his cloak tied around his neck even though the tail end was still kindling a small flame. His face was smudged with a black substance that Jayce assumed was Malum blood, but it wasn't much better than Inferneous.'

Inferneous looked to have more ash and soot on his face than anything, but his sleeves, along with the bottom half of his pant legs, were completely gone. He had gashes and cuts all over him that were also bleeding profusely and a large slash against his chest that Jayce could see through his tattered shirt. The weird thing is that Inferneous was smiling almost to the brink of laughter. He was looking at the ocean while Balast was looking at him with a gaze of simmering rage, but he looked too tired to act upon it, so it settled into an annoyed glare.

Inferneous greeted Jayce first, standing on his bare feet, grabbing Jayce's hand, and shaking it vigorously as they had just met.

"You survived! I knew I picked the right apprentice!" He let go of Jayce and shook his head, "Sorry, I'm still a bit jittery from the fight."

Jayce looked concerningly at both of them, "Are you alright?"

"Yeah, I'm fine. It looks like you broke your nose, though." Balast pointed out with his finger as he stood on his bare feet.

"Yeah, you also have a very bad cut on your-" Jayce stopped when he saw that the cut on Balast's head was healing at a rapid pace, and the blood was basically reversing itself back into his body, and the cut sealed itself.

"Oh," Jayce stepped back as Balast pushed past him, walking down the stairs. Inferneous followed him, and they kicked and levitated boulders out of their way, making a wider and clearer path to the shoreline. When they moved aside the last boulder, they found a small camp of about twenty injured people who weren't fast enough to avoid the boulders falling from the sky. As Inferneous and Balast walked forward into the crowd, there was a sudden silence from everyone around them, and most turned to stare at them. Balast paid no mind and walked over to where he saw Zack lying on a blanket on the sand.

"Oh my," he said, anger rising in his voice. He stepped over to him and immediately picked up both his wrists. He unwrapped the wood and cloth, keeping them straight, and put both hands on them. There was a golden flash, and Zack's wrists were no longer purple. Drathni, who was watching the whole thing, rolled her eyes and walked away to help the other injured, muttering jealous curses.

Before she got too far away, she muttered, "He hasn't woken up since he was shot out of the castle."

 Upon hearing this, Balast put his hand on Zack's forehead, and by his temperature, he could tell it was mana exhaustion. "He'll be fine." Balast stood up and turned to Inferneous, "But he could have been better if you hadn't blown up the whole castle! You Idiotic-" Balast couldn't finish his sentence because of his anger. "I'm going to leave the apologies to you because you can't seem to control yourself enough not to hurt the innocents around you." An Inferneous smile disappeared as Balast berated him, and his mood fell as Balast shoved past him, going back into the rubble of the castle.

Erica then came into his view and asked, "What was that?"

Inferneous shook his head, "It's none of your concern."

"It is my concern because I want to know why I got launched out of a castle like a catapult and almost died!"

"Ok, fine." Inferneous sat down on a rock and started, "We decided that we would face all the Malums in the castle. There, we thought there were maybe three to five thousand in the castle, and it turned out to be more than we thought-"

"Five thousand?!?!?" Jayce exclaimed.

"Yes," Inferneous sighed. "There were more, though, and we were able to take care of all of them because of our combined magical power, but I got a bit too excited and broke the magical threshold of- uh…" He looked up, rubbing his chin, and then waved his hand, "I forgot what Balast said, but basically, I blew it all up. I'm glad you guys got out in time because you would not have survived that. Hell... they couldn't survive it," he said, kicking the skull of a Malum.

"You speak of it like you didn't do it yourself," Rhinda said as he joined the conversation.

"Another one of those subconscious magic tricks," Inferneous laughed and nodded. "Yeah, sorry for endangering you guys like that. Let me know if there are any casualties."

"You can stop apologizing. We've dealt with worse than what you have put us through so far, as long as you get the civilians to safety in the end," Erica retorted.

"Of course." Inferneous nodded. "Let's start getting ready to set sail again-"

"Inferneous!!" Inferneous heard Balast yell out. "Come over here. There's something I need you for!"

Inferneous rolled his eyes. He stood up groaning and said, "Please find Holdren and tell him to find me so we can plot out our next course." Jayce nodded and ran off into the small crowd of civilians.

Inferneous walked toward where Balast was and found him observing an odd-shaped rock. Before he saw it, he felt a familiar magical energy resonating from the rock, and when he got closer, he saw that Balast was holding his hand over the stone, and there were strings of wispy magical energy flowing from the rock into his hand.

"By Angel's grace..." Inferneous said in awe. He knelt down next to the rock and put his right hand out, and strings shot up into his hand immediately. He jerked his head back in slight surprise, and his mouth opened at the energy. It felt as if Diadus was right there, reaching his hand out and holding his. The magic made him remember the strong grip and fiery power of the one who had taught him everything he knew about magic. Inferneous giggled at the feeling but snapped out of it when the rock broke in half and fell into two pieces. On one half, there were weird runic carvings glowing a nasty magenta; on the other, there were three strange objects. Balast sniffed, and Inferneous looked at him and saw a few tears he had shed. Balast quickly wiped them away and examined the three objects.

The first was a piece of red cloth that looked torn and tattered but was warm to the touch; the second was what looked like the skull of a cat, but there were a few too many holes where the eyes were for it to be a normal one, and the third was a rainbow-colored gem that on every facet was a different color. Balast easily took the items out of their engraved places and studied each individually.

"There's no way in Magia…" Balast started but didn't finish because he was too interested in what he was holding.

"What are they?" Inferneous asked.

Balast handed him the piece of cloth, and Inferneous understood immediately. "It's a part of Diadus' cape."

He felt the familiar magical energy circle through the object, still active and alive. "So that gem is Parquen's, right?"

Balast nodded to Inferneous as he pocketed the gem and said, "Feel this." He handed Inferneous the Malum cat skull, and Inferneous grew more confused when he held it.

"What… what is this?" he said, turning it around and examining it. "It feels the same, but it feels different from Diadus and Parquen's magic, too."

Balast took the skull away and rolled his eyes, "Yeah, you're no help."

"Ok, I'm trying to help, just be nice. Goodness," Inferneous said, staring at Balast.

Balast put away the skull and said, "Where's your ship? Let's get off this island so I don't have to think about your incomp-"

"Inferneous!" Holdren yelled out, running towards him with his hand and waving him down.

"Good timing." Inferneous said after grasping Holdren's hand, "Glad you're still alive."

"You too. I heard you took on five thousand plus Malums?" Inferneous nodded, and Holdren raised an eyebrow. "Well, I guess I'll take the castle sprawled over the beach as a sign you're telling the truth." He patted a rock and continued, "So, we have a slight problem."

"Skip the word and give me the bad news," Inferneous said flatly. Holdren winced and said, "You might want to see it yourself."

A few minutes later, Holdren, Inferneous, Balast, Jayce, Zack, Rhinda, and Erica were standing in front of a shipwreck, but not the kind you would usually encounter.

"How did that even happen?" Zack asked, rubbing his forehead. He was looking at a smaller, very dark wooden ship sitting inside a destroyed cargo ship. The masts of the cargo ship were splintered in multiple halves and were to the sides of the ship. People inside the wreckage were still trying to salvage what they could, but it was overwhelming to carry to the shore.

"So, we have decided to store as much as we could on the other boat because, surprisingly, it's completely intact. Even though almost pitch black, the wood hasn't even been scratched." Holdren added as they all stood looking at the confusion of the two ships. Balast shook his head and walked toward the ships, saying, "Ok, looks like because of Inferneous, we'll be stuck here for longer than anyone thought. Thanks, Inferneous." He put a thumbs up, not looking at Inferneous as he floated up to what used to be the front of the cargo ship and then down onto the dark wooded ship.

As soon as Balast's feet touched the wood, he felt the same kind of odd magic as the cat Malum skull in his pocket. As he walked up and down the ship, he couldn't help but be a little disgusted. It felt unfamiliar, which was a strange feeling for someone who had traveled and seen almost everything the world had to offer. He examined the wood and inspected every corner of the boat, making sure no Malums had hidden themselves inside the boat or anything else. When that was done, he grew bored but remembered that he had started building a school. He sat down near the helm and sat cross-legged on the wooden floor. In his mind, he searched the strings of magic flowing from him, followed a particular string that led to the stone statue that he had created, and looked through its eyes.

He observed that the first building had walls now and that people were still diligently working. It gave a bit of relief seeing things had not gone haywire while he was away. He turned the bust and saw the little tarp that the engineers had been working under had developed into a small shack with what he would see was a few more chairs and tables. He saw inside where Gareth, the others, and even some new people were all having a good time eating a nice feast in the sunset of the day. He couldn't help but smile and relax because of the comforting atmosphere. He decided to leave them alone, turned the bust back, and opened his eyes to the mess in front of him. He sighed, stood up and muttered, "One last test," he then raised his hand and shook it, and as he shook it, it morphed and cracked until scales covered it and three large dragon-like claws replaced his five fingers. He then swiped at the wood, and there was a bit of magical resistance, but he eventually sliced off a good chunk of the dark wood off the railing. He then caught the chunk with his other hand and popped it into his mouth. As he chewed the wood, he shook his hand again, and the transformation undid itself. He floated back down to the beach and yelled, "Ok, I've made a decision!" Everyone stopped and watched as he floated to the ground, spat out the piece of wood he was chewing on, and said, "We are taking the newfound ship. Make sure to stock it as fully as you can so we can sail by nightfall!" All of the working civilians and tiger masks looked toward Inferneous and Erica for confirmation, and Erica responded, "Follow this man's orders, and quickly!" while Inferneous snarkily added, "Were you a bit hungry, Balast? I think you should get some fruit before eating the ship." Balast rolled his eyes, picked up the wooden piece he was chewing on, and threw it at Inferneous. It bounced off his chest as Balast said, "It's not bitter. Now get to work, pleb, we have places to be."

Chapter 15

It was around midnight when the ship was fully out to sea and sailing among the dark waters. It seemed darker because of the deep coloration of the wood of the ship, and some civilians almost fell off the side because of it, too. There was no moon tonight, so there was no real light source besides the small fires that Inferneous had put on the rim of the boat. They had even added to the darkness in a weird way.

As the fires flickered on the main deck, Balast's imagination flitted with them. Butterflies made of the cinders of magical ash and mosquitoes larger than usual floated about his eyes in a dreamy battle where they flustered about in between each other's lines. There was only silence, and that made the hallucinations more real to Balast as he saw the silent battle between inherent good and evil. The butterflies floated about and darted in different directions with such grace it was hard to imagine them fighting for their lives, and then the mosquitoes swarmed them, not caring about the pursuit of life but the fast and heavy chase of death. There was no rhyme or reason to the battle; all Balast knew that there was a fight, and he wondered which side he should root for.

"Sorry to interrupt your delusions, but I have something to show you," Inferneous said, leaning on the rail right next to Balast. He then placed a coin on the rail and pushed it to him.

Balast picked up the coin and examined it. "It's round. Seems like the only thing special about it." He flipped it over and over and shook his head, "Probably useless." He then placed it on his thumb and flipped it into the air toward Inferneous.

Inferneous, in shock, grabbed it out of the air and slammed his hand on the rail. He closed his eyes and shook his head at the way Balast stared at him. "That's my fault. I should have told you the rules before giving them to you."

"The rules?"

"Yes. The coin is magical, and it tells the future if you get heads, and it disappears if you get tails." Balast stood there and looked down at Inferneous' hand. "Do you feel it?"

"Yes, but it's magic. It may just work on us, seeing that it is tails."

"That's a bit smart of you," Balast said condescendingly. "I guess we'll have to see."

Inferneous eyes widened as he pleaded, "Don't you know anything about this? Don't you even know whose magic it is?"

"Nope. I didn't even sense any magic from it, so raise your hand so we can be done with this problem."

"Actually, there's another rule."

Balast rolled his eyes at Inferneous before slapping his hand out of the way. There was a small burst of light, and a golden silhouette appeared in front of them. As the image unblurred, it revealed the image of a man with a hard jawline, a bit of stubble, and, most notably, a blue right eye and a brown left eye. In the silhouette, he was petting what looked like a cat with a ring of eyes on its head. He was standing, holding the Malum cat, and looking towards someone to his right. There was also a hand on his left shoulder. As Balast viewed the seemingly still figure, he couldn't believe his eyes. When he circled the figure, his mouth dropped open in awe.

"What do you see?" Inferneous said, looking at Balast.

Balast put his hand over his mouth, asking, "What don't you see?!?!" He pointed to the insignia on the man's military uniform, to the hand on his left shoulder, and a small part of a cape. "That is Prince Cordis Aureum conversing with Parquen and Diadus!!" Inferneous' eyes widened to the realization of what he was witnessing.

Balast put his hands on his head, and his smile dropped into a thin line pressed into thought. "This-this is revealing." He circled the image once more and continued, "I don't know how, why, or when this was, but this is going to be history-changing evidence."

Inferneous stared at the silhouette, then at the wooden floor and asked, "What were you thinking about when you flipped the coin?"

Balast raised an eyebrow and responded, "Well, I was thinking about how stupid it was for you to show me something as stupid as a golden coin when we should be worrying about who created this ship."

Inferneous was silent for a few minutes and then exclaimed while he put his hands on his head, "No Way!! Cordis Aureum created this ship?!?!?"

Balast grabbed the coin from Inferneous and examined it, turning it over in his hand. "What was the last rule?"

"Well, you were supposed to ask a question before flipping it, but it looks like it answered the question that was on your mind instead," Inferneous said, grabbing the coin back. "That's the end of the presentation, goodnight."

"Wait, tell me where you are steering this ship before I head below decks."

Inferneous rolled his eyes, "I thought you were smarter than this. I told you we came to the island by following the compass, looking for you and Castillus Grex so we could find a good place for the civilians. Now we are going to try it again without the globs of Malum blood on it, and hopefully, it will lead us to where we actually want to go."

Balast smirked and shook his head, "Don't get too far into the route. I have a faster, more magical way to take the civilians there."

Inferneous turned to Balast and asked, "Well, what is it so we won't waste time!"

Balast smiled and walked down the stairs to the main deck and said, "You'll find out tomorrow. Goodnight."

Inferneous glared at him and slammed his hand down on the helm as he returned his gaze toward the dark open sea, grinding his teeth and muttering angry retorts into the night air.

The next day came, and when Balast started to climb the stairs to the main deck, Inferneous pulled him up; as Balast stumbled up bit, Inferneous put his hands on his hips, saying, "Now tell me what you were on about last night."

Balast smiled, turned toward the front of the ship, and put his hand together, both of his palms touching each other. He then slowly slid them apart, and as he did so, what looked like lightning and electricity crackling appeared in front of him. The electricity then started to separate and show another place on the other side– a portal. As the portal opened as wide as a door frame, everyone on board could see to the other side, and so could the people on the other side see them.

Balast turned to Inferneous and said, "I have to follow the trail of magic from the third artifact because it's too important to sit around undiscovered. It also may have to do with our masters, so you are going to have to come with me," he waved his hand toward the portal and continued, "there's Castillus Grex. The portal will stay open for as long as I need it to, but I'm still a little drained from the fight, so please make sure you get the civilians and anyone else not willing to risk their lives through."

Inferneous sighed and nodded. He yelled for Holdren, and a door swung open behind him as Holdren answered, "What do you need?"

"I need you to gather the civilians and the High Shadow Ninjas from the decks below. Just tell them to drop everything and come above the decks." As Holdren nodded and trotted down the stairs, Inferneous yelled at the crew, "Drop the anchor! Everyone, gather in the middle of the deck!"

It took a few minutes for the sails to be let down and for everyone to get to the main deck, but when they did, Inferneous climbed the stairs to look down on them from the helm.

He cleared his throat and started, "Dear crewmembers." He uneasily shifted from his left to right foot, then shook his head, muttering, "No, this isn't right." He walked back down the stairs, joined the crowd, and started again, "It's been a good journey, but now I have to ask you all to go to Castillus Grex. A portal at the front of the ship will take you there instantly, and hopefully, you all can lead fuller lives there."

"If you enroll as a student, they provide full room and board if… you show a true passion," Balast added, interrupting Inferneous.

"There is that option," Inferneous continued, "I thank you all for accompanying me on my journey, but I'm afraid it will become too perilous for anyone not willing to risk their lives. So, with that statement, please gather anything you need and head to Castillus Grex."

And with that, all the civilians started to leave through the portal one by one. All the children, men, and women that had been with the High

Shadow Ninja clan each took their masks off and dropped them on the deck of the ship, leaving the pain and suffering behind them.

Before the portal closed, Inferneous approached Erica, "You are free to go if you want; I won't stop you if you go but know that I harbor no ill will toward you."

Erica looked around, and her gaze landed on Holdren, who was hunched over a table, examining some maps and using his compass. She looked around the ship and watched the mercenaries and the tiger masks work together, almost seamlessly working to run the ship. She looked back at Inferneous and shook her head. "I guess we are staying with you. I couldn't get used to life without the constant fear of dismemberment anyway," she said, closing her eyes and waving her hand dismissively.

Inferneous smiled and nodded, "Glad to have you aboard." Inferneous turned away and then turned back to Erica, asking, "Do you know any magic?"

Erica shook her head, "Magic has never really been my strong suit."

Inferneous nodded, "When we are at full sail, gather your best men and come to me. It's time for everyone to learn some basic spells."

An hour later, Inferneous was inspecting the inside of the captain's quarters, admiring the dark wood and its ornate carvings, when Holdren entered the room.

"Oh, there you are," Holdren said, surprised, "I thought you were below decks getting some sleep. You really should after staying up all night steering the ship."

Inferneous shook his head, "Why sleep when you could be looking at this amazing craftsmanship?" He smiled as he looked at the intricate carvings on the walls and floors of the cabin, and he ran his fingers through them, feeling all the grooves out. "This ship is very special, you know." Inferneous said, eyes glazed over, "I can feel that magic was used to make this, but the magic is foreign to me, so I can't exactly tell what parts are interactable."

Holdren looked around the room and shrugged, "I'll let you know if I find anything, but I came here to tell you they are waiting for you."

"Oh yeah!" Inferneous exclaimed, "I almost forgot" he then rushed past Holdren and stepped up to the deck.

In the middle were three tiger masks, four mercenaries, and Erica. Erica was sitting cross-legged in the middle of all of them and stood when she saw Inferneous emerge.

"Ok!" Inferneous said aloud, "Where is Balast?"

Erica pointed up behind him, and he turned around and saw Balast steering the ship.

"Someone has to make up for your laziness," Balast said snidely, "go ahead and start by teaching them how to sense magic. I'll help if they get stuck on the higher spells."

Inferneous raised his hands and then put them down, sighing and shaking his head. "Ok, whatever." As he walked between the idle mercenaries and ninjas, he muttered, "OK, everyone, get into a circle and close your eyes. We are going to start by taking deep breaths, and I want you to try to see through your eyelids."

One of the mercenaries raised his hand and asked, "How do we do that? I think once you close your eyes, you can't see, right?"

There were snickers from the other mercenaries, but Inferneous just smiled and politely said, "You aren't actually seeing. You are focusing your magic on your eyes so you can sense other magical presences near you. Just try your best."

A few minutes later, everyone was in a proper circle and was in varying stages of magical awareness.

It seems like the tiger masks are getting this more than the mercenaries… makes sense, though. Those tiger masks have gone through some rough training, to get that mask. Inferneous thought for a moment when an idea flew across his mind. He smiled and said, "Alright! Everyone find a partner. I want one tiger mask for every mercenary."

They all looked at him in confusion for a second before intermingling and talking out their pairs.

Inferneous left the group to sort it out for a second and looked around the ship until he spotted the two people he wanted. Jayce and Holdren were tying ropes to the mast and discussing ration sizes when Inferneous walked up to them and said, "Follow me. I have an important bonding activity for you two to complete."

"Bonding activity? Holdren and I are brothers now. What do you mean by bonding activity?" Jayce understood once he saw the two Tiger masks Inferneous stood between.

They both wore black gi's with red claw strike patterns and had their arms behind their back in a more formal position.

"These gentlemen are Shiro and Kuro, two very talented young ninjas," Inferneous said.

Nice to meet you.

Holdren and Jayce both scratched the inside of their ears in irritation.

"What was that?" Holdren asked.

We are communicating telepathically. The voices spoke again.

Holdren and Jayce both caught on and stared at the two boys concernedly. "Well, can you speak out loud instead of in our minds? It's irritating."

No. The voices said firmly.

Jayce looked at Inferneous with an annoyed stare.

Inferneous put a hand up, saying, "It's ok, we are all just getting to know each other, and we don't want to make anyone unreasonably uncomfortable."

"That really doesn't make any sense-" Holdren started,

"Ok, just go along with it," Inferneous said, putting his hand on both of the boys' shoulders. "This is Shiro and Kuro. They are two very talented boys that I think you guys would work well with."

Shiro and Kuro put their arms to their sides and bowed to Jayce and Inferneous. "It will be a pleasure to work with you," their voices resonated.

Holdren looked at Jayce.

Jayce scratched the back of his head, asking, "How are we supposed to tell you two apart?"

Shiro stepped in front of his brother and bowed slightly as they heard a slightly different-sounding voice in their heads: "I am Shiro, the Black Sword."

Kuro then stepped beside his brother, and they heard in another slightly different voice, "I am Kuro, the White Shield."

"Interesting names!" Holdren said as Inferneous started to tend to the other mercenaries and ninjas, stepping up to them. Holdren continued, "How did you gain those titles?" He was at least five or six inches taller than both of the boys, which Shiro and Kuro obviously saw as a show of intimidation.

Shiro replied calmly, gesturing to his brother, "Kuro is known to have an impenetrable magical defense that our enemies would refer to as the 'White Shield.' He once stopped six wyverns from attacking an ambassador's caravan for a whole month."

There was an odd silence as Shiro looked back at Kuro, and they looked at each other oddly for a few seconds before Holdren interrupted, looked at Shiro and asked, "And you?"

"Well, I'm known for my extensive campaign history, but-"

He was interrupted by Kuro, who stepped in front of him quickly and said, "He's known for his raw skill as an assassin and as a warrior. He once killed everyone in three towns searching for his target. When he didn't find him, he then killed everyone in the target's family, including the chi-"

Kuro stopped as he swung his head around to Shiro. This time, their stares were more hostile at each other, and it gave Jayce goosebumps just looking at them until Holdren interrupted them with another question, "Are you two communicating with each other secretly? If you are, then I'd rather be paired with someone else."

"That won't be necessary," Shiro said to him.

Holdren caught wind of his angry tone through the deepening of the mental voice and smiled, "Great." He said plainly, looking over Kuro's shoulder at Inferneous and the rest of the crew, asking, "Did he tell you guys what we are doing in these partner exercises?"

Shiro turned around just in time to hear Inferneous yell out, "Ok, everyone, get in a circle with the edges extending out to the edges of the boat! Yes, yes, just back up..." he ushered people behind him and sides of the boat forming a rough circle of mercenary and ninja pairs. He waved everyone to be silent and then started, "Alright! I want to thank everyone here for sticking with Balast and me on this adventure. I promise that you all will not regret your decision."

He then motioned to Balast behind him, and Balast walked forward and extended his hand with his palm facing toward the wooden deck. He retracted his hand, whispered under his breath, and then sliced the air with his palm. The middle of the circle then flashed a bright golden yellow beam to the sky, then extended outwards. Some flinched back as the light extended until it stopped a few feet in front of them. The light dissipated, and Balast sat cross-legged on the deck, gesturing for Inferneous to continue.

Inferneous then stepped forward, but as he did, the area that was just highlighted with magic blinked as Inferneous entered it. He nodded in satisfaction as he walked to the middle of the space. He turned in a circle, and without warning, he swung his hand in the direction of Balast, and a wall of flames erupted from the wood and flew at him.

The people behind Balast tried to quickly move out of the way, but Balast didn't flinch as the wall of fire approached him. Right before the wall reached him, the flames erupted upwards and dissipated as Balast continued to sit there.

The ninjas and mercenaries watched Inferneous and Balast in awe as the magic dissipated.

Inferneous then started again, "I'm sure all of you are talented in your own rights, but now that you have joined our journey, we need those talents to work in harmony to create a powerful team that won't falter against the evil of Malums."

He raised his hand, gesturing to the space around him, "Even though this boat is smaller than I'd like, we will be testing the limits of your abilities and your cooperation skills by having a few scrimmages." He looked around the circle and noticed that the crowd was not amused. They all looked uneasy about entering the ring, so he called out, "Zack! Jayce! Get over here!"

Zack was standing next to an empty barrel, eating an orange. When he heard Inferneous' call, he excitedly knocked over the barrel. He hesitated a bit before entering the circle, but he put his hand in first, giggling a bit from the tingling magical energy as he entered. When he was fully in, he ran over to Inferneous in excitement.

He looked around at the crowd and whispered to Inferneous, "This is really cool. Will you teach it to me after?"

"No, you probably won't be able to do this in your lifetime," Inferneous whispered back, patting him on the shoulder. He then looked around and spotted Jayce standing next to Holdren. He pointed him out, "Jayce, you better get out here before I think of some horrible training exercise for you."

Jayce sighed and stepped up to the circle. As he entered, he made a funny face and then sneezed as he jogged over to Inferneous.

He slapped Jayce on the arm, saying, "Good job not chickening out." He put his hand on his chest and then put his other hand on Zack's chest, and they started to glow a golden white. The glow didn't fade away when Inferneous took his hands off them and up.

"Ok, turn toward each other and prepare yourselves."

They both looked to Inferneous in confusion.

"Wait, what?!?" Zack exclaimed, spreading his stance and putting his hands up.

"You want me to…fight Zack?" Jayce asked, pointing at Zack in a panicked position.

"You can't leave the circle, don't worry about hurting each other, and by Angel's grace, Fight!"

Inferneous raised his hands, and the light barrier around the arena turned a scarlet red.

Zack looked back and forth between Inferneous and Jayce in a questioning manner as Jayce shrugged his shoulder, drawing his large broadsword.

"Shout when you yield," Jayce called out as he swung at Zack, who couldn't dodge because he was preoccupied with his disbelief in his morbid situation. As the flat of the sword left contact with his head, he flew a few feet backwards and rolled to a stop, his face facing the wood floor.

"I actually hit him?!?!?! Inferneous!!" Jayce looked over to Inferneous, who was still in the ring.

Inferneous shrugged, saying, "I guess he hasn't had much training yet."

Jayce scratched the back of his head and shook it as he walked over to Zack on the floor. Right before he got there, Zack stood up and turned to look at Jayce.

Jayce saw the look of betrayal on Zack's face as he stepped back and opened his mouth for an excuse, but all that came out was, "I'm sorry."

Zack shook his head as he tried to run out of the circle, but he bounced off the scarlet barrier.

Inferneous chuckled and ran over to Zack and raised his voice to address everyone, "You see, we are all going to participate in this sparring drill so we can get the full scope of everyone's abilities," he helped Zack get up and continued, "Zack is unharmed because the minute you enter this barrier, you will be protected by my magic. I'll call out who is next after Zack and Jayce finish."

He looked over to Zack, who was trying to get out of his grip, and he let go as he addressed him, "Don't be afraid of fighting. You'll be fine." He dragged him over to Jayce, who had walked back to the center of the circle, and he shouted, "Go!"

Jayce was a bit more hesitant this time, but he still swung, punched, and kicked at Zack, knowing he was going to be ok. Zack dodged, weaved, and started to outright run around the circle. He ran and then stopped when he was tired, but surprisingly, Jayce caught up and punched him in the gut, then slammed him with his sword, putting his full strength into it. Zack didn't feel much pain, but he was still thrown a few feet back. As Jayce approached, he scrambled and ran away again. That happened about two more times, with the crowd around chuckling and some outright laughing at the cat-and-mouse chase unfolding before them.

Jayce, seeing this, threw his sword at the barrier, causing the mercenaries laughing to go silent as Jayce yelled, "Shut it!" Jayce shook his head at them and then started to approach Zack again.

Continuing to run again, Zack took in large gulps of air as his tired body pushed itself to its limit. He stopped to catch his breath and looked to the crowd again in shame when his eyes fell on Balast– he was not laughing. He was staring at Zack, who could tell he was infuriated, but not at him. His eyes were dark with rage, but Zack could tell when they made eye contact that he had an idea.

As Balast made eye contact, he raised his hands to his stomach and then pushed them outwards, signaling something to Zack.

Zack didn't understand, so he slightly raised his hand before receiving a kick from Jayce, which sent him flying into the barrier.

As he fell down, he heard Balast behind him say, "You don't have to let them push you around anymore."

There was a crackle of magic Zack heard behind him, and he rolled around to lie facing the barrier. He saw Balast breaking the barrier and dropping a small metal rod into the ring. "That barrier that broke your wrists didn't come from nowhere. Beat him. The odds are in your favor this time."

Zack stared at Balast's determined and angry eyes and adopted his resolve as his own as he grabbed the metal rod.

Jayce stepped over to Zack, still lying on the ground and started, "Hey, Are you–"

He was cut off by the thundercrack of lightning striking his ribcage as Zack ignited his sword and sliced Jayce across the chest.

Jayce was shocked and was convulsing a bit from the lightning to give Zack enough time to get off the ground and deliver a swift kick to Jayce's gut, grounding him. As Jayce recovered from the shocks, he retreated and grabbed his broadsword. More cautious this time, he returned to the middle of the space, circling Zack.

After a few seconds of circling each other, Jayce lunged at Zack, but Zack was ready this time.

Zack dodged skillfully and continued shocking Jayce with his lightning sword.

As Jayce recovered from the shocking blade, he came back at Zack, but as he ran up to Zack, he rubbed the hilt of his sword, which glowed a bright red. He brought it above his head and yelled as he brought it down on Zack.

Zack caught unaware, reacted instinctively and cowardly, but as he did so, he brought his hands up to his stomach, and his eyes glowed a bright green. He then pushed his hands out as Jayce's sword was inches from his face.

Instead of a collision, Zack pushed outwards, and a green veil of magic pushed Jayce back and sent him flying to the other side of the ring. Jayce flew for a few seconds, then slammed into the scarlet wall and fell to the ground, unconscious. At first, the crowd was silent as Inferneous ran over to check on Jayce. He turned Jayce over to reveal that he had a bloody nose, and the blood was running down the side of his face. Inferneous shook him hard, and Jayce woke up with a groan. Inferneous, breathing a sigh of relief, touched Jayce's forehead with two fingers, and a magical fire appeared over Jayce's head. Inferneous set him down on the floor. He stood and slowly started clapping. He smiled at Zack as the crowd around started applauding as well. There were no cheers, but there was no more laughing at him or anything shameful about it. Inferneous put a hand on his shoulder as Holdren helped the already mostly healed Jayce limp off to the side.

"Nice moves. Did Balast teach you that one?" Zack glanced over to Balast, who had a finger over his mouth and was looking at Zack.

"No, I created that one myself," Zack said, smirking at Inferneous. "Oh wow! Looks like Balast has a knack for scouting creative magical talents," he said, escorting Zack to the side.

As soon as both contestants were out of the ring, Inferneous returned to the middle of the circle, raised his hands once more, and asked, "Who's next?"

There were many battles that began and ended that day, showcasing the crew's hidden talents and skills as everyone, whether ninja vs mercenary or friends against friends. A competitive aura began to appear amongst the crew, fueled by Inferneous' magic; some excelled more than usual. They were only halfway through when the sun started to set, and it got so dark that Inferneous had to light fires so he could see the fights.

After the last fight concluded, he announced, "Everyone, take a rest. We'll resume this tomorrow!" He waved his hand, and the area glowed brightly and then dissipated. As people flooded the deck preparing their separate meals, Inferneous set fires so the crew could sit around and stay warm. What used to be a dull murmur of assassins and soldiers talking in their own groups turned into a gathering of sorts.

As Inferneous sat down to eat, he was approached by Balast, who slapped the chicken wing out of Inferneous' hand and sat down, asking, "Why are you doing this??" Inferneous smiled and picked his chicken wing back up to have Balast grab it and throw it over the side of the boat.

"You know, we could have analyzed everyone's magical power one by one, but instead, you had to go the most chaotic way forward by having them beat each other up," said Balast.

Inferneous shook his head, "Have you been away from people for so long that you don't enjoy a good sparring match?"

"I have never enjoyed a sparring match in my life! Sparring matches are for people who want to size each other up in the most unintelligent-"

"Then why did you help me create the sparring ring? Huh? Why did you sit to the side?" Inferneous snapped back at Balast.

Balast took a deep breath and held up a finger to Inferneous in anger, "You put that 19-year-old mass of mercenary up against a 17-year-old orphan who is probably still malnourished and obviously doesn't know how to fight. Even if Jayce went easy on him, that was too much!"

"Balast," Inferneous said, turning his head from the fire before him to look Balast straight in the eyes and saying, "You need to let him have challenging experiences. He won't survive if he isn't constantly put up against difficult odds."

Balast grew enraged and stood up in anger, "He's my apprentice!! Don't force your master's crude and barbaric teachings on him."

There was a silence as the rest of the crew turned and stared in the direction of Balast.

"Continue on with your ignorance!" Balast yelled to the crowds as he stormed to the captain's quarters.

As Zack watched Balast storm off, he grew slightly unsettled. He turned his gaze to Inferneous, who had his hand over his face. He shook his head, supposedly of either embarrassment or disbelief in Balast's actions. He felt a bit of embarrassment because Zack knew they were talking about him. He looked farther past Inferneous and spotted Jayce talking with Holdren, and by his mannerisms, he wasn't happy either. Zack stood from the barrel he was leaning on and started to walk Jayce and Holdren. As soon as he was standing near their fire, they stopped talking and turned their attention toward him. Zack couldn't tell the emotions on their face from up close now because he was sweating a bit from the slight possibility that Jayce might be angry that he blasted him so hard.

"Uh... um," Zack stuttered.

"What is it boy?" Holdren asked impatiently, taking a bite out of an apple.

"I wanted to say I'm sorry for hurting you."

Holdren whipped his head around, looked Zack up and down and laughed. Jayce, smiling, slapped Holdren on the back and turned his focus back to Zack, but his face showed kindness.

"It's alright. That was a really cool spell you performed, and that lightning sword was… electrifying, to say the least."

Zack breathed a sigh of relief and smiled at Jayce's remark. Jayce pulled an apple out of a small pouch and tossed it to Zack. Zack caught it and looked at it, then at Jayce. Jayce slapped the floor and said,

"Why don't you join us?"

Zack immediately sat down and devoured the apple until a sliver of the core was left. Jayce was slightly taken aback by how fast he devoured the apple.

"Dang, you must have been starving!"

"It's a familiar feeling," Zack replied, tossing the apple core behind him. "Got any more?"

Jayce chuckled and reached into the small sack once more, found a piece of bread, and gave it to Zack, who shoved the whole thing into his mouth. Jayce shook his head in disbelief, watching the crumbs fall to the floor. Zack crunched the bread piece by piece until it was gone.

"So," Zack said, wiping his mouth, "Where did you come from, and how did you end up with Inferneous?"

"Well," Jayce started, "Inferneous basically captured all of the mercenaries and High Shadow Ninjas after we turned against him."

Zack looked at him in confusion, and Jayce shrugged, "We just accept it because it's Inferneous, you know? It's hard to question anything by people as powerful as them."

"I guess so…" Zack murmured, looking over to Inferneous lying down on the deck, fully asleep next to the fire.

"So, how did you meet Balast?"

"Hmm? Oh, I tried to assassinate him."

Jayce spit out the ale he was drinking, and the fire sizzled as it dissipated the drink.

"Yeah, needless to say, I failed. I still don't get why he didn't kill me, but he told me that I wasn't the first."

Jayce winced in second-hand embarrassment, but he frowned when Zack looked at him with a serious tone and asked, "Are you sure you're not mad? I kind of cheated with my wand…"

Jayce shook his head, "Definitely not. I'm more angry at Inferneous for even putting me against you. I'm also a bit peeved at my men for laughing at such a thing. They should know what I went through…"

He was silent for a few minutes until Zack broke it, asking, "What did you go through?"

Jayce sighed and leaned back, saying, "I grew up in an arena, so fighting and killing's the only thing I know how to do. Most of the matches I was given, I had to–" he looked Zack up and down and shook his head again, "I had to fight children like you. Mostly in groups, but still no less horrifying. I haven't killed anyone or anything since meeting Holdren and starting the mercenary group."

"Oh, I'm sorry," Zack said awkwardly, scratching his head.

"It's ok. I tend to try to dwell in the present." Jayce paused when he heard Inferneous yell that the fires were going to be cut down and that everyone should try to get some rest.

"Well, I have to go and start on a night watch, but thanks for coming over, Zack," Jayce said, standing up and walking over to Inferneous.

Zack nodded, and as he stared at Jayce, he couldn't help but wonder what else there was to him.

Chapter 16

As the boat rocked back and forth in the soft, dimly lit darkness of the nighttime, Erica awoke from a deep sleep. She had been drinking a bit of ale earlier despite her having stomach problems every time after in her past. She got up slowly and stepped over her tiger mask guards, all sleeping a tight circle around her, and leaned over the railing of the ship to expel the contents of her stomach. She heaved a large breath afterwards and leaned on the rail for support as she slumped down a bit. As she laid her forehead on the cold dark wood, she couldn't help but sigh to herself in pain from the stomach convulsions. She felt a soft touch on her back and jumped up only to fall back down on her rear. She looked up and saw that it was Drathni, and she calmed down, leaning her head back on the railing with a faint greeting,

"Hey."

"Regretting that alcohol?" Drathni said, removing her mask to reveal a tired smile.

Erica turned to look away from her and murmured, "Can you just get to healing already?"

Drathni sat down on her knees next to Erica, placed her hands on her lower back and said an incantation that made her hands glow a faint white. She sat there for a few more minutes and then removed her hands from Erica's back.

"It still hurts," Erica murmured quietly.

Drathni turned away from Erica and sat with her legs crossed and said, "I'm sure it does."

Erica didn't turn to face Drathni, but she could tell that Erica was scowling and rolling her eyes.

"Do you feel as though your leadership is invalid? Or even worse, non-existent?" Drathni said aloud.

Erica didn't move at first then turned to Drathni with tears in her eyes.

Drathni shook her head and placed her palm on Erica's face. "It's ok, it's ok."

"A leader shouldn't be like this. I'm not qualified anymore," Erica said, turning away from Drathni once again in sorrow.

Drathni sighed and looked up at the full moon in the dark night sky. As the small fires Inferneous had placed burned, they seemed to be complimenting the moon's grace instead of trying to overtake it as a normal fire would.

"Drathni, when morning comes, tell the others that I will not lead them anymore. Tell them that they don't have to follow me, and they can decide for themselves."

"What?" Drathni asked, turning Erica around with one hand to face her.

Erica's eyes were a bit puffy but her eyes were so dark that her despair leaked out and darkened her whole face and tone.

"I said I'm stepping down. While I'm still in charge, I'm asking nicely to inform them to get a new leader."

"But—"

"That's final!" Erica said, turning back over and shoving Drathni's hand off her.

Drathni stared at Erica, and then she shook her head, muttering, "Ok, this will be a good lesson."

The next day came in a seeming haste compared to most of the other days on the ship. The crew was still bubbling with chatter about who would be next to fight in the ring and some were betting food rations on who would be next or who would win, overall high spirits despite what they had been through.

Erica awoke to Rhinda waking her up and saying that they were called to a meeting near the helm. She sighed and rose from the hardwood floor and stretched. She groaned as she massaged the bruises on her side and started to walk up the stairs to the helm. As she stepped up, she knew there were more people here than she thought would be included. Inferneous was driving the helm while behind him, Balast, Zack, Jayce, and Holdren. Holdren waved to her as she came into his view, and she rolled her eyes as she turned to Inferneous and asked, "What do you want?"

Inferneous smiled at her, shook his head and then nodded in the direction of Holdren. "He wanted to tell everyone something."

Erica huffed and turned to Holdren, stepping over to the small table with a detailed map of the world and a smaller map of the ocean they were currently sailing in. As she stepped forward, Holdren shushed Jayce and Zack and got to the heart of the matter.

"I called you all here because of this," he pointed at an empty space in the middle of the world map. "This is where we are headed."

"To the middle of nowhere?" Erica replied.

"Well, no. There is a largely unexplored part of the world map that no one has dared to explore since a great wizard combined all of the ocean and land maps."

"That was my master, Parquen," said Balast.

Balast chimed in again, "He told me that he used magic to survey the world and combine the maps and that there was no place on Earth that he didn't know of."

"So why are we heading into a blank space on the map?" Zack interrupted Balast.

Balast shook his head, and Holdren shrugged.

Erica rolled her eyes in frustration and continued, "So we don't have any idea why there is a blank part of the map that was made however many years ago, and we are going to sail straight into it? This is amazing."

"At least it's a step up from sailing in circles," Rhinda chuckled behind Erica.

"Keep your voices down, we don't want the crew to be alarmed—"

"If they weren't already panicked by what we've been through already I'm sure they wouldn't mind being lost for a little while."

"Well, anyways, drop the anchor!!" Inferneous yelled to the crew, taking his hands off the helm and turning around to face the others. He smiled, put up two fingers, and said giddily, "It's time for round two. Who's going to be in the exhibition match for today?"

Everyone looked around nervously, not wanting to be chosen to fight.

Erica then rolled her eyes because she knew everyone was going to have to fight some time or another. "I'll go first. It's not like I'd get to humiliate you in a duel anyway."

"But I won't be–" Inferneous tried to reply, but Erica had already stormed off to the main deck.

"Well, ok. Who is going to be her partner?"

"I will," Rhinda said, stepping forward.

"Are you sure you want to fight her? My magic is kind of stretched thin, but we can wait a bit for it to get stronger."

Rhinda started down the stairs and reassured Inferneous, "Don't worry, I've sparred with her before."

Inferneous followed him quickly and replied, "But you can't go easy on her. These fights are subtly establishing a kind of hierarchy among the crew, and if you don't show all of your power, some of your men might take you for granted. Plus, I need to see everything you can do so I can know everyone's abilities just in case things get deadly."

Inferneous passed him and looked Rhinda dead in the eyes. "And I need you to be something more than a walking brute."

Rhinda's eyes darkened, and his gaze hardened, obviously offended by the remark.

"I know you and Erica are partners, but now we are all your partners. As soon as you see her buckle, you stop."

Rhinda scoffed, "She won't buckle, unlike you. I know her from her prime years."

He brushed past Inferneous and continued, "Don't worry about me holding back or injuring her. Worry about healing me after she's done."

As Inferneous watched Rhinda walk away, he shook his head with a tinge of worry. He then yelled out, "Alright! Clear the main deck. Round two is beginning!!"

Inferneous hadn't seen so many moves so fast. The crew was excited to see the next round of fights and displays of magic. "Well, it looks like the crew's excited today. Balast?" Inferneous turned around and extended a hand to Balast.

Balast then walked past him and extended both his hands and raised them into the air quickly, and as he did so, a dark translucent purple wall shot out of the wood and extended towards the sky. Lightning popped inside the wall and sometimes curled out to slightly shock some of the crew as it stood, but even without that, it was a daunting barrier.

"I think I'll create the barrier this time," Balast said, looking at Inferneous intently.

Inferneous raised his eyebrow and started in defense, "But you haven't learned much about barrier magic. Your barrier probably isn't strong enough–"

"I have the same base power source as you, so it should be fine."

"No, it's not–"

"If you're not confident in my abilities, let's try it out." Balast stepped inside, and the barrier blinked into a teal blue and stayed that way.

Inferneous followed Balast warily, confused as to why Balast was acting this strangely. He stepped toward Balast and whispered, "What is this about?"

"This is for trapping my apprentice," Balast hissed at him.

"But I told you–," Inferneous tried.

"Then let me be the one to make that decision. Now..." Balast snapped his fingers, teleported to the other side of the space and yelled to him, "...now let's try putting on a show and demonstrate a good percentage of our power to our crew and set our place in the hierarchy, hmmm?"

Inferneous rubbed his face and started to walk to the opposite side of the space, and when he turned back around, his face was filled with annoyance and anger. "Fine! Let's play a game of Summoner Ball."

There were murmurs of confusion and excitement as the crew watched Balast and Inferneous.

"For those who don't know, Summoner Ball is a simple game where you have to hit the other summoner with a ball of energy. For this game, we'll just use two balls and Balast and I are both summoners."

"Get on with it already!" Balast yelled out. He clapped his hands together and drew them apart slowly. As he did, there were teal streams of electricity arcing between his fingers and eventually settling in the middle of his palm, and after he fully pulled his hands apart, he had a moderately sized ball that was glowing teal translucent with arcs of lightning inside it.

Inferneous scoffed and raised his right hand and concentrated on it. In a flash, a moderately sized ball flashed into existence, wreathed in a ceaseless flame.

"Fine then, GO!"

Inferneous and Balast then disappeared.

The crew looked in confusion as the space in front of their eyes was visibly empty.

There was a minute of silence until Zack spoke up against the murmurs of the crowd and asked, "Where did they–"

He was interrupted by a thunderclap and the flash of a blinding light from the middle of the area in front of them. The sky darkened to a hue of black, and the clouds parted in the sky as a beam of light descended from the heavens and touched down on the boat. The boat started to shake violently as it started to spread outward toward the barrier. As it crept forward slowly, the waves around them lost their gravitational pull and started to float above the boat, creating walls of dark teal water.

As the light reached the barrier, it shook like panes of glass holding back the winds of a hurricane. It shook and shimmered but held as chaos was unfolding outside and inside of its realm.

As Zack held on for his dear life to the railing of the ship he saw in the middle of the space two dim figures. As he continued to stare, they became clearer, and Zack recognized them as Inferneous and Balast. Balast was holding his energy sphere against Inferneous' energy sphere in what appeared to be a struggle to touch each other. Balast was closer to the floor and was struggling to push against Inferneous, who wasn't touching the ground at all. Instead, he was almost wholly bathed in flames and was pushing his sphere against Balast's.

In a desperate attempt, Zack started to scream. He yelled out anything he could: curses, insults, song verses and pleas for his life, trying to get the attention of the two wizards, but nothing worked. He screamed some more, but it was all silenced by the loud roaring of the sea, sky, and magic pounding and charging the air with a pressure that everyone could feel, crushing their mind and souls.

As he watched Inferneous gain the upper hand, Zack knew that there was really no stopping them. For a second, he lost hope that they would stop. He weakened his grip on the railing, and soon, he was flying away from the ship into the deep waters of Magia.

Balast was occupied with Inferneous, but he was watching Zack in the corner of his eye, and when Zack flew away, his stomach dropped. He strained harder and harder against Inferneous, but when he looked into Inferneous' eyes there was nothing but a fire that would never quell. Inferneous was gone, and what replaced him was a molten desire to win and destroy. Balast realized his dire situation and did the only rational thing he could do.

He gave up.

As his muscles slackened and he retracted his magic, the barrier burst with the ear-splitting sound of glass shattering and wood tearing apart; the boat blew apart.

But Balast didn't let that happen.

Before everything blew apart, he had woven a spell inside his summoner ball, and as it unraveled, time rewound itself, and as he opened his eyes, he was back looking at Inferneous talking to Rhinda on the main deck. He was walking down the stairs, and he passed them as he gained a sense of horror and relief at what Inferneous had done. He stayed silent until Inferneous spoke and asked, "Hey, lend me your magic so I can see what the crew can do."

Balast quickly slapped his hand away and, while turning his back, said, "You killed all those people at Valde Cruz."

Inferneous was stunned. The color drained from Inferneous' face as Balast walked back to the captain's quarters and slammed the door.

As Erica got ready, she couldn't help but glance around her. The ninjas around her were conversing and generally not paying very close attention to her, but she knew that wasn't true. It was a ninja's job to look uninterested in a target and then snap to laser focus on a dime, so it was usually hard to tell. But as she continued to stretch and get ready for the fight, she noticed that they really seemed to be getting along with the mercenaries. Even though most still had their masks on, she could tell that they were acting far differently than they would ever be around people like her, especially in the days when the High Shadow Ninjas were actually a threat to anyone.

She turned back to face her opponent once Inferneous put the golden barrier up and she grew angry when she recognized the person she was facing, and it was not Inferneous.

"Hey!" she yelled to Inferneous, "I thought you were going to fight me?"

Inferneous shook his head as he entered the ring, "I already know my limits and skills. I also know most of what you can do, but I'm having you fight because I think you are a capable leader."

Erica stalled for a second and stuttered, "W–what?"

As Rhinda entered the circle, Inferneous stepped back and yelled out, "I don't have magic at hand to shield both of you, so go easier than I told you to."

And so, the battle started. Rhinda and Erica had been friends ever since she got her tiger mask. He was an outsider at first, but just after a year of being with the High Shadow Ninja, he gained their trust, gained his special rhino mask, and joined the ranks as her second in command. They had sparred plenty of times before and their ninjutsu's were not that different from each other.

Erica struck first with a few heavy kicks to Rhinda's head. He blocked and dodged as well as he could, but he knew Erica's kicks were fast and strong, so they would eventually catch him somewhere, hopefully in one of his trained parts, like his stomach, which could receive most of the blows. As Erica grew more aggressive, she realized that she was the only one really attacking.

Rhinda was blocking and dodging around her attacks as well as he could with an occasional break of his defense where Erica would land a blow to his side or rarely his face, but he did not go on the offensive once.

Erica stopped attacking him and shouted, "What is the meaning of this?"

Rhinda fell to one knee in exhaustion and replied earnestly, "Your pride has gotten the best of you, Erica." He stood up and threw his rhino mask on the ground in front of Erica to reveal his sweaty face. His hair was slightly falling in front of his face as Erica looked him up and down. "Why would you step down as leader? And even worse, why would you cower and tell Drathni to do it?"

Erica found herself avoiding his gaze as she put her hands up again, ready to start her offense again. She backed up and got a running start, and as she ran full speed toward Rhinda, she jumped and kicked him right in his face.

Rhinda stumbled back and held his nose as it was bleeding profusely. Rhinda spat out a wad of blood on the deck and shook his head, saying groggily, "You don't understand what we are or what we were."

Erica gained a running start again, and this time, she wrapped her legs around Rhinda's torso and crossed her arms into a chokehold from behind.

As Rhinda struggled and stomped around, Erica struggled to keep her hold. When Rhinda fell to his knees, grasping at Erica's arms and for air to breathe.

Rhinda was at a loss for air, and his vision was growing blurry and darker by the second. He fell toward the ground, and as Erica's feet uncoiled around his torso and landed on the ground, he heard Erica whisper quietly, "It's better this way. I never deserved it in the first place."

Rhinda lost it. Ignoring the obvious lack of oxygen in his brain he stood to his full height with Erica so surprised she loosened her grip. He took advantage and took a breath, restoring clarity and sight. He then jumped up and fell backwards onto Erica. As all of his weight crushed Erica, all the breath left her lungs, and she completely released Rhinda.

Rhinda, in a fit of rage, turned and grabbed Erica by the ankles and threw her a few feet away. Erica was trying to catch her breath, but when she finally did, it was too late.

Rhinda barreled into her, knocking the air out of her lungs once more. As they rolled, Rhinda gained his footing. He picked up the dazed Erica and hoisted her body into the air. As she tried to move, her legs flailed until Rhinda yelled out and slammed her to the ground.

The crowd went silent as Rhinda breathed heavily, bleeding from his nose and a bit from the corner of his mouth. Everyone held their breath and stared at Erica's unmoving body. A few seconds later, she coughed and breathed in deeply. She sputtered on the ground, too weak at the moment to sit up. Rhinda watched her and then slowly started to approach her.

Inferneous got up quickly, watching them knowing High Shadow Ninja customs. Rhinda was going to end Erica's life. He started to run toward the crowd around the ring, intending to get there before Rhinda could do anything, but halfway pushing through the crew, Balast put a hand to his chest. Inferneous looked at him in a questioning manner, and Balast didn't acknowledge him but instead looked Inferneous in the eyes and turned his attention to the space. Inferneous looked back in restlessness, and what he saw surprised him.

Rhinda walked up to Erica and crouched down to look at her. Erica was still lying on the floor recovering from the attack when she heard Rhinda step to the left of her. She turned her head to him, and when she looked at his face, he had tears in his eyes.

"You got all of those villagers to safety but you forgot you have to protect us as well. Just because we have been with you for years doesn't mean we've been saved, too. There were so many things that were wrong with the High Shadow Ninja clan, and you knew but it was all you knew. You still have a job to do. Don't cower away from your duty."

Rhinda stood, wiped his mouth and nose of blood, and walked out of the circle, leaving Erica lying on the deck in the middle of the circle.

Balast set his hand down, and Inferneous rushed to Erica's side, shaking her for a response. She sat up and slapped away Inferneous' hands angrily. She had a slight cut on her forehead that was bleeding profusely, but any attempt that Inferneous took to heal her, she just slapped away.

When Erica was fully upright Inferneous was going to ask if she could walk but instead tried to grab her arm. She shoved his arm away and gave him a look that Inferneous had seen a few too many times. He stepped back and said, "Tell me when you're ready to be healed."

"Drathni will do it," Erica replied gruffly, adding, "continue on with the matches. You find the ninja who watched me will be extra strong today."

She was right. Inferneous continued with the matches, this time with magical shielding as Balast had come back and offered his silent aid. But as the matches progressed, he saw that the ninjas were overly aggressive. In more than a few matches, he had to pull the ninja off of the mercenaries because they were bent on destroying their opponent.

"That concludes the matches. Thank you, everyone, for putting your very best in!" Inferneous said with vigor.

After everyone turned their attention away from him, his mood dimmed significantly. The day he had gotten the idea to have the fights, it seemed like a great idea, and the first day of putting it into practice reinforced its positive sides but today proved that maybe it wasn't the best of things to do. As Inferneous started to set up magical fires, he thought over and over about Erica's loss to Rhinda and the reactions of the ninjas afterwards. The morale was still high, but there seemed to be weird tension when any of the mercenaries brought up Erica or Rhinda in their conversation.

As Inferneous sat down next to his fire, he couldn't help but overhear a tiger mask and one of the mercenaries converse over dinner.

"Man, your punches are so strong! I almost blacked out when you hit me in the jaw! Good thing we had the magical protection, unlike that first girl." The mercenary said before biting into a freshly cooked fish.

"Don't talk about the High Shadow like that!" the ninja scolded. They were silent for a bit until the mercenary started again,

"So, who is this High Shadow?" The ninja shook his head and replied, "The High Shadow is just a title for the leader of our clan. Erica, or the moon dragon, depending on how you know her, was the highest-ranking officer left alive after Inferneous, in his relative youth, killed the High Shadow, his apprentices, and his son. We've been through a lot with her but she should be treated with more respect than you speak of her."

"I think she should be treated with less. Honestly, after what Drathni told us, she's lost faith in us and herself." Another tiger mask joined in. He sat next to the mercenary, took the remaining fish that he was eating, shoved it all into his mouth and pulled out the bones seamlessly.

"I say Rhinda should lead us; he's fit to with that display of strength earlier today."

"Don't get any idea, Ark. You just want to cause chaos," the first ninja replied angrily.

"Well, at least it would be something entertaining, unlike you, Jaz," Ark responded.

He turned to the mercenary and asked, "Name and denomination?" The mercenary looked uncomfortable and responded, "Uh, Aiden, what's a denom- um…"

"Who did you get on this ship with? What group are you a part of?" Ark spat impatiently.

"I'm a mercenary, but I don't think our group really has a name. Some of the others suggested that the whole ship should have a name since we were traveling together," he answered.

Ark sneered and then sat back and rubbed his chin.

"I guess we all should have a name. Something with ninjas and wizards …."

"How about the high shadow wind pirates?" Jaz chimed in.

"Too long and convoluted," Ark said, shaking his head.

"What does convoluted mean?" Aiden asked.

"Maybe the mercenary shadows? I don't know…"

"How about the Ninjirates?" Aiden said.

Ark's eyes lit up, and he smiled at Aiden.

"That sounds nice, but what does that have to do with mercenaries?"

"Well, we kind of do anything, and we're on a ship right now, so we are kind of pirates in a way…" Aiden mumbled.

Jaz tipped his head to the side, rolling it over in his head. "Really? Ninjirates? I feel like something more sophisticated is needed–"

"I think that is a wonderful name!" Inferneous turned around and joined the conversation. He grabbed the base of their campfire, and it dropped to the wooden floor from its floating position. As it did so, all the campfires on the main deck started floating slowly toward Inferneous' campfire.

"Everyone come and gather around. I have an announcement to make!"

Everyone slowly stopped their conversations and gathered in a circle as their campfires merged together until there was just one huge campfire. Inferneous stood up and walked around the huge fire as everyone gathered, and as he had everyone's attention, he started,

"I've decided since we are all traveling together, we should all have one group name to symbolize our closeness as a crew. We will be named The Ninjirates of Magia!"

There was silence, but as a few seconds passed, there were murmurings of approval as people pronounced it and tried to guess the meaning.

"That's a terrible name! The High Shadow Clan should remain on its own!" Ark yelled out. A few of the crew members were shocked, and some of the ninjas agreed, yelling out protests in agreement with him.

"Why would you say that? You just like the name a minute ago?" Inferneous said, very annoyed at Ark, who was laughing as the crew argued. There was a commotion as Inferneous tried to calm the arguing groups down, but everyone immediately went silent when a voice from the crew yelled,

"Silence! The High Shadow Ninjas are nothing anymore!" Erica shouted, standing up.

She had a large scar on the top of her forehead and a few bandages on her face, but she didn't look like she wasn't serious. Everyone, especially the ninjas, stared at her intently as she continued speaking. "The High Shadow Ninjas were powerful and the best of their kind, but they are now the best of the past. We have lost hundreds and thousands of troops and almost perished from our enemies more than once. Now that we are here in the present, we don't have to live like we are still strong. It's not the name that matters. It's the people that carry on their legacy that matters. Through the name of Ninjirates we can continue to live out our lives in reverence of what was lost."

She paused a second as her gaze reached Rhinda and Drathni sitting opposite of her and continued, "I thought that I was unfit as a leader because we were weak, but I now realize that I tried my best and that I shouldn't stress over the past but put my efforts toward the present and future. The only thing I can truly say is that all of those who were once a part of the High Shadow Ninja clan follow my decision."

There was silence for a few seconds, and then the ninjas all cheered. Before this the ninjas were always calm and calculated but Erica's speech had them elated. So elated that even the Mercenaries felt it and started to clap and cheer as well.

For the first time ever, Inferneous saw Erica honestly smile. Inferneous wiped away a tear, seeing Erica smile. As they continued to cheer, Inferneous whispered a small spell, and drinks appeared in almost all of the crew's hands and he raised his and yelled out, "A toast to The Ninjirates of Magia!!"

"HUZZAH!!" the crew replied, all taking a drink of the wonderful tasting alcohol in the never-ending magical cups. Inferneous smiled widely, enjoying the moment, but from the helm, Balast watched them all in somber loneliness.

"They simply haven't lived long enough," he whispered to himself.

Chapter 17

Inferneous woke up with a strange tingling sensation everywhere on his body. He sat up from the hard wooden floors of the main deck, groaning as he did so. He had fallen asleep on the ground after drinking more liquor than any normal man could in just a few hours.

As he sat up from the ground, he looked around, but all he could see in every direction was a wall of mist. He could only see a few feet in front of them in either direction as he stood and turned around. He started to walk forward, following the grain of the dark wood at his feet. He continued walking forward warily until his foot hit a soft object. As he struggled to stay upright, he looked down and realized it was just an out-cold mercenary. The mercenary shifted in his deep slumber, mumbling, "A few more minutes…" before going still again.

Inferneous sighed in relief when it clicked in his brain that he wasn't dead and that there were other people on the ship with him. He looked around again and realized that there were others strewn about the ground, hopefully just asleep, but Inferneous went over to a ninja lying on the ground and put a finger up to the ninja's nose. He felt the warm air of the ninja's breath confirming he was alive, so Inferneous moved to the next body. He checked the bodies that came into his limited vision for a good amount of time, and Inferneous sighed with relief as all of them he found were just asleep or unconscious. The odd thing was that no matter how hard he shook the bodies, they wouldn't wake from their slumber. Inferneous stumbled over Rhinda's still form and eagerly shook him, "Rhinda! Wake up!" He yelled out, trying to rouse the burly man, but he didn't even twitch in response.

He checked Rhinda's pulse and found the slow thrum of his heart, confirming he was alive too. Inferneous then stood and put his hand on his chin in deep thought.

What in the Angel's name is happening here? Everyone is asleep, but how could they sleep with this buzzing feeling I'm getting? I can barely think straight... he rubbed his forehead as he felt a slight headache starting to form between his eyebrows. He jumped when a hand patted him on the back from behind, saying, "Getting overwhelmed by the magical energy?" Balast said, walking past Inferneous and checking Rhinda's pulse, too.

"So, it isn't just me," Inferneous frowned at Balast, smiling from his successful jump scare.

"But that doesn't mean everyone else can feel it either," Balast replied, standing up from Rhinda's body to inspect another. "What are your guesses?"

Inferneous put his hands on his hips, looking around and exclaimed, "I can't see anything with this mist; let's see what I can do to get rid of it."

"Don't," Balast said flatly, "you won't be able to control it."

"Why?" Inferneous said, snapping his fingers. A small flame appeared on the tip of his finger as he continued, "I don't see anything wrong–" he was cut off as the small flame exploded into a whirlwind of fire and enveloped the air around them. Balast reacted quickly and waved his hands in a zigzag pattern, and the fire subsided almost as quickly as it had raged. Inferneous looked at Balast as Balast patted flames from his cloak, and Balast gave him an angry stare.

"You must have brain damage from all that alcohol," Balast said angrily as he finished patting out the rest of the flames. Inferneous looked around and noticed the mist had cleared the whole main deck, but it was slowly starting to creep back as time passed.

"Are we moving? Who's steering?"

"I was, but it's been hours, and I still can't tell North from South." Balast looked around and noticed that the whole Ninjirates crew was scattered across the deck and that he and Inferneous were the only ones awake on the whole ship. The Ninjirates crew were all scattered about the deck in a seemingly random order, but as Balast continued looking, he noticed something odd.

"Inferneous," he called him over to the front of the ship. When Inferneous was next to him, he waved his hand to the deck and asked, "Who would you say has the most magical prowess besides us two?" Inferneous raised an eyebrow and then stuttered, "Uh, I would say Drathni, I guess. She has been in frequent use of her powers since the start so she has to be the best magic user among them." Balast folded his arms as he continued to stare intently at the deck.

"And where did you wake up?" Balast asked Inferneous without looking at him. Inferneous looked around and realized he was right where he had first awoken.

"It was right here..." he said slowly, his mind working when he recognized a pattern in the alignment of the Ninjirates crew.

"You see it now?" Balast said, more a matter of fact than an actual question. They were standing at the front of the ship, and from there he realized the order from the front to the back of the Ninjirates crew was separated by magical capability. At the back, there were mostly former mercenaries and ninjas, but as they traced up, Inferneous could recognize some ninjas and mercenaries that had performed magic during the fights he had held. They were ordered relative to each other in strength only exactly how he had categorized them inside his head.

"The magically exempt are at the back, and the magically adept are in front. That would make sense, but why is Rhinda in front of Drathni?" Inferneous asked, looking down at their feet where Rhinda lay at almost the very end of the ship.

"So, if I was laying here, where did you wake up?" Inferneous asked, pointing to the Balast.

"I woke up in the captain's quarters, but I went to bed early and by my own will. Did you fall asleep at the front of the ship?"

Inferneous shook his head, "I like sleeping in the middle of the deck or at the helm if we decide to sail through the night."

They both remained silent as they looked down at Rhinda in confusion and wonder. As the next few minutes passed by, the mist resettled onto the deck, making it hard to see more than a few feet in front of them again.

Balast broke the silence, saying, "I'm going to go check the captain's quarters because I have a theory that it might be magically reinforced. Keep trying to wake up the crew and don't even think about using magic!" he walked away into the mist as he pointed at Inferneous giving him a glare.

As he walked through the mist, he had to keep looking down to make sure he wasn't stepping on any of the crew members accidentally. He hit his head on the wall when he finally reached the back of the boat and cursed as he traced the wall until his hands found the handle. Opening the door, as soon as he entered, a sense of relief flooded through him. The dark purple wood of the walls calmed him on multiple levels as he passed by them and sat in the large black chair in the corner. He closed his eyes and almost fell asleep with the weird amount of calm he was feeling, and as soon as he noticed, he jumped up and slapped himself in the face to wake himself up.

Why am I so relaxed? It's almost as if the room was trying to calm me….

He walked the length of the wall and examined them, but as he touched the wall, he felt a familiar buzz in his body. From afar, the wall looked like it had wallpaper designed with small swirls and odd squiggles, but as Balast looked closer, he saw and felt that the designs were intricate carvings in the wood. Balast traced them and realized that he hadn't seen anything like them. His master, Parquen, would always create new runes like he had new magic runes here and there when he was just scribbling on a napkin, so new runes weren't surprising, but he usually shared all of his runes with him until his death. These runes were different and foreign to him, though.

They couldn't be Malum runes because they are too ornate, and none of them match my own…

Balast stood back from the wall and crouched, putting his elbows on his knees and his hands on his face. He stared at the runes like they would speak and tell him the secrets to magic and life in mere moments, but nothing spectacular happened as Balast stared at the wall, rubbing his head.

Things aren't making much sense these days, he thought.

He remembered all that happened over the past few weeks and scratched his head harder. From hiding in Parquen's legacy, teaching the next generation of magicians things that they'll never master in their lifetime of training to gallivanting after a whisper of a forgotten, painfully present, past. He thought back to the day before and found a scathing burning memory that gave him a headache which, when he thought about it, gave him a splintering headache.

These headaches aren't helping me think, but I can't help but think of that time flash. They have been happening far too often...

He snapped out of his thoughts when Inferneous burst through the cabin door half stumbling, half falling off the stairs into the room with as much commotion as he possibly could. Balast shook his head, thinking.

How is he the person that Diadus chose?

"I can't wake anyone. I've tried water, violent shaking, and even a bit of pinching. Not even magic can awaken them." Inferneous said after he regained his balance.

Balast stood, shook his head then said, "Well, I don't know what to do then. These runes are unknown to me. There is definitely something magical happening here, but I can't pinpoint what exactly it is..." Balast put both of his hands on his head and scratched his scalp voraciously with a deep, angry sigh.

Inferneous looked at him with mild worry as Balast made angry noises. When he stopped, Balast looked at Inferneous and asked exhaustively, "What about the coin?"

"What about the coin?" Inferneous asked. Balast rolled his eyes and slapped his forehead, "You have a magic coin that gives you answers, and you don't think to try it? Where is it?"

Inferneous frowned at him, dug into his pocket, and held up the coin to Balast.

"I don't trust magical items as much as you do, so no, I don't think to use it. I'd rather solve my own problems than turn to random chance..."

"It's not random chance. It's divine intervention. Have you forgotten how we got these powers?" Balast retorted, snatching the coin out of Inferneous' hand. He turned the coin over in his hand, examining it and its odd curvature. Most forms of currency on Magia were either triangular or rectangular in shape but this coin seemed to have an odd circular shape to it with grooves on the edges, supposedly so you wouldn't lose grip of it. As Balast examined it once more, he thought better of using it.

"Where did this come from?" He turned to Inferneous, holding up the coin between them.

Inferneous shrugged his shoulders, "I got it from a random band of pirates that tried to attack me. The one deckhand I brought with me didn't tell me where they got it or where it came from. He just told me how to use it," he folded his arms and leaned on the wall as he continued, "so, are you going to flip it or not?"

Balast looked at the coin for a moment before extending his arm out to Inferneous to hand it back, saying, "No, you're right. This coin is an unknown magical artifact. That means that the magical capabilities of it are too dangerous to comprehend." Inferneous took the coin and shrugged, mumbling, "Ok…"

He put the coin in his pocket and asked, "So what are we going to do now?" Balast started up the stairs and exited the cabin, saying as he left, "We are going to continue to follow the magical trail."

A few minutes later, Balast was at the helm with the piece of Diadus' cape, the cat Malum skull, and Parquen's magic jewel rating on the railing. Inferneous was holding his hand out in front of the boat with fire spewing out of his hands, dissipating the mist so Balast could at least see the span of the boat while he sailed. It had been a good four hours sailing around in the mist, and little had come of it. Inferneous stopped spewing flames in front of the ship and, turned around and yelled to the helm, "I think we should try using the coin now!"

He saw Balast shake his head, and he yelled back, "Why not?!?!? It's been four blasted hours already, and my arms are starting to get tired of this!!"

"There is no way we can know what will happen! Especially in this magically supercharged place!" Balast yelled as he stared down at the deck. He glanced at the three artifacts, and seeing as they radiated a much stronger aura of magic because of their surroundings, he should have been able to pinpoint exactly where they were leading him, but instead, all he sensed was just an overwhelming sense of dread and worry. Four hours and nothing. Balast began to wonder if he was just losing his mind over this.

"I'm going to try seeing if the artifacts react to the runes in the captain's quarters!" Balast yelled to Inferneous as he scooped the three artifacts up in his arms, carrying them down the stairs and into the rune-marked room.

As Inferneous watched Balast go in, he started to doubt himself. He had said that he would like to solve this problem himself, but in reality, it would be a thousand times easier to just… flip a coin. He reached into his pocket and sighed as he flipped the coin into the air. It shined brightly as it came down into Inferneous' hand again. Heads. "What- what do we do here?" he asked in the open air.

A small inscription appeared on the back of the coin, and it said, "Say these words: *Afferte me ad rationem desiderii mei.*" Inferneous took a deep breath and spoke the words into the open air.

Balast was enjoying the calm and silence of the captain's quarters when he heard a tinkling sound like coins hitting a stone floor. He turned around and saw nothing had fallen over in the room. There was barely anything besides a few food crates and maybe a weapon or two, but everything was completely still. He turned back around to look at the wall and realized that one rune in front of him was glowing a dark pink. Balast crept forward and touched the rune, and suddenly, all of the runes in the room were glowing. Balast backed up to the middle of the room, and his mouth dropped open in awe. He had only seen runes on the walls and some on the table, but now they covered everything from the sealing to the undersides of the chairs. He would have stayed, but he had a thought that the runes could be incineration runes, so he quickly ran out of the captain's quarters to find Inferneous outwardly panicking.

"Balast, the crew are disappearing!!" Inferneous yelled out as he looked around for another crewmate. Balast watched as, before his eyes, the mist came upon Zack, who was lying on the ground in front of him and covered him wholly. A few seconds later, the mist retreated, and Zack was gone. Balast put his hands on his head and then pointed to Inferneous, who was looking around at the crew as they disappeared, one by one, into the mist.

"You–you…" Balast said, anger building.

"What did you do this time?!?!?!" Inferneous started, "flipped the coin and–" then he realized what Balast had said.

"This time?!?!?" He was offended by Balast's choice of words, which created a divide in his mind. One half was reeling over the tone of Balast, and the other half was still panicking and trying to find a quick solution to the problem at hand. It all came out when Inferneous screamed, raising his hands into the air to shoot fire from his open palms. This fire was an angry spew of black and blue flames that eviscerated the mist far faster and better than his previous spells. But it was futile. As Balast tried to wave away the mist, but his attempts were even more fruitless.

As Balast and Inferneous tried their best, the number of crewmates dwindled drastically. Most were taken without the pair even knowing, as the fog was still too thick to even begin to see through. Soon there were only two of them left standing on the deck of the ship.

There was dreaded silence as Balast and Inferneous stood back-to-back, panting from their unsuccessful efforts to save the only people that trusted in them wholly. They stood there for a few minutes before they realized that nothing was happening in particular. Inferneous stopped producing flames and stepped back, letting the fog encase him whole. He felt the tingling sensation of persistent magic in the air. Balast shifted behind him, and as Inferneous stared blankly at the chalky whiteness of the mist, he asked, "So why isn't it taking us?"

Balast waved his hand through the mist and sighed, replying, "Maybe we are already there?" Balast continued waving the mist angrily until he saw a faint purple glow piercing through the mist. Balast winced to make sure he wasn't imagining things, then turned and tapped Inferneous on the shoulder. "Look," Balast said, pointing to the light.

"Don't touch me," Inferneous said, jerking his arm away from Balast as he walked toward the light. Balast rolled his eyes as he followed behind him. They reached the light at the same time and gazed upon the glowing doorway of the captain's quarters. Inferneous, without hesitation, opened it and was temporarily blinded by the purple lights.

When Inferneous and Balast stepped fully into the cabin, they were shocked to find not only a cabin but a large hall. It would have been pitch black inside if there weren't hundreds of huge glowing purple runes lining the walls. Well, they weren't exactly walls.

As Inferneous stepped through the door, his mouth opened in shock. As Balast's jaw dropped, he smiled. His mind was a jumble of emotions, but surprisingly, the most prominent one was excitement because Balast had no idea what was happening. He stepped forward and tried to lean on the wall but his hand met nothing solid and passed through the space between two glowing runes. He examined his hand in shock as he pulled it back. It felt like a thick soup, and as he pulled his hand back strings of darkness melted off his hand and back into the walls.

"What is this?" Inferneous said, slightly annoyed and slightly amazed as he continued walking down the long hall, looking up. There was no ceiling; instead, there was just an inky blackness lit by the glowing runes. "By the Angel…" Inferneous said, walking forward.

He snapped out of his shock when Balast pushed past him and started to run down the hall.

"Wait!" Inferneous said, running after him. As they ran Balast noticed a weird and odd sensation at the back of his mind. It was like he had just woken up from a long nap, and he didn't know what time it was. He stopped as he came up to a short flight of stairs and the door to the captain's quarters. Inferneous stopped behind him, slightly winded from the run. He also looked in confusion at the door. He turned around and looked back down the dark hallway, but even with the glowing runes, he couldn't see down the long hallway. "Didn't we just–"

Before Inferneous could finish his sentence, Balast had already opened the door. Balast stepped up the stairs, and as his eyes adjusted, he gasped audibly. When Inferneous followed him, he exclaimed, "Why is the sky black?"

The sky was pitch black and the sun was so dim it was only radiating half of the moon's light. As Balast and Inferneous stepped on the deck, they couldn't take their eyes off the sky. As they looked up, they could see the sun but it seemed like it was closer than usual. As Balast trailed its light downward, he noticed the ocean water was pitch black and scattered rocks were everywhere. Between the rocks and beyond murky water, he looked at the horizon. He could barely tell the sky from the water if there wasn't a light shining directly under the sun. Balast raised a hand to perform a far-sighted spell when he heard a voice to his right, "The ocean is beautiful, isn't it?"

Balast turned slowly to his right and lunged to hug the young boy whose voice he recognized was Zacks.

Zack was shocked, but he awkwardly hugged him back. Balast pulled back with tears in his eyes and asked, "What are you doing here? H–how?"

"What do you mean? We've been together for a few months now. By the way, Holdren was looking for you." Zack replied, turning around to point to the other end of the ship.

Balast turned around and saw the whole crew doing their regular work maintaining the ship, tying knots, pulling the sails, and counting their supplies. Balast was sure they weren't there before. His emotions flitted from overjoyed to confusion as he walked through the crew working. He saw them, but for some reason, they looked odd. They were somehow brighter, almost dimly glowing from head to toe, each and every one of them, making a stark contrast from the dark world.

"How are you all here?" He asked, turning around, making sure everyone was accounted for.

"What do you mean? It's not like we can go anywhere else. Besides, it's nice we get mostly bright sunny days instead of storms," Holdren said, walking up to Balast, shielding his eyes from the dim fake sun above like he was actually having trouble looking up at it.

"Do you not see what I'm seeing?" Balast said to Holdren, putting his hands on his shoulders and looking him in the eye."

"The sky is black, and the water is even darker! We aren't on Magia anymore!" Holdren seemed to stall for a second, looking up once more at the fake sun with his hand raised, then to Balast. He seemed to darken into a more realistic color for where they were.

"What in the world…" Holdren said, looking up at the fake sun with a stunned expression. Soon, it was like a ripple effect, and everyone on the ship began to realize they had no idea where they were. There were gasps of shock as they all came out of the strange coma. Balast was just about to issue orders when Inferneous forcefully turned him around and yelled in his face, "Balast!! Who are you talking to?!!?"

Balast snapped to Inferneous and shoved his arms off his shoulders.

"What are you talking about?!?!? They are all here. Can't you see them?" Balast waved his hand behind him at the crew, but Inferneous was getting very angry. When Inferneous stepped into the darkness of the deck, he had gone up to the helm of the ship and started to try to steer ship when he saw Balast was talking to seemingly nothing. He had hurried down to the deck, worried for his friend, when he received Balast's answer.

"Who?!?!? Do you mean–" Inferneous' face went blank with anger, "if this is a cruel setup for a joke, you've reached new lows."

Balast face dropped, and he replaced it with an angry one, "What are you talking about? Can't you see them?"

Inferneous looked around and raised his hands, "I don't see anyone. If you really just want me to admit it, I flipped the coin."

Balast froze in place, staring at Inferneous as he heard the words. "There was an incantation on the back, and I read it alright? I didn't think this would happen, but I think there is a way to get the crew back–"

Inferneous had never really been caught off guard since he had gained his powers, so you could consider Balast extending his hand to slap Inferneous the first time he had ever been hit by another living being. Inferneous didn't even think before he struck back with force. Balast watched in definite slow motion as time slowed for him the incoming flaming fist of Inferneous. Even though he could easily predict the incoming attack, time was still slowed, making moving a complete impossibility for Balast. His mind flourished with thousands of spells as even in slow motion Inferneous' fist, which had started at his side, was now almost touching Balast's face. Fear and instinct had nothing to do with the automatic green barrier of defensive magic that came over Balast. He skillfully implemented the barrier and then tripled it as Inferneous' fist broke through the first, sending magic shards toward Balast.

Time then resumed.

Jayce was enjoying the sunshine as he was hauling ropes back and forth on the ship. He had removed his armor pieces, unclasped his weapons belt, and rolled his green shirt sleeves up to help the crew with tending to the ship. He had just tied the last knot needed for the sails when Holdren called out the shift change. As the others he had been working with turned to take a break, other crew members walked and ran forward to replace the others. No one came to replace him, but that's because he had said not to. Most mercenaries had volunteered to give him a break multiple times, but he refused politely, saying he 'gets seasick if he stops moving.' Even if this may or may not be true, his men respected and admired him more for it. He wiped his forehead, which was slick with sweat and leaned on the railing to look up at the billowing sails and whispered, "Thank the blacksmith, this is a wonderful day."

He heard a yell and then got smacked in the face with an orange. Zack was a few feet to his right and had thrown it like he was trying to stone him, so it hurt a bit when it made contact.

"Why are you trying to murder me?!?!" he yelled over to Zack, who was keeled over in laughter. He walked over and threw the orange back at him, but Zack quickly caught Jayce's throw as Jayce approached though Zack was shaking his right hand because of the pain caused by the powerful throw.

"Dang, you have a good arm on you. Ever cut a person in half with that arm?"

Jayce frowned at Zack's insensitive comment but then smirked and replied, "No, but I would cut you down to size but you're too short?" Zack shook his head, smiling at the joke.

"You won't be so tall after I beat you with my wand again!"

Jayce shrugged, "I don't think I could get any shorter than you."

Zack bristled at the comment and it was Jayce's turn to laugh out loud at him. When he stopped, he took the orange from Zack's hand and before peeling it, he realized that it wasn't only an orange. There was the orange rind of an orange on one side but on the other was half a lemon somehow attached to each other.

"What the heck is this?" Jayce said in between giggles.

Zack grabbed it back and started to peel it while explaining, "It's both a lemon and an orange. It's sour and sweet together. I learned to bind things together from Balast, and I thought this was a great idea but in hindsight…" he dropped the rinds and bit the top of the combined fruit and made a face as he swallowed. "I have made a mistake," Zack said and then both laughed. When they were done, Zack started to separate them.

Jayce looked around and asked, "Where are Balast and Inferneous? Have you seen them?"

"Not since last night. I was having too much fun, but they seemed to be at odds after Erica's battle. Holdren told me to go get Balast, but after I couldn't find them, I assumed they would show up sometime," Zack replied and with a fizz of blue lightning, the lemon and orange halves split apart. He gazed at them with satisfaction and then frowned, "Shame they can't get along; I would really like to get more lessons on magic."

Jayce nodded, looking behind him and said, "Yeah, and I'd like to actually get somewhere. Those two are so alike, but they don't mix ever since we've been with them, they don't mix. Especially when they argue." Jayce looked back at Zack, and he grabbed the lemon and took a bite out of it. He recoiled, making faces at the extremely acidic taste, and Zack laughed again.

"How about we lead the Ninjirates then? When they argue, we'll go and do something fun." Jayce looked at Zack, saw the mirth in his words and smiled. "Of course! That's how it's always been, anyway. No one would stand up to us, not even Erica."

Zack smiled and stood, walking over to the railing to look over the sparkling teal ocean and sunshine.

"The ocean is beautiful, isn't it?" Zack said, smiling at Jayce. He would have responded but was cut off by Balast's arms wrapping around Zack. Zack was a bit surprised as he turned into the embrace. He looked back in slight confusion to Jayce but Jayce didn't see his face. He saw Balast's face and got very worried. Balast's eyes were starting to tear up as he hugged Zack and as Jayce looked at him, he knew something was wrong.

Balast stopped hugging Zack and asked, "What are you doing here? H– how?"

"What do you mean? We've been together for a few months now. By the way, Holdren was looking for you," Zack replied, turning around to point to the other end of the ship.

Jayce still stared as Balast looked to his right, and his eyes got wide. "How are you all here?" he asked, turning around and looking at all of the crew.

"What do you mean? It's not like we can go anywhere else; besides it's nice we get mostly bright sunny days instead of storms," Holdren said, walking up to Balast, shielding his eyes from the sun above having trouble looking up at it.

"Do you not see what I'm seeing?" Balast said to Holdren, putting his hands on his shoulders and looking him in the eye.

"The sky is black, and the water is even darker! We aren't on Magia anymore!" Jayce, puzzled, looked at Balast and then back at Holdren, who was now looking at the sun with his hand down.

"What in the world…" Holdren said, looking up at the sun in an odd fashion. A few seconds passed by as Holdren stared at the sun and Jayce grew more confused when he stared at other people who also grew entranced by the sun. Soon, most of the crew were staring up into the sky, unmoving. Jayce finally snapped out of looking at them and turned to look at the sun but he didn't complete the motion fast enough. As he moved his head past Holdren he was blinded by a white flash and was knocked back by a gust of heat. He collided with the mast and grunted his pain as he slid to the deck. He opened his eyes to see what happened, but instead of the sunny, bright skies he was just enjoying, he took in the dim onyx black of the sky and ocean. He sat there shocked at the change of scenery, but not for long as he realized that he was on fire. He scrambled, trying to put the flames out, but he realized that they didn't burn or hurt him. He quickly stood and saw Inferneous standing in front of the captain's quarters and his head was completely on fire. The flames burned differently, though. What was once bright and beautiful flames were now more smoke, and of what little fire you could see, dark black specks came out of them. Jayce looked back to Inferneous and realized that not only was his whole head on fire, but he had a crown of black flames around his temples. Balast scared Jayce a bit as he stood up, and Jayce realized that Inferneous must have blasted back Balast because there were dark streaks in the wood that ended at Balast's feet. Jayce stopped analyzing the situation when he saw all the crewmates scattered between them. He quickly turned to his left and saw that Zack was quivering from fear at what he was seeing, but he was still standing.

"Zack!" Jayce yelled out.

Zack slowly turned to him, wide-eyed but listening.

"Get the other crewmates to safety!! Wake up, Rhinda!" he pointed ahead of Zack to the form of Rhinda leaning against the rail of the ship.

Zack glanced back and forth between Rhinda and Jayce, then nodded his face in determination. Before he set off, he pointed to behind and to the left of Jayce.

Jayce turned seeing Erica struggling to stand. He turned to Zack and nodded, and they ran over to help the Ninjirates crew.

Balast swore he was dead for a few seconds before he skidded to a stop in the middle of the deck. He blinked away the pain and found himself still well into the land of the living, which disappointed him more than he thought. He realized he held his shaking hands up in a defensive position but felt a burning sensation on his upper chest and neck. He looked down and saw that his clothes were burnt off, revealing bubbling black and charred skin and blood. As Balast continued to look at it, though, he could see his magic naturally flow over the dead skin and start to repair it. In mere seconds, the skin was a new light pinkish color.

Balast looked back up and saw what he dreaded. Balast had known that Inferneous had a spirit living inside him from the beginning, but that was all he knew. The thing standing in front of him was definitely not Inferneous and Balast needed to find a way to get rid of it.

"Balast," Inferneous whispered, turning his burning head toward the defensive Balast.

Balast was surprised the thing could speak. He was about to reply when all the flames glowed except the dark crown around his head.

Inferneous' usually dark orange eyes were now a burning blue, which amplified the seriousness of his tone. "I am completely in control of this being inside me. The one thing I am not in control of is your remarks. I want to forgive myself for those hundreds and thousands of lives that we ended at the Aureus Empire, and I want to stop being human and be a perfect wizard like you would appreciate, but I'm afraid that's impossible. I want you to know," Inferneous raised his right arm and pointed at Balast staring him in the eyes. "That if we continue this fight, our friendship won't only end, but one of us will die."

Balast shifted backward as Inferneous pointed at him, then stopped crouching and rose to his full height. "I'd rather die fighting the person who ruined my life than continue living with his ignorance."

Inferneous would have shed a tear, but the flames that burned after Balast finished his sentence billowed and roared, evaporating even the water molecules in the air. "I wish we could go back," Inferneous said as his head became engulfed in flames again.

Balast tensed as the flames rose around Inferneous and dropped behind him to make a cape entirely out of flames. Inferneous outstretched his hand, and a broadsword of white flames materialized in it. Balast decided to take the offensive before Inferneous did and stepped forward, pushing his hands forward. The air in between them rippled and then grew hazy in an instant.

Inferneous couldn't see anything in front of him, so he slashed at the magic spell with his flaming sword and found that the space in front of him was no ordinary space anymore. As his sword entered the space his sword slowed and continued to slowly move along the space no matter how hard Inferneous pushed or pulled.

Balast took this opportunity to walk through the space unaffected by his own spell, and as he exited, he launched two orbs of light at Inferneous. As his momentum carried him forward, he turned and started to throw kicks at Inferneous to try and finish him.

Nothing landed. Inferneous easily dodged both orbs and simply released the flaming handle of his sword to dodge Balast's kicks. Balast was a bit off balance as his left foot collided with nothing, but he turned the balance into momentum and put it all into a punch headed straight for Inferneous' face. Inferneous dodged his punch, but this time, instead of just sidestepping it, he stepped back and came forward to deliver a crisp blow to Balast's stomach, blowing Balast back into the space he had created.

Balast almost threw up from the force of the punch as he tumbled back, but he found that he couldn't. When he removed his hands from his stomach, his hands were slightly covered in blood. He looked down and saw that there was a gaping hole in his flesh, and he was pretty sure his organs were showing. As he stumbled back, though, it healed slower than the last injury, but he was soon able to empty the contents of his stomach. As he sat up, he realized he couldn't see Inferneous through the gray area. Before, he could see almost every detail of him shining as he was ablaze but now the brightness was gone, until he looked up.

There, in the space above the area, he conjured. He was looking down at Balast with a sad look, almost like tears would be streaming down his face if he weren't aflame.

Balast glared in anger and yelled, "You aren't more powerful than me! Don't act like you're sad! You know you can't–"

"No," Inferneous said, shaking his head lightly, "you know better; you just never gave yourself time to think." Then Inferneous raised his hand, conjured a flaming spear, and hurled it at Balast.

Balast had felt the heat of the spear burning his eyes as its tip was aimed at his forehead, but it never landed its mark. Balast careened to the side as Jayce barreled into him, effectively saving his life.

Balast stood up and pushed Jayce off of him, saying, "I had that boy. Go save someone else right now."

When he was finally up, Jayce grabbed Balast's shoulder, turned him around and backhanded him across the face.

Balast was shocked and didn't register that Jayce had yelled in his face, "WHAT ARE YOU DOING?!?!"

Balast's vision focused on Jayce, and his face was one of mass desperation and anger.

"The crew are scared for their lives right now!!"

Jayce turned Balast around to point out the pairs huddled, some limping to the helm to escape the battle. "You two need to stop right n–" he was cut off as Balast shoved him back, and two more molten fire spears collided with the wood between them.

Balast then turned to Inferneous, still flying in the sky, and started throwing bigger mana spheres at him. Then he launched himself at Inferneous, propelling himself by slowing spaces of time as he literally stepped up to Inferneous.

Jayce was beyond mad now. After he helped Erica get all the crew out of their way, Jayce just looked back at the fight and saved Balast just in time. The response enraged Jayce; he got the courage to yell at Balast, but it was useless because they were already in the thick of their fight. Jayce ducked and dodged flying flaming projectiles and magical orbs as he ran to the other side of the ship and helped out Zack with more crewmates. Zack was helping a mercenary along but was struggling because of the weight. When Jayce reached him, he wrapped the mercenary's other arm around his neck and sped up the process. When they reached the railing for the stairs to the helm, he and Zack let the mercenary take himself up. As they turned around, they witnessed the full breadth of the fight at hand.

Balast was zipping around Inferneous in a storm of man flashes and magic while Inferneous floated in one place, reacting impossibly fast to Balast's attacks and not even flinching at one.

"Balast is overwhelmed," Jayce said under his breath as he saw the few attacks Inferneous dished out seemed more hesitant and cautious. They both moved at speeds faster than Jayce could track, all he could see was them materializing and then hearing the sound of them shattering magic protection spells or slamming themselves into the wood of the deck. It was like different colored lightning everywhere.

Jayce clenched his fist, staring up at them, and made a decision that he was sure to get him killed. But first, he turned to Zack and started, "Zack, I want you to protect–"

"I'm going to help you stop them. Don't ask me to stay behind; the only person who's really cared about me all my life is about to be killed by his best friend if we don't do something."

Jayce closed and opened his mouth to retort, but Zack took out his wand, and his lightning spell sparked to life, lighting his determined features.

"Are you coming?" he said, looking back at Jayce.

Jayce stood and nodded as he unsheathed his broadsword.

They weaved and dodged the projectiles as they moved underneath the raging battle, and as they did, the battle got more and more intense. It grew harder and harder for them to see the wizards as they flew back and forth fighting. There were now multiple areas Balast had created in the air and on the gray ground, and they had to move around them lest they be slowed, but luckily, they didn't stumble into any on accident. When they were right under where the two powerful wizards kept clashing constantly, they both looked up and questioned what to do.

"What do we do now?" Zack asked, yelling as loud as he could because of the deafening sound of the roaring fire and the loud crashing of magic against magic.

Jayce shook his head, saying, "I don't know." He looked up, trying to think of a way to reach them as he looked back down at Zack though he realized that Zack had picked something up along the way to the middle of the magical storm. It was a shining golden round coin. Jayce remembered Inferneous telling him about it and realized that it was the answer.

"Flip it, Zack! Ask it what to do!" Zack looked up at Jayce with a look of confusion, and Jayce shouted, "Do it!" Zack then put the coin on his thumb and flipped it into the air. The coin shined, and Jayce caught it. He opened his palm, and it was a head. As he showed it to Zack, he looked expectantly at him, but Zack just stared at the coin, visually stammering. Jayce realized he didn't know what exactly to ask, so he did it himself.

"What do we need to stop Inferneous and Balast?" The coin showed bright, contrasting the darkness of their world, and then a passage appeared on the coin.

"For the only answer to your perilous plead, you and your people have all the gifts you will ever need."

Jayce at first questioned what that meant, but then he got a very good idea. "Follow me, Zack! We are going to need a little more help than this!"

Balast was now wishing he was dead. Inferneous' flames were an impenetrable wall of fire that nothing could penetrate. The battle had exponentially increased since they started, but Balast knew his speed was not proportional to Inferneous' reaction and response time. Every time Balast threw any type of attack at Inferneous, whether it be lightning, wind, or even fire, he would easily dodge it and instantly retaliate. Balast, in the span of a few minutes, had become closer and closer to death than he had in his whole life as spears nearly impaled him, and he almost succumbed to the voracious flames that caught and stuck to his skin like an animal, biting into him, trying to consume him whole. He never let it, though, using water magic to put it out. The pain and closeness to the brink of death didn't bother him as much as the glimpses of Inferneous' face through the flames. Inferneous looked to be sadly watching Balast and outwardly hesitated every time he threw an attack. He was nowhere near straining. Balast, in anger, summoned a windstorm, and the ship was now a whirlwind of flying debris thoroughly mixed with a dark grew mix and flashes of lightning and fire. As Inferneous threw another flaming spear, Balast weaved into the gray storm to avoid them.

As Balast waited inside the gray, he decided to engage Inferneous in conversation and yelled, "You know I trusted you back then! But you just left without even listening to me!"

Inferneous turned around, looking at the gray as he replied, "And I trusted you to be strong enough not to want to abandon all the people still in the city! Why did you want to run?"

Balast hissed out, "I didn't run; I came to you instead!! Your arrogance was going to get the people we could have saved killed! Did you really think we could take all of those Malums?"

"Do you seriously still doubt what we can do? We are blessed by the Angel and trained by the ones she chose to give her blessing to; there should be nothing that can stop us." Inferneous looked down at his flaming hand and shook his head, saying under his breath, "Or there should have been."

Balast circled Inferneous in the storm as he talked, looking for any sign of a breach in his defense, but could not find anything. "The flames were too high, his reaction time too perfect..." Balast sighed as he accepted an idea he had been mulling over since the battle started.

Balast stepped out of the storm behind Inferneous, saying, "I want to end this battle now."

Inferneous turned around, the flames around his head lowering to his collar.

"Really?" he said hopefully.

Balast glared at him as he floated forward. He stopped when he was close enough to feel the flames off Inferneous and then raised his hand.

"One last game of summoner ball." His hand exploded with green, blue, and teal energy, swishing and crackling with the storm as it grew to about the size of a human head.

Inferneous raised his hand, and a flaming ball of vibrant golden fire grew to the size of a watermelon.

"No holding back," Balast hissed at him, glaring at Inferneous' magical orb.

Inferneous then raised his hand above his head, and the ball grew to the size of a large boulder. It illuminated the dark world around them, lighting the water to brownish and outshining the dim sun. Inferneous watched as Balast cock back his arm, preparing to lunge at him; he closed his eyes and lowered his hand. The massive orb started to descend as Balast lunged forward, arm outstretched at Inferneous. The orbs clashed, and a white flash blinded both of them. Inferneous looked away from the flash, but Balast continued to stare into the magic as he struggled to push against it. He believed he was dead when the pressure subsided, and he almost fell to the ground when he heard a voice calling out to him. His eyesight adjusted, and he found Zack floating in the air in front of him.

"Zack?" he questioned weakly.

Zack just stared at him until he broke the silence and said, "You need to let go."

Balast wondered what that meant until he saw that his hand was still holding onto a half-formed magical orb. He slowly released the magic, and it dissipated. He looked over Zack's shoulder and saw that in front of Inferneous was Jayce.

Inferneous was thoroughly surprised that Jayce was holding up his hand, which controlled the massive magical source above him, but what surprised him more was the continued pulse of magic he felt radiating from his apprentice. He looked down and realized his magical fire armor was dying out, and the bottom of the magical orb was unraveling where Jayce floated under it.

"You two are both the biggest fools I've ever been with."

Inferneous opened his mouth to reply when Jayce looked up, and Inferneous realized his eyes were glowing golden and no irises showed.

Even though he only met golden glowing eyes, Jayce's fury was still palpable as he cut off Inferneous before he could even start, "Don't say a word. Calm down now, or I'll make you."

Inferneous didn't think anyone would have ever tried to intimidate him successfully, but Jayce did the job pretty well as the orb above them started to disintegrate into the sky.

Inferneous started to descend as Balast and Zack did, and when they touched the ground, Inferneous realized that Zack and Jayce were holding onto Balast and himself to keep themselves afloat. He also realized that the whole crew was surrounding them with partly terrified and partly angry faces. They then rushed forward to hold Inferneous and Balast's arms. They brought them side by side as Zack and Jayce stood in front of them.

"What are you doing?" Balast asked angrily. He was sweating hard as the strain from the battle was still taking a toll on him, and he slightly struggled against the crew's arms, but he stopped with a huff of exhaustion.

Zack looked at Balast, and his face furrowed with worry but it hardened when he looked at Jayce.

Jayce's eyes stopped glowing, and he breathed winded from his magical exhaustion but his face looked furious. As Jayce turned and looked at Zack, they nodded to each other and faced Inferneous and Balast.

"This is a mutiny," Zack said, looking Balast, then Inferneous in the eye. "Your actions have been childish and not in the interests of the crew, so Jayce and I are replacing you two." Zack turned to Jayce and whispered a bit quieter, seeing he was angrily staring at both of them, "Go easy on them."

Jayce folded his arms, then wiped his face, looking up at the sky as he thought over the multitude of choice words he had for them, and then came back to Inferneous and Balast with more calculation mixed in his anger.

"I thought you two would have solved whatever you two had going on civilly, but I was mistaken," he sighed in anger and stuttered half a word before covering his mouth and shaking his head.

He gained his composure and continued, "You have proven too dangerous to remain above decks. Take them below and leave them with a few days' ration, then lock the door."

Inferneous was dumbfounded in shock as he and Balast were dragged down to below decks. The last thing he heard before he was thrown down the steps was the quiet words of Zack as he said, "Without them, I don't think any of us are going to leave this place alive."

Chapter 18

Balast had been below decks before for meager things like snacks or to retrieve certain crewmates from slumber so they could perform their duties, but he was just starting to look at the bunk beds Inferneous had built into the hull, dusty now, in a new light. Or a new darkness, you could say. It was almost pitch black, and with the little light that showed through the floorboard, it was constantly blocked by the shuffling and moving bodies of the crew as they moved about the ship and continued to run it.

Without us, Balast thought, scowling at Inferneous on the other bunk, just staring at the boards above him. They had not spoken a word, and Balast tried his best not to even breathe in his direction but failed. As Balast watched Inferneous, he tried to analyze what he was thinking and process his thoughts. He realized that he was still in shock that the crew had mutinied. The thought of Zack and Jayce's faces when they announced it were, I would say, almost opposites. Balast could tell that Jayce was almost out of his mind, which was a new look on the usually calm and level-headed young man he knew. The more he thought about it, though, it made sense. Balast couldn't imagine leading anyone without at least something admirable or fearful about them.

As Balast continued to stare at Inferneous, he still couldn't pick up on any emotion. Inferneous just laid there, almost corpse-like. He could only tell he was alive because of the occasional orange flicker of flames as he breathed in and out. If that was an indication of anything, Balast believed that Inferneous was angry, but as long as he had known him, magic lived inside Inferneous as much as outside. It wasn't really showing off his feelings, but when it was, it usually appeared in some animal form. His attention was drawn above him when a crew member crossed the boards. The board made more noise because the person who was crossing over it was Rhinda.

Rhinda started walking up the stairs to the helm and saw Holdren steering the ship with Jayce, Zack, and Erica leaning on the platform's railing. "So, where are we going?" Rhinda asked, crossing his arms as he walked to the middle, facing Erica.

Erica smiled and shook her head, saying, "That question is never going away, is it? We are all just caught in this cycle of perpetual disorientation…" She looked to the black horizon and then back at Rhinda's hard gaze. She then tipped her head to Zack and Jayce and said, "It's their ship; ask them."

Rhinda turned to them and saw Zack fondling the wide-brimmed wizard's hat Balast had given him. Jayce was just staring at the ground radiating a kind of pulsating energy Rhinda couldn't put a finger on.

Zack spoke first, "We decided we are just going to head to the light on the horizon because there really is nothing else, we can do." Zack dropped the hat on the ground with a small sound of surprise, and as he picked it up again, he continued, "We never really were disorientated like Erica said; it's just that we placed our trust in the most powerful people we knew."

"Those fools," Jayce spoke up, uncrossing his arms. "Or, more accurately, us fools."

"Don't blame any of us for what's happened, including yourself. We are only at the whim of the blacksmith at this point," Holdren chimed in, not turning back from the helm.

Suddenly, the ship shook violently to the right and then swayed back over as Holdren hissed, "Disregard that; there are apparently many jutting rocks in the water, but it's almost impossible to see them in this darkness. Honestly, I gave this ship less credit than it deserves; we would have sunk by how many rocks we've grazed if we were on a regular ship. Must be something special in the wood."

Again, the ship shook violently and swayed left, this time making Rhinda step back into a sturdy stance, keeping his balance. Rhinda looked past the mast into the dark horizon until he found a dim line of light shooting up to the dim sun.

"So, we are just going to stumble through the dark then?" Rhinda summed up as the boat stopped shaking.

Jayce nodded solemnly as he turned to look out at the darkness. "It's really all we can do. We don't know the danger that is posed by us being here, so we'll just have to keep moving."

Rhinda nodded his head as he couldn't say much to the honest answer. He stared at Jayce, looking out at the horizon and then down to Zack, who had slumped to the deck, sighing as he rested his head on his tucked-in knees. "What about Balast and Inferneous?"

Jayce's shoulders tensed, and Zack tightened his curl as Rhinda said those names aloud.

"We leave them locked up," said Jayce instantly.

"I don't think we should leave them locked up," Rhinda replied to Jayce's quick and angry response.

Jayce turned around, and his face was contorting in ways Rhinda had never seen before. "They stay in the crew's quarters because I said so, Rhinda. Plus, it's common sense in case they have another outbreak."

Rhinda raised an eyebrow at him, "Common sense? If they have another outbreak, then the interior of our ship is as good as gone. How is that common sense?"

"Do you have any ideas? Would you like to deal with people who could kill you in under thirty seconds? I don't know if you were conscious, but did you see and feel the magic that was radiating off them when they were fighting? They weren't just going ta' have a nice ol' fistfight; they were going to kill each other and also the rest of the crew!" Jayce exclaimed. He glanced over to Zack, who had started to shiver a bit because of the realization of where they were hit him like a tsunami. Jayce's face dropped into a deep sorrow as he looked back at Rhinda. "Are you willing to take another chance with that kind of power? Are you willing to trust them again with your life, if not all of ours, for a hopeful dream?"

"It's no dream, it's people. You have ceased to think of them as people if you ever did in the first place. You're young, which gives you that excuse, but Erica and Holdren," Rhinda looked to both of them respectfully, and they avoided his gaze, knowing his intention. He shook his head in disappointment. "Both of them appear to agree with you. It's a very childish thing to think that people with power you can't fathom are something more than human on the inside. I'll work with Balast and Inferneous on their problems as long as you'll promise me one thing." Rhinda stepped forward to Jayce in his rigid stance.

Jayce wanted to back up but was surprised when Rhinda embraced him in a hug. Jayce's hands unclenched in shock as he felt Rhinda's thick arms embrace him in a softness he never thought of from a man of his stature.

"Don't give up hope. You've been doing an amazing job as a leader. You've shown more courage than both Balast and Inferneous combined on this journey." He let Jayce go and started down to the main deck, leaving Jayce with his hands clenched, now contorting in opposite ways as he closed his eyes, holding back emotions.

It took a day and a half before the Ninjirates entered waters that were lit by the bright light source. The sky was now a muddy sunset color as if the sky had been beaten to a red pile, thrown in the mud then returned to its place above. It was more welcomed than the cold black expanse the crew had been experiencing for the previous day and a half.

"It's like we are deep underground, not too close but not far enough from hell itself," Arc, a former tiger mask, had said concernedly on his break from ship work. "It's cool."

As Jayce overheard his comment, he frowned in distaste. He then proceeded to tie a knot to a peg on the mast. The ship suddenly shook and swayed to the right. Everyone on the ship held onto something this time as the tilting and swaying didn't stop for a good five minutes.

This can't be rocks, Jayce thought just as the shaking ended and everyone went on with their work. He let go of the mast and walked to the helm where Holdren was teaching Zack about map making while Erica held onto the helm, pretending to know how to steer a ship. She was doing a good job of it until she slightly moved the wheel, and her cool demeanor fell apart and worry filled her eyes, questioning if she did something wrong only for Holdren to come over and slightly adjust the wheel and smile kindly at her. Erica was instantly calm as soon as Holdren redirected her. Jayce could have sworn she moved the helm to the right on purpose to garner Holdren's attention once more. Jayce blew it off as his imagination as he greeted Holdren and started with a question. "When do we arrive?"

Holdren scratched his head, and his face scrunched into a tight ball in obvious pain.

"Just tell me, the only thing worse that could happen is if we all lost our memories and had to start over from square one," Jayce said tiredly.

Holdren sighed and said, "We aren't moving. Or we are going as slow as a snail with a bad knee."

Jayce sighed and motioned for Holdren to continue. "What's stopping us? The supposed 'Rocks'?"

Holdren winced again at his comment and continued, "There are no more rocks."

Jayce was surprised that he was correct and stared at Holdren to continue, but Holdren just stared at the black water over the railing of the ship. Jayce tapped him on the shoulder, and he jumped a bit as he turned toward Jayce. Jayce looked Holdren in his wavering gaze and asked carefully, "Tell me what's in the water, Holdren."

Holdren rubbed the stubble on his chin nervously when he replied in shaky sentences, "I think there is a Malum in the water. The rocks and sways in the ship are probably trying to steer us away or just directly stop us from gaining ground, so to speak. I asked some of the crew members, and they said they saw something moving in the water, and I didn't believe them until I saw what I thought was a piece of seaweed or something then the water underneath it rushed it away."

Jayce's brow furrowed, trying to comprehend what Holdren said, and then his face grew hard when he asked, "So this thing is large enough to keep a ship from progressing but smart enough not to destroy the ship in the process."

Jayce folded his arms in thought, and after a few seconds, Zack chimed into the conversation, "That doesn't seem like a Malum."

Jayce turned to him with a hand raised, asking, "How do you mean?"

Zack responded, "Malum are pure evil and love destroying everything they can. If it truly is a Malum, then it would have either sunk our ship or hopped aboard to try and eat us all."

"So, what's stopping it?" Jayce asked

"Either the presence of Inferneous and Balast, which makes sense because of their outburst, or because of some ulterior, most definitely evil, motive."

Holdren nodded and frowned as he voiced a question. "What if it was attracted to the magical energy they released? We didn't seem to have turbulence in that illusion we were in. It definitely started after we started heading in the direction of the light, too."

Jayce cursed softly at the new problems sprung by the fallacies of the wizards but kept any other nasty thoughts to himself. "If it was them, we only have to add to the list of problems those wizards have created. Prepare to have a hard time handling the ship; I have a Malum to kill."

Jayce then walked off, yelling to the crew, "Everyone get to your battle positions!! There is a Malum on the way!"

The crew was jarred to life as the word Malum shook the last of the slight foggy confusion that had muddled their minds away. They scrambled to different preplanned positions, some drawing their weapons while others gathered their strength for magical purposes. As soon as Jayce saw everyone was ready, he peered down into the black waters and waited. It was a long five minutes where no soul moved. Some crew members shifted from foot to foot, anticipating the action. Jayce gathered his strength, and as he did, he felt a cold and burning feeling rise from the sole of his foot through his actual soul all the way to the center of his forehead. His face contorted in an unreadable expression. As he closed his eyes, his veins glowed an electric yellow. He breathed in deep and yelled, "Come on!!!" As he yelled, a pulse of yellow energy exploded from his body, blasting an invisible field of magical energy all around him. It then shot outwards and passed over everything. As the magic passed over the crewmates, they all felt rejuvenated and ready to fight, and those who were gathering their magical energy felt overfilled with magic as the wave passed. The water, on the other hand, reacted violently. The shockwave caused the water to boil and pop like it was superheated. A wall of water stretched far enough to pass over the whole ship and at least twenty feet in all directions before it dissipated. There were a few more minutes of silence, but time passed by quickly because of the energy boost Jayce had given them. Then, the ship was struck violently on its starboard side. A few crew members were thrown up off the deck into the air from the hit, but this time, they were ready, and all landed back on the deck safely. The ship rocked dangerously to its side but remained afloat as Holdren strongly turned the wheel to try and steady it.

When the boat slipped back to a more upright position, Jayce finally caught a view of the monster. Its skin was almost darker than the water around it. If its dark purple scales didn't lightly glint from the sun, Jayce was sure he wouldn't have seen anything at all. It quickly slithered through the water away from the boat, and Jayce got to see its full length. As it parted the waters, seemingly fleeing, Jayce could see that it was at least six hundred feet long and twenty feet thick. Along its back, several sharp spines lined its vertebrae and every twenty feet, he could see an appendage or fin flash by.

Jayce turned around to see if everyone was ok, but instead, he met Zack's worried face. "Are you ok? You've been glowing oddly since yesterday, and that blast didn't look controlled. It did help the others react faster, though; I bet without it, half of the crew would have fallen off the ship."

Zack looked out to the horizon, and his face changed from concern to horror as he pointed behind Jayce and yelled, "It is coming back!! Get do—" he was cut off as the boat rocked violently to its side again, but this time when it swayed back over it was weighed down by something large.

When Jayce stood to his feet again, he stepped back in shock as he gazed upon the serpent leaning on the side of the ship, half its body out of the water. Its face looked like the blunt edge of a blade as Jayce saw its outline looking down at them from the dark sky. While Jayce continued staring, he realized its head was growing and shrinking like it was almost breathing. Jayce then remembered a spell Inferneous had taught him and covered his left eye and spoke the magical spell, and his vision zoomed up to the monster: his mouth dropped in horror.

The head was just dozens of open pores that breathed and writhed as the monster moved. As the crew members started to fire magic projectiles or, even worse, throw their weapons at it, Jayce yelled out as he turned around, "That's not the head!!"

When he was fully turned around he saw, as they were distracted by the smaller tail of the beast, the real head was watching menacingly from the other side of the boat. Its real face had long tendrils radiating off it and two large spikes with purple rings all down the length of them. It had two glowing purple tongues that flicked intermittently in and out of its mouth, tasting the air for its prey.

Jayce tried to point to the monster, saying, "The real face is there! Hey, look–" he stopped when he realized no one was listening. No, it wasn't that they weren't listening; it was more like they were entranced with the tail than anything else. He ran and stopped a crewmate from jumping overboard to try and attack the tail, and when he looked at the former mercenary in the face, he saw two purple rings in his irises and realized that this wasn't any normal attack.

Jayce then got angry as he shouted to the head behind them, "Fine, I'll take care of you myself!!" A pulse of magic radiated off him as he ran toward the large Malum, readying a ball of magic between his hands. He then leaped off the deck and hurled the ball right at the Malum's face.

Zack was standing still from shock as he watched Jayce attack the horned Malum, but when the pulse of magic from Jayce snapped out of it and realized he had to help in some way. He ran toward Jayce as he saw him jump off the deck, trying to attack the head. Zack knew he couldn't possibly just stab into the Malum and not fall into the murky water, so he stretched out his hands and created a green magical platform for Jayce to land on. When he did, Zack saw Jayce look back at him and nod thanks as he turned and hopped back onto the ship. Zack then ran up to him and asked, "I've never seen a Malum like that before!" he yelled as the Malum suddenly bellowed and roared.

"It seems to be creating a distraction using magic to hypnotize the crew into thinking its tail is its head." Jayce said while looking up at the monster and then at the crewmates who weren't really even attacking the tail anymore; they were just standing there yelling insults or just saying 'Attack' in a weird trance. Among the crew, he saw Erica and Rhinda shaking people, trying to wake them from the trance.

They walked toward Erica as she was slapping a former ninja hard, yelling into his face, "Wake up!!" Jayce put a hand on her shoulder to stop her from yelling, and she snapped to him in rage at first, then recognized his face.

"What's going on here?" she asked, obviously still mad. She then looked up and shook her head at the horned Malum. "Why is it just sitting there keeping the men entranced? More importantly, how do we get rid of it?"

Jayce was about to speculate on it when Holdren stopped next to Zack and started, "The Malum is trying to keep us away from the source of the light. It's turning us away from it, and I can't control the ship anymore."

Jayce realized that the ship had been slightly turning away from the light source.

"I don't think this Malum is like the other ones," Rhinda said, stepping past Jayce so he could get a better look at the Malum.

At first glance, when he looked, it was flicking its tongue in and out while its ringed horns pulsated a dark purple, but when he stared longer, it suddenly stopped moving. The Malum turned to face him specifically. While the others were talking, shouting, and barking orders, Rhinda walked to the tip of the boat and back as he watched the Malum seemingly watching him and his every movement.

"What can we even do against a Malum as large as that? I've never even seen…what is Rhinda doing?" Erica said as she raised a hand, pointing to Rhinda, walking back in forth, looking at the Malum.

"Rhinda, what–?" Jayce stopped and followed Rhinda's line of sight and saw that the Malum was following his moves closely. They all watched as Rhinda ran to the front of the ship, and the Malum's horns swayed to continue following him.

"Why is it only following you?" Zack asked when Rhinda approached them again.

Rhinda, still watching the Malum, shook his head, saying, "I have no idea. I haven't done anything special since we got here." He waved his hand at the Malum, and it remained in the same place, continuously staring at him. He put a hand to his chin in confusion, and then he got a brilliant idea.

"What if it's following my magical aura? Considering I'm probably the most magically powerful and experienced besides Drathni," Rhinda looked over to the frozen hypnotized crew and saw Drathni still frozen.

"That doesn't make sense, though. Inferneous and Balast are still below decks, and it hasn't sensed them," Holdren replied.

Rhinda furrowed his eyebrows as he stared deeply into the Malum's face and shook his head, "It must be something with the line of sight and whether it has you under its mind control. Anyways, hand me a weapon. I have a theory to test."

Erica fished through her gi and removed a one-sided throwing axe painted a dark shade of red and handed it hilt forward to Rhinda. Rhinda nodded his thanks and placed his other hand on the blade, and then the blade started to glow a yellow-golden color. He took a step back toward the helm, stretched his arm back and threw the axe to the other end of the ship. They all watched as the horned Malum turned to follow the axe until the magic dissipated. Rhinda smiled and nodded, saying silently to himself, "I knew it."

"So, it can't tell the difference between you and something you imbue with magic," Jayce said after retrieving the axe and handing it to Erica.

"So, do you think it would follow you if you left the boat?" Erica asked Rhinda after re-sheathing the axe.

Rhinda grimaced at what Erica proposed. "I don't think me leaving the ship would rid us of the Malum. It's trying to stop us from getting to the light on the horizon; it's not just here for me."

They were silent for a bit as they tried to think of a solution then it was broken by Jayce walking to the edge of the boat and throwing a ball of energy at the Malum. The attack had no effect on the Malum and made Erica raise an eyebrow at what Jayce was doing, but Jayce walked back over, and Erica saw a spark in his eye.

"Rhinda," Jayce unsheathed his broadsword and held it up to Rhinda, "Can you imbue your magic into my sword? I want to try something out."

Rhinda nodded and placed both his hands on the broadsword. He closed his eyes, and a few seconds later, it started to glow golden, just like the axe.

"Thanks, now watch this." Jayce ran toward the edge of the ship, and right before he reached the railing, he threw his sword at the Malum. It flew in the air for a couple of seconds until it sliced cleanly into the Malum's flesh. The Malum recoiled, and the boat rocked as its body thrashed about. Jayce smiled as the crew started to move about. The hypnotism faded away, but he didn't stall when he turned to Rhinda with his hand out and said, "Let's kill this thing."

It had been a few minutes since the last time the boat shook, and Balast was worried almost out of his mind. He was sure that if the crew and Zack were in danger, they wouldn't hesitate to release him and Inferneous to handle it, but from how Balast was remembering, Jayce looked like he would be mad at them for a long while. Inferneous didn't seem worried, but truly, Balast still couldn't tell what he was thinking or feeling. He had been tempted the first day they were put below decks to try and magically peek into his mind, but he was already pushed to the point where he would half whisper a spell and almost lose consciousness as he mustered the remaining magic.

So, instead, he just watched Inferneous from the opposite bunk in silence. Inferneous didn't move until a crewmate came down and delivered their rations, which were cut in half, probably by Jayce's orders, but even when he sat up and received it, he didn't speak or look at Balast. It wasn't coldhearted or cruel like he was cross with Balast, but it was more of a melancholic ignorance like Balast was dead, and he was mourning the loss of his friend.

Balast couldn't understand Inferneous in the least, so he just brushed it off as a random sadness. Balast was definitely still angry at Inferneous to the point that the last two days passed faster for him, and all he could think about was the mistakes of the past. As he started to whisper a spell and had trouble finishing it, he finally got a slight burst of brief relief as the light spell worked, and a ball of light rose from his finger and lit the room. He looked at Inferneous with a defiant smile but found him still lying in the same position in another world, another sad world. Balast's vain smile faded into a still simmering anger as he canceled the spell, and the room went dark again. "Didn't we used to be stronger?" He said aloud, still looking at Inferneous. "I remember when we used to slay ten Malums with a flick of a finger, and we used to take care of bandits blindfolded for fun. Remember that? Now we are just old men parading around like children, acting like we are still that powerful."

Silence followed his remark. Balast then shook his head, anger flaring up after no response. "It just seems like after you messed up, my magic hasn't been the same." He muttered, lying down in the cramped bed. He stared up at the wooden frame of the bed, and his thoughts turned to his master, Parquen.

"They didn't ever get along either, did they? I always saw them through the corner of my eye or after we went to bed, giving each other harsh glances or arguing under the impression that we were asleep." Balast looked over to Inferneous, who was still unresponsive and shook his head again. "I never knew we'd become just like them. No, we're actually worse. Not even responding or acknowledging each other like children. At the very least, you could respond to show that you care."

Balast then stood and walked to the middle of the room and stared at Inferneous long and hard. "I'm waiting!" Balast said, tapping his foot impatiently.

Inferneous did nothing. Balast was about to yell at Inferneous when he felt a wave of magic pass over him as the boat rocked violently. He was thrown back into the bunk as the boat rocked, and then he heard multiple footsteps rushing about on the deck above him. Balast's worries came flooding back as the ship started to rock back and forth. After a few minutes of tossing, turning, and shouts of battle, the boat stopped rocking, and there were cheers. Balast was confused for a second, but after the cheering died down, all was back to the quietness of the crewmates working the ship once more. Balast stood once more and peered through the floorboards to see Jayce and Rhinda standing together, talking about something, but he didn't really care what they were saying; he was looking for an indication that Zack was ok. He was back at ease when he saw Zack coming behind them, smiling and talking fast, excited about something, but Balast just sat back down on the bunk bed, sighing in relief.

Rhinda didn't know what Jayce had up in his sleeve when he asked him for his magic, but he could trust the smile on his face. As Rhinda locked arms with Jayce, he smiled and said, "Alright, what's the plan?"

"Just channel all of your energy into me; I think I can drive this thing away," Jayce said, walking to the middle of the main deck. He lifted his arms up, stretched them up to the sky, then centered his palms at his chest. A gust of hot wind blew away from him in all directions as his veins started to glow white under his skin, and then he yelled out, "Stand back, everyone! Rhinda, now!"

Rhinda then welled up the majority of his magic in the palms of his hands and pointed his palms toward Jayce. He was about to send a volley of magic toward Jayce, but he was caught by surprise when the magic started to flow freely from his hands toward Jayce. It was an odd feeling having the magic flow out so easily. Rhinda watched as the magic was pulled out of him like silk out of a spool; it flowed into Jayce's chest. As it did so, Jayce started glowing golden, the same golden Rhinda's magic was.

"Look, the Malum sees you!!" Zack shouted out.

Jayce looked up from his concentrated ball of magic and saw that the Malum was staring directly at him. He smiled in anticipation as he continued to feel the power of Rhinda's magic inside him. The small ball of magic between his palms then hardened into a golden orb, and Jayce knew it was time. He then yelled out and slammed his palms together, crushing the glowing orb. Everything went silent for a few seconds, and then an explosion of magic radiated from the center of the boat.

When the ship stopped rocking from the recoil of the Malum and the explosion, Rhinda noticed that the air felt different. It was warmer, so warm that it felt like Rhinda was moving slowly through a thick soup. The thing was that he could feel and audibly hear his thoughts like the air itself had become an extension of himself. He snapped out of the shock when he felt a ripple in the air and saw that Jayce was no longer on the ground. He was floating inches off the ground, and his veins were glowing all golden, and there were runes covering his face. Rhinda stepped back when Jayce's eyes turned to look at him, and he heard in his head, "This feels really good!" in Jayce's voice.

Rhinda couldn't believe what he was seeing as Jayce flexed his back, and a pair of golden feathered wings appeared behind him. Jayce turned around and raised his arms, gawking at his magically heightened state and then settled into a smile when he saw the Malum. He then flew with the speed of the wind and slammed headfirst into it. There was a loud crunch as one of the Malum's horns snapped off and fell onto the deck of the ship. Jayce backed up, rubbing his head in pain, then looked up to the Malum and found that it was already uncoiling itself from the ship. Jayce watched for a few minutes as the Malum dived into the water behind it and swam away. Jayce yelled out, "Yeah, I did it!!" but while he was celebrating, Rhinda started to feel faint.

Jayce was in the air, still celebrating, when Rhinda collapsed to the ground. Jayce turned around as he heard Rhinda's body hit the floor, and before he could react, he felt the warmth leave the air. Jayce's nose started to bleed from both sides, and before he could react, his wings disappeared, and he lost consciousness, falling to the deck below. As soon as the magical field Jayce created disappeared, everyone else on the ship took a breath.

Zack coughed as he asked, "What was that–Jayce!!" he stopped and yelled out as he saw Jayce fall to the deck. Zack outstretched his hand and caught Jayce with an upside-down green magical shield, breaking his fall. He bounced off of the shield, and his body ended up half off the side of the railing, leading Zack to run as fast as he could to catch Jayce before he fell off the ship. Erica helped him out, grunting as they pulled the heavy young man up.

Holdren noticed Rhinda collapse and decided to tend to him, seeing that Erica and Zack were taking care of Jayce. The crew, shaking off their shock, then sprang into action, helping them, and soon they were back on course. Zack was sitting with Jayce at the base of the mast when Jayce woke up with a start. Jayce stood up, immediately looking around until he saw Zack staring at him dumbfounded.

"Did you see that?" Jayce asked excitedly. "That was awesome!! I didn't even know I could do magic until yesterday…" He then sighed, sat back down, holding his head and wiping his nose on his sleeve. When Jayce saw the blood, he looked at Zack in surprise.

Zack nodded and smiled, "Yeah, that was awesome, but you definitely have lost a lot of blood from that nosebleed."

Jayce nodded and smiled. Drathni soon came over to help him, and after she healed him, she informed them that the captain would like to see them.

"The captain?" Zack questioned. "You mean Holdren?"

"Yes, the crew has been calling him captain lately. I forget you guys call him Holdren," she responded while collecting the bloody rags she had used to stop Jayce's bleeding nose.

"He says it's important though."

"Then let's get going," Jayce said, standing up and shaking in an uncertain balance. When he was stable, he started to walk toward the helm, calling over Erica, who was dealing with the crew issuing orders.

"What? The crew needs something to do so they can forget about what just happened, "What do you need?"

"Holdren has something to tell us. It has to be something about the light on the horizon, so you need to know," said Jayce.

He and Zack walked off, and she reluctantly followed. When they got to the helm, Holdren looked a little more worried than he usually does. Once he saw them, he just pointed to the front of the ship and said, "Look! The light has gotten closer! Here," he passed a spyglass to them.

Holdren handed it to Jayce, but Zack grabbed it out of his hand and leaned over the edge of the ship to look at the approaching light.

"It's an island! A big one, too!"

Erica grabbed the spyglass out of his hand and looked through it, and for the first time, she smiled. She looked to Holdren, who was also smiling ecstatically, and said, "Looks like you can actually steer a ship."

He nodded thanks as she handed the spyglass to Jayce. Looking through it, he exclaimed, "It looks like we made it. And all by ourselves, too."

Chapter 19

Rhinda awoke to his whole body hurting. His eyes remained closed as he groaned in pain, feeling like he just fought a whole war by himself. He opened his eyes to a significantly brighter sky than he remembered when he was fighting the Malum. He sat up and looked around to see jags of darkness stretching up out of the ocean and reaching toward the sky; some touched the clouds, which were now visible to the naked eye because of the increased light coming from whatever was ahead of the ship.

"You're up," Rhinda heard Jayce say to his left state, relieved.

"Sorry for using your magic up like that. I didn't know... Well, I don't really know how my magic works. I'm glad you didn't die, though."

Rhinda rested his back up against the railing of the ship and let a long sigh out as he started to gain full consciousness.

"Let me know next time your plan includes doing something life-threatening."

"But I didn't even know though. You can't hold it against me. I just had a taste when Balast and Inferneous were fighting and–"

"How are they?" Rhinda interrupted Jayce in the middle of his sentence.

Jayce's face grew hard, and he crossed his legs and rested his head on one arm. "They are still down there. I didn't send anyone down there, but they have no reason to even think of leaving the ship lest they break their way out of served meals daily."

Rhinda looked at Jayce and then looked past him at the latch that led down into the ship where Inferneous and Balast were held. He then shifted his gaze back to Jayce, whose face was now contorted as he gritted his teeth. His eyes were pointedly at the floor, and his fist was clenched.

What Rhinda perceived was the lasting anger of what Jayce thought of the powerful wizards. Rhinda sighed and stood up, wobbling with disorientation and a bit of nausea. Jayce stood quickly, reaching out a hand to help, but Rhinda raised his hand to stop him. He turned to Jayce, and as he looked him up and down, he realized there was a large stain of blood on his right sleeve, and he asked, "Are you ok? Whose blood is that?"

Jayce looked down and shook his head, "Yeah, I was a bit roughed up after falling from the sky. Drathni did say that I only lost a good amount of blood but I will be fine if I don't exert myself."

Rhinda nodded and turned around to look over the side of the ship and saw that there was a clear path between the obsidian rock struts that protruded out of the water like the ocean tried to spew out the darkness within it. As Rhinda's eyes were unfocused, he realized that something odd was happening in the scene.

"Why are the pillars moving?" he asked Jayce, mildly concerned.

Jayce looked over the side of the ship and said, "They are moving?" Jayce didn't see anything as he looked up at the pillars.

Rhinda pointed at the water and said, "Not up there, but they are moving under us, and it looks like they are going past us, like they are enveloping us."

Jayce looked down and saw the ripples of the ship's wake going outwards as they moved forward, but then they collided with multiple smaller wakes around the bases of the rocks.

"Wow, that is super odd; we should go tell Holdren about this."

Jayce started to walk toward the steps when Rhinda raised his hand and said, "Go ahead, you got it. I'm going to tend to an important situation."

"What situation?" Jayce asked, very confused.

Rhinda looked up at him with a gaze that was torn between pity and harsh judgment as he said, "Someone has to sort these two overpowered children out."

Balast was growing tired of being cooped up below decks and was seriously thinking of just opening the hatch and seeing what was going on. He had considered what the crew and, most importantly, how Zack and Holdren would react if he just defied their mutiny. This had been his first time ever captaining or co-captaining a ship, and he wasn't stressing about the fact that he was a bad captain but more about how he was a bad mentor. The options of what the crew could do would come down to just accepting him or trying to rebel against him. With the crew Inferneous had picked up along his travels, Balast wasn't so keen, but they would just heartily agree on his presence above deck.

He was standing up, now pacing the length of the small walkway between the close-quartered beds that were crowded with food supplies and other necessities they had taken from the massive cargo ship and stuffed inside this smaller ship. He paced toward the small ladder that led to the trapdoor above him and then turned back to pace toward the walkway leading to the supply of food stuffed in the very back of the cabin. When he turned around, he saw someone climbing down the ladder. By the man's large and muscular structure, Balast could tell it was Rhinda.

As Rhinda turned, Balast noticed his face was paler than usual. He didn't say anything but just stared at him, and Rhinda stared back until he sighed and sat on one of the ladder rungs and asked, "Are you guys done fighting?"

Balast smiled and shook his head, saying, "I'm not, but my counterpart looks like he is." Balast kept shooting hostile glances in Inferneous' direction just to get the same response of morbid silence.

Balast turned back to Rhinda and smirked as he asked, "So, what happened without my supervision? Anyone dead from Jayce's mistake of putting us down here?"

Rhinda's eyes furrowed as he smiled in a twisted disbelief in Balast's attitude. He then resettled himself with a quick retort, "No. Jayce handled the situation pretty well."

Balast scoffed and chuckled as he responded, "Then why are you almost completely drained of magic? And also, you look like you just ran laps around the ship and didn't breathe through it."

"What does that mean?" Rhinda squinted his eyes in confusion.

Balast raised a hand, and a mirror pointed towards Rhinda, showing him that he was as pale as a freshly dead man. Rhinda stared at the mirror for a second, realizing he hadn't seen his own face in at least two years. He slowly reached his hand up to touch his pale cheek, but before he did, he also realized what he was doing.

"He required a bit of help, but I was willing," Rhinda said, staring at Balast sternly.

Balast dropped his hand, and the mirror disappeared with a shimmer as he folded his arms. "What could he possibly do to drain you of that much mana? He doesn't even know magic."

Rhinda smiled and sat back on the stairs. He sighed, saying, "Well, he does now. But that's not the point of why I'm here. Are you two going to even try apologizing for the childish scuffle you had, which put the lives of your crew in danger? I know because of the flaming spears and other random magic you two threw around, people were injured, and without Drathni's amazing healing skills and the bravery of your own apprentices, everyone was able to even survive that mess—"

"You must have an amazing sense of duty calling someone at least fifty years older than you childish," Balast scoffed.

Rhinda stood and faced him as his voice lowered, "Some children just grow older. You're a prime example of one. But even so, I think you have enough maturity to acknowledge that, whether you wanted to or not, there are people on this ship who will not make it through this hellish dimension you brought us to."

He paused to step back and address Inferneous, too. "I don't know what you two are even fighting about, but from how I've experienced you working with others, I know that you two can work this out even if this feud has been going on for longer than I've been alive."

At this point, Inferneous sat up in the bed he had been lying in and spoke up, "It hasn't been going on for quite as long as that," he then looked Balast in the eyes as his voice dropped into a lower, sadder tone saying, "but it has felt that way."

Balast rolled his eyes, exclaiming, "Oh, he's awake! I thought he was in a coma from some sort of mana deprivation, but it looks like his feelings were just hurt."

Inferneous ignored his comment, looked to Rhinda, and nodded. "I thank you for coming down here and thinking about us. You show wisdom beyond your age by your actions."

He turned to look at Balast and then shook his head in sorrow, continuing to say, "I think you are right. We are very childish, so I would like to ask you to guide us to a middle ground and hopefully communicate to the crew why we would be better above deck."

Rhinda blinked in surprise, but his gaze settled as he made up his mind. "I will help you. I think the best way to get the crew to start to trust you again is to open up to them in a respectable manner. We can solve the problem here, and then I'll prepare them for your speech." He stood up and climbed partially up the ladder to peek out to the upper deck, and he saw the sky gradually growing lighter each minute. He climbed back down and addressed them both with an urgency in his voice. "Ok, tell me about the past you have together, but quickly, I think we are approaching our destination faster than I thought."

Zack was caught between extreme boredom and a creeping sense of either excitement or anxiety. He figured it was probably both from how shaky his hands were. He was holding all too tightly to his wand as he stared at the almost blindingly bright horizon through the forest of obsidian black pillars that barely avoided the ship. Zack looked at them in awe and in an unidentifiable fear in his gut, saying that something wasn't right about them. He brushed the feeling aside, thinking he should take a walk around the ship to ease his nerves. He made his way down the stairs and passed a few crew members also gawking at the obsidian pillars and spikes while some sharpened their weapons in preparation for whatever the ship was going to face. Zack passed all of them, absorbing the anxious atmosphere, when he found himself at the door to the captain's quarters. He slowly pushed the door open to reveal a room glowing with purple runes across every wall and piece of furniture. He couldn't recognize the runes, but he noticed a small skull on the table in front of him. It was glowing the same faint purple of the runes but seemed to pulsate more than the runes on the walls around him. He picked the skull off the table and felt the cold, chalky feel of the bone, and as he held it, he felt a peculiar energy radiating off it. He felt the magic deep in his chest react strangely to the artifact, and as he continued to stare at it, he grew entranced in the ridges. He almost threw the artifact across the cabin when Jayce burst through the door.

"There you are! We've been looking for you for an hour now! I thought you had fallen overboard!"

Zack opened and closed his mouth in confusion, but Jayce didn't wait. "Come on, Zack, let's not stall any longer."

He pulled Zack out of the room into the bright upper deck. He turned his head to Zack, saying, "We need to get some rope and ladders to make sure everyone gets off the boat safely–"

"Even us?" said Balast, standing directly in front of Jayce.

Surprised and angry, Jayce replied, "No, not you..." he looked past him and saw Inferneous to Balast's immediate right and the rest of the crew lined up, seemingly waiting for something.

Rhinda stepped out of the crowd and came up to Jayce, and said, "You need to listen to what they have to say."

"And if I–"

"Don't make the mistake of thinking we can get out of here by ourselves." Rhinda cut Jayce off before he had the chance to refuse.

Jayce's gaze hardened as he stared at Rhinda and then at Balast. He shook his head and walked past them to join the rest of the crowd, with Zack following close behind him. Once Jayce was with the crowd, he raised his hand to Rhinda and yelled, "Get on with it! The sooner we get out of this cursed place, the better!"

Rhinda turned to Balast and Inferneous and raised a hand toward the crew with a hopeful look on his face.

"We wanted to apologize for our foolish actions that endangered the crew, especially when we entered this new and dangerous place." Balast started putting his hands together in a contemplative manner. "There are a multitude of things that could have gone wrong, but you all, as a crew, have bonded and worked together to survive the challenges life has placed in front of you."

Balast looked to Inferneous, who then started to speak, "We do want to be good leaders and have as good as a relationship that all of you have with each other, and all we simply ask is if you can forgive us for being human."

There was silence for a good minute as the crew silently contemplated until a familiar and angry voice broke the silence with frustrated yells, "Is that it? Congratulations on how well we did, and then a desperate try at an apology?" Jayce retorted. "You two are the most magically powerful humans on the planet, and you don't know how to admit your wrongs. No wonder you fought each other!"

"Jayce!" Rhinda started scolding, "Sheath your tongue! Their plea is true, and I must remind you we are not in a place to disagree." He said, stepping forward adamantly.

Jayce stepped forward to separate himself from the crowd, and with a scowl on his face, he replied, "Who do you represent here, Rhinda? Some sort of prophet told them to silence the people so the gods could gain back their status. We took care of the Malum ourselves and you still think that we are just a bunch of lost children in need of guidance?"

"Jayce, we never have tried to harm you or have had an ill intent towards any of the crew; why–" Balast tried to reason with Jayce, but Jayce cut him off.

Jayce pointed to the bright light in front of the boat and continued, "We are making so much progress for you to ruin it by bringing up your past mistakes!"

Balast thought he could finish his sentence, but the more Jayce's words echoed in his mind, the more shocked Balast became. The words that came out of Jayce's mouth shot through Balast more powerful than any attack Inferneous or any Malum could throw at him.

Seeing the effect his words had on Balast, Jayce turned to Inferneous to do the same when he felt an elbow lodging deep into his rib cage. He staggered back in pain as he saw Zack retract his elbow, shaking his head.

"It's time for this to stop." He said as he stepped forward from the crew. "Truly, I think we all need to be reminded of each other's humanity time and time again. It's undeniable that no one can ignore that Inferneous and Balast are the most powerful people on this boat, and no matter what we as the crew do, we cannot stop them from enacting their free will upon us." He turned around to face the crew and raised his hand as he finished, "I would rather have a forgiven ally than a lenient captor. Raise your hand if you would reinstate Balast and Inferneous as captain and first mate of the ship."

There was more silence until a shuffling of feet as Erica, Holdren, and Drathni stepped forward and raised their hands. Erica rolled her head around, stretching it as she said, "I was waiting for you guys to come back above deck; I don't think I want to lead another band of people because I know how that ends…" Erica then folded her arms and looked at Jayce with a glare. "Rhinda is as right as he's always been; I suggest you heed his warnings, Jayce."

Jayce clenched his fist, raised it, released the tension, and dropped it to his side, dismissing his anger, saying, "Fine, If the crew wants your mistakes back, I won't stop you; in fact, I can't stop you." He turned to Balast and Inferneous and gestured behind him to the crew, "But I can try to keep you accountable for their sake."

Inferneous, at first frowning with worry, settled into a challenging smile, stood, walked over to Jayce, and held out his hand, "I can help you with that."

Inferneous' hand set aflame with a dark purple hue. When he turned his palm upward the fire retracted to form the shape of a dual-headed spear about the size of a fork. "This spell will help you keep me in check," he looked back at Balast, who was staring off into the distance and then back to Jayce. "And consequently, it will also keep Balast in check,"

Balast looked toward Inferneous and he scowled at the purple flames.

"You know what you are about to do is forbidden."

Inferneous scowled back. "What should be forbidden is us abusing our power once again." Inferneous said turning back to Jayce whose eyes were locked uneasily at the weapon spinning in the palm of Inferneous's hand.

Looking at Inferneous' hand, Jayce got an uneasy feeling, the unusual coloring of the flames, the weapons scaled down form, and Balast and Inferneous's words told him that this was no light matter. *Like this wasn't already a heavy subject.* With that thought Jayce's then his courage kicked in. He grasped Inferneous' hand tightly, looking him in the eye. Jayce winced in pain as he looked down and saw that the spear had righted itself and was now sticking out both his and Inferneous' hands. A tinge of apprehension flicked across Jayce's face as he looked back at Inferneous, who still had a dangerous smile on his face.

"This spell will allow you control over me in the event something like that ever happens again, as long as you agree to one thing."

Jayce looked down and saw that the spear had now melted on the back of his hand, and he hissed in pain as an insignia of a flaming spear embed itself into his hand.

"And what do I have to agree to?" Jayce asked, holding his composure by gritting his teeth in defiance.

Inferneous' smile softened as he gazed at Jayce in a sad manner. He said, "To keep your end of the bargain, to hold us to our word and to protect the crew as best as you can."

Jayce met Inferneous' eye again and held it as the words instantly left his mouth: "I agree."

Inferneous unclasped his hand from Jayce's as he examined the burning scar mark identical to the back of Jayce's hand and nodded in approval. "The deal has been sealed."

There was nothing but the whispering of the crew for a few minutes. They all returned to their positions, and Holdren yelled out directions, "Lower the sails and lower the anchor! Land is too close for comfort!!"

A few minutes later, the boat rocked as it connected with the black sand and dirt, dragging its hull across the dark shore. As soon as the anchor was down, Zack was the first one on the sand. He knelt down on the wet sand, and when he held up a handful of the black grainy material, something felt off.

Jayce slid down the rope and came up behind Zack, wondering what he was doing.

Zack stood up and turned as he heard Jayce behind him and said, "Hey, Jayce, look at this sand; it's really odd." Zack waited for Jayce to come over, and then when he was close enough, he moved his cupped hands over to Jayce.

"What is it?" Jayce asked, looking at the sand in Zack's hand. "Looks fine to me."

"I swear it doesn't feel as normal as it should here; take it from me," Zack said as Jayce raised his hands under Zack's hands.

Zack then opened his hands to let the sand fall into Jayce's. He was shocked when he looked at his hands. The sand that wasn't touching his skin had fallen into Jayce's hands, but all the sand that was touching his skin was forming lines all across his hands and even after he tried to wipe them off on his clothes, they did not disappear.

"This sand is really odd," Jayce said, dropping the sand to the floor. "It seems to be alive or something."

Jayce looked at his hand thoroughly and saw that the sand was uniquely standing up. It looked more like black flakes of ash as the sand remained rigid on his skin. He heard a few more people descending the rope and warned them not to let their skin touch the sand because it was very clingy.

Zack turned around as he saw Balast levitate down from the ship's rail and showed him his outstretched palm.

"What is it?" Balast asked curiously, looking at Zack's outstretched hand. When he got closer to Zack's palm, he grimaced and jerked his hands away from him.

Seeing Balast's reaction, Zack grew alarmed and asked, "What is it?!?!"

He stepped toward Balast, and Balast stepped back, his hands outstretched to keep Zack at a distance as he replied, "Calm down, it's not lethal. It's just…" he made a face of disgust and prepared a water spell in his hands as he continued, "You are not going to like what I'm going to tell you—"

"Good God!! Is that Malum flesh?!?! What in the Angel's name…!!"

Inferneous had just jumped from the side of the ship to the beach of disintegrated Malum flesh, sending the sand under him to puff into the air, and before he could recognize it, it was already covering most of him.

Balast rolled his eyes at Inferneous as Zack half grinned at the exclamation. His mirth changed to disgust when he fully realized what Inferneous had said. He coughed and gagged as he tried to wipe the sand off his sleeves with no progress.

"Here, it won't wipe off easily. It's attempting to rebuild itself by siphoning the magic out of you. Just stay still, and I'll get it off." Balast said as he grabbed Zack's wrists together with one hand palms up. He waved his other hand over them, and with a blue flash, the flesh particles softened into a fine powder and slid freely off Zack's hand.

Zack wiped his hands together for good measure as the substance fell through his hands. He sighed in relief and thanked Balast as Balast went over to Jayce to do the same.

The last person to come down the rope off the ship was Holdren with the magical compass, a piece of blank paper, and a lead pencil. He yelled out for everyone to gather around, and as all of the crew started to gather, he walked over to Balast and Inferneous and asked, "Alright, what's next?"

"Well, first, you can put that map away because it's likely that you will never come back here if we even find a way out," Balast said, grabbing the magical compass out of Holdren's hands.

"Well, maybe I could at least map it out for you guys; if you come back, it could be useful."

"This island isn't that big, and I wouldn't think that there are any more islands because this one was so heavily guarded. Anything of real importance is here," Inferneous chimed in as Balast examined the magical compass.

The compass was spinning in an odd way. It first was rotating clockwise steadily, but once it pointed in the direction of the bright light, it reversed itself to go counterclockwise, seemingly bouncing off a magical barrier.

"Well, the only thing we can really do is go towards the light, right? What could be on the island that was worse than that Malum?" Jayce said, walking up to them.

Inferneous chuckled and wiped his nose at Jayce, saying, "There literally could be any number of worse things, but if that were true, they would have already made themselves known."

"So, let's just continue to explore the island and find the light source. If something happens, we'll all be there to face it," Jayce responded.

"But what about the ship?" Holdren asked, concerned.

"The ship is an inanimate object; if we leave it, we leave it," Balast quickly responded. "We need to get moving; no one knows the effects of just being here. Having Malum flesh as sand is the biggest sign that we could just die from being exposed to this place for too long."

There was silence from Jayce, and Inferneous shrugged at Holdren.

"I guess that settles it; let's get moving," Inferneous said as he started to walk to the golden light on the horizon.

It took around twenty minutes of walking before anything remotely interesting appeared on the horizon. As they walked, Balast observed their surroundings, barren in a nervously dark and blackened hue. Nothing was visible beyond at least forty feet behind and to the sides of them because the light they were walking toward illuminated their surroundings to reveal light fog. The light fog became unable to see through as the light bounced off the water droplets floating through the air.

As they pushed forward, the island started to grow thinner and thinner until it was only about two men apart from the shores of the dark black water. Jayce started to notice that it was growing a little crowded and realized that Inferneous had said this was a tear-shaped island. He ran forward to the forefront of the group where Balast, Inferneous, Holdren,

Zack, Rhinda, and Erica were leading everyone. He stopped running when he was standing behind Inferneous and asked, "How did you know this island was tear-shaped?"

Inferneous turned his head, replying, "Well, the magic, of course."

Jayce rolled his eyes and continued, "Well, how with your magic did you know?"

Inferneous smiled and said, "Well, most of my magic works on physical touch, so anywhere I set my feet, my magic gets information for at least fifty miles. The only place it doesn't work is on a boat."

Jayce folded his arms, half-satisfied with the answer.

A few minutes of silent walking went by until Zack broke it and asked, "How long will it be until we get there?"

"It's right over this hill, but before we go over, I need that Malum skull from you," Balast said, halting his walking and holding out his hand.

Zack stopped immediately, shyly pulling the small skull out of his pocket and asking, "How did you know?"

Balast replied, "That artifact has led us here; you think I wouldn't keep track of it?"

Zack slowly put the skull in Balast's hands as he nodded. "It was glowing brightly with purple runes when I found it in the captain's quarters. I thought it might do something important, so I brought it along."

Balast nodded as he held the skull with both hands. "That is a good rule of thumb; a lot of important magical events happen where you cannot see them." He then started to scale up the hill and gawked at what he saw as he got to the top.

The hill wasn't just on their side of the island, but it was more like a crater. In the center was a ring of white obsidian obelisks with black runes running down their length. None of the obelisks were straight; instead, they were all leaning toward the light within them. As they got closer, the light in the circle of obelisks seemed to grow infinitesimally brighter, as if its shine could light the darkest of night skies.

As Balast descended down into the crater, he felt a burning sensation in his hand. He looked down and saw that the Malum skull he was holding was glowing bright purple with white runes now across it. As he looked down at it, he realized that the ground underneath him was also smoldering. Small tendrils of smoke rose from the crater surrounding the ring of obelisks, like the light itself was constantly burning the ground. Balast had the urge to continue forward, but as he stepped, a hand came down on his shoulder. He looked back and saw Inferneous nodding back to the crew. Balast looked back at the ring of obelisks, then turned back to Inferneous and nodded. They both then walked back up the hill and to the other side.

The whole crew of the ship had funneled around the base of the hill and were starting to rest on the ground from exhaustion. Jayce and Zack were about to start scaling the hill when Balast came down and stopped them halfway. When Jayce looked up at Balast's face, his stomach dropped to his feet. Balast had a face of pure and unfiltered terror; his eyes were glazed over, and his mouth half agape, as if his mind was still comprehending the image he had just seen.

"What did you see?"

Jayce heard Zack's shaky voice ask Balast. He looked over, and Zack was shaking so badly that he couldn't believe he was still standing. Balast didn't respond immediately to Zack, but Jayce saw him regain consciousness and look softly at Zack after a few seconds. His face then contorted into a mix of anger and sadness as he stared at Zack, showing obvious signs of fear. The emotions were not so much pointed at Zack, though, but they were more reflective.

"I... I don't know what in the Angel's name is in there, but it is something more powerful than me or Inferneous." he stared at the ground and murmured, "It might be the Angel herself."

Jayce's worry was growing almost as much as his curiosity, but his worry won when Inferneous came down; he was holding his hand up to his nose, and blood was falling through his fingers.

"What happened?" Jayce asked Inferneous as he walked past them.

Inferneous stopped, and his hand glowed bright orange, and a sizzle could be heard as the blood evaporated off his hand. He turned to Jayce, and Jayce noticed with horror that one of his eyes had a bit of blood trickling out of it.

"Balast is right, but it's not the Angel. Whatever is between those obelisks turned pitch black obsidian to be as white as the northern snows, maybe even whiter."

Inferneous turned and continued walking down the hill as he said, "I don't think it's dangerous though, even though we had reactions to it; if it truly was meant to harm us, we would be dead already."

Jayce grew hives at the thought; he partly didn't believe such power could exist, but what could a mortal like him know?

"So, what are we going to do?" Jayce asked as Inferneous massaged his nose.

Through his rubbing, he replied, "Well, I'd prefer if none of us would go, but we are going to need help getting over the wall of obelisks."

"Why can't you just blast through them?" Jayce asked as he acknowledged Rhinda and Holdren walking up behind Inferneous.

"There's far too much magic in that crater. If Balast or I were to cast a spell, we would run the risk of either imploding or exploding."

"Well, that is rather violent," Holdren said with a defeated sigh. "Ok, how much help do you need?"

"Only a few people. I would say Balast, Jayce, Zack, and I, but we might need one more."

"Okay," Holdren said, "I'll go with you. Go ahead and go in while I break the news to Erica."

Inferneous nodded, and they separated with Holdren as he went back to the crew.

He found Erica helping out with distributing rations, and he pulled her to the side. She asked, slightly annoyed, "What is happening? Have they found a way out?"

"No, not yet, but I wanted to come over here and tell you that we are going to check out the light, and we need you to stay here and take care of the crew while we do it."

Erica's face slowly grew pale as the words left Holdren's mouth and entered her ears.

"No, I am coming with you," she said adamantly.

"No, you are not; it's way too dangerous down there for you-"

"You can't know that until I've tried! What did Balast and Inferneous say about it?" Erica said, turning around and starting to walk towards the crater.

"They said that if this magic was hostile, they would have been dead the moment they entered the crater."

Erica stopped dead in her tracks as Holdren relayed the information. She straightened her angry posture, turned back to Holdren, and replied, "I don't care if I die as long as we can provide for the crew. Plus, if you all die, they would be in the same position with or without me."

There was a cold silence as Erica looked off in the distance and Holdren recognized what she really thought of herself.

Holdren then stepped toward Erica and said adamantly, "You are an amazing leader, and if there was anyone else more suited for the job by themselves, it is you." He gently grasped Erica's hand and pulled out the magical compass, then continued, "This is the last thing my father gave to me before my whole clan was killed; when I leave this with you, I bet my life on coming back." He took her other hand, set it on the compass, and squeezed it tightly.

Erica was left speechless as Holdren turned away to jog up to the top of the crater and disappear over the ridge into the light.

Balast was constantly in need of either physical touch or mental distraction the whole time they were descending into the crater. Every time he looked up to see how far they were, he grew enraptured by the obelisks in unison with the light and magic in the air. The only thing he thought while his mind was taken from him was an infinitely repeating question…

"What is it?" Inferneous said, grabbing Balast by his left shoulder and slowly turning him away from the center of the crater.

Balast's consciousness returned to him in a slow fashion, and his eyes were unglazed so he could finally see Inferneous standing in front of him. He remembered where he was and what he had to do, and a dulled sense of fear set in the bottom of his stomach as he raised his left arm, grabbed Inferneous back and said with a serious tone, "Keep doing that, I might not come back if I stare into the light too long."

Inferneous nodded grimly, and as he did so, his eyes watered. He felt a sharp pain in his nose, and another nosebleed came through. He lifted his right arm to keep the blood from spilling, and Balast got a glance at his almost fully bloodstained sleeve. Most of it was fresh, so Balast knew that he wasn't the only one struggling. He looked back to see that Rhinda, Jayce, and Zack were looking back at Holdren, who was just catching up with them.

"How are you all doing?" Balast asked as Holdren was close enough to hear.

Rhinda nodded and said, "I'm good."

The others looked at him pained, and Balast prepared himself for the responses.

"I can't feel anything," Jayce said worriedly. His face was flush red, and so were his hands, so he almost looked like a cooked lobster. Balast had never seen anything like it before. Inferneous stepped forward, pinched one of Jayce's hands, and asked, "Did you feel that?"

"No, not at all; oh, and I cut myself on the way down, and something weird happened; let me show you." He pulled out his sword and promptly sliced his palm, and Balast flinched a little, but his emotions rapidly changed into awe as the deep cut healed instantaneously. No blood even fell out of his hand. It was as if he was healing before the blade even breached his skin. Balast couldn't think of any explanation.

"Well, there isn't any pain, is there?" Balast asked.

Jayce shook his head, and Balast continued, "Then we can move on, Zack."

He turned to Zack, who was looking at the ground oddly, and Balast stepped forward to touch him when Zack suddenly stood up straight, rubbing his eyes and asking, "What happened?"

"Were you just asleep? How could you fall asleep in a place like this?" Balast scolded him.

Zack started to tear up and cry as Balast stopped talking. Balast was taken aback as he would usually talk back or just ignore him, but this time he was bawling like a baby. When Zack abruptly stopped crying, he looked around and realized what had just happened.

"I don't know what the heck just happened, but I'm starting to hate this place more and more," Zack noted.

Balast continued, saying, "It looks like you are experiencing heightened emotions. This place seems to be affecting us in odd ways. Holdren, what are your symptoms?"

Holdren shrugged and replied, "I'm fine, I guess. There is nothing particular to note."

Balast nodded, then shook his head, "I guess we'll be fine as long as Inferneous doesn't run out of blood."

Balast looked to Inferneous, and Inferneous shook his head, saying, "I'll be fine."

Balast nodded, nodded his head toward the crater's center, and started to move toward it again. A few minutes passed as they continued down, and they stopped a few times to either wake up Zack or snap Balast out of the strange trance he kept falling into.

As soon as they reached the obelisks, though, the odd thing happening to them ceased. Inferneous sniffed, then sniffed again and spit a bloody clod to the ground and put his arm down. No more blood rushed from his nose, and he sighed under his breath with relief, "Thank the Angel, that was terrible."

Zack was now wide awake, and Balast seemed more ok and was not drifting off at all. Balast touched the white obsidian and winced as golden bolts of lightning shocked his hand away. He started to walk around the perimeter and said, "Follow me; look out for any cracks in the wall."

They all nodded and started to circle the perimeter with him. They all carefully moved along the obsidian obelisks, careful not to get shocked; they examined the cracks where the jagged pillars crossed and where they were rooted. Zack tried to squeeze into some of the bigger holes, but they all ended in failure, with him being shocked by a verbal exclamation.

When they eventually reached the other side of the wall, Zack was the first to notice a strange marking on two obelisks. As Zack analyzed the two pillars, he realized they were not the same. They were both standing completely straight into the ground and midway up the pillars, there was a strange sigil glowing purple. "Hey guys, look at this–" he approached the obsidian pillars, and he flinched slightly as he reached out his hand, expecting a shock, but nothing came. His hand touched the obsidian's warm surface, and he felt a sense of relief as he felt the jagged grooves of the markings.

He slightly jumped when Balast came next to him and asked, "It's not shocking you?" he put his hand on the obsidian, and Zack saw an unprecedented focus across Balast's face. "Wow, that is…" he got closer to the obsidian, put his face on the rock, and stepped back in awe.

"Did you find something?" Inferneous asked as he came around the obelisk round.

Balast replied, "This magic is more than remarkable; it's so potent it could disintegrate us but so controlled it chooses to make the stone warm instead."

Balast smiled at Inferneous and Zack and said excitedly, "I have to find out what is in here." He started to examine the rock up and down, careful where he touched it in mild fear of electrocution. Holdren and Rhinda came around a few minutes later, and Inferneous filled them in on what Zack had found.

"Did you find anything on the sides?" Inferneous asked them as they approached.

"No, nothing. We tried fitting through the bigger holes, but of course, we couldn't fit," Holdren replied, standing next to Inferneous. "What about you?"

Inferneous folded his arms and pointed in front of him at Balast and Zack, checking around the pillars. "It looks like there's an odd marking on those pillars. Also, they stand up completely straight, unlike the rest." Inferneous remarked.

"It looks like a cat," Rhinda said, tilting his head sideways.

Balast looked back and exclaimed, "Oh! Rhinda, come help. Try to move the pillars to the side; it looks like they can slide away."

Rhinda nodded and stepped toward the pillars, putting his hands in the crack down the middle, and he pulled as hard as he could, but they didn't budge. He tried again, making sure his stance was strong, but the pillars did not move.

"Didn't know what to expect there," Rhinda said, massaging his fingers and turning to Balast. "Try using that skull you found at the Malum castle."

Balast raised an eyebrow questioning Rhinda; he replied, "Why?"

Rhinda said, "Because it is a Malum skull, and the markings look like a cat. It wouldn't hurt to try."

Balast shook his head as he pulled out the Malum skull and pointed at it. "This Malum skull could potentially set off any traps set to protect the magical power inside of there. We can't just-"

He stopped when Rhinda grabbed the skull out of his hands and said, "You worry too much." He fiddled with the skull, and as he pushed it up against the obelisk, the obsidian melted around the skull and enveloped it. The markings started to glow a dark purple, and the pillars reverted to their natural black.

The markings on the sides turned white as Rhinda turned to Balast and said, "See? Progress." Rhinda then walked up to the pillars, settled his stance, and started to pull the pillars apart. As he struggled, they all watched, holding their breath as the pillars started to budge. Just before he stopped to breathe, Rhinda's finger slipped, and the pillar cut his palm, and a drop of his blood was enveloped in the stone. Rhinda stepped back, wincing in pain, but before he could say anything, the pillars were forced to the side by a magical force, and they were all blinded by what was inside. Balast covered his eyes at first, but when they adjusted to the bright light, he saw two statues. The first was a man on his knees with a pained expression, reaching out for a floating smithing hammer that was made of what looked like obsidian gilded with gold. The man was wearing royal garb and a cape, and he had an abnormally large golden birthmark on his left temple.

Balast stepped forward so he could view the whole of the next statue, which was a massive Malum with five tentacles with mouths on the ends of them and spikes protruding off its upper body. The bottom half was all a mess of dark tendrils. It was floating like a hammer, but it was higher up and leaning over the first statue. There were more tendrils reaching around the first statue as if it were trying to capture the man but were repelled by an unknown force.

"Angel's grace," Balast said, stepping forward into the ring of obsidian pillars. He stepped in front of the first statue, and he recognized the face of the man all too well.

"It's Corvus Aureum, the lost prince." As the rest of them stepped into the circle, magical writing appeared above the statue of Corvus and the floating hammer he was reaching for. Balast read it aloud,

"'My soul will not be touched, and I will not die. Instead, I will live.' I said as the demons in front of me disintegrated with screams of agony, and a giant beast with eyes all over its body, red hard skin, and large horns descended in front of my eyes. The beast wore a white tunic and carried a flaming battle axe. Behind them, I could hear a loud chorus of singing beyond that of human capability, and behind them shone a light so bright I could only see the figure's silhouette. I cried in pain and joy as the beast floated over and put its large clawed palms on my face, and I felt my soul being lifted into the heavens. I saw a small woman with blonde hair and blue eyes welcome me as I approached the place where I would worship The Welder forever."

Balast finished wiping away a tear that had escaped his right eye. None of them could fathom what was in front of them, especially those who didn't know its significance.

"Who is Corvus Aureum?" Zack asked curiously.

Still staring at the statues, Jayce replied, "He was the last prince of the Aureus Empire; he disappeared sixty years before the Empire fell. It is known that his disappearance was what started the downfall of the Aureus Empire and what finished it was…" he stopped looking at Balast and Inferneous who were both now grimacing at the statues.

"At least we know where he went," Holdren said softly, circling the statues. "So, is the hammer the source of the power, or is it the statues themselves?"

Balast took a minute to answer as he got over his awe and analyzed what was in front of him. "I think it's both, but I can't feel as much magic inside the circle, so maybe the pillars are just amplifiers, but still…" Balast looked up and closed his eyes to sense the flow of magic, and in the darkness behind his eyes, he saw that the pillars were shooting light and magic into the sky, but he couldn't see anything else because of the potent magic blinding his vision. "I truly don't know, but what I can assume is that it is the hammer."

"What would happen if we took it?" Jayce asked, stepping forward to grab the hammer.

Inferneous was there before he could stretch out fully, and he stopped Jayce from touching it. "I can assume that we lose all light this place gets or, even worse, the reality collapses in on us."

Jayce took his hand from Inferneous' grasp and asked, "Well, it should take a good minute, though. Can we escape and get back to Magia? Maybe we can escape through the cracks if this reality starts to crumble?"

"Don't assume about multidimensional travel; that's how you end up as flat as parchment paper. The truth is that that is a possibility, but of course, it's dangerous," Balast said, walking around the statue and analyzing it some more.

"It really doesn't matter either way," Rhinda said, folding his arms. "This is our only source of light in this whole hellscape, and I don't think we can risk the crew's lives sailing in these dark waters and fighting whatever comes at us. Worst case scenario, it's a Malum that is stronger than the one we faced."

Holdren nodded in agreement. "Truth be told, we are fumbling in the dark." He stepped back, hands raised in a defensive gesture and finished, "I trust you two with whatever decision you make; I just suggest we hurry because who knows what would come of us staying here too long."

Inferneous locked eyes with Balast as Balast completed his analytical circle around the statues. Balast returned the look and sighed as Inferneous shrugged, reached out, and grabbed the hammer.

Silence followed as the hammer left its position. The silence was interrupted by a sneeze from Rhinda, which surprised everyone else.

"Sorry," Rhinda said, wiping his nose.

Balast sighed with relief; he didn't realize he was holding in and reached out his hand to Inferneous to ask, "Can I see it?"

Inferneous handed the hammer to Balast, who raised it to his eye level to examine it. It was decently heavy, as you would expect a smithing hammer to be, but any ordinary person could tell this was not an ordinary smithing hammer. No smithing hammer would have gold inlaid inside the handle all the way to the flat of the head. Balast was finding it odd that there were strips of silver inlaid also, but he was even more surprised when he turned the hammer upward and found that on the head of the hammer, right on the flat space, was an insignia. An alpha and omega infinity symbol with a large sword and another contraption he had never seen before crossed each other in a sort of arms insignia. The strangest thing, though, was that Balast had seen the insignia before.

"So, what's the verdict?" Inferneous asked.

Balast looked up and realized they were all staring at him and waiting for a response. He handed the hammer off to Inferneous and said, "It's a normal hammer, but it looks more ceremonial than anything."

"Ceremonial?" Holdren asked, confused, "I've never heard of a ceremonial hammer before."

"They are quite common in the eastern forests, especially between warriors. Most of those tribes have strict rituals about weapons and their crafting," Rhinda said, surprising Balast with his knowledge.

"Yes, you are correct. How did you know that? Most eastern knowledge is highly gatekept,"

Rhinda shrugged, "My grandmother taught me; she said my father was well versed in these things."

Inferneous' gaze grew critical as Rhinda relayed this information. Balast looked at Rhinda, glanced at Inferneous, and then went back to Rhinda.

"Remind me to talk to you when we get back to the ship," Balast said as he headed toward the gap between the obelisks, "Come on, let's get back to the ship and try and see if anything has changed in our surroundings."

Everyone followed as Balast exited the obelisk ring and stepped back into the crater. It seemed brighter now that they were outside, but maybe it was just because his eyes were adjusting to the darkness. As soon as everyone was out of the obelisks, they started climbing back up the crater. They had made it halfway up when Inferneous started to bleed from his nose once again. The other symptoms returned as well, but Balast was having a much easier time because he wasn't staring at the obelisks anymore, so he helped the others climb to the top. He gave a sigh of relief when Erica greeted them at the crest of the ledge and managed to get Drathni to help stop Inferneous' bleeding.

"Told you we would come back; now give me my compass," Holdren said playfully.

Erica refused, saying, "It was your duty to come back; I'll be holding on to this so you come back every time." Then she hurried away from a mildly shocked Holdren to go inform the rest of the crew to pack up their supplies and head back to the ship.

The process went smoothly as the crew packed their temporary camp up and started the trek back to the ship, leaving only a few scraps of trash here and there. Balast and Inferneous were behind everyone, making sure that nothing came behind them. As they were beginning to leave, Inferneous looked to Balast, and Balast's looked him in the eye and sternly said, "Don't say anything; things have already gone better than anticipated."

Inferneous playfully looked shocked and replied, "I wasn't going to say a word! See now it's your fault if–" he stopped when suddenly he couldn't see Balast anymore. He, in fact, couldn't see anything. Simultaneously, Balast and Inferneous raised their hands, and a ball of blue light formed in

Balast's hand, and flames erupted out of Inferneous.' They both looked back and were blinded by the flash of light that came from the crater. When their eyes adjusted, they saw a massive orb of light as big as the moon start to rise into the sky. It grew smaller and smaller ascended, and once it was barely visible in the sky, it turned purple, and the sky itself imploded. The orb collapsed in on itself, shot a wave of purple wavelike magic across the dark sky, and slowly dissipated. Balast and Inferneous stepped back as their minds exploded with a series of images and emotions overwhelming them. They held their heads as the psychic attack continued, but Balast was able to yell out, "Everyone, RUN!!" As the ground beneath them started to shake and broil. The sky was slowly tearing apart like old fabric, revealing thousands of black writhing figures behind the scenes, spilling Malums and pieces of rock from the sky.

The ship was pulsating purple and crimson through runes engraved in its dark wood, and no one felt like they were going to live a few minutes longer, even if they were running as fast as they could. Everyone was running to the ship as the ground beneath them was crumbling like a freshly baked cookie.

Inferneous was a bit distressed and confused about what was happening and why, but he set his feelings aside when he saw a crack open under a mercenary and swallowed him until he was only holding on with one hand. He immediately rushed to help him but couldn't reach him in time, even with his speed. The ground closed up, and the mercenary was lost to the angry, rumbling earthquake; Inferneous cursed loudly and held his head in regret. He screamed out, and flames erupted from his eyes, feet, and hands. Suddenly, he was the fastest one in the group. Flames weaved between the Ninjirates crew as Inferneous micromanaged each of them into the safest route possible to ensure they made it to the ship.

Zack had mounted Jayce's back and was creating a large shield to cover the crew from the massive chunks of earth falling from the sky. He was growing a bit tired, so he yelled out to Balast, "I'm running out of mana here!"

Balast was at the front of the group with his wand morphing and forming it to slice any rocks that got into their path, but he looked back for a split second and reached his hand toward Zack.

Zack felt an overwhelming warm presence inside him and then sat up straighter on Jayce and reinforced the shield with the newfound mana Balast had given him.

As Balast continued to cut and split rocks, he looked ahead and saw their ship being tossed around in the murky black waters from the massive chunks of land falling into it.

From here, he saw that the anchor was loosening, so he called out, "Inferneous! Get the anchor! Rhinda! Replace me!"

Rhinda stepped in front of him, and his hands glowed a bright red as he activated his spell and started slicing through rocks like butter. Inferneous ran ahead, grabbed the anchored chain to the ship, and pulled it out of the water with a struggle. Balast continued to help the others not meet their death, and as he did, he glanced back and saw nothing. The altar where they were just at was nothing; the whole other half of their world was slowly falling into the void.

"By the Angel," he muttered in awe. He turned toward the ship and saw Inferneous with his heels dug at least a foot into the earth, holding their ship from drifting into the abyss.

The first person to get to the ship was Holdren, and as he reached the edge, he reached into his pocket for his compass, but he didn't have it. He looked back and called out, "Erica!! The compass!!" he raised his hand as Erica, who was helping a mercenary up, saw him, and she quickly reached into the folds of her robes, pulled out the compass, and threw it. Holdren swiftly caught it, and when it touched his hand, the compass glowed, and two swords materialized in the air in front of him. He grabbed onto one and threw the other onto the deck of the ship.

As he launched himself over the troubled waters, he yelled, "Libi!" and was teleported to the ship's deck. As he rolled onto the ship's deck, he smiled at his success. It didn't last long, though, because he had a job to do. He quickly grabbed a rope ladder and threw it over the side of the ship, tying the end to the mast. Once everyone had gotten on the ship, Balast took the helm and spun it as hard as he could. The ship slowly turned and, even against the massive tide, crept forward.

It was a tense few minutes as the ship and crew worked and strained to escape the void until Balast yelled, "Inferneous! This ship is going to need a bit more to get out of here!"

Inferneous nodded at him and then went up to Balast and grabbed ahold of the helm. Fire erupted from his arms, engulfing the helm and spreading across the whole ship. The back of the ship then lit on fire, the flames roared, and the ship was propelled forward. When they started gaining actual traction, Inferneous let go of the helm and, breathing heavily, sighed.

Balast regained the helm and nodded in approval to Inferneous. Inferneous waved his hand and smiled shyly, "It was nothing."

The Ninjirates crew were all still a bit high-strung, so every rock that fell close to the ship was taken with extreme caution as if it was trying to hit the ship, but Balast skillfully avoided them.

As Balast guided the ship. He saw that there was a dense fog starting to form to the right of them. He remembered how they got here and, in a last-ditch effort, wheeled the helm to the right, heading straight for the fog.

He let go of the helm for a second and called out to Inferneous, "Inferneous!!"

Inferneous, who was keeping the sails from flying away from the ship because of the tearing winds, looked back at Balast in response. Balast struggled with the helm and shouted out, "Get to the captain's quarters!!"

Inferneous looked ahead of the ship, saw the fog, and nodded. He quickly ran a ring around the mast, acquiring rope burns as the sails struggled against his strength and tied down the rope. The ship lurched to the side as it collided with a large rock, and the crew hit the deck to avoid being thrown overboard.

"Everyone, hold on to something!! We're almost out!!" He yelled out as he rushed toward the captain's quarters. He looked up at Balast, still steering the ship, and a conundrum appeared.

Inferneous looked over the side of the ship and saw a massive whirlpool in front of the ship and under the fog. The crew would disappear with the fog, but Balast has to be gone by then, or they all might not make it back.

Inferneous didn't know everything about the fog but knew that it didn't take him or Balast when they entered this place.

He looked around the deck and spotted Holdren, drenched, curled against the stairs hanging on for his life. Inferneous made his way toward him and yelled out, "Holdren!! I need you to take over the ship!! Can you do it!?!?"

Holdren hesitated for a moment, and then he nodded with stern discipline. "Aye, Captain!!"

Inferneous grabbed his arm, smiling and pulled him through the rocking of the ship all the way to Balast at the helm. Balast and Holdren held onto the wheel, steering it toward the fog together. Then Holdren yelled out, "I got this!!" and swiftly took over, pushing Balast out of the way.

Balast and Inferneous wasted no time and swiftly jumped over the railing onto the main deck and barreled through the door as the fog started to envelop the ship. The silence of the magical tunnel was deafening compared to the howling winds they came from. They stopped to take a breath, but as they did, the door behind them turned black and exploded into a vortex that started to suck the purple runes that lined the tunnel. Inferneous was already moving before the first rune fell into the abyss, but Balast was a bit awestruck. The vortex almost reached him before Inferneous pulled him back.

Balast regained his senses and started running with Inferneous, heading toward the white-outlined door at the end of the hallway. The vortex grew faster and faster until it was at their heels. Balast put his foot on the door frame as soon as the vortex sucked away the last rune. He looked behind him and instinctively reached out to catch Inferneous, pulling him through the door frame. As they landed on the deck of the ship, the door slammed behind them, and dark tentacles squirmed back inside the door as it did so. A loud bang sounded behind the door, and then there was an explosion. Then, the door was silent.

They stared at the door, Balast still gripping Inferneous' forearm tightly when Inferneous 's eyes adjusted to the sunlight. Balast sighed in relief as he smelled the salty, clean air of Magia's oceans and stood up, pulling Inferneous to his feet, too. He turned around and saw that the crew were all appearing one by one. First, there was a silhouette of mist, and then it solidified into a crew member.

Balast lurched forward when Inferneous put his arm around his neck and laughed heartily, "That was awesome!!" his face then dimmed as he scanned the crew, "Is this all of us?"

The Ninjirates crew looked around and noticed that their numbers looked fewer than when they had entered, and when they were done counting, there was a somber tone in the air. Balast rushed off, pushing people aside until he saw Zack sitting next to a winded Jayce and Rhinda. Inferneous headed to the helm just as Holdren materialized out of the magic mist.

Holdren was still drenched, as all of them were. Inferneous hugged the shocked Holdren, still holding onto the steering wheel.

As they all gathered on the deck with Inferneous and Balast in the middle, there were solemn faces, and a few tears shed as if a few had not made it.

"We mourn the passing of our comrades with an offering of magic," he balled his hands and then opened it, setting free three eagles made out of glowing crimson fire into the sky. Balast, at the same time, made a sign in the air and then opened a magical book and tore three pages away to have them fly away in the wind too.

"Their memories will live on through our emotions, adventures, and ultimately our lives." Inferneous continued. He bowed his head and shook it, murmuring, "They will be missed."

There were a few minutes of silence before the group dispersed and returned to their normal duties. When the sun set, everyone gathered on the deck around the big fire and had a big feast. They brought a large roast from the storage and heated it over the fire in celebration of making it out of the pocket dimension.

Inferneous, with four kebob sticks of meat and a few fruits, sat down next to Balast, who was carving little runes into the ship's wood and said, "That was horrible; I thought we were going to die there." With his mouth full, Inferneous whispered, "What did you see when the grave exploded?"

Balast pushed Inferneous' face away with a disgusted face but answered his question, "I saw a series of images and then something…disturbing."

"You saw yourself in a black void in the jaws of a Malum, dead."

Balast whipped his head around and stared at Inferneous who was staring into the magical bonfire with vigorous anger. "How did you know?" Balast asked calmly, not immensely surprised but more curious.

"Well, I guess it's obvious. We both saw the same thing, but the thing is, why? And was that a premonition of what is to come?"

Inferneous scanned the Ninjirates crew and shook his head, "No. It won't be."

Balast eyebrows furrowed in concern as he slouched back and listened to what the other Ninjirates were talking about. There was small talk going around, but the most overhanging topic that Balast could hear through the mutterings eventually made itself known through Holdren.

He drank a swig of alcohol before he said over everyone, "What are we going to do now?"

Everyone quieted down to murmurs as they looked at Inferneous and Balast sitting together. Inferneous took a big bite out of his kebob and shrugged his shoulders.

There were audible groans and complaints as Inferneous kept shrugging, saying, "What were you guys expecting? I'm only a bit different than when I kidnapped all of you to be my crew!"

There was a mix of laughter in the crowd now as most still complained.

"How about we visit Castillus Grex! We can see how the civilians are holding up!" Holdren shouted.

Erica, who was right beside him, shook her head, looking at Balast with a pained look.

Balast nodded and answered, "That sounds like a great idea! We set sail at dawn!"

The Ninjirates cheered in unison, not because of the order, but because they now had a new destination and adventure to pursue.

Balast woke up feeling extremely good. He sat up from his levitation, and his feet landed gently on the floor of the captain's quarters. He smiled as he saw Inferneous sprawled across the floor with a blanket and a straw-filled pillow. He walked around the room for a bit to stretch his legs, dragging his hands across the ornate detail of the wood and then walked out of the door to greet the salty air. He greeted every crew member and helped out a bit with rigging the ship, striking up a conversation with the crew about what they wanted to achieve in the future. He got a varied number of responses, but the most common answer was simple: "I don't know." Balast thought over this as he greeted Holdren, who was diligently steering the ship and also making sure they stayed on course.

"Hey," Balast smiled and waved.

"Hey," Holdren smiled back.

Balast looked him up and down and saw that Holdren had been doing this for a bit.

"Let me take over for a bit; you look a bit tired." Holdren laughed, turned to Balast, holding his hand open, and said, "Be my guest."

Balast took over, and Inferneous sat at a small table with a large map to the side of the helm. Balast looked over and raised an eyebrow asking, "What's that? You look more tired and stressed looking at that than you were steering."

Holdren nodded his head. With an uneasy face, he said, "This is supposed to be a map of the world."

"Wow, really?" Balast glanced over to it and with raised eyebrows, said, "It looks a bit small."

"That's exactly what I was thinking," Holdren said, picking up the map with both hands. His arms were a good distance apart, but he could still hold it between both hands.

"Almost every capitol city and small town, sea and river, Pub and Inn; what is this?!?!? Who made this? The artist must have been to every place or somehow gained information thousands of miles apart." He set the map down, and Balast glanced once more at it, and this time, he caught an insignia that he recognized very well.

"My master made it," Balast said to Holdren nonchalantly.

Holdren turned to him with an eyebrow raised. "You had a master?"

Balast nodded and tapped the bottom right corner of the map. A small golden book appeared on the yellowed edge of the paper, and its pages opened to reveal a decahedron.

"That's my master's mark. I bet there's one somewhere on those swords or the compass you have, too, but that's definitely his."

Holdren pulled out his compass, flipped it over, and saw the insignia reveal itself and he nodded in acceptance. "So, how did your master map out the whole of the world?"

Balast laughed loudly, saying, "It's not so much how. I bet he did it just for fun." Balast looked over to the map again and nodded to it. "Looks like it adds the current buildings in progress, too," he pointed out a half-finished building insignia and under it said, "Balast's unfinished school."

Holdren's jaw dropped in awe.

"Man, you wizards sure are amazing."

Balast smiled and shook his head. "I guess we are."

That evening everyone was gathered around the fire Inferneous had created once more; Balast was sitting next to Erica and decided to interrogate her. He approached her with an orange, and as he extended his hand out toward her, he asked, "Do you like oranges?"

She grabbed the orange and bit into it, peel and all.

"No, I don't, but I've learned to get used to it. It's better than scurvy."

Balast sat next to her and shook his head in disgust, "I don't think I've ever seen anyone eat an orange as you do."

"It was quite frequent between the High Shadow Ninja clan. It showed the cleanliness and discipline we had."

Balast nodded, showing obvious confusion in the custom, but he brushed the look off his face as his mind was drawn to other things. He looked away for a moment, then looked back at Erica and asked, "What do you want to achieve in life?"

Erica blinked at him and shook her head, asking, "Why the sudden depth in conversation? I thought you and Inferneous were just aloof souls killing a Malum every now and then."

"Well, I do have aspirations for the future, unlike most of your soldiers."

"Well, of course. You have been free to do what you want because you have no type of leadership in your life anymore. I'm sure you had no aspirations with Parquen."

Balast smiled slightly, "So you have been listening in on our sessions?"

Erica smiled coyly, "Nope, they have." She pointed behind him, and a few inches away were two tiger masks who immediately turned around to face Balast.

They bowed while cross-legged, and Balast shook his head at Erica. "They really have no autonomy, do they? You dictate everything they do and say, don't you?"

"Most things, yes, but they have been growing more personal tendencies like talking to people. I'm most surprised by how Inferneous got Shiro and Kuro to talk. They haven't spoken a word since their first few days of training."

Balast looked over the two young ninjas conversing freely with Jayce and Zack, laughing and sharing food, and Balast smiled.

"But you're right in a sense." Erica admitted, "These people are very indebted to me. They will follow me to my death and most certainly sacrifice themselves for me just to uphold rules by what once was a corrupt group of old men who wanted power." She balled her fists and put them against her temple in anger and then lowered them as it subsided. "I judge my mistakes by the lives I've ruined in the wake of my own greed for power, and what I aspire to do in the future is fix those mistakes by having the people who follow me gain lives of their own."

She tapped her fingers on the hardwood of the ship as she looked up and saw Rhinda sitting alone, eating a piece of bread. "Sometimes I lose hope when it comes to certain people…" She glanced back over to Shiro and Kuro, smiling and laughing and saw that they were calling over to

Rhinda. She watched as Rhinda came over and started conversing with them, smiling. Erica then gave a smile of satisfaction. "I guess I won't have to worry then."

Balast looked at her and, seeing the rare smile on her face, nodded in understanding. He stood and started walking towards the captain's quarters with a quick "Goodnight" to Erica.

She wasn't listening, though, as she enjoyed the sight of the people in front of her.

Chapter 20

"Land Ho!!" Zack yelled out from the top of the sails. "Now, can someone help me down?"

Balast had just gotten up, and somehow, Zack had performed a levitation spell and was hanging on to the sails.

"Are you just saying land ho to get attention?"

"No, I do see land, but I did also want to get down from here."

Balast shook his head and snapped his fingers, and green sparks flew between them and then up to Zack.

"How did you manage to do that?" Inferneous said, glancing at Balast as he walked past him.

A few seconds later, Zack started to slowly drift down, and when he was firmly on the ground, Balast snapped his fingers again and asked, "Are you going to do that again, or do we have to strap you to the anchor?"

"No, I won't mess with magic that I don't have under control yet," Zack reluctantly replied.

"No, only practice magic around me or Inferneous. Nice wording, though; your mind tricks won't work on me because I know you think you have everything under control." Balast smiled at Zack as he gave a shocked face.

"But I do have everything under con— What is that!!"

He pointed to the sky, and Balast gazed in horror as a Malum flew straight into the mast of their ship. The world started passing by slowly for Balast as he saw the front half of the ship buckle and splinter under the weight of the Malum. He saw the mast snap in half and plunge into the ocean. The Ninjirates succumbed to the Malum's black skin, and the boat started to sink into the water. He watched as he and the other half of the crew were launched into the air from the impact. He looked to his left and saw the sharp point of the mast, and then Zacks's body was on a collision course straight towards it when he snapped.

"No," he said aloud. The singular word was so loud that it seemed all of time had stopped. Balast shook his head and realized that, in fact, time had stopped. He blinked, and then he was back on the ship's deck.

"Land Ho!!" Zack yelled out from the top of the sails. "Now, can someone help me down?"

Balast had just gotten up, and somehow, Zack had performed a levitation spell and was hanging on to the sails.

"So, where you just saying land ho to get attention?"

"No, I do see land, but I did also want to get down from here."

Balast shook his head and snapped his fingers. Balast felt weird dizziness, then sneezed and spat on the deck, tasting the tangy salt of his own blood. He wiped his nose on his sleeve and saw a red streak go across his sleeve. He stared at his sleeve and thought, what just happened?

"How did he manage to do that?" Inferneous said, glancing at Balast while he walked past, then stopped and saw the blood, "You ok? What happened?"

Balast looked at him, confused, and said, "I don't know." He then pressed his hand to his nose, snapped his fingers, and continued to walk with Inferneous to the front of the ship.

As he walked forward, Balast started to feel uneasy. He then turned around, pointed at Zack, and said sternly, "Don't practice magic like that when Inferneous and I aren't around."

"Fine," Zack scoffed. "I had it under control though."

Balast then reacted ahead of time this time. He raised his hands, and a golden barrier appeared. It spread across the whole front of the ship a second before a massive Malum slammed into it. The boat was rocked backward, and Balast was thrown back from the impact. He slammed into the mast but held the spell as the Malum clawed at it. As the Ninjirates crew tried to regain control of the ship, Inferneous took action. He balled his right fist, and in a second, a large spear made out of fire erupted out of it. He then took a step back and threw it through Balast's spell and pierced the Malum in the head. The Malum was unfazed until Inferneous waved his hand to the left, and the spear ruptured out the other side of the abomination's skull. The Malum then screamed in pain and sunk into the water. Balast sunk down to the ground, coughing a bit as his hand glowed brighter, indicating more healing power.

Inferneous came over to him and started to heal him as he asked, "How did you know that was coming?"

"I don't know." Balast heaved and wiped his bloody nose again. "I saw everything happen in slow motion, and then time rewound itself, and I acted…" He heaved again, and his mouth moved, but no noise came out. His brow was furrowed in confusion, but he was too tired to expand upon any theories.

Inferneous stopped healing him and pulled Balast up to a standing position, saying, "Well, a good thing. Now let us see what's going on land." He walked away, and soon everyone was working double time to make the ship go max capacity.

Balast walked to the front of the boat and whispered a short spell. His eyes turned white, and then he could see everything on land. He was shocked to see multiple fires raging across the land. The structures were worn down, beaten, and burned with carvings of dark runes on the side of the buildings.

"Get this boat moving as fast as you can!!" Balast yelled out.

Inferneous then took charge of the helm and burst into flames, "You got it!" His flames enveloped the helm, and just like in the Malum dimension, the boat sped forward, pushed by Inferneous' magic.

The docking was rough, to say the least. As they came into the port, the wooden ports were crushed under the speed and weight of the Ninjirates ship. As they continued to plow through the docks, eventually, the ship slowed in the rough sand.

Balast was the first off the ship as he fell, then floated down to the burnt sand. He ran as fast as he could and started to look around; he then realized he didn't need to run anymore. He recognized the shapes of the buildings he used to teach in. He walked forward more, and as he entered a broken brick wall, he realized it was his living quarters. The bed had been thrown across the room, and the dresser had burnt to ashes. He could see the small footprints of a child strewn across the room and then the deep gouges of the earth in the walls that signified a darker entity. He stumbled forward through the debris and opened the half-burnt door to the courtyard, and he grew weak at the sight. Hundreds of bodies were thrown about; blood splayed on the walls, the empty faces of the dead. Balast shakily stepped forward through the doorway, pushing away what had been the hallway ceiling chandelier, and stood, mouth agape in horror. He took another step forward, but instead of progressing, he felt something under his foot. He looked down but snapped his eyes back up as they welled with the sight of headmaster Corbin's top half. He continued to walk forward and found that the bottom half of the fountain was still intact. Inside it was the melting remains of a single Malum mixed in with the remains of one of the teachers. In the teacher's hand, there was a small item. Balast picked up the small stone and dropped it immediately when his hand started to burn profusely. Balast pulled up his sleeve to see no flames, but the angry black scar was writhing back and forth. He almost blacked out in pain, but when he closed his eyes, he saw the whole battle happen in front of him. It was a bright day when it happened, but the Malums still swarmed the campus. Multiple people were barricading the doors, but it was a futile attempt because the Malums just climbed over the walls and started to wreak havoc among the students and teachers. In the midst of the carnage, he saw that the teachers were using bits of magic, but they didn't have much experience using it, so their attacks fell through.

Though it seemed like the viciousness and malice of the Malums would kill everyone, Balast saw that the Malums were more reserved, and they seemed to be just grabbing the children and dragging them away into portals under the ground.

He was shaken out of memory, and he opened his teary eyes to Inferneous, who grabbed him by the shoulders. When Balast's eyes adjusted, he looked at Inferneous and wept. Inferneous held Balast tightly as he gritted his teeth in frustration. A few minutes later, Balast regained his composure and walked outside of what was Castillus Grex to face the Ninjirates crew with Inferneous at his side. The crew were scouring the wreckages looking for survivors, but there was nothing but corpses and burnt remains of buildings.

Inferneous called them together and addressed them as a whole.

"What has happened here is a travesty, but there is still hope." He turned to Balast, and Balast started, "I saw a vision of the past. The Malums attacked this place, but they did not come for chaos and kill like they usually do. They were more restricted, and they had a purpose behind their actions; seldom good can come from them, though."

"So, what are we going to do?" Jayce spoke up. "They can't get away with this."

The Ninjirates roared in approval.

Inferneous raised his hand to calm them and pointed towards the sea. "We scour this place for anything that might point at where they have gone, then we go and rescue the taken innocents and destroy the Malums behind this!"

The Ninjirates cheered more as they disbanded and started searching more fervently, looking for any traces of Malum and human tracks. The sky grew lighter as the smoke died down and the fires quelled to reveal a bright, cloudless, sunny day.

"Such contrast to the lives that were lost…" Balast said to Zack as they brushed aside more wood, turning it to charcoal.

"It's like God doesn't even care."

Zack shook his head at the sky.

Balast looked over at him and said, "Don't say that. If anything, it's a blessing we got here this fast to try to save them."

Zack's eyebrow raised, "I didn't peg you as religious."

Balast sighed, "It's a bit complicated, but I guess I was raised a bit like that."

"How so?" Zack asked, getting ready to hear another whole backstory, but they were interrupted by yells and screams to their left.

Balast stood and saw Inferneous looking around. They made eye contact, and Inferneous then pointed to the mountain horizon. In the midst of the broken buildings, there was a massive shadow moving across the landscape at a very fast pace. Balast wiped his eyes and activated his magic eyesight, and he zoomed in on the shadow.

"Oh," Balast said with disdain. He looked over to Inferneous and waved him over. When he was close enough, Balast started, "It's a Bellua Bestia."

Inferneous scoffed. "Really? I had hoped they would send something more dynamic."

"Hold on," Balast held his hand up to stop Inferneous' thought as he squinted at the beast once more with magic. "It looks like it's been equipped with a special type of armor. It looks like shade cascade armor, flail, and longsword."

"Oh, never mind. That's very dynamic for a Malum. Anyways, do you think it's intelligent?"

"Almost one hundred percent."

"Darn it. Looks like we'll have to keep it alive," Inferneous said, taking off his shoes.

"Um, why are you taking off your shoes?"

Inferneous said nothing and just winked.

"Come on," Balast said as he walked toward the direction of the Malum. There was a faint rumbling that turned into the thunderous steps of a large and malicious being. When it came within range of sight, it jumped in the air and slammed into the ground right in front of Inferneous and Balast. Everything was launched into the air except them, who stood unnerved by the massive figure. When everything, and everyone, fell back to the ground, the Malum spoke in guttural tones that no ordinary person could understand. To Inferneous and Balast, it was as clear as day.

"Are you Inferneous, the infinite flame and Balast of the river of time?" it yelled the question in their faces. Its breath reeked of fresh blood and rot, but Inferneous and Balast still stood unflinching.

"Is that what they call us among your ranks?" Inferneous looked to Balast with a smile on his face. "I'm flattered."

"Me too," Balast said, smiling back. The Malum's eyes were covered by the intensely black armor covering him, but Inferneous and Balast could tell that he was a bit angered.

"I will assume that you are the great wizards and move on to massacre your friends and family first."

Inferneous looked to Balast, and Balast looked back at him. They looked at the Malum and said in unison, "Sure."

They both raised their hands to the Ninjirates crew, and Balast said, "Be our guests."

They could tell the Malum was more confused now because it hesitated to step forward, but it eventually did. It approached the Ninjirates crew, who were standing their weapons ready for the fight of their lives when the Malum turned and whipped its flail and swung its sword to try and slice and smash Balast and Inferneous, but they were blown out of his hand by an orange and teal blasts. The weapons flew away and crashed into the dirt on either side of it.

Balast shook his head, saying, "It's pitiful. This is the pinnacle of Malum intelligence," he turned to Inferneous, who was already wreathed in flames, and said, "I'll stall him; you do your thing."

"Got it," Inferneous said before backing up.

Balast walked toward the Malum, and it reacted with a swipe of its claws, which Balast blocked with an outstretched hand. The Malum tried to recoil but saw there were green runes and rings around its claws, keeping it in place. It tried to retaliate with its clawed feet, but Balast outstretched his hand again and stopped it in its tracks. Balast then flew over to its other arm and did the same thing, and yelled over his shoulder, "It's ready!"

Inferneous had backed up all the way to the edge of the town limits, which was about a mile from where the Malum had made its stand. He used magic and saw that Balast was waving him down, so that meant it was time to remove its heart. Usually, it would take a long time to break through shade cascade armor, but with this new method, Inferneous was sure to get the heart. And this was the fastest way possible.

As his flames died down, his feet burst into flames, and he lowered himself to the ground, then started to run toward the Malum. The speed grew exponentially, and soon, for every step, he was covering at least twenty feet. He laughed out loud as he left a trail of fire behind him, and right before he reached the Malum, he jumped, retracted his fist, and punched straight through the Malum. Not only did he punch straight through it, but his whole body also went through the torso of the Malum. The blood splattered all over the Ninjirates crew as Inferneous went crashing into a building.

As Zack wiped the Malum's blood from his forehead, he smiled and laughed out loud. "That was awesome!!" He ran over to the building where Inferneous crashed and gave him a hand to get out of the rubble. Inferneous breathed hard, and then revealed in his hand was a large purple heart-shaped rock. It was pulsing with purple energy, and it moved ever so back and forth. "Dang, that's huge."

"Yeah, one of the biggest I've seen," Inferneous said, dusting himself off.

He walked back over to Balast, who was sitting on top of the Malum's face, tapping his foot on its eyeball. The Malum was grunting in extreme pain, and its eyes darted around frantically as Inferneous approached with its heart.

Balast kicked his heel into one of the Malum's eyes and yelled, "Stop squirming. You may have a chance to escape from your wretched existence if you answer our questions."

The Malum couldn't speak because its mouth was magically sealed, but it didn't look too menacing in the position it was in right now. Inferneous climbed up the leg of the monster and joined Balast on its face, nodding to Balast to release its mouth.

Balast waved his fingers, and a bloodcurdling scream came out of the Malum. Birds in the distance were disturbed by the caliber of the scream. After it was done, it breathed a heavy sigh. Balast, Inferneous, and the rest of the Ninjirates crew unplugged their ears as the Malum stopped.

Inferneous shook his head from the sound and said sternly, "Don't do that again." He stood over the Malum's other eye and sat down on a large armor plate under its eye.

"Ok, so first question–"

"Where are the students??!!" Balast interrupted, putting his foot deeper into one of the Malum's eyes. The Malum screamed in pain again, but the duration was shorter.

After Inferneous uncovered his ears, he waved his hand to the angry Balast staring down at the Malum and said in a nicer tone, "Calm down; we won't get anything out of it if we continue to hurt it more."

Balast looked up at him with anger on his face but saw that Inferneous had the same anger in his eyes but was hiding it beneath his cool demeanor. Balast removed his foot from its eye with a sickening squelch of fluids and shook them off as Inferneous continued his questions.

"Why did you come here? Actually, why have your kind come to this hemisphere? Didn't our masters clear out this land of your kind?"

The Malum breathed heavily and replied, "We were avoiding this land for as long as we sensed the vast magical energy that you withhold. After the great disperse, most of us assumed that you were dead."

"The great disperse?" Balast questioned. "What is that?"

"It was when the Aureus empire fell." Inferneous put together. "When that Innominatus blew, it probably dispersed its energy to Malums throughout the realms. Must have been a burst of power and intelligence for most of them." Inferneous looked to Balast, and Balast looked away, shaking his head.

"Bad memories aren't meant to be relived."

"But it looks like we are going to have to revisit the idea. It was completely our fault–"

"Next question!" Balast interrupted Infereneous.

Inferneous sighed and continued, "Ok, where are the people you abducted, and what are you monsters going to do to them?"

The Malum wheezed and let out a loud booming laugh. It wasn't as loud as its screams, but it was enough to make everyone wince at its cold and raspy tone. "They will be sacrifices. A miracle has happened, and we must complete it."

"What miracle?" Inferneous questioned.

The Malum laughed again. "Basileus Rex will live again."

Inferneous' mouth dropped open, and Balast punched the armor on the Malum's forehead, and it cracked but cut open Balast's skin. Balast then took his bleeding hand and took the Malum's heart from Inferneous while pushing him off.

Inferneous didn't have time to react as he fell to the ground. He landed on his feet and immediately yelled to Balast, "What are you doing?!?!"

Balast ignored him and looked the Malum in its eye, whispering in a dark guttural tone. The blood from his hand then started to form strings with spiked points at the end. Balast knelt down and put his palm to the Malum's slimy skin, and the red tendrils of his blood pierced the heart of the Malum. The Malum's eyes rolled back as it opened its mouth in pain.

"Oh no, no, no, no," Inferneous said as he tried to jump back up to the Malum's head, but he was then slammed to his side by the Malum's hand. As Inferneous went flying into the nearest building, the Malum regained its composure but didn't rampage. It stood up but with its head back to keep Balast from falling off. Balast stopped speaking and dropped down from the Malum.

Inferneous immediately ran over to him, dusting himself off in anger, and yelled, "What in Angel's grace are you doing?!?!"

He was about to continue to chew out Balast when the Malum lunged at Inferneous. He flinched, and his arm ignited fire as he prepared for the impact, but nothing happened. He looked at the Malum, and it was trying to grab Balast, but it seemed it couldn't. Balast put up his bloody right arm, and Inferneous saw it was almost completely black, and it had red tendrils from it to the Malum's heart in his hand.

"You didn't…You can't…?!" Inferneous stuttered in disbelief at what he was seeing.

"Yes, I can," Balast said, putting his arm down.

The Malum was grunting and digging its claws in the dirt, trying to get to Balast, but to no avail. It stopped when Balast turned to it and started laughing nervously as it said, "Binding magic won't work the way you want it to be mortal. You'll be indentured to me forever with the kind of magic you have!"

"No," Balast said calmly. "You are indentured to me." Balast then concentrated, and the red tendrils from his arm pierced the Malum's heart more.

The Malum fell to the ground, coughing up black ooze, and as it slowly recovered, it lowered its head to the ground to stare Balast in the eye and said, "It's all your fault. You already know."

Balast said nothing as he squeezed the Malum's heart until it crumbled in his hands. The Malum writhed and clawed at its head, screaming until it slowly stopped and melted into black sludge that gurgled and popped.

Balast turned to the Ninjirates crew and said, "Harvest its armor. It may be the only chance you have for survival where we are going next."

"Balast, what is happening?" Inferneous yelled at him as he grabbed him by the shoulder.

Balast shoved his arm off and said, "It's all our fault."

"What do you mean?" Inferneous asked, looking Balast in the eye.

Balast visibly looked drained and had bags under his eyes as he looked at Inferneous in despair. "We killed all those people, and our past actions are about to kill more."

"Tell me what you mean!!"

"We broke the Malum king's prison!! Cordis Aureus's grave was keeping the king's energy contained, and now all the Malums in the world are going to try to revive him using the lives of the magically awakened!!"

"W–what?" Inferneous eyes then opened wide to realize what Balast had said. "By Angel's grace, what have we done?"

While Inferneous was realizing their situation, Jayce, Zack, and Erica approached them. Jayce saw Inferneous in shock and asked, "What's wrong?" He turned to Balast and blacked up in mild shock. "Balast, you have a dark ring in your eye right now," he said in a low voice.

Balast nodded his head. "Yeah, I know." As he started to walk back to the ship, he said, "Don't follow in my footsteps."

Inferneous gained his senses and yelled out to the Ninjirates crew, "Hurry to the ship; we have to set sail immediately!! If you are having trouble integrating the armor, go to Holdren for help!" He gestured to the ship and lowered his voice to Zack and Jayce, "We are going to have a talk on the ship; follow me."

They nodded, and as they followed, the rest of the Ninjirates crew followed, and soon, they were out at sea again.

In the captain's quarters, Balast, Inferneous, Holdren, Erica, Zack, Jayce, and Rhinda sat down at the round table in the mile with maps and compasses in dead silence. The walls were thick enough even to keep the roaring tide and the creating wood at bay. Balast was in deep thought, fingers intertwined, elbows on the table, and eyes unflinching, staring down at the table with his darkened features. His arm was still a dark black and purple, and his irises still had a black ring around them from the binding magic he had performed on the previous Malum.

Everyone but Holdren and Erica were staring at Balast in an awkward phase of anticipation, but nothing came for the few minutes they were sitting there. Holdren wasn't fazed because he was continuing to track the course of the ship across the sea, and Erica wasn't trying to pay attention at all.

Inferneous grew tired of waiting and asked, "Ok, do you even know where we are going?"

Balast then turned to look at Inferneous with awe in their eyes to make Inferneous realize the irony in his words. "Ok, hold off with the stares for now because the world is at stake here."

They all turned back to Balast, and he shook his head. "It's too late."

"Spare on the drama and tell us what you're thinking," Erica said with an impatient tone.

Balast slammed his hand on the table, causing purple light to ripple from his hand across the table. Everyone except Inferneous visibly jumped in their seats.

Balast was about to speak, but he shook his head and clenched his fist on the table. "They are going to group at a spot that has an abundance of life energy or, even better, a place where a lot of people lost their lives."

"So where was the last place a war happened?" Holdren asked.

"No, no real war has happened in a long time. I made sure of that," Balast said, looking up to Inferneous.

Inferneous sighed, "They are going to the ruins of the Aureus empire. There isn't a doubt about it."

There was a bit of silence as Holdren furiously started charting the multiple maps, and then he stopped when he started writing on a blank piece of paper.

Balast put a hand over the paper and shook his head. "I already did the calculations in my head. There isn't a way we could make it with the time we have left."

"But have you considered alternate routes? Maybe–"

"I appreciate the effort," Balast said, looking Holdren in the eye. "But I already know every way, every black stream, every magical solution…" He trailed off into silence and then stood out of his chair. "We set for the mainland immediately."

"But–" Holdren raised a finger.

"I said no–" Balast said, trying.

"What about the civilians?" Jayce asked,

"We just can't s–" Balast said, trying again.

"What about the crew?" Rhinda asked.

"We'll just–" Balast tried again, his anger rising.

"What about everyone else?" Zack asked.

"I'll figure–" Balast tried to reply faster.

"Who are we even going to go to?" Erica asked.

"You have to–" Balast tried one last time.

"What about us?" Inferneous asked.

Balast slammed both hands down on the table this time, and it glowed dark purple energy again as he snapped, "I don't know, and I don't care anymore!! All of you can ask all the questions you want, but no answer will be provided because this is it!! This is the end!! Make your amends with yourself and know that you couldn't have done anything about it!!" He then kicked his chair back and stormed out of the room.

There was more silence as everyone watched and heard him storm out to the deck and up to the helm.

They looked around at each other in awkward silence when Inferneous spoke, "Don't be alarmed. We'll figure something–" he stopped when he looked down at Holdren's map and saw something irregular in the movement plotted out of their ship. "Is this where we came out of the Malum dimension?" he asked Holdren, pointing down at the small circle.

Holdren nodded and pointed to a dot a bit behind it, "This is where we were when we entered. It may not look like much, but this is a smaller map."

Inferneous stood there for a second, looking at the paper. Then, he looked at Holdren with a fire in his eyes and a smile on his face. Holdren smiled, too, as he continued, "It's called space dilation, and we could make it there if we take a small risk." Inferneous set the map down on the table, and as he started walking out of the room, he said, "Continue plotting that course and get your men ready for the fight of their lives."

As he walked outside, he saw that the crew were looking uneasy and avoiding their gazes from the helm. They all looked a bit traumatized from just seeing Balast in the state he was in, which made Inferneous solidify his resolve. The sun was starting to dip below the horizon as Balast leaned against the railing of the ship. Inferneous approached slowly before he put a hand on Balast's shoulder, and Balast slapped it away.

"You always like to put a hand on my shoulder like a father and his son; it's annoying."

Inferneous shrugged, "I can't help it; I'm a physical person."

"You sure are," Balast said, scoffing. "If only you could become smart enough to use it wisely."

Inferneous ignored the insult and looked Balast up and down, analyzing his terrible state. His arm had gotten worse; it was an angry black all the way to his shoulder. The black rings around his irises had grown larger now, so it looked like he had targets for eyes, and he looked even more tired than ever. Inferneous looked to the sunset, set his head on his hand, his elbow on the railing, and asked, "Do you remember when we first met each other?"

The question put off Balast, and he shook his head in confusion. "What?" he asked, looking at Inferneous.

Inferneous smiled and chuckled. "My first thought was, 'Man, he looks ugly.'" Inferneous then burst out laughing and slapped his knee.

Balast shook his head and resisted the urge to smile. He eventually gave in and started to smirk as he replied, "And I thought the exact same thing."

Inferneous was hunched over the rail, crying with laughter.

Balast couldn't help but laugh a little at Inferneous' amusement and the humorous tale of their youth. When Inferneous stopped laughing, Balast's smile faded into a distant sadness as they stared at the sunset once more.

"I bound the Malum to me. That's why my appearance is deteriorating. I did it because I needed all of the information the Malum had and because it also gave me a connection to all of the Malums." Balast covered his left eye and winced in pain as his eye turned black from what looked like blood seeping from his arm. He stared into the distance, and his vision muddied and clouded until he had a clear vision of every Malum on Magia. He hated what he saw, but he pushed on as a pounding headache mounted behind his eyes. He looked left, right, up, down, and everywhere, looking for a clear place where the Malums were holding prisoners until there was a Malum with a clear view of ruins with humans in cages. He recognized the ruins, and as he tried to examine them closer, the other Malums in the picture snapped towards him. They all then leaped at the Malum Balast, who was viewing through, but before he experienced that, he quickly put his arm down.

"I know where they are," Balast said, calmly shaking off the fear he had felt of being devoured. "They are at Valde Cruz."

Inferneous sighed, putting his hand over his face in a smile. "Everything leads back to there, doesn't it?" Inferneous stopped leaning on the railing and looked at Balast, still looking out at sunset, and shook his head.

"None of this is your fault. And even if it was, it's as much as my fault for all of those lives that were taken at Castillus Grex or even Valde Cruz."

Balast continued to look at the horizon in shame, but Inferneous continued, "I love that you take everything upon yourself and make yourself out to be the most responsible, but that doesn't mean that you are wrong for having questions. I have questions about the survival of every single one of the people who decided to stick with us, and I count the missing people every time we come back to the ship–"

"I know!" Balast said, snapping at Inferneous with rage at first but then with grief, "I know it's over because now I'm even questioning if I can do it in my own power! I never thought I'd have that question in the back of my mind ever again, but now–"

"It doesn't matter anymore if you can do it!" Inferneous interrupted fervently. "It matters what you will do!" Inferneous extended his hand to the lower deck and asked, "If you really don't believe you can save the stranger on the road, then what about the ones closest to you?" Inferneous took a breath and softened his tone as he asked, "What about me? Or even better, what about Zack?"

Blast stared at him with a rage that told Inferneous he had struck the right nerve. "You're his first role model!!"

Inferneous smiled and laughed, "We both are! Zack and Jayce are now our duty to train and protect, to face the world and its many challenges, and you question if it's in your power to save them?" Inferneous put his fist out to Balast, and it burst into flames. "We've both spent too much time with them, and we've both spent far too much time hiding in our own corners of the world from our mistakes. Don't question what you can do; question what you will do."

Balast, at this point, was angered beyond belief, but instead of lashing out, he punched Inferneous' burning fist. As he held his fist there, staring at Inferneous, the flames traveled up his arm, burning away the black and tarnished skin and restoring it to healthy, powerful skin. It then retracted itself back to their fists, and the flames stopped in their motion like they were frozen in time.

"I won't question it; we are going to rid this world of Malums, no matter how long it takes."

Inferneous softly smiled as he said, "Glad to see you're not a coward." Inferneous turned and yelled out to the deck, "Ahoy, Ninjirates!!"

"Ahoy!!" They answered back.

"We are going to go fight for the lives of everyone you've ever known or loved, as well as your fellow crewmates, so take this time now to reflect on the glorious lives you have lived; all mistakes, failures, and mess-ups are nothing now. All of you will be immortalized as warriors!!"

There was continued cheer from the crowd.

Inferneous finished off by saying, "Now set sail for Valde Cruz!"

Chapter 21

"There isn't a way to get there in time!!" Balast said with an angry deposition. "I'm a wizard whose talents extend to manipulating time and creating portals across the world, and I'm saying there isn't a way to do that!"

"Then we find a way! Are you even trying to get to where we are going? It seems that at every opportunity, you want to give up everything!!" Holdren shouted angrily back.

Balast, Holdren, Inferneous, Jayce, Rhinda, Zack, Erica, and Drathni were all in the captain's quarters witnessing, some participating in an argument about their course. Everyone was sitting in purple chairs they had found below decks except Balast and Holdren.

Balast was at the head of the table, clenching his fists so hard that his knuckles were white. He was staring down at an old map of the world where Valde Cruz was still a major landmark. They couldn't find a world map where Valde Cruz wasn't an irrelevant unnamed ancient ruin, so Balast had to search through his bag and find a map that may have been older than most of the people at the table.

Holdren was standing on the left side of the table between Rhinda and Erica, staring at Balast with wide, angry eyes. He had plotted a course for the ship, and he was saying that they could make it there in a good week, but Balast had fallen back into a pessimistic state when he deemed that was too long. Thus started the heated argument.

"Both of you need to stop yelling at each other!! If we are going to solve this problem in the least amount of time possible, arguing isn't going to make anything better! I believe both of you know this, so this is shameful behavior!" Inferneous, who was at the foot of the table, said, standing up to yell at both of them at the same time.

"What are our magical options, Balast? I could use my powers to accelerate the ship, so we could probably cut the time to get here in half." He said as a small flaming ship made its way across the map, leaving a trail of magical fire mapping their route.

Balast sighed and said, "I can portal us into the Intervallum seas, but no further."

Inferneous tapped the table, and the flaming ship teleported further towards Balast with a green flash.

"Why can't you teleport to Valde Cruz? Haven't you been there before?" Jayce asked.

Balast shook his head, closing his eyes in regret. "There was a point where I wiped my own memory trying to forget what happened at Valde Cruz; in truth, I can't even remember what it looked like in its prime."

He looked down at the map, and Jayce couldn't tell if it was immeasurable anger or deep sorrow that showed on Balast's face. "That would still only take a week off the course; we would need to do that at least three more times to get there in a good two to three days."

"Then we will. Balast can check out the area using double space, and I can make the ship go faster than normal when we can't use his portals." Inferneous said, standing up from the table. "We should be able to get there in a maximum of three days."

Holdren opened his mouth to talk, but as he looked at the magical ship teleport and burned its path across the map, he closed it.

"Well, now that we have that settled, what are we actually going to do about the Malums?" Erica said after seeing Holdren's reaction. "Every time we have dealt with a Malum, the crew has been almost absolutely useless. We need to teach them ways of defending themselves so we don't add to the slaughter when we get there," she said with her usual angry tone, but Balast saw another emotion flick across her face.

"We can put protective spells around them to protect them from the toxic magic of the Malums but we won't have time for them while focusing on getting us there–" Inferneous explained.

"No," Balast said, cutting Inferneous off. "While we rest, we can teach some defensive skills."

"As captains, that is the least you could do," Jayce commented. "Your crew should be priority number one; plus, Erica has a point. We are going to be the ones fighting alongside you while everyone else runs away."

Inferneous bowed his head and raised his hands as he said, "My apologies, you're right. It might be a little strenuous for us, but I think we'll be fine, right Balast?"

Balast smiled and shook his head, "I won't; you will." He sat down and continued, "Ok, we will meet again on the third day when we arrive. Now, everyone except Inferneous, please leave because I have to speak with him privately."

Everyone stood except for Balast, who was already sitting, and Inferneous, who sat down as everyone else exited through the door behind him. As soon as they were alone, Balast pinched his fingers together, and the table they were sitting at shortened. Inferneous's chair followed the table until he and Balast were less than a foot away from each other.

"I want you to know that this is really, really bad. Exactly three times worse than the last time we were at Valde Cruz–" they both hissed in pain as their scars burned in an angry fester. As Balast winced through the pain, he continued asking, "Can you feel that? That is the feeling of our death slowly approaching."

Inferneous growled and said angrily, "That isn't true, and you know it! Those visions we saw in the Malum dimension were false premonitions. They were created to discourage us from destroying them."

"But it's the realist possibility."

The pain stopped, and Balast and Inferneous stopped holding their arms in pain.

"It's more likely that we die fighting the remaining Malums of this world. Don't you think there was a reason why Parquen and Diadus told us to choose apprentices as soon as we could? They died fighting, and so will we." Inferneous sat back in his chair and sighed. When he did, flames hissed out of his mouth, showing that it was a more exasperated sigh than anything. "And you say this all for what? Do you enjoy thinking about the worst possibilities?"

"I say this to tell you to start transferring your power to Jayce and to make sure that we are on the same level." Balast looked Inferneous in the eyes and continued, "If anything happens...if everything happens, tell me that we can trust each other to stay strong and do anything to save as many people as we can."

Inferneous gazed apprehensively at Balast, and then his gaze softened, and he looked to the table. "This is what our mistake was last time." He looked up to Balast, who was still staring intently at Inferneous, waiting for an answer. Inferneous smiled and, held out his scarred hand, and said, "I promise that whatever happens, we'll be together when it does, truly; that's all that matters."

"You're missing the point–" Balast tried.

"No, you're missing the point," Inferneous interrupted. "The truth is that if we aren't together, everything bad happens. If we stay together, mind and soul clashing, we can navigate through anything and everything that comes our way. Saving our crew? Done. Ridding Magia of Malums? Done. Fixing the mistakes of our past? Easy."

Balast grabbed Inferneous' hand with his and started, "I can get behind that, but there are more important things than us."

Balast looked past Inferneous and saw a small foot slip through the door at the last second. Inferneous smiled because he knew what had happened behind him. "There are more important things than us, but if we can't take care of each other, then we won't ever take care of those important things."

Balast nodded as he looked back at Inferneous. He squeezed Inferneous' hand tighter and whispered, "Promise me you won't let them die. If worse comes to worst and we need to be of one mind and soul, promise me you prioritize them over everything."

Inferneous grew serious and squeezed Balast's hand back and said, "To the end."

"And to forever." Balast finished as they unclasped their hands and stood from the table.

Inferneous stepped aside as the table lengthened back to its original size, and he looked Balast dead in the eyes one last time before he exited the room.

The air of both excitement and dread was inversely affecting members of the Ninjirates as they made their journey across the Oceans of Magia. Between the switches of Inferneous' acceleration of the ship and of Balast's portals, the crew changed their resting rotation to thirds to accommodate training.

"The Malum structure looks complicated in their shifting forms, but they are quite simple," Balast said. He was standing with his back towards the captain's quarters, facing a small crowd of about ten people. Jayce and Zack were in the crowd, intently listening to Balast's teaching, refreshing their memories about Malum's offense and defense.

"The most vital point of a Malum is their core," he waved his hand, and magical lights appeared and formed into the writhing shape of a Malum.

A glowing purple orb moved steadily back and forth inside the image, mimicking the motion of a Malum.

Balast pointed to the purple orb and continued, "This is a Malum core. If this is destroyed, your problems will be solved. The question is how."

He waved his hand again, and the image zoomed into the Malum core, showing a hard-shell casing shaking with troubled energy. "All Malum cores are unbreakable by human hands, but through magical means, you can get close. You won't have to worry about destroying them because you'll be accompanied by either Inferneous or I. The point is to always aim for the Malum core. Doing damage to this will keep you alive until we can get to it."

He waved his hand, and the lights disappeared.

"Any questions?"

One ninja, who Balast recognized as the troublemaker called Arc, raised his hand.

"Yes, Arc," he said as the young ninja stood up.

"If these Malums are so dangerous, how is it that we've easily defeated them every time we've come in contact with them? Even when you guys were below decks, we easily got rid of one."

Balast frowned and replied, "That was an excellent exception, and that wasn't any normal Malum. I believe that Malum was magically created by a very powerful person."

"Ok, so? How are Malums even created anyway?" Arc responded with enough attitude for Balast to magically push him into a sitting position.

Balast sighed and conjured up another spell, starting to explain, "Malums are the manifestations of desolation, cold death, and vast dark space. Ever since the first hordes of Malums descended upon Magia from the stars, all the races of this planet have fought tooth and nail to keep them from taking over."

He raised his hands, and magical lights arranged themselves into a picture of absolute war chaos. Streaks of red trailed from the sky to the ground, so crimson from the bloodshed that a ripened apple couldn't compare. Many recognizable figures of Magia's history appeared, trying to save their fallen comrades and fighting against the monsters. Every dark space was dotted with eyes, claws, or viscous tentacles, yielding that no shadow was safe. The light from the sun shining through the dark clouds allowed respite but did not incentivize hope. The figures were crowded with fearful soldiers trying to get a slim chance at life beyond their current darkness.

The brush strokes of the clearing image were frantic as if the artist was painting straight out of a fevered premonition.

Balast spoke, "Then came along the Angel of Magic, who granted immense power to three people." The image changed to show an image of three men. "Diadus Karkale, Parquen Valter, and Corvus Aureum."

The picture showed each man, all wearing grim faces, standing next to the others, seemingly talking about something of rather grave substance.

"We don't know much about Corvus…but we have found that he is connected to the Malum dimension more than we know. There is much I have to speculate and investigate to even get a logical answer for why he was even there–" Balast stopped when he realized he was trailing off.

The crew members were talking amongst themselves, so he clapped his hands together, and the image folded upon itself and disappeared.

He raised his voice, saying, "Enough speculation of the past. I'm going to teach you how to deal with a proper Malum with magic you've never seen before. Now, everyone, give me some space to work."

The crew members who weren't already standing jumped to their feet and backed into the empty space of the main deck. Balast rubbed his hands together, racking his mind on how the spell was going to work. He pulled out his magical bag, reached into it, and his hand emerged with a single piece of parchment. He focused his magical energy on the tip of his finger and started to race it furiously along the piece of paper.

When Balast was done, he held up the piece of paper to the sun and nodded his head in satisfaction.

"Alright! No one makes any sudden movements when the spell is activated. Move only when I tell you to!"

He put his left foot back to steady himself and gently threw the piece of paper to the middle of the deck. The paper flopped and blew about in the wind for a few seconds before abruptly slamming down onto the wooden deck with a hard slap. As he watched, the paper started to float up slowly, and the side where Balast had written was adorned with blue runes.

The runes started to shift and change, a dark purple substance beginning to pour out of the parchment until it was surrounded with a violet, viscous liquid. The liquid grew in quantity and size as the spell continued, reaching a height taller than most of the crew members. Suddenly, it stopped.

As they all stared into the now swirling mass, Balast said once more, "No one moves until I tell you."

He raised his hand, and the liquid splattered all over the ground. What remained wasn't the parchment paper but a Malum. The crew gasped and gaped, but no one dared move. The Malum was half-humanoid, having the upper torso and head of a man, but instead of eyes, there was a mangled black crown with four spike horns on its head. The Malum's bottom half was large and round, like a spider's abdomen. For limbs, it had only spiked tentacles.

Balast smiled at the ingenuity of his own spell as he saw the fear radiate amongst the crew. He stepped toward it with a hand raised as it twitched and convulsed in ungodly directions. "This is the least intimidating thing you will be facing where we are going."

He grabbed one of the Malum's horns and stared at its disfigured face. He shook his head in morbid disgust as he realized how awful he really had made it.

He dragged it forward a bit and gestured to the crowd, saying, "Zack! Come and touch." He said, pointing him out in the crowd.

Zack furiously stepped back, trying to hide amongst the others, but Jayce put a hand on his back and shoved him forward. As Zack stumbled forward into the open, he turned back and saw Jayce smiling with a thumbs up. Zack made a face that conveyed all the negative emotions he could through a piercing gaze and gritted teeth before snapping back to anxious fear when the Malum groaned creepily in front of him.

"In order for any of you to survive the battle, we are heading to the first thing you need to learn: resist fear," Balast said to the crew. He turned back to Zack and whispered, "Go on, trust me."

Zack hesitated, his hand shaking as he reached toward the hideous being. When he made contact, the Malum shuddered violently, and Zack retracted his hand before Balast could stop him. Balast almost breathed a sigh of resignation when he saw Zack reach out a second time and feel the Malum again.

He rubbed the dry skin and furrowed his eyebrows as he sensed the waves of liquid magic under Malum's skin. He removed his hand and looked toward Balast with disgust but also a morbid curiosity.

Balast smiled back at him and whispered, "You look confused."

Zack nodded and whispered back, "This isn't a real Malum, is it?"

"Yes and no. I'll explain in a minute." Balast stepped back from Zack and shouted out as he raised the Malum's head, "Anyone else wants to come and touch?"

The crowd was still hesitant. Balast looked around and dragged the Malum with him; some flinched and took steps back. Balast frowned and shook his head. He turned around and, with a sickening pop and crunch, ripped the Malum's head off. Everyone gasped in disgust as the body fell to the floor.

"I want you all to listen to me and take these words to heart…no, further than your heart. I want each and every one of you to look into your soul and ask yourself what keeps you from running away." He was silent for a moment, then started again, "You have been given many attempts to leave this ship and all of the troubles it comes with, but you all have stayed here for a reason. You are about to face absolute death, and you are afraid of just one of its many tentacles? Let me tell you, whatever you hold dear in your heart should take precedence FIRST over the fear that you harbor for Malums. From experience, I know." He revealed his left forearm and showed the pulsing black scar. "That if that fear shows itself on the battlefield, you will not survive. My own fortune barely saved me. I may not have lost my life, but…" He looked down at his hand wistfully, then continued, "I lost something that was important to me."

There were a few minutes of silence before Balast came back from the plane of his own thoughts.

"Anyways," he said, dropping the Malum head. "Jayce, Zack, Shiro, and Kuro, all of you come and stand near me. Bring your weapons. You will be good examples of how to work together."

Shiro, Kuro, and Jayce grabbed their weapons and separated themselves from the crowd. Balast walked over to the Malum's body and, with a crunch, shoved his hand deep inside its chest, pulling out the piece of parchment the Malum had formed around. He stretched it out and poked a small hole with his fingernail in the middle. When he did, the Malum's body melted to the floor and turned to black ash. Balast walked over to where the body once was and dropped the parchment paper on it.

"Are you four ready?" Balast asked as he walked past them to lean on the door of the captain's quarters.

They all nodded, and a teal blue barrier rose at the edge of the crowd, cutting the four off from going anywhere else but the space inside it.

They all looked back at Balast, and Jayce asked, "Why the barrier now?"

"Well, because now I won't be restricting the Malum's power. The Malum you four will be facing will be as realistic as I can make it. Not just in looks and texture."

Jayce heard a loud popping sound and whirled around to see that a new Malum had formed around the parchment. This Malum was very different from its predecessor. As the crowd outside the barrier gawked at the Malum, Jayce analyzed the new being. It was at least seven feet tall and had at least ten tentacles on each side of its body. Instead of a head, it had two intertwined horns, and instead of any kind of leg, it was firmly anchored to the deck.

He took a step backward, and immediately, Shiro and Kuro disappeared from his peripheral vision as three tentacles lashed forward at the group.

Jayce pushed Zack out of the way of one tentacle and then spun around, drawing his axe to slice the tentacle aiming for him. His eyes widened with shock as his axe rang like a church bell as it struck the hardened Malum flesh. He grunted as he was pushed back into the magical barrier from the force of the attack. Jayce regained his breath and quickly rolled away as another tentacle slammed into the barrier and shattered a hole through it.

Jayce looked back and saw Balast with his mouth slightly agape, and he yelled, "What kind of Malum is this?! Can you turn the difficulty down a little?"

Jayce dodged another tentacle, and it slammed onto the deck but didn't pierce through.

Balast closed his mouth, and it started to twitch into a curious smile.

"The barrier will heal itself, and I believe you can do this." He sat down cross-legged, leaning on the wall of the captain's quarters, and continued, "Have faith in you and your crewmates, and you are sure to survive our next battle."

Jayce didn't have time to argue. A shrill yell echoed behind him. He turned around as a lump of panic rose in his throat.

Zack was wrapped in tentacles and being raised into the air by the Malum. Jayce gritted his teeth and stepped forward in preparation to run to his aid, but Shiro was faster. He saw a black and orange figure zip up and down across the tentacles, and Zack was suddenly on the ground, removing cut-up pieces of tentacle from his robe.

Shiro was beside him with two knives in each of his hands. He looked at Jayce and yelled out, "Do you know how to perform magic?"

Jayce nodded and started to run the length of the barrier as the tentacle chased him and attempted to impale him. As he ran, he ducked, dodged, and slid until he met Shiro in the middle at the opposite end of the Malum.

"I know magic, but I can only draw power from others. If I do that.."

He dodged a tentacle, then swiftly stepped forward to cut it when another tentacle came from his blind spot. His muscles tensed, bracing himself to be impaled, but Shiro stepped in and caught the tentacle between his forearms.

Jayce saw a red glow flash between his shoulders and hands, and then the tentacle burst to pieces.

"Whatever drawbacks it has doesn't matter; minimize them and do it!" Shiro said, then rushed forward toward the Malum.

Kuro joined him, and they rushed the Malum together, dodging and slicing the tentacles off one by one.

"Jayce!" Zack ran up to him and held up his wand. "I have an idea."

While Zack explained his plan, Shiro and Kuro were struggling to handle the Malum. As each tentacle was cut, another took its place, coming at them at an array of angles. Shiro dodged left to avoid one tentacle, then backflipped to avoid another. In midair, he blocked a third spiked tendril and didn't regain his balance when falling back to the deck. Two tentacles started to head toward the downed Shiro, but Kuro was already slicing the tentacles off.

"Get up, Shiro! Your form is slipping!" Kuro yelled, annoyed.

He dodged a tentacle and backed up toward Shiro. He kept moving, grabbing the back of Siro's gi and dragging him to his feet. They both dodged to the side as two tentacles slammed into the ground between them.

Kuro looked at Shiro and yelled, "Pay more attention to your footing!"

Shiro looked down and realized he was standing on the viscous black liquid that the Malum secreted. He traced it with his eyes back to the Malum. Where it had started was at least five feet away.

"Pay more attention! It's trying to absorb the whole of the deck!" Kuro shouted and quickly jumped backward, avoiding the growing slime and shooting tentacles.

He gained his footing and then looked up to see Jayce rushing into the slime, recklessly slashing anything he could, even if it resulted in his foot slipping and Kuro having to save him by deflecting a tentacle.

"Jayce, don't–"

Jayce interrupted Kuro as he sludged forward. "Keep the tentacles at bay! We have a plan!"

He looked to his right and saw that Zack had his eyes closed in focus as a ball of lightning energy flashed between his hands.

"Shiro! Protect Zack! They have something planned!"

Shiro nodded as he sliced a tentacle off and headed to defend Zack. Jayce continued to trudge forward, blocking and slicing tentacles as viciously as he could muster as his feet sunk into the Malum slime on the ground.

He didn't have to do much, though, because Kuro was covering him. A blue aura covered Kuro's hands as he threw six silver knives into the air. They magically flew around Jayce, protecting him from incoming attacks. As Jayce stepped forward, getting closer and closer to the Malum, the attacks increased. With the help of Kuro's knives, he was able to get within striking distance of the main body of the Malum.

"Zack, now!!" Jayce shouted out, and Zack cried out in excretion as he shoved the ball of electric magic into the ground.

The electricity surged forward and burned the Malum slime on the deck, making it recede all the way back to the main body. The magic then went everywhere, and it was about to electrocute everything but Zack when a wave of hot energy came from Jayce. His face started to bear magical runes that pulsed a bright orange. The magical lightning immediately ceased, and around half of the Malum's tentacles shriveled up and disintegrated into ash on the deck.

"Rush now!" Jayce yelled out, but everyone was already with him.

They all surged forward at the Malum, weapons, and magic in sync. Kuro waved his hand, and the knives surrounding Jayce flew and impaled the remaining tentacles of the Malum's body; Shiro sliced the bases of the tentacles, leaving the Malum with no one to attack. Jayce ran forward and slashed the Malum down the middle, revealing the parchment paper, and finally, Zack pulled out his wand. It morphed into a short sword and pierced through the paper until the hilt was touching the runes. The Malum stilled, convulsed, and then promptly fell to the ground, turning into a pile of black ash at the feet of the four.

All of them were heaving with exhaustion as they stared down at the Malum, their victory not registering in their mind. Suddenly, applause erupted from around them, making Jayce come back to the reality of what he just did. He smiled as the runes faded from his face and the barrier around them lowered. Balast walked over to them, picked up the parchment paper, and slapped Jayce on the back with a big smile.

"You did it. Congratulations on defeating your first Malum." He examined the parchment paper, noting the gaping hole through the middle, crumpled it up, and lit it on fire.

He then turned to the crowd and said, "Take this example and replicate it among yourselves. That was an excellent example of taking an unexpected problem and solving it. This is what you will need to survive."

He turned to Zack and continued, "Your plan was simple but effective. You are most definitely ready to receive the Angel's blessing, so give me your hand."

Zack's eyes grew wide in shock as he gave Balast his right hand. Balast circled the back of his hand with his finger, and a golden circle drew itself over it.

The circle spun and flipped until multiple circles appeared and created a golden glowing ball that shrunk, leaving the image of a girl with large feathery wings protruding out of her back above his hand. The image then transmogrified into a being Zack's mind recoiled at before finally transforming into a golden sword.

The sword then descended and pierced Zack's skin, drawing a droplet of blood. Then, it disappeared into thin air. Zack rubbed the back of his palm as Balast let go, and as he looked up at Balast, he realized something was different about him. He seemed slightly shorter, and his form slouched a bit as the magic faded.

As Balast saw the spell work itself through, his eyes glazed over, and he remembered when he received his powers. He remembered the pain of the cut being overridden by his childhood ambitions coming true, and he remembered everything he thought he would become. But it was now overshadowed by Zack's smiling face.

He stepped back from Zack, slowly fading out of his memories into the real world, and Balast leaned against one of the posts in exhaustion. Zack stepped forward to help Balast, but Balast raised a hand as he pushed himself away from the post and stood fully upright.

"It's funny…" he said with a slight chuckle. It feels like a weight has been lifted off my back, and I can finally rest a bit more easily. He thought, staring at his hand.

Stretching and groaning, he turned to face the rest of the crew and said, "Alright, now that you have witnessed what teamwork and trust in your crewmates can do, I want you to follow their example." He walked past Jayce and said, "Ok, you handle the rest; call me if something goes wrong."

Then Balast swiftly entered the captain's chamber and closed the door behind him with a yawn.

Inferneous was growing a bit wary from propelling the ship, so he was relieved when he saw Balast walk up the stairs to the helm. Inferneous let go of the flaming helm, and the magical fires he had lit dissipated immediately, bringing the ship to a cruise and eventually a complete stop.

He met Balast at the crest of the stairs and commented, "You look more tired than usual. Was training the crew that laborious?"

Balast laughed and shook his head. "I just gave Zack the Angel's Blessing, that's all. If I'm this tired after transferring the blessing, I am curious to see what happens to you."

Inferneous smiled, but in truth, this statement worried him. He patted Balast on the arm and said, "Good luck," as he passed him, descending the stairs.

Balast grabbed Inferneous' arm lightly and said quietly but with a grave tone, "They may be trained in dealing with Malums, but they still lack the conviction and understanding of how grave this is. Please, do your best to make them understand."

Inferneous looked Balast in the eye and saw that this may have been the first time in forty years that Balast had genuinely asked him for something. Inferneous nodded solemnly and continued down the stairs, leaving Balast to his thoughts.

"Take your time; I'm going to start on the teleportation runes." He heard Balast say as he left, but he didn't acknowledge it because he was focused on creating an effective speech.

At the bottom of the stairs, the crew was gathered together around the centermost of his magical fires, and there was a murmur of conversation between them. When Inferneous reached the fire, they circled around; the murmurs dwindled until everyone was silent and paying attention to Inferneous. Inferneous dimmed the fire a bit to alleviate the crew's eyes. He looked up for a moment, gazing at the stars glinting in the deep, dark velvet sky.

"I wanted to thank all of you for staying on this journey with Balast and I. You all could have, and most likely should have, chosen better lives outside of the crazy demon hunting he and I are tasked to do."

There were a few chuckles from the crowd as Inferneous continued speaking. "There...is no way to put this lightly; I want all of you to understand the gravity of the fight that we are going into. So, I will ask a question first…"

Inferneous turned to his left, pointed out Shiro, and asked, "What would you do, Shiro, if Kuro died in your arms?"

Shiro stood up immediately and replied, "Avenge him."

Inferneous nodded. "That is what I expected you to say. Appropriate for any usual situation."

Kuro, who was sitting next to Shiro, pulled Shiro back down, shaking his head in mild embarrassment.

"Don't shun your brother Kuro. I know you would do the same for him in a heartbeat, but that is the problem. In this situation, you are wrong."

The crowd hissed murmurs in confusion. Inferneous turned around and started to talk over the murmurs. "Erica!" he said, seeing Erica surrounded by ninjas, lying on her side, barely paying attention.

She sat up when she heard her name, raising an eyebrow to Inferneous.

"What would you do if one of your men was eaten by a Malum to save your life?"

Erica didn't hesitate either as she said, gesturing to the ninja around her. "I would avenge them. We would avenge them."

"You see, that would be wrong, too."

The crowd grew louder in outrage. Inferneous let them talk it out for a minute, hearing the different disputes on why his claims were nonsensical and even downright immoral.

He was fine with most of the complaints coming from the crowd until he heard someone say, "We didn't sign up for this!"

Inferneous raised his hand, and the central fire exploded with a new rage, quieting everyone.

Inferneous yelled out, "You all signed up for this! This is what was entailed when you agreed to stay on this ship and, most importantly, with the crazy people Balast and I are!"

He took a deep breath, and the fire settled down to its original size. He turned around and faced Shiro once again, "In the very real chance that Kuro dies, you don't avenge him in the way you are used to."

He turned and started to walk around the fire, waving his hand at the crew. "Whoever you care for that is here on this ship has a very real chance of dying a horrible death to the abominations called Malums, and if that is to happen, you. Move. On! You move on with the memory of that person in your heart, and you remember that they chose to stay on this boat and dedicate themselves to the adventure of their lives!"

Inferneous turned towards Erica and continued, "What would you do if one of your men died for you, Erica?"

She didn't answer right away, but she waited as if it were a rhetorical question.

After a few seconds, she confirmed it was a real question, and she answered, "I would retreat for the moment–"

"No," said Balast, shaking his head. "As a leader, you remain calm and take account because every death in battle is one that was either caused by idiocy or foolishness. You see, I need you all to understand that all of you are no longer here for yourselves or the ones you are indebted to. When you named yourselves as one crew on one ship, you no longer apply that singular set of mind. When you became Ninjirates, you became one of the Angel's blessed, therefore, one of the people who are going to save Magia."

There was silence from the crew as they absorbed his ending sentiment. Inferneous turned around to make sure everyone was paying attention. As he finished his rotation, he nodded in satisfaction. "Thank you for taking this seriously and thank you all for accompanying us on this journey. Win or lose, these final months have been an adventure I could never forget," he finished, walking back to the helm.

The murmurs returned when Inferneous reached the top of the stairs; Balast raised his hand and yelled, "Stop! Watch where you are stepping!"

Inferneous froze and looked down to see that he had almost stepped on a cylindrical blue rune that was pulsing evenly. Inferneous slowly looked up around the helm and saw that there were runes on almost every square inch of the platform, and the number of runes only increased.

"Looks like you were busy," Inferneous said, stepping into the rare empty space on the deck. "You sure you have enough runes? And also, how come you can step on them, and I can't?" Inferneous asked, seeing Balast standing directly on a square-shaped rune.

"I can step on them because I made them. Having you step on one is like putting a hot coal on a piece of paper. Why are you impending on my progress anyway?"

Inferneous got a good standing and replied, "I was hoping you would help cast protection spells on the crew. I'm not well versed in them as my magic does it automatically."

Balast sighed as he finished one last rune on the helm. He turned around, folded his arms, and asked, "Did you talk some sense into them?"

Inferneous raised an eyebrow. "Were you not listening to the uproar while I was speaking?"

Balast shook his head. "I got all of these runes done because I put myself in a temporary state of time contraction."

"What does that mean?" Inferneous asked.

"I sped myself up to get these runes done. I underestimated how many I could fit on this platform," Balast said, looking around at the runes. But I just need to make sure you drill it into them because from how many runes I have here, we might just come out of a portal on top of Valde Cruz."

"What?!" Inferneous asked semi-excitedly. "What do you mean by that? I thought you said it would take at least–" Inferneous tried.

"It doesn't matter what I said before. I misjudged, and now, if I activate this spell, we will be there by tomorrow morning," Balast said, cutting him off.

"What matters is if they understand the gravity of what we are getting ourselves into. When I tested them with my hyperrealistic magic doll, many of them got injured in the process of defeating it." Balast paused, looking out at the horizon.

"Which means that many are to die when we get there." Inferneous finished Balast's sentence. "But that is expected. There isn't a battle without casualties," Inferneous said, adjusting his stance so he could get closer to Balast without ruining a rune.

Balast looked down at the hundreds of runes he had created and shook his head at the impending future. "I thought that all of them would leave with the civilians, but I became skeptical when a lot of them stayed with Erica. I am still confused about why Erica even chose to stay," he said, turning around and observing the full deck of people conversing and eating.

Balast could tell, even with the crew spending months on the ship together, that the crew was divided. On the left side, there were more people, mostly ninjas, surrounding Erica, occasionally offering her food no matter how much she refused. Holdren sat next to her, along with some of his men, enjoying their time in her company. On the right, there was an even mix of ninjas and mercenaries scattered around the deck, but most were huddled around Jayce and Zack, who conversed freely with them.

"They are divided," Balast said as Inferneous stepped up next to Balast to look down at the crew.

"What do you mean?" Inferneous asked.

Balast pointed out the left and then the right, saying, "It's disproportionate how many people are on each side, and it's telling. Erica still has the allegiance of almost all the ninjas while the mercenaries are still wary of them."

Inferneous smiled and shook his head. "You see division on the surface, but you have to really look closer, Balast. You see." he gestured toward the left side. "Holdren and his men are making themselves comfortable with the ninjas. They are probably liking the more regimented ways of them." He then pointed to the right and said, "Maybe the mercenaries keep to themselves, but the ninjas that are between them get to exercise a type of freedom they haven't experienced before."

He sighed and looked to Balast, whose eyes were glazed over in sorrow. Inferneous straightened himself and breathed the melancholic emotion that washed over him.

"We both are afraid of losing control again. I know that you are more afraid of losing the people who have devoted themselves to this cause, but the only advice I can give you is to stop mourning future losses and instead enjoy who is here now." Inferneous then stepped awkwardly over the runes, back over to the staircase, and asked, "Are you going to help with the protection spells?"

Balast was silent for a minute, then wiped his face and said, "Yeah, I'm coming."

"Everyone gather around! You will receive your instructions now," Inferneous yelled out from over the railings of the helm platform. He turned around and smiled as he saw the small number of people around a table with a map of Valde Cruz sprawled across it.

Holdren, Erica, Rhinda, Drathni, Jayce, and Zack stood at the ready, weapons in hand. Inferneous stepped toward them and slapped Balast on the back, signaling for him to start.

Balast grunted and glanced at Inferneous but shook it off as he started, "Alright, we don't know exactly what state Valde Cruz is in, so we are playing it by ear at first. Any information that we receive must come back to me unless in dire situations. This current plan that I am going to outline to you six is what is going to happen if everything is as bad as I think it's going to be when we get there, understood?"

Everyone agreed and watched him as he outlined with magical writing on the map certain points.

"Where we are going to be coming into, there will be a large sandbank littered with stone and rubble from the building, which is cut off from the east and the west by two corroded watch towers. We are going to first clear that sandbank and set up a healer's station. Anyone you cannot heal you will teleport to Castillus Grex with these rune papers."

He waved his hand, and a stack of papers as tall as a chair thumped on the table in front of Drathni. They all glowed with a greenish-blue hue and had runes marked across them.

"The crew will be split into three teams, with two of you leading each of them. Inferneous and I will be flying back and forth doing what we can."

He looked to his right. "Holdren and Erica, you two will take your allotted men and head along the wall of the western tower. Whatever you find, you report back." He looked forward and continued, "Rhinda and Drathni, you two will be defending the sandbank. You will be the safe haven for any civilian, and you will teleport them back to safety."

They nodded, and he looked to his left and hesitated for a moment. Jayce and Zack were rigid with excitement. Jayce's eyes shone with a fearsome resolve and a dangerous bite to fight, but Zack's determined stare was hopelessly laced with fear. He felt a nudge to his side by Inferneous and snapped out of it.

"Zack and Jayce, you two will go along the wall of the eastern tower. Do what you can to get information." Balast stood back up and looked over the map with unsure satisfaction. "Any questions?"

Everyone, even Inferneous, raised their hands.

Balast looked to Inferneous, rolled his eyes, and pointed to Holdren. "We'll start with Holdren."

They all put their hands down as Holdren started, "How are we going to communicate? This is nearly three cities in one since it was an empire capital, right?"

Balast thought for a second before he spotted Shiro and Kuro out of the corner of his eye.

"You won't need to. I'll set up surveillance when we get there, and if something goes wrong, Inferneous or I will let you know personally."

He then pointed to Erica, and she asked hesitantly, "Are we to kill every Malum we see?"

Balast shook his head at the question. "You would never be able to; the priority is the humans. The second the last human is found; you go back to the sandbank and teleport out of Valde Cruz. Do. Not. Hesitate."

He said the last three words with a weight that everyone could feel from their stomach to the soles of their feet.

He turned his attention toward Rhinda and shook his head.

"No questions here."

Balast nodded as an odd respect was gained from the words spoken by the large man. Holdren raised his hand again, and Balast turned back to him, saying, "I thought you already asked a question?"

"Are we only allowed one? I wanted to ask if we each should take a teleportation rune just in case anything happens?"

Balast looked at the pile of papers and then back at Holdren as he shook his head.

"I want to make sure that every civilian gets out."

"But what if we come across a civilian on the way?" Erica chimed in.

"Then you protect them with your lives until they can run towards the beach—" Holdren and Erica were about to interrupt Balast again, but he raised a hand as he said, "I can't make any more right now if something happens, Inferneous and I will be there."

Holdren sighed and nodded as he folded his arms in minor frustration. He looked towards Erica, and she glanced back and forth between the stack of papers and Balast. Holdren's brow furrowed for a second until he saw Balast then turn to Drathni.

In a soft voice, the elf asked, "What do we do about our own?"

"You mean the injured?" Balast asked.

Drathni nodded, looking down at her hands, which were lithe but still frail.

"I may not be able to heal as many as I would like to." Balast sighed as he saw the aged ninja start to doubt her abilities. He walked over to her and cupped her hands with his, and a bright green light shone between them. He then walked back to the head of the table as Drathni clenched her fist, a well of magic shining from it. She seemed shocked as she looked up at Balast, but then she bowed deeply.

"No need to heal anyone but the injured civilians. I made sure the protective spells were also regenerative with time."

He grew uncomfortable as Drathni stayed in a silent bow to him, so he moved on to Jayce.

Jayce struggled to speak, starting and stopping a few times before asking, "What if we can't defeat a Malum?"

Balast would have responded if Inferneous hadn't stepped in and said strongly, "I'll be there. Don't worry about falling short; we'll pick up wherever you leave."

Balast nodded his head. "That is what we are going to be doing the whole time."

Jayce looked satisfied with his answer and nodded with thanks.

Balast finally turned to Zack, who asked without remorse, "What if no one makes it?"

Even though no one was in it during the silence that followed, the shifting postures and eyes of everyone around Balast gave the deepest pit of hell a voice.

Balast closed his eyes as flashes of a past life tore across his vision. He pushed through them until he saw Zack clearly in his vision again. He opened his mouth in a sad attempt to respond, but instead, he closed it and stared sternly at Zack.

"I can't say this out loud, but if any of you die," Balast started, as everyone started to hear him in their minds, looking around the deck.

"I will try my best to resurrect you…but because of the unholy monstrosity of the beasts we face, that is the most unlikely thing to happen. If any of you die, the least I can do is recover your body and give you a funeral better than any king. In truth, I would be surprised if one of us, including Inferneous and I, didn't die today."

He turned back to look at Zack and said aloud this time, "I will die first before that happens. And If I don't die first," he pointed to Inferneous, saying, "he will."

He pointed to Holdren, saying, "He will."

He pointed to Erica, saying, "She will."

He pointed to Rhinda, saying, "He will."

He pointed to Drathni, saying, "She will."

He pointed to Jayce, "He will."

Balast finally pointed to Zack. "The question is, Zack if all these people die and you are the last one standing against the last Malum, battered and broken, with the world on the balance, will you?"

Zack opened his mouth to say something, but nothing came out.

Balast stood as Zack closed his mouth, then he turned around and addressed the rest of the crew. "Ninjirates!"

A roar of acknowledgment came from them.

"If this is the last day we are here on Magia…if this is the last day we draw our breath as living beings…if this is our last day as Ninjirates, do not forget what your brother and comrade died for! Don't forget what is at stake, and remember that even in the afterlife, we will have one hell of a story to tell!!"

The Ninjirates roared in approval as they drew their weapons in agreement. Balast divided them accordingly, then turned back around, grabbing the helm, whispering an incantation. Suddenly, blue runes covered every inch of the ship from top to bottom. Then, a large portal spiraled open below the ship. The ship swayed side to side as it descended into the portal.

The shaking didn't stop as the portal reached over the sails and spiraled back to close, taking the blue runes that covered the ship with it. As the ship continued to rock, Balast eventually focused his eyes on the horizon and gasped at what he saw. The sky was a mess of scattered dark blue lightning clouds that all swirled to a point high above Valde Cruz. At that point, a black circle grew at a slow rate. The water was a sickly green, constantly churning from the boisterous breaths of fierce winds.

"Inferneous take the helm!" Balast yelled.

Inferneous immediately grabbed the helm as Balast left and set the ship ablaze. Flames flew across the railings as the ship started to gain traction against the wind and seas.

"Mast the sails!!" Inferneous yelled out to the Ninjirates. They all rushed to pull the sails up so the wind wouldn't hinder them.

As soon as it was done, it seemed like a knife was through butter. They all approached the sandbank rapidly, the wind almost blasting them off the ship, the sea bucking and jerking them to and fro. They were almost there when Balast glimpsed black shapes forming a line in the water.

"Inferneous! There is a Malum underwater!" Balast magically told him, but Inferneous was in a trance.

As his flames danced against the winds and the sea, a wicked smile grew on his face, and a golden light glowed in his eyes.

He yelled back to Balast, "Whatever dares to confront this ship, and I am going to find out what danger it is in!"

As they sailed forward, the black shapes in the water rose and connected, forming a giant shark with eyes covering it. For every eye, there was a sharp row of teeth and fins. It leaped out of the water and let out a deafening screech, forcing everyone except Inferneous to cover their ears in pain.

Infereneous laughed harder as it shrieked and dove back into the ocean. "What an un-original formation!! You can't possibly think that will stop ME!!" He turned the helm to the starboard side as fire enveloped the front of the ship.

As the ship turned, the Malum followed and collided with the front of the ship, turning it completely in the opposite direction.

The Ninjirates were thrown all about the ship, some even thrown into the sea. Balast was one of these, but he activated a spell and gained his footing in the air. He dashed back towards the ship and landed back on the ship next to Inferneous.

Drenched and shaken, he yelled, "I don't think– Inferneous! I don't think you can–"

"I CAN KILL IT!" Inferneous replied, spinning the helm to the port side.

He then pushed Balast into the helm and started to walk to the starboard side. He pressed his hands together, and the rain hissed and sizzled off his skin as a large spear formed in his hand. He raised it up and placed his right foot on the railing, aiming at the dark waters.

As Balast regained his senses and continued to steer the ship, he realized the front of the ship was facing the west tower. He tried to turn the ship, but before he could, the ship collided with the Malum again. When the ship stopped rocking, Balast looked over to where Inferneous was standing and saw that there was no one there at all. He grunted in frustration and continued to struggle with the helm.

Suddenly, he was blinded by a bright flash. He looked to his right and then up into the sky and saw a massive, flaming phoenix with its wings spread. Inferneous was at the center of it, spear in hand and a broad smile on his face. He saw Inferneous raise his spear as if waiting for something.

Balast felt the Malum hit the boat again, and another flash blinded him as the phoenix dived into the water. There was a thump next to him, and Inferneous pushed Balast aside to regain the helm. He had a rope of fire wrapped around him that immediately bonded to the ship when he grabbed the helm and turned it away from the Malum.

Balast looked around, seeing what he could do as the ship.

"Ok, you have to do something," Balast thought to himself, trying to stand after Malum slammed into the side of the ship once more. When he stood, Balast saw that at the front of the ship, a line of fire led all the way down into the sea, and he was being pulled by something. As they sailed a bit forward, suddenly, Inferneous wheeled the helm, and the ship turned. The flame rope suddenly went limp. The point of the ship burst aflame, and the flames turned into a pointed spear.

Balast looked back at Inferneous, who smiled and yelled, "Brace for impact!" as the ship lurched forward.

At the same moment, the Malum leaped out of the water and became impaled by the flaming spear at the point of the ship.

Inferneous laughed in triumph as he sailed forward and hollered, "LAND HO!"

The ship lurched again as it hit the sandbank, driving the fire spear into the Malum until it pierced the opposite side. The flames then receded, and Inferneous turned to Balast, smiling.

"Good Job," he said, shaking his head and spitting out seawater. He slapped Infereneous on the back, "Get everyone off the ship now."

Inferneous nodded and jumped off the side of the ship to land on the sand. It was only twenty minutes before everyone was on the beach.

"Alright, Ninjirates, you know what to do! For Magia!" Balast yelled, "For Magia!"

They responded, all heading in separate directions.

Balast watched them all go, but he picked two out of the crowd and called them back. "Shiro, Kuro, come back over here! I have a different job for you two!" he yelled out.

They came back quickly, their footsteps barely leaving an imprint in the wet sand. He reached out in front of each of them, interacting with their protection spells, and whispered a few spells. They both shook their heads as their eyes dilated, and suddenly, both Shiro and Kuro could see a good mile in front of them easily.

"I want Kuro to go to the west tower and Shiro to go to the East tower. You two need to inform me of everything happening so I can intervene when needed."

"I don't suggest we do that," Shiro said to Balast.

"I'm afraid you have to. You guys are going be the reason we succeed, alright?"

"But–" Shiro started,

"Shiro, please, this is important," Kuro interrupted.

Kuro bowed to Balast and then hurried away to the East tower. Before Shiro could object, Balast was already heading into the city.

Shiro shook his head as he started to run toward the West tower, hoping Kuro would be ok.

Balast couldn't help but stare vacantly at the ground as he ran toward Valde Cruz's outer suburbs. His memories constantly bashed him as he saw hundreds of skeletons, broken buildings, and scorch marks on the once powerful and bustling city. Black lines streaked from a point every so often, usually a window, and pointed toward the middle of the street, repainting the picture of endless fires and ceaseless death.

He continued to walk, oddly stepping over the broken cobble of the road until he stopped at a large black hole in the ground. He stopped and took in his surroundings, noting every burnt frame, broken stone, and cursed claw mark on the ground.

His nightmares hadn't gotten every detail correct, but his emotions replicated the memories perfectly. As he gazed down the road as far as he could, he could still see all the way into the city's center, where Aureus's castle lay in ruin. He could still see the mixed faces of fear and malice from the rushing citizens and the absolute horror of everything falling to the Malums.

"It is larger in my nightmares," Inferneous said aloud behind Balast, who flinched in reaction.

Inferneous walked up beside him and looked down into the black pit, waving his right hand over it. The black scar that showed through his clothing was reacting violently, bubbling underneath his skin, and spiking every time he moved.

"You too?" Balast asked, revealing his left arm, which his scar was rolling like waves that got larger as he moved. "I guess it makes sense. This is the point where it happened, and it's even more active with magic," Balast said as he looked up toward the black swirling orb in the sky.

Now that he was closer, he could see that it was exactly above the Aureus castle, and it indeed was growing larger as they watched.

Inferneous lightly tapped Balast on his scarred arm with his, and Balast looked up to see Inferneous smiling.

"I'm glad to be here again with you," he said mirthfully.

He continued forward and jumped over the gaping hole to continue deeper into the city. Balast continued shaking his head, but he couldn't hide his smile as he jumped over the chasm to walk beside Inferneous once again.

The crew was shaken but still aware of where they were as they started to come off the ship. As they survived the crazy captaining that Inferneous performed to kill the Malum, they were all vigilant and cautious of the beach. As Balast observed the crew, he sighed and started counting heads. He jumped and started to float upwards, gaining a better elevation and overall sight of the city, and started to gain some information. He looked to his right and saw Jayce and Zack with 19 other Ninjirates going to the eastward tower.

The bigger the group, the less people should perish… he thought. His stomach churned as he lost sight of them behind a charred building ruin. He looked to his left, noting the whole section of people assigned to Erica and Holdren's group summed up to seventeen people.

The smallest group but the most capable, all in all, they shouldn't lose too many. Balast thought as he finished counting the group going westward. When Balast divided them on the ship, Holdren remembered hearing him mumble to himself about the numbers, saying, "I'll take from Erica's group in order to get some more people for Drathni and Rhinda. Erica and Holdren should be able to handle themselves anyway."

Although Holdren thought this was a good idea, it didn't give him as much confidence as he would have expected.

He snapped out of his thoughts as he came across a blackened and burnt doorway. He crept forward into a building, both swords drawn. He lightly pushed the door, and it slowly cracked and creaked before falling to the ground and splintering into pieces. Everyone in the party turned to look at Holdren, who was surveying the room for any trouble. When he was done, he looked back and shrugged as an apology.

He continued forward down the street, traveling in silence until he looked ahead. He turned to ask if anyone saw what was ahead, but the ninjas that were around him were long gone. He cupped a hand over his mouth to call for them when Erica grabbed his arm from behind and dragged him through a burnt windowsill.

When they settled, Erica held a needle to his throat in complete silence.

Holdren choked a bit, trying to say something, but she pressed it a bit deeper into his skin and hissed, "Stop struggling and be quiet, or die."

Holdren stopped moving, dropped his swords to his sides at the hiss, and they sat there for a second. He was going to break the silence when a dark shadow started to pass over the street, making what little sunlight breaking through from the stormy sky obsolete, rendering them blind for a few seconds until it passed.

As the light started to filter back in, Erica let go of him and crept up to the window, glancing out of it from an angle.

Holdren sat up and scrambled over to the window to see what she saw, but Erica shoved him against the stone wall as soon as he stood.

"What are you doing?!?! Have you never been silent in your life??"

Erica whispered loudly to Holdren. Holdren gained proper footing and whispered back, "Yes, but I haven't been taught to hide from the enemy like this before," he responded, a bit surprised at Erica's roughness.

Erica half-shouted and half-whispered, "I guess you aren't smart enough to realize that taking your enemy by surprise is the best course of action! We don't need any idiotic casualties!"

She carefully peeked her head out of the window, and Holdren saw her eyes widen as she tilted her head up to the sky.

"What does it look like?" Holdren asked Erica.

She looked back at him, then back out the window, and did it once more until Holdren walked over to the window himself to see the horror of the being.

It was jet black and seemingly bigger than the sky itself. A colossal, abyssal falcon that could easily stand as tall as the building they were standing in was soaring above the clouds circling the plaza ahead of them. Every time it passed by it was as if the massive bird simply caused nighttime itself, but instead of seeing tiny sparks of stars, skulls of every variety along with writhing tentacles and multitudes of small wings dotted the creature's feathers. The most terrifying part, though, was that it didn't flap its wings like a normal bird; in fact, it didn't move its wings at all. Caught in perpetual glide, the bird circled impossibly over them, ever so still but ever so menacing.

Holdren shook his head and lowered his gaze from the horror to see a black figure on the opposite side of the road walking in an odd fashion. Holdren instinctively dropped below the windowsill as he realized what he had just seen. Erica did the same at the same time Holdren did, but it still looked like she was going over the image of the flying Malum. He couldn't blame her because he was instinctively trying to forget himself, but that would have to wait. Holdren picked up both his swords and started to breathe at a quick pace, reading himself for battle; when he started to rise, Erica stopped him.

She pulled him down, peeked her head over the windowsill, and pointed out the building behind the humanoid Malum. Holdren peeked over the windowsill and saw that on the other side of the street, inside a ruined house, were three ninjas. They were hiding in the shadows, eyeing the Malum, seemingly ready to fight. One of them made a hand signal in Holdren's direction, and Erica responded with a hand signal.

They backed further into the shadows after Erica's command, and the Malum continued to limp forward, not knowing what had happened. Erica turned to Holdren with a scowl and started, "We should leave."

"What? We just got here. What about the civilians?" Holdren said, peeking his head out of the window and checking their surroundings.

"Holdren, those people are most likely dead already–"

Erica was interrupted by a shrill, piercing scream that made the group tense harder. Holdren crept further inside the house and quickly opened a few doors until he got into the next house, closer to a plaza. He pushed past rubble until he could see through a hole in a boarded-up window that faced the plaza directly. At least thirty Malums were walking around. Most were humanoid, limping around with constantly bubbling black blood for skin and spikes sticking out of their back. Occasionally, there was a dog-like Malum that growled in devilish tones.

As Holdren watched them all closer, he realized that they weren't randomly walking around. They were almost in neat lines coming in and out of a building to the left of the plaza. The building was made out of what looked like thick green glass that was covered in moss and foliage. Holdren looked closer and realized that mostly the humanoid Malums were going into the building. He then looked to the other line and saw each Malum was holding what looked like glowing rose petals. Holdren noticed a faint purple glow coming from inside a greenhouse.

He snapped back to a human woman as she screamed again, "Get off of me!" She screamed, pulling away from three humanoid Malums who were harassing her.

As Holdren watched the woman struggle, he realized that the way she was moving was odd. The woman was holding something, too, holding her arms close to her chest as she turned her back to the Malums attacking her. Holdren watched in horror as the Malums attacked the woman, hitting her over the head with their hands and making her crouch down to the ground in defense.

Holdren realized what she was holding when another shrill cry pierced the air, and the sounds of a baby crying made its way around the plaza. Holdren stood to open the door to the right of the window, but Erica grabbed his arm to stop him.

"Don't. We are outnumbered."

Holdren turned to Erica, and when she saw his face, she flinched backward. This was the first time she saw Holdren truly angry, but before she could recover, he was already out of the door. Holdren opened the door calmly and walked out into the open, passing several Malums, only focused on one thing.

He unsheathed his swords and sliced the first Malum off of the woman, then he kicked the next in the face, sending it rolling to the ground. He struck the third Malum in the face with the butt of his sword, then ran it through with the other.

He leaned down and helped the crying and battered woman up, saying, "Come on, I'll get you out of here."

The woman slowly got up, looking at Holdren with wide, scared eyes. As she stood, she glanced around and saw that the Malums were starting to surround them. She stepped closer to Holdren, fearfully clutching her child as the Malums started to approach. Holdren was prepared to fight the Malums, but as they approached, a seed of doubt sprouted. He remembered that he couldn't just fight; he also had to protect this woman and her child.

"Holdren, run this way!" Erica shouted from inside a nearby ruined building.

Holdren gently nudged the woman. "Run towards the building, now!"

The woman did as he said, and they started to make their way back across the plaza. Holdren sliced through every Malum that came close to the woman or blocked her path, making sure to stick close to her.

By now, the animal-like Malums were taking notice of them.

Holdren screamed, "Duck!" as a Malum hound launched itself at the woman.

The woman ducked, and he swung above her to slice the Malum in half, letting the two pieces fall to the ground as they continued toward the building. As they entered the house, a ninja closed the door behind them, and two more held their backs against it, and Malums started to break it down.

Erica looked queasy as Holdren came through the door and started to pick large pieces of debris off the floor, stacking them near the windows in an attempt to keep the Malums away. As he did so, he yelled, "Does anyone have a portal rune? We need to get this woman and her child to safety–"

He was interrupted as a Malum hound burst through the window and attacked the closest ninja. Holdren swore as he drew his swords again and stabbed both into the hound, pinning it to the ground. Breathing heavily, he yanked his swords out and turned to continue barricading the window.

"Again, does anyone have a portal rune?" he yelled out, finishing the barricade and returning to the Malum, taking one sword out and slicing its head off.

He looked around at the ninjas, and most shook their heads. Holdren swore again as he heard a loud crash in the room across from him and the vicious gurgles and growls of Malums spilling through.

"Everyone follow me; there should be stairs somewhere around here!"

They all funneled into the hall that Holdren started to run down. Holdren smiled as he came up a flight of stairs that looked sturdy enough but also frail enough that he could collapse with a good hit.

"Everyone to the second floor! Find a path to the roof if you can," Holdren ordered.

Holdren stood at the bottom of the stairs, ushering everyone up, when Erica stopped to face him.

"What are you doing?" she asked.

"Helping everyone stay alive. Thanks for helping." Holdren replied sarcastically. "Now, help everyone along; it's better if we can get to a point where we at least have a bit of open space."

"What, you think the roof is a good place to go? You forget there is a giant flying Malum in the sky!"

"What do you want me to do, huh? You want me to give up and die? Is that it?" Holdren snapped.

Erica was taken aback at his harsh response. "Well–"

"No, all you have done since we got here is say we should leave. It looks like you didn't get what Inferneous or Balast told us."

He saw the last mercenary run past him and turned to run up the stairs. Erica followed him closely, and as they were halfway up, the thumping, banging, and growling of the Malums flooded the hall they were just in.

They both hurried to the top of the stairs, but as the Malums started to climb, Holdren raised his hand, gathered his strength, and shakily whispered a spell. A large bolt of energy formed at the palm of his hand. He laughed in surprise and wonder, then fired the bolt at the stairs. The Malums crawling up the stairs fell to the ground floor, and the stairs collapsed on top of them.

"When did you learn to do magic?" Erica asked.

"Inferneous taught me a few spells," Holdren replied as he turned away from the stairs, walking down the hallway of the second floor.

One of the mercenaries waved at him at the end of the hall, so Holdren and Erica headed down to the last door of the hallway and stepped into a small-scale library with a ladder in between the bookshelves. They climbed the ladder and, upon reaching the roof, were met with strong, cold winds. As Holdren and Erica saw that everyone was on the roof, they stepped over to look down at the plaza and saw that most of the Malums were still ferrying the odd rose into the well in front of the greenhouse.

"We need to destroy whatever is in that greenhouse!" Holdren yelled over the now howling winds.

A dark shadow came over the roof, and everyone on it looked up to see the underside of the flying Malum in finer detail.

"But first we have to deal with that."

Chapter 22

Jayce walked out into the middle of the street, battleaxe drawn and ready for any Malum encounter. But there was none. The rest of his troupe came around the corner and filled the street, making sure that anything that popped out at them couldn't get past them. Zack ran and stood next to Jayce, gripping his metal wand tightly as if it were a cherished item rather than a potential weapon.

"Keep your eyes out for anything suspicious; if you spot a lot of them, alert the others quietly so we can get a surprise attack ready," Jayce said, looking to his left and right, making sure everyone heard him. "Alright, let's move forward."

They all started to move forward cautiously, observing every windowsill, broken door frame, and rooftop, making sure there were no surprise attacks from any direction. There were a few men who turned around, walking backward slowly, making sure there were no surprises from behind as they continued forward down the street. A good five minutes down the road, Jayce started to relax, holstering his battleaxe over his shoulder, but as he continued into the empty street, he still held onto the hilt of his sword.

There isn't a way that we don't come across a Malum in this city... his thoughts were interrupted by a voice, making him jump and turn to his right.

"Jayce?" Zack tapped Jayce on the arm while continuing to survey their surroundings.

"Yeah?" Jayce responded.

"What did you think of what Balast said?"

"About what Zack?" Jayce said, looking down the road and noticing a curve to the left.

"You would die to protect me?"

Jayce turned his head and saw that Zack was shaking all over.

Jayce turned and grabbed his shoulder, looked Zack in the eye, and said, "Yes, I would."

Jayce continued down the road as he continued to say, "All of us would…but what Balast asked wasn't just a question on what you would do if we died, but a question of what you believe in Zack."

"What do you mean?" Zack said as Jayce moved to the left to slowly scale forward along the wall.

"When you asked the question 'what if everyone dies,' it implied that you didn't believe in the cause that we are fighting for."

Jayce kicked open a burnt wooden door, peered inside the house, and came back out, saying, "And if you don't believe in fighting for Magia, it's possible that you could be a burden to us. That's just common sense, but I think that Balast also wanted to instill something in you. As his apprentice and all…if you don't believe in your crew and fighting for Magia, you are definitely unfit to be an apprentice of one of its protectors."

Zack continued behind Jayce, thinking over what he said.

Jayce started again, though not finished. "In truth, though, it's a sentiment that all of us struggled or still struggle with; the only thing that really matters is that we try. In my personal opinion." Jayce turned to Zack and said, "We can do anything, especially with those crazy old wizards on our side."

Zack smiled, shaking his head, and Jayce smiled back. He turned forward and stopped dead in his tracks as he noticed the end of the street ended in a plaza, but he wasn't grimacing because of the city street plan. In front of a fountain filled with what looked like a black soup of human body parts floating inside it, there was a large set of armor. At least four feet taller than everyone in their group, it was not armor any of them would even be able to lift from the looks of it. It looked like it would tightly fit something as big as the Malum that attacked them at the charred remains of Castillus Grex, but less thick and hollow. The armor seemed to absorb light itself and was covered in small spikes. The large helmet on the Malum's head had four horns sprouting out of the crest of the helmet and intertwining into the air to create a deadly spike that, by just looking at it, you would get stabbed.

"Malum!" Jayce yelled out, mistaking the armor for a large still monster. "Advance slowly! We don't know if this is an ambush or not."

The group grunted in approval and started to walk cautiously toward the still-supposed Malum. When they reached and entered the plaza, Jayce realized that the armor was not animated by anything. He stepped up to it, signaling the others to spread out. He stared upwards under the large helmet. The armor was as black on the inside as it was on the outside, maybe darker.

He stepped closer, seeing the spiky texture of the armor, and reached out to touch it when a booming voice echoed, "Hast thou brought thyselves as sacrifice? How the weak hast fallen further…"

Jayce hurriedly backed up as the suit of armor slowly started to expand, growing in height and width until the slits between the helmet were filled with an inky, black substance and shining purple, slitted eyes.

It took a step toward Jayce and knelt down to his level. "Doth freedom hold thy soul, yet crave the cell of eternity? Or hast thou come in search for our monstrous arcaneness?"

Jayce's eyes widened as he stepped back further, whispering to himself, "It can talk."

"Correct." The Malum stood gazing at the whole group like they were sheep ready for slaughter.

It raised its hands to the sky, and a black void opened above its helmet's crest. The being reached inside of the portal, retrieving a gigantic blade that had a gaping hole in the center and its hilt covered in large spikes that pierced the Malum's skin, causing the black liquid to spill over the blade. As it did, the hole in the center of the blade grew covered with blood and a large, slitted eyeball formed in the center, blinking slowly as the Malum slammed the sword into the cracked stone of the road.

"Thou feeble souls, my sword thou shalt not face. Thy spirit shall face the temptation of fate," the Malum said, letting the sword stand on its own. "The decision is yours now, mortals."

Jayce looked back and made sure that everyone was accounted for, then raised his great axe up and stared into the Malum's eyes as he made his demands. "We don't have to fight if you free the humans you have captive."

His demands were backed up by a persistent cry from the rest of the group to agree. Jayce started to smile, confident that the Malum would back down.

"Thou shall forever hold thy peace," the Malum said as it stood.

Jayce watched it arise, and as it did, it swung its right hand, sending Jayce to lie in the burnt brick wall of the house behind him. Immediately, the whole group rushed the Malum, weapons drawn. The Malum clenched its metal greaves and threw punch after punch, sending the mercenaries flying. Zack ran to Jayce, who was now on the ground, bleeding from the mouth. Zack shook him profusely, and Jayce stood up quickly, realizing what was happening.

"Jayce, this Malum is beating us with only his fists; we should go–" Zack tried.

"Don't. Don't say those words. We just got started."

Jayce picked up his sword, sheathed it, then drew his battleaxe and ran towards the Malum, jumping into the air. With his speed, he sliced his battleaxe into the separated part of the Malum's armor between its arm and wrist in two clean strokes. Two pieces of the armor fell to the ground, clanking with hard thuds. Jayce grew hopeful and raised his battleaxe to swing again, but the Malum lashed out and landed a kick to Jayce's side, sending him flying into another building. Zack watched as Jayce fell to the ground again, then helped him up.

Jayce was bleeding from both nostrils, and as he wiped the blood away, Zack could see a large bruise forming on his cheek. Jayce, grabbing his side, winced and continued back toward the Malum without a second thought. Zack watched Jayce grab a mercenary's arm and pick him up, yelling something about persistence, and then start heading toward the Malum.

He picked up another mercenary saying the same thing. Then, all three of them rushed forward to attack. The first mercenary used his sword to slice at the shin guard of the Malum as the second went for the other leg. Jayce jumped onto the Malum and swung his battleaxe at the crevice between its legs. He successfully severed one leg before being grabbed by Malum's right hand and thrown back where Zack was standing. Jayce sat up, coughing and spitting out a wad of blood, to see the Malum's limbs float back to the main body and reattach themselves. He cursed as he stood, grunting in frustration and pain. All of their group was scattered around the plaza, haplessly knocked out or too hurt to move.

"Now cometh the hour for thy final breath," the Malum said, picking up the nearest mercenary by his head.

Zack and Jayce watched in horror as the Malum started to squeeze the mercenary's head. His screams started to echo off the houses as Jayce started limping forward. "Stop! Don't you dare!" He tried to run but couldn't. He held his arm to his side, wincing in pain.

Jayce looked up, and the Malum had turned to Jayce and Zack with the mercenary's face turned in their direction.

"This doth present the thing thy heart did seek."

Zack sank to the floor, covered his ears, and closed his eyes as Jayce witnessed the Malum squish the mercenary's head and drop his lifeless body to the ground. Jayce screamed, as yellow runes appeared flaring brightly on his face as he stormed the Malum. As he got closer, the Malum stepped back, slightly surprised. This allowed Jayce to get close and land a blow to the Malum's breastplate.

His battleaxe glowed bright orange and sliced into the armor as the Malum stepped back, leaving a large rip in the armor that the Malum didn't or couldn't heal straight.

Jayce landed on the ground and continued his assault, trying to catch the Malum's shin guards, but stopped when he heard the groans of the men around him grow into cries of pain.

He looked around and saw lines of yellow-looking dust coming off the men and filtering directly to him, fueling his rage and magic. Instantly, his power dissipated, and the runes faded off his face as he deactivated his magic, wincing with a retractive pain. The Malum rushed forward, eager to take advantage of the opportunity. As it reared to send Jayce flying with a kick, it instead met a green bubble of magic. The bubble shattered as its kick connected, but behind it, no human presented themselves.

"Thou run from thy own fate. Show thyself; thy destiny awaits," the Malum called, looking around.

Jayce and Zack were hiding in an alleyway behind the Malum, crouched low in the shadows watching.

Zack, panicking, asked, "Jayce, what do we do? If it can't find us, it's most likely going to start killing the rest of the group, and we can't take it by ourselves…"

"Don't give up yet, we can do this! I think I have a plan."

Jayce peeked out into the street and saw that there was no Malum in sight. He scanned the perimeter carefully, but he saw nothing but unconscious people and the dark fountain.

"When I say run, you go to the biggest building in the plaza, alright?" Jayce said to Zack, still observing the plaza.

Zack nodded, and Jayce suddenly ran out into the open.

Before he got halfway to the fountain, the Malum dropped seemingly from the sky behind him, sending him to the ground just from the sheer shockwaves sent by its landing on the ground. Zack gasped but patiently waited as he saw Jayce get up and start running toward where they first entered the plaza.

"Thy destiny awaits!" The Malum called out to Jayce as it caught up in only two strides to Jayce.

"Now!" Jayce yelled out as he reached under his armor and pulled out a piece of parchment paper with a glowing blue rune on it.

Glowing yellow runes appeared on his face again, and the paper set aflame, turning to dust in his hand. The runes on Jayce's face then turned blue, and he smiled as he stopped in front of the oncoming Malum. Jayce's change in demeanor didn't faze the Malum.

Instead, it rushed forward and stomped on Jayce as hard as it could. As it removed its foot, it didn't see a splattered mess of human remains; it saw only the crumbling pavement. The Malum lurched forward as a searing pain bloomed from its back; turning around to see what caused it, it saw Jayce starting to fall back to the ground with a smirk on his face.

"Tricks doth thy play, matters not," the Malum said, rushing toward Jayce again.

Jayce nodded, and a portal opened behind him. As he stepped back into it, another portal opened at the opposite end of the plaza on the steps of the largest house. The house was taking up at least three spaces of a normal house and had a good three floors to it, perfect for the plan Jayce had in mind.

"Follow me; I have a destiny to reap," Jayce said, quickly stepping inside the house through the massive double door that was the entrance.

The Malum followed in hot pursuit and didn't bother to stop for the front wall of the house. It burst through the wall and was immediately assaulted in the shins by Jayce. The slashes burned, but the Malum didn't care to find out where Jayce was. Instead, it resorted to destroying the center of the mansion so it could get enough room to move properly. It moved and swung back and forth, making a circular hole through all three floors with a good ten-foot radius around itself. When it stopped, the building was a mess. Wood was mostly on the ground, the floor piling up around the Malum's feet.

Nothing showed itself, so the Malum screeched, "Thy destiny is ready to be sown! Show thyself!"

"Up here!" Jayce said, stepping to the edge of the roof.

The Malum's head snapped up to see Jayce leap from the roof, the runes covering his face glowing orange now. The Malum reared back, ready to blow Jayce out of the sky, when it felt its legs blown from underneath itself. Out of the corner of its eye, it saw a figure holding its hand out, casting a barrier spell into its legs and pushing them from under it. As it fell to the ground, the only place to look was up, and it saw Jayce come down right at its neck level. Jayce swung as hard as he could and saw a flash of purple lightning flash by his face as his battleaxe connected with the Malum flesh between the cracks of the armor. There was a flash of white and yellow, and Jayce felt his battleaxe sever through what remained of the Malum's neck.

Breathing heavily, Jayce stood, leaving his axe in the wood between the now splintered wooden panels. He stepped back from the Malum and looked up to the sky through the three floors of the house, then down to Zack, still standing to the side of the Malum, hands outstretched from the spell he cast. When Zack's eye met Jayce's, he stood straight and started to smile warily.

Jayce removed his battleaxe from the floor and slung it over his back as he continued to the broken entrance of the house. Zack followed him out into the courtyard. Jayce's smile dropped when he remembered that their whole group had basically been beaten within inches of their lives. He hurried out of the building and down the stairs worried for his men, Zack closely following him. As he descended, he grew relieved seeing his men grouped at the bottom of the stairs. They turned to him and raised a weak cheer in celebration.

Jayce continued down and yelled over the crew's exclamations, "Is everyone ok? Anyone need a healer?"

Every person apart of their group had bruises and cuts all over their bodies. Some even had broken bones, but none raised their hand. Jayce reached into his armor once again to retrieve another parchment paper with glowing blue runes, but this time he let it drop to the ground. As soon as it hit the stones, the parchment was shredded to pieces, sparked with an arc of blue lightning, and then swirled into a human-sized portal.

"OK, all of you just filter through this portal. Healing is on the other side."

Some protested with groans, but Jayce continued, "I have eyes. You can't be fine after taking a beating from a Malum of that caliber. Now line up to get into the portal."

The group quelled their protests and started to filter into the portal as Zack reached the bottom of the stairs. He stood by Jayce and watched the injured crew step through the portal.

"Zack, come with me; we need to check out this fountain," Jayce said, walking around the portal towards the intricately carved stone of the fountain.

Jayce and Zack stepped up to the edge and gazed at the horror of the fountain. The pitch-black liquid swirled towards the center and forced itself upon the intricately carved stone, climbing its way up the upper level where usually the water would flow out. The liquid seemed to be thickest at the bottom level, where it pooled until it was only inches away from overflowing.

"Wow," Jayce said in disgust. "I–don't know what to think of this mess."

He stared at the pillar in the center of the fountain and followed it down to its base, thinking whether he should destroy it or not.

When he looked at the liquid, he glimpsed a flash of white and gagged when he saw it. "Was that—"

"Those were bones," Zack said, shaking his head. "I don't think anyone survived here. We should destroy this and regroup with the others."

"Yeah," Jayce said, raising his axe. Grunting, he swung his axe, striking the center of the fountain.

It cracked and then crumbled into the black pool, sinking until it was fully submerged. A scream sounded behind Jayce as Zack noticed something in the dark water. A large round object pulsed a gradient of dark purple as it surfaced. Zack's mind shattered to a thousand different thoughts, all panicked, as he realized that he and Jayce had not come close to finishing either of the Malums.

"Get down!!" Jayce screamed, pulling Zack to the ground as a large black object passed over them.

When they stood, Zack looked ahead of him and saw the remains of all of the men who hadn't gone through the portal. They had been cut cleanly in half, leaving only Jayce and Zack alive. Zack didn't feel Jayce's hand shaking him, but he heard his words.

"We can knock it down again! Do the same thing you did last time–"

They were both sent flying as the Malum swiped its claws at them, roaring in anger.

Zack groaned as he came to. He started to push himself up but faltered as a pain in his chest blossomed. He staggered and fell but continued to rise, pushing through the pain.

As he stood clutching his side, his vision focused on seeing the Malum in its full breadth. It had lost all of its armor except for its spiked helmet, its body now just viscous liquid mixed with dark shadows standing in the center of the plaza. It looked like the Malum had just been summoned from hell; its eyes were bright red, pulsing with audible thump. The Malum looked up towards the sky and slowly lowered its head until Zack was in its sights, making sure to brandish its previously unseen mouth, bristling with fangs longer than any blade.

Zack took a step back, looking around until he saw Jayce; his forehead gashed, and he stopped. Jayce wasn't moving, and Zack couldn't tell, but it looked like he wasn't breathing either. Zack's breathing started to get faster and faster as his thoughts scrambled for an answer, a reason for why they forgot the most important thing about a Malum.

Those days of training really led to this? All of that preparation…to just forget to destroy the Malum's heart?

His eyes grew wide as he realized that the Malum was now only five feet away from him. Its footsteps were no longer making any sound because there was nothing making contact with the ground. Zack raised his eyes to the Malum's face, which was now smiling in hideous mirth, smiling at Zacks's helplessness. At that moment, a thought pierced Zack's mind and delved into his heart and soul.

This is what Balast meant. All his allies are dead, gone, or unconscious, with no hope for survival and one last, lonely stand. One question showed through his mind as he stared at the Malum looming over him.

Will you?

It echoed back and forth in the seconds of time he stared death in the face, reverberating across his whole body, across everything that mattered. Zack looked down, stepped forward, and drew his wand, a lightning sword sparking from the action. The Malum laughed as it stepped back, getting ready to enjoy its electrified meal.

Then the silence snapped, and the Malum screeched as it careened towards Zack.

Zack broke into a run towards the Malum, and before it came down on him, he yelled out, letting the air know, "I WILL!"

His sword sparked out as the Malum crushed him under its weight, slamming, slashing, and ripping.

Erica would have had more solace facing a hoard of at least human-like beings but was utterly terrified of what she was witnessing in the moment. She watched in fear as the sky blacked out into a mass of dark matter that had purple lightning flicker across it as black tentacles with sharp points descended down to them.

Caught by surprise, a ninja behind her suddenly flew into the air as a tentacle quickly wrapped around him and pulled him into the sky. Erica turned around to see that it wasn't only one person that got caught. Multiple tendrils of sharp, inky darkness had descended and quickly started to entangle most of the other people on the rooftop.

Holden yelled out as a tentacle almost took him up, but he acted quickly, putting his swords between the tentacles and his armor so as it constricted, it severed itself on the blade. He fell to the rooftop with the writhing piece of Malum and stomped on it for good measure before he turned and dashed for the woman holding her child. He watched as the tentacle spiraled down towards her and knew he wasn't going to reach her.

He planted his feet and threw the sword in his right hand, yelling out, "Ridituis!" as he did so. His sword glowed orange hue, and suddenly, he held both his swords in the air above the woman. He spun in the air, sliced the tentacle up and dropped back to the roof with the tentacle into four different prices. The woman crouched down and shielded her baby as Holdren landed, but he reassured her by holding a hand on her back.

"Let's go back down; we can find you someplace to hide," he said, gesturing toward the ladder. Erica stopped him as she held out a piece of parchment paper with blue runes on it. She looked away as Holdren looked up at her furiously, then snatched the spell out of her hands and activated it. The woman hurriedly dashed into the portal, and as it closed, Holdren stood and brushed past Erica, looking up at the Malum and questioning how to take it down. Erica looked behind, then saw their crew struggle against the tentacles, failing miserably, and she noticed the ladder down into the building was moving erratically, signaling that they were completely surrounded.

"Holdren!" Erica yelled out to him, pulling his arm back from the ledge of the roof. "We have to get out of here! Half of our men are captured by that thing. We should wait for Balast and Inferneous to–"

"No!" Holdren yelled back. He stepped toward Erica with anger, annoyance, and a third emotion Erica couldn't capture in the moment.

"What happened to the Erica, who was willing to take on the world for her men? What happened to the Erica, who fought one of the two most powerful wizards in hand-to-hand combat despite knowing she couldn't win?"

He shook his head, then looked up at the Malum, saw the men slowly absorbed into the skin of the Malum, and grimaced.

He looked back down at Erica, unsheathed his sword, and handed it to her. "Just because you are in the care of someone more powerful than you doesn't mean you are completely useless. Now I am going to get captured by the Malum, and when I yell out, you need to say 'Libi,' ok?"

He didn't wait for her to respond as he started to yell at the Malums above them. "Over here! Give back our men!" He ran over to the ladder into the house and kicked it so it no longer rested on the hatch to the rooftop. The Malums below hissed in defiance, but Holdren didn't mind them. His chance had come. A particularly large tentacle was spiraling down to the roof, and Holdren ran to the back of the building. He got to its edge and looked to the next building, noting it was too far for him to even attempt to jump to.

He turned around with his sword facing the tentacle, smiled and yelled, "Get ready to throw!"

Erica was following him from a distance, dodging smaller tentacles and looking for a proper opening. She acknowledged Holdren's cry by backing up and planting her feet, her arms behind her, readying for the throw.

Holdren looked up to the Malum and said under his breath, "Curse you," and jumped off the building.

Erica lost concentration for a moment as she watched Holdren fall out of view, but as she saw the tentacle go after him and the flying Malum dip down and reveal its back to her, she didn't hesitate. She grunted loudly as she sent the sword flying in an arc. Erica's heart dropped when she saw how hard she threw it despite its weight. The sword flew high over the Malum, and she couldn't see if it had landed because the Malum had started to rise back up into the sky. Erica saw that Holdren was being raised into the air by the tentacle that was chasing him.

A quick breath of relief escaped Erica, but she didn't relish in it because she knew she had to free him before the Malum absorbed him into itself. Holdren's left arm and sword were pinned to his side as the Malum squeezed him so hard he felt his bones grind together. He cried out in pain, clawing at the tentacle with his free right hand until he looked up and saw Erica moving.

Erica reached into her gi and pulled out a hand axe, yelling out, "Holdren!" She then threw the axe at him, and he caught it by the very edge, almost dropping it. Instead of letting it drop, he used the momentum to slice the tentacle around his left arm, freeing him to cut the part of the tentacle holding on to him.

He fell down to the roof once again, landing on his feet, but as he landed, his ankle bent in a way that guaranteed pain. Erica knelt down, wrapped his arm around her neck, and lifted him up to his good leg.

"Say it now," Holdren said through grunts of pain as they dodged the Malum's tentacles, actively trying to catch them.

"What was the word again?" Erica said, taking them back down to the ground as a tentacle swiped at them.

She then remembered just as Holdren yelled it out and said in unison, "Libi!"

A bright orange light that appeared in front of Erica zipped past and temporarily blinded her.

When Erica opened her eyes, she could barely keep them open as the raging wind blew against them. She felt Holdren rise, and as he did, she raised her hand to shield her eyes from the wind. She saw him with a hand in front of his eyes reaching toward her, his gaze beckoning something more of her. His eyes glowed a dark orange color as she grabbed his hand, and they started to trek across the back of the Malum. As Erica looked ahead, she saw that there was a purple light emanating from somewhere on the Malum in front of them. They were making good progress when Erica suddenly realized that she was now starting to walk uphill. When she looked behind her, she saw almost half of Valde Cruz.

"We need to hurry!" Holdren said, picking up the pace even though his ankle was visibly swelling.

The ground suddenly lurched as the Malum flapped its wing once, almost sending Holdren and Erica back down to Valde Cruz. They climbed and climbed until they both stood above a large, pulsing purple orb barely under the black tar of the Malum's skin. As they both stared at it, the same question came into their minds.

Looking back down at the ground and then at Holdren, Erica asked, "How are we going to get down? Is this thing just going to dissipate once we kill it?"

Holdren stared hard at the Malum core and shook his head.

"Doesn't matter," Holdren said, unsheathing his sword, cutting through the skin of the Malum. It receded to reveal the black and purple orb firmly seated in the Malum. He raised his sword to pierce it when Erica stopped him.

"What about the men? They are still being held in the Malum's body! We can't just–"

"Erica!" Holdren said, pulling the sword away from her. "This was never about our survival. This wasn't even about the survival of the men."

He grabbed her hand as he looked her in the eye, then put the sword in her hands as he said, "This is for everyone who doesn't know what is happening here. For the innocent, hell, even for the worst people out there. I know you would have died for less in the High Shadow Ninja clan, but now we have a definite purpose right now."

They both shifted their stance as the Malum flapped its wings once more, breaking through the clouds and allowing them to see nothing but the beauty of the sun's rays bouncing off the clouds in the intended mystical majesty of Magia. Holdren looked out at the scenery and then back at Erica, who had a single tear rolling down her face as she looked down at the sword in her hand.

Holdren grabbed the sword's hilt right under Erica's hand. She looked at him, and he looked back. They nodded once, raising the sword as high as they could, and then pierced the Malum's heart. As the sword pierced the heart, they had to push harder, as it only made it through the first layer. They both screamed out in pain, anguish and fear as the sword broke through the final layer, exploding outwards. The Malum jerked backwards and promptly started to separate into balls of Malum flesh, which started to fall to the ground.

Erica was barely awake as she passed the clouds, but once she was clear of them, she started to scream in panic. After a few more seconds, she lost her breath and flipped in midair to see her incoming doom. The ground was approaching slower than she would have thought, but it was still terrifying; she was free-falling without a plan. She was about to resign herself when a large dark chunk of Malum flesh passed by her. Inside was one of her men, conscious and struggling to free himself from it. She looked around her and saw that in every fifth flesh ball, there was one of her men inside, and they all were awake and struggling.

She shook her head and moved her arms and legs together so she could properly control herself midair. She leaned to her left and grabbed the arm of her soldier, who, in shock, yelled out in fear. Once he saw Erica, he cried out in recognition. Erica wasn't paying attention to him, though; she was already locked on to another one of her men, and she was leaning towards them, dragging the man she was holding onto with her.

The Malum flesh connected, bringing the two men together. They saw each other, then looked at Erica, and immediately started to lean with her to the next man. She had gathered five men as they continued to fall, and she was working on the sixth when she saw Holdren flying through the air, doing the same as Erica. He only had two people, but Erica's determination was solidified as she saw him and then she looked down.

The Malum flesh broke most of her fall, and the men were freed as the flesh broke apart once again as they hit the roof of the greenhouse. Some of the glass panes shattered and fell through, taking some men with them, but Erica bounced off the Malum flesh and landed on the edge of the building.

She coughed up blood, rolling to her side in pain. She opened her eyes and quickly threw herself to the side just before a large chunk of Malum flesh smashed through the glass she was just lying on.

As she was running, she saw Holdren falling. His trajectory was set just in front of her, but he had nothing to break his fall. In front of Erica, there was also nothing but the edge of the building. Her eyes widened as she quickened her pace, locked on the edge of the building, determined to catch him. She looked back up but didn't see Holdren as he was falling too fast for her to follow, she dived in a desperate attempt and just as she reached the edge her hand brushed Holdren's, then she watched him fall down to his death.

Zack was sure that it would have hurt to be smashed to bits and pieces, but it looked like it wasn't as painful as he had thought it would be. He opened his eyes slowly, removing his hands from in front of his face to see why he hadn't been scattered across the ground. He was shocked to see that the Malum was suspended in front of him, seemingly paused as if time wasn't passing for it. When Zack looked around, he noticed that the clouds weren't moving.

"I'm glad you got to truly understand what I meant," Zack heard a voice say. He turned around just as Balast embraced him, hugging him tightly. He furiously hugged him back, breaking down in Balast's arms.

They stood there for a few minutes until Zack recomposed himself. He looked up to Balast and saw his tired eyes pulsing with a teal glow. Zack stepped back from him and asked, "It happened again."

Balast looked mournfully to the right, and his demeanor changed from a soft, happy smile to a teary wail of despair. Zack followed Balast's gaze and saw himself on the ground. He was torn to shreds, barely recognizable, smothered with his own blood, which painted the ground around him.

Zack's attention snapped back to focus on Balast, who was on his knees, hands covering his face, tears streaming down his cheeks. Zack stepped forward shakily and touched Balast on the shoulder.

"Balast?"

Balast stood abruptly, wiped his nose, and then thrust his hands in front of him; blue and teal runes covered his arms as he whispered multiple spell incantations. He stopped, looking at the living Zack, and with a determined look in his eyes, he said, "Don't worry, you won't have seen me like this. I won't let this happen to you again."

He pulled his sleeves up, revealing runes carved into his skin, which were scabbed over and solidified. He crossed his arms, then pulled them apart, and three orbs appeared in front of him: red, black, white, and grey. A blue flash blinded Zack, and suddenly, he was back in front of the Malum. It all came flooding back to him, and he started to panic. Zacks's breathing started to get faster and faster, and his thoughts scrambled for an answer, a reason why they forgot the most important thing about a Malum.

Those days of training really led to this?

All of the preparation for nothing. His eyes grew wide as he realized that the Malum was now only five feet away from him. Its footsteps were no longer making any sound because there was nothing making contact with the ground. Zack raised his eyes to the Malum's face, which was now smiling in hideous mirth, smiling at Zack's helplessness. At that moment, a thought pierced Zack's mind and delved into his heart and soul.

This is what Balast meant. All his allies are dead, gone, or unconscious, with no hope for survival and one last lonely stand. One question showed through his mind as he stared at the Malum looming over him.

Will you?

It echoed back and forth in the seconds of time he stared death in the face, reverberating across his whole body, across everything that mattered.

Zack looked down, stepped forward, and drew his wand, a lightning sword sparking from the action. The Malum laughed as it stepped back, getting ready to enjoy its electrified meal.

Then the silence snapped, and the Malum screeched as it careened towards Zack. Zack broke into a run towards the Malum, and before it came down on him, he yelled out, letting the air know,

"I WILL!"

Another larger arc of electricity flew past Zack as he charged, and a large gust of wind blew past him, striking the monster down.

Balast appeared in front of Zack and started to wave his hands in different directions, dictating where the wind should go. The Malum was suddenly suspended in midair, being thrown around by the magical wind Balast was conjuring.

Balast stopped using his left hand and instead started to prepare another spell that manifested itself in the form of a toxic green ball that bubbled and produced green smoke in the palm of his left hand. He split his focus between his hands until the Malum got thrown close enough to the ground that it dug its claws into the stones. Contorting with pain and strength, the Malum buried its claws into the sides of the tower and flung them at Balast in a desperate attempt to free itself. Balast stopped throwing the Malum around with wind magic and walked toward the Malum, seemingly not needing to dodge because none of the rocks even remotely hit him, landing on either side of him or breaking into smaller pieces before they hit their mark.

He ran forward, swiping his right arm downward, causing the wind to slam the Malum to the ground. He got up close to the Malum and slammed the green ball directly into the Malum's helmet. The Malum screamed in pain and lashed out at Balast, but the time mage dodged flawlessly, locked onto the Malum's helmet, watching it suffer. He extended his arms and pulled them apart, and with magical force, he started to tear the Malum in half from the inside out. Like another curtain, the Malum was ripped open, screaming and wailing in excruciation.

Balast stopped when there was a hole large enough to fit a person inside of the Malum, then slowly turned and started to walk back to Zack. The Malum collapsed, still writhing in pain when Balast reached Zack.

Zack found that in watching Balast kill this Malum, he had never seen Balast really try to destroy something. Even when he saw Balast fight against Inferneous, it wasn't like the hatred that drove him now. When Balast stopped in front of him, Zack tried to compare his fear to the Malum, that gut-wrenching, nauseating fear he felt before. He thought back to that moment and forgot it completely. As Balast stood in front of him, he felt his face grow numb, and his limbs turned to stone as Balast's fist clenched and unclenched to the exact rhythm of his heartbeat. At that moment, he found that he would rather face the Malum again than stand in front of Balast.

"My wand," Balast said, extending his hand.

Zack slowly dropped the metal rod into Balast's hands.

Balast silently walked back to the Malum as his wand started to disintegrate in his hand. The particles of the wand sparkled in the air, but instead of floating away, they hovered right over Balast's hand, following him closely. Midway between Zack and the Malum Balast stopped.

"Do you wish for mercy?"

The Malum heaved its answer, "You..doth dare... Me to ask... For thy mercy?"

Balast's eyes narrowed at the Malum.

"Yes, or no?"

The Malum managed to stand up one more time and bellow in Balast's face, "You are no greater than I, mortal! You—"

"Good," Balast said, facing his open palm toward the Malum.

The floating dust of his wand floated toward the Malum and into its skin, silencing the Malum. The Malum stepped back, crumpling into a ball, then started screaming again, long and loud heaves hinting to the unfathomable amounts of torture it was going through. Spikes formed and melted off the Malum as Balast watched it with a cold gaze.

A smirk slowly appeared on Balast's face as the Malum stopped struggling, fell to the ground, and exploded. Malum flesh flew high into the air, splattering on almost every surface and coating the five-foot area around it with black blood. Balast magically cleaned himself as he walked over to Jayce, who was lying on the ground, and put a hand on his neck. He had started to glow white, and as Zack got there, Jayce sat and gasped awake.

Zack kneeled down to help Jayce sit up as he started to breathe and panicked erratically.

"What happened–?" Jayce looked around and saw the remains of the Malum all around him, the remains of the men who were in his group, and then Balast's blank face.

Jayce stood, turning to face the aftermath of the battle, and asked, "How many men made it to Drathni and Rhinda?"

Balast glanced to the right as if something or someone had appeared there, then looked back at Jayce. "Eight."

Jayce walked forward and retrieved his battleaxe, slinging it over his shoulder. Then, he grabbed a hand axe from the ground. He remembered how they all wanted to stay initially, and he shook his head slowly.

The portal was still open, swirling with blue electricity, and as he stared into it, he couldn't help but ask, "Balast?"

Balast turned to him and replied, "Yes?"

"Was it worth it?"

Balast looked down at the ground and then back to Jayce's face, solemn in the familiarity of the feeling and the gruesome sight of the battlefield.

Balast could only match his gaze and reply, "It's what we make of it."

Jayce looked away from Balast, shaking his head once more as he entered the portal. He was greeted by the fresh spray of ocean water mixed with the smell of blood. There were a few sheets spread around in rows; some had blood spatters over them, but all were empty. He looked up to see Drathni and Rhinda sending one of his men through a portal. Behind them were seven of his other men with different bandages covering them.

I guess I'll have to tell them what happened… Jayce thought as he walked toward the group.

As Holdren fell to the ground, he couldn't help but smile at the thought of his whole life. From unsuccessful gladiator to a father figure and co-savior of the world? An interesting fate he would never have thought up. An interesting fate that he wouldn't have thought was in store for him. He embraced the notion with grace and waited for the inevitable.

Suddenly, he was jerked upward. He felt a hand grab his ankle, and a familiar warmth radiated from it. Suddenly, he was flying upward instead of spiraling downwards.

"I didn't know you could fly!" Holdren heard a familiar voice exclaim; he strained his neck and looked up to see Inferneous, covered in magical armor made from his token flames, smiling down at him.

"I didn't know either!" Holdren replied as Inferneous flew back to the greenhouse rooftop.

"Well, that was a terrible first try; watch your head," Inferneous said as he slowly set Holdren down on the roof and landed next to him.

Holdren tried to stand but fell, leaning on his arm. Inferneous put out a hand to him, and Holdren nodded in thanks as he stood on his good foot.

He stumbled once again as Erica ran over and wrapped her arms around him, hugging him so tight that the breath was forced out of his lungs.

"Whoa!" Holdren said as he hugged her back to regain his balance.

He looked down at Erica, who was silently sobbing into his shoulder, and sighed, looking around for the rest of the men. He saw the broken glass and then heard the unsheathing of weapons as the men who had survived the fall were preparing to fight the Malums inside the greenhouse.

He looked to Inferneous and asked, "How many survived?"

"All but four. Some are injured, so we need to get down there," Inferneous said, walking to the edge of the glass to look down on the situation the men were in.

Erica let go of Holdren, took a deep breath, leaned down next to Inferneous, and asked, "What's the plan for getting down there?"

She looked toward Inferneous, and the crown of flames on his head glowed brightly as he turned and grinned at Erica.

"Follow my lead."

Inferneous stood up and walked between Holdren and Erica; as he did, tendrils of his flames wrapped around them until they each had a fiery outline about them.

Inferneous looked at each of them and said, "Now jump!"

They all jumped off into the greenhouse, and instead of falling normally, the flames around them burned bright, letting them descend to the ground gradually enough for even Holdren to land on his good foot.

As soon as they touched the ground, they were bombarded with Malums.

Two humanoid Malums immediately grabbed Holdren and Erica as they landed. Inferneous waved his hand, and a wave of fire blew around the room, disintegrating the Malums and making the glass shake.

As they looked around, they realized that the greenhouse was unusually dark for a building made with glass panes for walls. The building's interior wasn't anything too uncommon: shelves lined with wilted potted plants, pots of dirt lined against the walls, and a counter near the front for recreational use.

"Where are my men?" Erica asked, pacing around the counters and tracing the walls.

"Over here!" Holdren said, waving his hand in his direction as he pushed away debris in front of a wooden door at the back of the greenhouse.

The back wall was made out of a dark stone Inferneous didn't recognize until he slowly walked forward and touched it. Instead of a cold, smooth surface, his hand melted through the wall into a warm black liquid, making Inferneous yank back his hand.

"Holdren! Erica! Wait!" he tried to call out to them as they opened the door and stepped through.

As Inferneous stepped to the doorway, he saw a purple light flash its outline, and then the door closed by itself. He didn't waste any time as he kicked the door down with a flame-wreathed foot. The walls cried out as he stepped inside the room.

He wrinkled his nose as he entered. The smell itself could kill any regular person, but it wasn't the only danger the room had to offer. Inferneous gazed at the disgusting evil of the room, multiple rotting corpses scattered around the floor, seemingly interwoven between strange roots.

His eyes trailed down the roots as he recognized a pattern of small purple flowers on each corpse and branch. They all trailed to a meeting point right at the back of the room. Sprouting out of the wall, on top of a small hill of bodies, was a large Lifeweed blossom. It glowed so deep purple that as Inferneous got closer, the room seemed to darken instead of brightening. Also, as he got closer, he realized that the nearer to the flower, the less decayed the corpses seemed.

He saw Holdren and Erica lying unconscious in front of the flower, their faces pale and gaunt. Inferneous stepped forward to carefully inspect them and winced as he felt the all too familiar tug of magic being drained from his body.

He looked at the flower, then back at Holdren and Erica. He placed his hand in front of their face and felt a small wind coming from each of them, making each of his steps surer as he stepped over plant and human alike. As he stood up and continued toward the flower, he saw more half-dead ninjas and mercenaries strewn about, weapons drawn, but their arms too weak to lift them towards the flower.

Inferneous stepped towards the life weed blossom and analyzed it by lighting a small fire in his hand. He watched as the magical fire seemed to lean towards the flower as if being blown by an invisible wind. The flower was large enough to drain a few people of all their magic, but with the Malum wall, anyone could have been tricked into coming into the room.

As Inferneous moved aside, the more rotted bodies trying to find the stem of the flower, he realized another horrid fact. The bodies would never have been directly under the plant because no one would ever have the magical or physical strength to climb under it and die.

The Malums have been feeding it and were planning to use it to feed the Malum in the fountain, he thought.

He moved a skeleton away from the base, and in recognition he reached out and grabbed the stem of the Lifeweed blossom and pulled. He could feel the magic start draining faster as he pulled harder, the flower fighting hard to remain alive. With one last heave, he uprooted the flower. Its petals lost their hue and wilted, breaking off and disintegrating into black dust. The center bud of the flower yet remained glowing as Inferneous scooped it out of the dust and slammed it into the ground. Like glass, it shattered, and Inferneous had to shield his eyes from the flash of magic.

He felt a rush of magic returning to him, and as he removed his arm from over his eyes, he saw Holdren, Erica, and all of the soldiers waking slowly, already looking healthier than a minute ago. Inferneous sighed in relief as he pulled Holdren and Erica to their feet.

"What happened?" Holdren asked groggily, holding his head and blinking slowly.

"Lifeweed blossom. Almost sucked both of you dry of magic," Inferneous said, smiling and patting him on the back.

"Come on, we still have to take care of the fountain outside." He walked back to the doorway, but as he got closer, he saw where the doorway was; instead, there was now a black wall.

Inferneous smiled and shook his head, mumbling, "Stupid Malums…they really don't understand…" He waved his hand around his body, and he went up in orange flames.

When the flames died down, his body was covered in a fiery orange armor. The armor glowed faintly, radiating heat. Inscribed into every piece was a sigil of fire, and when it pulsed orange, Inferneous walked straight into the wall. The Malum's flesh burned away, igniting the whole wall in orange flames. As Inferneous reached the other side, the wall collapsed into black ashes, just like the Lifeweed blossom. Inferneous smiled wider as it did and said, "They don't understand. They won't ever stop me."

The soldiers and ninjas stepped out into the greenhouse led by Holdren and Erica as Inferneous threw the greenhouse doors open. A ways away from them was a small group of five ninjas surrounded by ten humanoid Malums. They scratched and hissed at the ninjas, and the ninjas fought back, trying to keep a steady defensive formation, but Inferneous could see the slack in their legs and the sweat on their brows. "Hey!" he yelled out.

The humanoid Malums turned in his direction, and he waved his arm, a spear made out of fire manifesting in his hand. He threw it at the first Malum, and it immediately disintegrated, leaving only a small human-sized Malum core on the ground.

He looked behind him and yelled, "Crush the cores! I'll handle the rest!"

Inferneous then leapt into action. As the Malums rushed toward him, he made light work of them, splitting his spear in two, and the halves morphed into two broad sabres. With a caterwaul, he started to slash and cut his way through them. His form was impeccable, with one-step strength radiating out of him as he cleaved one Malum's head clean off with his left hand. With his right, he pushed through to stab another two Malum's in the chest. Both Malums didn't even disintegrate by the time he had moved on to the rest. With a flick of his right wrist, three Malums fell, missing their heads as they disintegrated, and with his left, he cleaved through four, separating their torsos from their legs.

He settled in front of the Ninjirates that were surrounded, swords raised, ready for more but he looked around and only saw Malum cores scattered around the ground.

He turned around and smiled at the soldiers, saying, "All right! Quick, crush the Malum cores before–"

He was interrupted by a loud roar behind the Ninjirates, and they all turned around in fear to see that six Malum hounds had just arrived. The largest one stepped forward and, with a guttural growl, sniffed a Malum core. Without hesitation, the hound devoured it, swallowing it whole. As the hound looked up, its body violently contorted, spasming and shaking. Spikes burst out of its back and maw, causing Malum's blood to spray across the gravel. It was over in seconds, but the change was permanent.

Three horns stuck out of the top of the Malum's head, making for a crude crown. The Malum raised its head and revealed its now massive fanged maw, drooling with slimy and grotesque anger. It raised its head up to the air and howled loudly, the other Malums immediately joining it in its cry.

Inferneous yelled to the Ninjirates, "Destroy the cores! Don't let Malum's consume them!" When he turned his attention back to the Malums he saw the biggest one was significantly closer and was staring him down. Inferneous stared back, racking his mind on what the Malum was capable of now that it had consumed a core. He was about to run and handle the other Malums, but a slight itch in his right hand stopped him. He lowered himself to the ground and placed his palm on the ground.

A circle of flames slowly rose from the ground as Inferneous held his hand there, and when he removed it, he ran as fast as he could. The Malum quickly started to dash after him, but just as it leaped over the circle, a large burst of flame came out of the circle. As the Malum flew to the side, a large wolf made of fire was left in its place.

Inferneous smiled as the wolf and the Malum engaged each other, knowing that would keep the Malum at bay. He turned his attention to the fountain in the center of the plaza. It was now void of human remains. He jumped on top of it, summoning a large ball of fire, and slammed it into the fountain. The fountain shattered to pieces, causing a large amount of viscous black Malum blood to spill across the gravel. All of a sudden, the sounds of Malums roaring and swords clashing against spikes stopped. He looked around and all the Malums were staring at him. They all were seemingly frozen as he held the Malum core he found inside the fountain in his hand. Before he could think, all the Malums in the square rushed after him. Immediately, Inferneous tried to create a ring of fire, but as he raised his right hand, he saw the canine Malum's jaw close over his forearm. He didn't feel the pain because a panic had set in his stomach as he turned, trying to get the Malum off his arm to be faced with three more humanoid Malums. He kicked one of them in the chest, and his foot ripped through the torso of the Malum, but the Malum continued to move, tearing at his leg. At this point, the rest of the Malum's piled on top of Inferneous as he fell to the ground.

The other Ninjirates watched in horror as the malus continued to pile onto Inferneous, compacting more and more until all of the Malums were one large shell of a writhing black mass. Holdren, wide-eyed and furiously worried, yelled out, "Inferneous!" and started to run toward the black mass. Someone grabbed his arm, and when he looked at what was stopping him from freeing Inferneous he saw it was Erica. "Let go! Inferneous is going to die!"

"No, he won't," Erica said in a low, calm voice as she eyed the black pile with what Holdren believed was an odd jealousy.

"He's never needed our help, and for as long as I've known him, he has never needed much of anyone's help." As Holdren followed Erica's gaze back to the pile, he noticed that the color of the pile had changed suddenly. It was pitch black when he had just laid eyes on it, but now it was a bright purple. It wasn't that the Malums had changed color, though; at the edges, it was still a pitch black, but at the center of the pile, it seemed almost a searing white. That's when the smell hit him. A putrid smell, worse than the smell of anything rotting for thousands of years and then being thrown into a fiery furnace. A smell that made Holdren gag, but as his nausea cleared, he realized what the smell meant. Erica put a hand on his back and said plainly, "Back up," as the pile started to glow brighter and brighter.

Holdren stepped back a few feet away just as the top of the pile formed a bubble on top and popped, releasing a heat that would have burned Holdren if he were closer. All the Ninjirates covered their eyes from the heat and light emitted. Through his fingers, Holdren couldn't help but look as the fire shot up and out of the pile in a straight line into the sky. As it reached just above the height of the buildings, it expanded into a cross beam, and the extremities of the flames formed a phoenix. The fire, although white hot, had a dark orange hue to it as the phoenix soared about. It circled the plaza once, then rose up higher into the air and dived back down into what remained of the pile. Another bright light shined as the Malum remains were incinerated, leaving Inferneous standing in the middle of a scorched radius. His head was adorned with a crown of flames again, and his eyes glowed a dark orange with white irises. He stepped up and out of the small burnt crater he had created and stretched his back as the crown dissipated and his eyes turned back to normal. He then wiped his hands off as a handful of dust rolled off onto the ground. Inferneous stood and walked over to Holdren and sighed as he said, "It's done. We are done here."

Holdren slouched in relief as he reached out his hand to Inferneous. Inferneous shook his hand at first but then was surprised to find that Holdren pulled him in for a hug. As Holdren stepped back, Inferneous nodded, saying, "Thanks for saving my life. I hope I can repay the favor."

Erica remained silent as the exchange happened, but after they were done, she made sure to yell out, "The fight's not over! We still have to go to the ruined castle and make sure that that black orb in the sky isn't a potential magical bomb." She pointed upwards and Holdren and Inferneous looked up to see that the orb was larger than any magical orb Inferneous could summon.

Inferneous looked toward Erica and nodded, "You're right. Get the men together and assess their wounds. Bring the extremely injured to me and—" Inferneous stopped as he covered his left ear, and his eyes widened as new information was presented to him magically. He turned quickly towards Holdren and Erica, saying, "Get the rest of the men to the castle; the rest of the Ninjirates will meet you there. Move as fast as you can; I don't think we have much time!" Then he burst into flames and flew off towards the West tower.

As Balast watched Jayce and Zack regroup with the rest, he put a hand to his ear and said, "What do you two see?"

In the crumbling towers of the East and West towers, Shiro and Kuro looked over Valde Cruz. Shiro couldn't believe how much he could see from the east tower. From the tower, he could see deep into the Intervallum sea and he could almost see the icecaps of the southern mountain ranges. To his left, he could see all of Valde Cruz, which was beautiful even if it was all basically in ruin. To his right, he could see miles of rolling hills, plains, and patches of forest decorating the beautiful landscape of Magia. He was sitting on the edge of the crumbling tile roof of the tower when he heard a buzz in his ear.

"How are things around the city?" Balast half said half barked into Shiro's ear. Shiro was used to it by now, but he was especially sensitive to it because of what he had just witnessed Balast do.

"There hasn't been much. Stray Malums have been roaming the streets, but I only count about fifteen to twenty. They seem to be looking for more humans." Shiro looked up and judged the size of the black orb in the sky. He shook his head as he relayed, "The orb has grown big, very big."

"I can see that. Kuro, respond! I need to know what's happening with Inferneous!" Balast yelled, no longer speaking to Shiro.

A few seconds passed before Shiro's brain started to work again. "Wait, Kuro and Inferneous aren't responding? What–" he stopped when a bright light blinded him to his left, and then a wave of heat washed over him. When he could see again, the breath left his lungs as a phoenix made of flames soared past the tower, almost burning and knocking Shiro off the tower. He watched as the phoenix circled the city and then dove back where it came from, right where Holdren and Erica's team was supposed to be.

"Kuro! Kuro! Are you there?" Shiro heard Balast start yelling, "Inferneous, answer me! Did you help Kuro? He asked for help minutes ago! I think the Malums are–"

Suddenly, Shiro couldn't hear Balast anymore. He waited for a second, thinking the magic was going to return, but it didn't. Shiro looked back out to Valde Cruz and realized that what he had seen before was not the same as now. Everything looked much smaller, and he couldn't even see the finer details of the west tower anymore. He shook his head, questioning what was going on when he heard the crunch of tiles behind him. He quickly turned around to see nothing but a loose roof tile fall off to the ground far below. He snuck forward to the missing tile space and checked around the pinnacle of the roof, making sure nothing was there. Once he made a full rotation, he sighed and started to climb down into the watchtower. The watchtower wall only had two openings, one which served as a lookout and the other was to light the harbor. Shiro lowered himself down to the lookout window and swung himself into the building. He stumbled forward a bit and his heart jumped a bit when he remembered that a good quarter of the floor had collapsed in, leaving a gaping hole that fell to the base of the tower. Shiro stepped back to the wall, but as he did, a deep growl sounded behind him. He turned around quickly but not quick enough as a spike pierced through his shoulder as a Malum limbed into the room. Shiro reacted quickly, and his forearms glowed red as he smashed the part of the spike still connected to the Malum and fell into the hole. He turned around mid-air, and his hands scraped and tore at the wall, slowing his momentum. He came to a complete stop as he held onto a loose stone with his left. He winced in pain as he came to a stop. His hands were scratched so badly that a few of his nails had fallen out, but even though the pain was excruciating, he would rather hold on than fall to the base of the tower. Shiro looked down and saw nothing; he was still high enough where the floor was still not visible, and all he saw was a misty darkness. He struggled to pull himself up, but just as he looked back up again, he saw the full breadth of the Malum that attacked him.

The Malum was currently taking the form of a large jaguar, but instead of limbs, it was just large spikes that it drilled into the tower walls to keep itself upright. Shiro scrambled to get a good grip on the stone he was holding onto as the Malum crawled closer, a guttural growl rolling through his body, making Shiro put more pressure on his hands. He was almost over the stone when there was a quick grinding sound, and the stone fell loose. Shiro curled into a ball as he felt the wind rush past his face, hoping to somehow survive the fall, he turned in the air until his forearms were facing the ground. As the seconds passed by, Shiro awaited death but hoped for something better as he plunged into the mist. As soon as he was through, he saw the rubble of the staircase that used to be and prepared for the worst. Shiro stared at his oncoming demise until the arms of Balast embraced him.

Shiro was surprised that Balast caught him, and as Balast set him down, he couldn't help but look up as the Malum that was chasing him roared out and detached itself from the wall, plunging down towards them. Shiro started to back away but Balast stood his ground. He crouched down, and on the dirt floor, he drew symbols, and when he was finished, they glowed a dark red. As the Malum plunged down, the rubble around Balast started to float and rotate, forming spikes upward. Balast watched in satisfaction as the Malum squirmed in the air, helplessly impaling itself. The rocks were formed in a swirled spike pattern, so as the Malum slid down the spikes, it not only impaled it further but splayed its flesh so far that its core was unprotected. Balast quickly shot a beam of light out of his hand, and the Malum stopped moving as its core disintegrated. He then turned to Shiro and grimaced as Shiro fell to the ground, bleeding profusely from his shoulder. Balast dropped to his knees, making sure Shiro didn't gain a concussion on a nearby rock.

Balast whispered some words, and Shiro's wound started to heal rapidly. As he came to, a question formed in both their minds, but Shiro voiced it first, "What happened to Kuro?"

Balast stood immediately turning left to face the direction where Inferneous and Kuro should be.

"Inferneous! Answer me! Kuro needs help immediately!"

"He's dead."

Balast took a step back, shocked. "What happened?"

Inferneous was covered in black Malum blood, and his face was covered in mild grief as he carried Kuro's body toward the rest of the Ninjirates. Balast answered his own question when he saw that Kuro had multiple wounds piercing his chest and arms. They were at the gates of the massive husk that was the Aureus empire's castle. The sky had grown darker, almost to the point of being nighttime, as all of the Ninjirates came together on the main street of the Aureus empire that directly ended in front of that gate. There were even still shadows of cartwheels imprinted on the road for how many people traveled the road. Balast stared at those shadows as Inferneous gently set Kuro in the arms of Shiro. This was the first time Inferneous was glad that the previous members of the High Shadow Ninjas still wore their masks. He didn't believe that he would have been able to control his powers if he could. Currently, Inferneous was engulfed in flames that burned so hot they were turning a white-orange color. The crown of flames on his head had larger spokes and flames than Balast had seen before.

Balast walked in front of Shiro and handed him a teleportation scroll and, without saying a word, strode forward to the large white iron gates of the Valde Cruz Castle. As Balast walked up to the doors, he observed that most of Holdren and Erica's men were leaning against walls or leaning on their weapons as they looked very drained from whatever they went through on the west side of Valde Cruz. He stepped toward Erica since Holdren looked too beaten and winded to speak.

"How many men do you still have?"

Erica looked at him and looked back at her men, then replied, "14 or 15. We are exhausted, though. We can't take on any more Malums."

Balast shook his head. "There's no going back now; this is the last part of the city to clear. Plus, you have Inferneous and I."

Erica's disdain didn't need to be hidden at the moment, but she still looked up at the door, trying to hide her innate fear.

"I promise you," Balast started, looking back at Inferneous and back at her. "We will finish this, no matter what." He yelled out, "We are going in now, everyone be on your guard!"

Balast and Inferneous stepped up to the door, and they nodded to each other. They pushed both doors open; loud screeching sounds came from both doors as they swung open to reveal a huge sunken dining room. It was almost shaped like a coliseum; the ceiling was so high up that you couldn't see the top, and the stairs ran an oval shape across the floor. Most of the stairs stopped just below the doorway, but some went higher to the second floor, which had railings for more spectators. As the Ninjirates cautiously entered, they marveled at the room for a second admiring its beauty, until they reached the top of the staircase and saw what was in the pit.

It was clear that there would be a deeper circle of stairs but they couldn't see them now. It looked like a large oval concavity with large steps downward and with stairs, like a small coliseum. But instead of an open area at the bottom, it was a black pool that filled halfway up the stairs. Larger than all the other fountains, this was almost a lake of black liquid. As Inferneous stepped forward, he covered his nose in disgust.

"By the angel, what is this?" he said, stepping towards the edge of the pool. As he did, the lake started to bubble and churn. As bubbles rose to the surface and burst out into the air, so did a large spiked tentacle. The tentacle had mouths along the length of its body, and as it rose, a chorus of shrieks sounded out, all of them sounding all too human. The Ninjirates all reigned and covered their ears as the sound tore and echoed throughout the castle.

Uncovering his ears, Balast yelled out, "Split up!" as the tentacle raised up and started to fall in the Ninjirate's direction. They all scattered out of the way of the tentacle as it first slammed through the wall and then through the door frame, smashing it to pieces. Balast and Zack went right, climbing the stairs to the second level to avoid the tentacle, while Inferneous and Jayce went to the left, staying on the ground floor. The Ninjirates split on their own occasion, but they all watched as they moved out of the one charged straight at the tentacle.

Rhinda fired up and started to glow a faint yellow as he dashed toward the tentacle. He ran forward, and as he reached the beginning of the flight of stairs, he leapt and sliced into the base of the tentacle. Inferneous laughed out loud as everyone else watched cut into the tentacle over and over again.

"That's it, Rhinda! Jayce, join us!" Inferneous said, stepping off the railing to fly toward the tentacle with a flaming sword forming in his hand. Jayce was about to join them when he heard a small cry behind him. The balcony was large enough for multiple tables to be set around, but it extended deeper into the castle. He heard a small cry come from behind doors slightly smaller than the front doors and he didn't hesitate to remove his foot from the railing and run toward it. As he reached the door, it burst open, and a humanoid Malum tackled him to the ground. He struggled as the Malum clawed and tried to bite him when Holdren cut it in half with his battleaxe and helped Jayce up. The Malum flopped to the floor, still trying to claw at Jayce, but he planted his heel firmly in its skull. Holdren defended him once more as another Malum came rushing at Jayce from inside the room. Holdren was able to behead this one and he grunted as he did so.

As the Malum fell to the ground, Holdren looked inside the room and yelled out, "There's people in here!"

Jayce stepped forward and saw that in the room they had revealed there were around ten people against the back wall, but in the center of the room was a fountain. Jayce immediately went into the room to destroy the fountain but was attacked by two more Malums hiding behind the doors. He cut off the first Malum's arm but wasn't able to dodge its other, earning a scratch on his face. Enraged, Jayce freed his left arm and punched the

Malum that scratched him, freeing his right hand; he then swung back at the Malum to his left, knocking it back a few feet. He then took his battleaxe to the right and sliced it in half by the waist. He smashed the Malum's head into the ground, and when he turned around, Holdren had already taken care of the other Malum. They nodded at each other as they stepped toward the fountain and smashed the central pillar, destroying the fountain. As it collapsed on itself, Jayce searched for the core of the fountain. The base started to leak Malum's blood onto the floor as Jayce drug his battleaxe through the blood, searching for something that wasn't there.

Holdren was helping the civilians get out when he looked back to Jayce and asked, "We have to get the civilians out of here!"

"The Malum core isn't here!" Jayce stared down at the Malum blood, now covering a good portion of the floor. "We have to destroy the core, or else this Malum may become something else."

Holdren ushered out the last civilian before yelling out, "It doesn't matter! All the civilians are out. Let us go help the others!" Holdren then stepped forward, but as he did, he stepped on the Malum blood.

Jayce then turned in horror to see the blood rise like a wave and cover Holdren. He fell to the ground, clawing at his face; he didn't dare open his mouth to yell out because of the fear of the Malum entering his body, so as the seconds passed, he clawed harder and harder. Jayce dropped to his knees and hesitated on trying to free Holdren lest he get covered himself.

"Someone get Inferneous!" he yelled out.

Erica, who was helping the civilians escape, heard his call and yelled out, "Inferneous! Jayce needs help!"

Inferneous, fighting the large tentacle with Rhinda in the middle of the room, stopped immediately in the air and glanced to the door and saw Holdren being consumed by the Malum blood; rushing over, he raised his hand to cast fire over Holdren. As Inferneous approached, the Malum blood retreated back into the room, flying past Jayce, it settled behind the broken fountain.

"I don't know what that is, but we need to find a way to destroy it. Where's the Malum core?!?!" Inferneous asked as Jayce helped Holdren, who was coughing, trying to gain back air.

"There wasn't one. I don't know what's happening, but it didn't have one. I destroyed the whole fountain and couldn't find it."

Inferneous's flames flickered, and he turned back to see Rhinda climbing to the top of the tentacle. Inferneous watched as Rhinda stabbed into the tentacle once more, and the tentacle jerked so wildly that he lost his grip on the handaxe he was using. Inferneous didn't hesitate, and before he knew it, they were both about to plunge into the black pool below. As Rhinda's body submerged into the pool, he prepared himself to feel the cold embrace, but before he reached the water, he saw a glint of a sharp gem out of the corner of his eye. He turned his head to face it, but the leg mid-air suddenly grabbed him. He was then flung to the ground, but he rolled and started to fly again; looking up he saw that Balast was floating above the water, looking down at where Rhinda had just fallen in. Inferneous was about to scream at him when the water started to bubble, and Rhinda emerged from the water. Inferneous stared at Rhinda in shock as Rhinda stood up, walking on the water.

"Did you see it?!?!?" Balast asked, dodging another swing from the tentacle.

Rhinda, who seemed to be glowing yellow all over, looked up to Balast and nodded. "It's directly under it!" He then retreated back to the front of the building as the tentacle kept trying to hit one of the Ninjirates.

Inferneous noticed as he observed the tentacle that it was flailing much more now and was less directed and more frantic ever since Rhinda fell in.

Balast landed in front of Inferneous and, in a hurry, relayed the information, "The tentacle's Malum core controls more than the tentacle. We need to destroy it. Can you do it?"

Inferneous smiled and immediately nodded. "I may need a boost, but we need to get up high."

"Let's go then," Balast said, flying up toward the tentacle and slashing it.

The tentacle flailed in his direction as Inferneous flew to the other side, sending fireballs into the base of the tentacle. Circling the tentacle, Balast and Inferneous flew up into the heights of the castle. When they were fully above the tentacles' reach, they both saw everything. From their height, they could see through the darkness of the pool to the very bottom. Right under the tentacle was a large purple shard that pulsed with every movement of the tentacle. Inferneous looked to Balast, raising his hand, readying to destroy the tentacle. Balast was going to do the same when a shiver of cold air blew down on them from above. Inferneous didn't feel it because of his flames, so Balast was the only one to look up and see that there were multiple smaller tentacles descending from the ceiling. Balast flew above Inferneous and brought out his wand. He threw the wand upward, splitting into many splinter-thin discs and slicing the tentacles, but more followed as the others regenerated.

As Balast sliced more, he looked further up and saw another large shard embedded in a sticky black ink that the tentacles were attached to. He realized what he needed to do and yelled out, "When I say, send an explosion behind you and destroy the core!"

"Ready when you are!" Inferneous yelled out, smiling eagerly.

Balast continued slicing the tentacles that got too close, monitoring which ones regenerated slower and trimming the ones that regenerated immediately. His eyes widened when the pattern changed, and everything fell into place as the tentacles surrounded him.

"Now!" Balast yelled.

Inferneous let out a war cry as he threw a ball of fire behind him and descended to the tentacle below. The ball of fire exploded, propelling both wizards. Balast flew upwards through the empty space the tentacles had made to try and surround him. Because of the explosion, it propelled him past the tentacles, and as he soared upwards, he reared back, gathering his want, and smashed the core. A loud boom echoed as Inferneous plummeted down and slammed the large orb of magic into the tentacle, splitting it in half and smashing through the submerged core at the same time. The castle shook as the tentacle fell, curling up into the pool and disintegrating into black smoke. As Balast flew down after the Malum at the top disintegrated, he discovered that not only did the tentacles disintegrate, the whole pool evaporated as well, only leaving the shattered husk of a Malum core. The Ninjirates gathered at the bottom of the stairs in a marble pit as the castle continued to shake and rumble.

"Everyone get outside! The castle might collapse!" Inferneous yelled out, sending them all running back to the crushed entrance.

They made it through as the top layers of the castle caved in, sending chunks of rock and dust into the walls. There was silence as the dust settled. When it did, Zack came up behind Balast and asked, "Is it over?"

Balast then looked up to the sky, and as the dust cleared, the large dark orb wasn't just still there; it was almost blocking out the sun with its size. Balast shook his head in frustration.

"I don't know what that thing is, and it's big enough that I can't imagine what it will do to us." He reached into his back pocket and brought out the rainbow-colored gem. It was slightly calming to feel Parquen's magic resonating from it.

"If we attack first, we are better off. Hurry up." Inferneous said, his flames bursting impatiently.

Balast nodded. "Hold your horses; this will only take a second." Balast held the gem out in front of him and uttered a few words that echoed throughout the Ninjirates' ears.

A faint glow set into the gem, and then it turned a bright white. Balast then dropped it on the ground with a small plinking sound.

As Balast stepped forward and looked up, Inferneous started, "Well, it's about time we–" he stepped back a shockwave of energy reverberated from Balast. Zack was knocked down from the blast, and everyone was blinded for a second as Balast stood there.

The light faded as soon as it came, but the silence didn't. Everyone stared at Balast as he stood there, a bit hunched over but relatively fine. Inferneous stepped toward him but stopped when the gem Balast dropped floated into the air and started to flash thousands of different colors in an instant. Colors of great magnitude and hue showed along with colors Inferneous had never seen before. The colors eventually slowed until the gem went clear then it shattered, sending shards in all directions. Inferneous dodged a shard that came his way but saw that a piece embedded itself in Beast's face. He was baffled because Balast could easily block it, so when he stepped toward Balast he was shocked to find Balast seemed to be comatose while standing.

"Balast!" Inferneous said, shaking him.

Balast awoke immediately and hugged Inferneous tight.

"What was that? Balast, what's going on?" Zack said, standing up. He saw Inferneous' face contort into a rage as Balast held him close and whispered something into his ear.

Zack was going to ask what happened again when he covered his ears. A large crack echoed across the land, making the wind blow towards the sea. The Ninjirates looked up and saw the orb had had a massive crack down the middle. They watched in horror as three large clawed hands pulled open the orb like a shell. As one half of the shell fell towards the ground, the other half shattered, and large thin pillars of obsidian shone through. Zack's eyes grew wide as he heard gasps from the other Ninjirates as a Malum exited its cocoon. It had a ring of large worms around its neck, each rotating around, mouths gaping open, showing rows of thousands of teeth. The Malum had the torso of a man but instead of flesh, it was covered in the skulls of every beast of Magia. The arms were wreathed in shadow, barely seated in reality, in contrast to the hands, which were mostly large blades capable of cutting forests in half. The head wasn't made out of Malum flesh at all but just a conglomeration of sharpened pitch-black horns. No eyes presented themselves; you could only tell it was a head by the mouth with thousands more teeth that almost extended into its chest cavity.

Zack closed his eyes many times in the face of the horror, but in the same respect, he couldn't keep them closed because of the abhorrent beast. Instead, he looked toward Infereneous and Balast, but it only lasted for a second as he saw that between them were two wispy lines of magic. An orange line was coming from Inferneous' chest, and a teal line was coming from Balast; where the lines met, a small golden orb floated above them.

Zack gasped as Balast looked at him one last time and said, "You will understand later. I'm sorry."

Balast then snapped his fingers, and instead of a white flash, the world went impossibly dark for Zack.

As Zack opened his eyes, Balast's face was still etched into his mind. The emotions that Zack saw crisscrossing across Balast's face were terrifying because they weren't completely logical for a person like Balast. Out of the mixture of anger, disappointment, and overall sadness, Zack saw a look of uncertainty that made Balast's face turn from the most powerful wizard, in Zack's eyes, to a normal, flawed man.

It took a minute before Zack blinked again as he realized that he was no longer a Valde Cruz. The area was, but he could tell they were surrounded by wood and moss because the smell was uncannily fresh. He bent down and felt dew on the grass underneath him, and he recoiled as the dew was colder than he would have thought. He heard rustling behind him, and as he turned around, lights from above them lit the room. Zack covered his eyes as they adjusted, but when they did, he saw that surrounding him was Jayce, Rhinda, Holdren, Erica, and Drathni. They were all blinking and looking around like they had just walked into a room and forgotten why they did so.

"Jayce?" Zack said softly.

Jayce looked toward him and then looked around again.

"Zack...what happened? I thought we were–" He completely turned around, scratching his head as he observed their surroundings. As Zack did so, too, he saw that the lights above them were just floating orbs of magical fire. They didn't flicker or wane, though; they kept a consistent stream of light. The walls were interwoven stands of trees, not rigid as usual, but they all flowed together like strands of fabric. There were pieces of leaves and trigs sticking out of the wall; as Zack got more familiar with the room, though, these random sticks and leaves were platforms leading upwards into the darkness above the orbs of flame. They seemed to be in a circular pit of some sort. Everyone was now fully conscious that they were not in Valde Cruz like they had been a few seconds ago, and the first one to ask the question was Erica, "Where in Magia are we? What did Balast and Inferneous do?" she said, stepping towards one of the walls and touching it. She recoiled as the wood wall reacted, and with a great creaking, the wood unwound itself to reveal a passageway. Standing directly in the middle of that passageway were Inferneous and Balast.

Balast was wearing his wide-brimmed red wizard hat, and Inferneous was wearing an actual set of armor instead of his magical flame armor, which caught the attention of everyone. Something was wrong. Along with the odd choices in fashion, they all noticed they had a pale blue outline to them, not so much like a ghost's, but they looked like they were not fully settled in this reality.

"Hello," Inferneous and Balast said in unison.

Zack grimaced and stepped back. "Those are most definitely not Balast and Inferneous."

Rhinda stepped forward and examined Inferneous, responding, "Of course, they aren't, but that isn't the real question here." Rhinda waved his hand toward Inferneous and Inferneous blocked it with a hand.

"I know this might seem uncanny, but I ask you to please follow us. There is a tale to tell," Balast said, eyeing Rhinda.

Inferneous smiled and turned around to head down the dark tunnel. Zack was the first to hesitate as the rest seemed to walk forward with them. As they all walked down the dark hallway, the only light source they had was the light blue silhouettes of Balast and Inferneous. They followed them as they took two turns down the hallways until a sloped appeared, and at the top, there was a bright, warm orange light that showed through. They couldn't see what was in the room until they reached the crest of the ramp. As they entered, Zack's mouth dropped in awe. The room was huge, and on every wall, there were thousands of books on thousands of shelves. On the ceiling lighting, the whole room was an upside-down tree that was on fire, constantly burning. It emitted a soft warmth making Zack realize he was so cold he was shivering. He couldn't look at the tree for too long because of its brightness. He looked down, seeing Balast and Inferneous stop in the middle of the room. As Zack walked further into the room he tried to read some of the book titles to see if there was anything of use. The main pathway was very wide, so he wasn't able to discern anything of use, really.

"The story starts at the beginning of Magia when only two things floated in the Aether of nothing: God and magic. There were…"

"Stop." Jayce stepped toward the fake Inferneous, who had started speaking. "We don't care about whatever fancy story you have to tell us. All we care about is that you explain where and why we are here."

"Well, you are here because you were born on Magia. Magia was created–"

"What he means is that you can skip all the way to the part where we blackout at Valse Cruz. We don't want to know the history of everything, just the history of the Ninjirates," Rhinda spoke adamantly.

As he did, Inferneous' expression changed. His head tilted to the left as if he were listening to someone speak into his ear. He then looked to Balast, and Balast nodded.

"Balast and Inferneous are dead."

No matter how warm the room was or how bright the flames were, they could not stop Zack's blood from running cold or stop the world around him from going back to a familiar darkness.

"What?" Zack and Jayce said in unison.

"They have sacrificed themselves for the greater good," fake Inferneous said with an unwavering tone. Zack sank to his knees as tears flowed down his face.

Jayce stepped back and chuckled, but then something snapped as he realized that there wasn't any reason for the copies of the wizards to lie to them. He then started, "There isn't a way they could die. I mean–" Jayce looked around. The thought had never crossed his mind and now it felt like it was burning a hole through him and his reality.

Erica stepped toward the fake Inferneous and started screaming, "You're lying! There is no way that Inferneous could have died! There isn't–" She stepped back as memories cashed past her eyes as the fake Inferneous stared at her blankly. She stepped back more, and Holdren caught her as she almost fell to the ground. She put a hand over her mouth as her eyes watered in horror.

Holdren helped Erica up and said, "Prove it. Those two would not have died unless they wanted it to happen."

The fake Inferneous and Balast turned back around and continued, "This is the library; it will be the source of your wisdom for the years to come. Over half of this library is written by Balast himself. The rest are all the books they could find, spanning from all over Magia."

All of them followed except Zack. He sat there unmoving, and Jayce was the only one who looked back to see him still sitting there. He ran back and grabbed Zack's arm, "Come on, we have to figure this out."

Zack went limp in his hands, eyes glazed over in disbelief and sorrow.

Jayce sighed, then grunted as he picked Zack up, carrying him on his back. When Jayce caught back up with the rest they had reached the far wall of the library. Between two bookcases that reached about fifteen feet up, there was a large space. On the wall in the space, there was a glowing rune that looked like an Angel's wings.

"This library may contain the world's best scholars, but if you want to know the truth about this place, you will need to go to the helm, where you will have all the materials you need to direct the ship."

"The ship?" Rhinda asked. "We are on a ship right now?"

"Biggest ship I have ever been on or in," Holdren said, looking around. "Prove it. No man could build a ship this big. I've seen banquet halls smaller than this."

The fake Balast placed his hand on the wall, and the insignia glowed brighter and disappeared. The wall unwound itself and showed another incline. They walked through, and as they came to the top, they were astonished. At first, the room seemed dark, but as their eyes adjusted, they could see thousands and thousands of stars. Even Zack couldn't help but look as Jayce carried him into the room. Seemingly, there was no ceiling; the floor was made out of grass but all they could see above them was stars. As they looked down a bright light blinded them as huge sails of light appeared in front of them over an impossibly large deck of a ship. It was all made out of twisting trees, and they couldn't even see the front of the ship where they were. There was no land, oceans, or even a sky, just the varying sizes of stars and planets.

"Oh my god," Rhinda said, taking it all in. "We aren't even on Magia."

The fake Inferneous nodded and waved his hand. As he did, Holdren and Jayce had to move more toward the center of the room when five tree roots came out of the ground. More came out, but they only surrounded the originals to make two tree root stands on the left and right, with one at the head of the room. As the roots settled, lights appeared over them illuminating the tops of them. Looking closer Rhinda saw that each tree root had a book propped up by a different colored flower.

"This is all we can show and tell," Balast said, waving his hand to summon his wand. He walked toward Jayce and stood there waiting for something.

Jayce set Zack down and said, "I think he has something for you." Zack stepped forward with a shaky breath toward the fake Balast.

"Zack, I want you to have my wand. Please make it your own and use it to defend those who have been abandoned and forsaken, just like I did for you. Become a man that is capable of handling those who need and refuse help with extreme care."

Inferneous then walked up to Jayce and pinched him lightly on the shoulder but kept his fist there as he said, "Jayce, you are a leader capable of ruling a fine empire already, don't fall for it. Kings want the kind of companionship and camaraderie you exude; they only lose it because they grow too far from the people they want to affect." He removed his fist and burned onto Jayce's chest was a runic insignia of a magical flaming crown.

The fake Balast and Inferneous backed up to the front of the room, and Balast continued, "And one last parting gift, from the both of us to Magia."

Inferneous then continued as they raised their hands to chest level, and a golden orb started to glow in front of them, "We never want anyone to suffer from a separation like us, so we want to bless Magia with one last spell as a farewell."

The golden orb between them started to reach the floor as it grew in size. The wind started blowing toward the fake Balast and Inferneous from seemingly nowhere as they charged the spell. Then, they both stepped forward and thrust the magic toward the group, and they were all blinded as they were consumed with their magic. When they could see again, they were in the same room, but all that was left on the floor was Balast's burgundy wizard hat and a small pile of sparkling golden ashes.

"I don't know exactly what happened, but it looks like we won't be seeing them again," Rhinda said, stepping forward to the book at the front of the room. He looked up into the empty space of the stars, and all at once, he realized what was happening. Turning around to face the others, he nodded solemnly. "It looks like they really are gone. I don't–" He looked at the ground as if it would leave his feet, then looked back towards the others.

"They didn't even leave us a proper explanation."

"You can't say that," Holdren said, stepping forward. "They gave us a whole library full of information! We have to find the truth for ourselves."

"We shouldn't have to do that though! The least you could do as a wizard with power as they did is to at least make better magical copies of yourselves!"

"Stop!" Jayce said, coming between the two of them. "We are somewhere unfamiliar, and we need to orient ourselves. The one thing we do now know for certain is that Balast and Inferneous are gone. No matter how abandoned we feel, we can't ignore the months of protection and care they gave us while trying to eradicate the Malums." He went around and examined each book until he picked up one and gave it to Rhinda.

"The title of that book is The History of Magia by Balast. They did give us explanations."

Rhinda turned the book over and nodded. "You're right."

Jayce then nodded but continued, "I don't believe there is a way for them to still be alive if they left all of this for us. Something bad must have happened, and we can't ignore that by saying they abandoned us because in truth." He picked up the book from the front of the room and squeezed it tightly. "In truth, they are still here with us. All the times where they were strong for us, all the times they became weak for us," Jayce faltered as his voice shook.

Zack then chimed in, "They became weak for us so we could become stronger." Gripping Balast's wand tightly, he said, "If they were to die for us, that means they wanted to make us live longer."

"They tore us down when we thought we couldn't get any higher," Erica said, wiping her tears away. "To show us that we were limiting ourselves the whole time."

Drathni then stepped forward and said, "They cared for us as a whole, not showing favorites for one, but showing favor for all." She then looked to Rhinda, who was looking down at the book in his hands with an angry misunderstanding. He then said as he opened the book, "They overcame their own problems so that they could solve all of ours. They were truly honorable; I cannot lie."

Jayce nodded as he said, "Yes. The question is now, are we going to run away? Or are we going to do our best to follow in their footsteps and be true Ninjirates?"

There was silence as Rhinda flipped through the book and then started to read aloud what Balast and Inferneous had done in their final moments.

Epilogue

Balast had never felt this old before. He sat up from the broken piece of rubble and stretched, multiple bones creaking in protest. He scratched his chin which now had a full beard grown onto it, scruffy and unkempt. He grabbed his wand and it formed into a knife as he raised it up to his beard. A quick slice and the hair fell toward the ground but stopped just before it touched the cobblestone of Valde Cruz. He sighed and looked up behind him to see the Ninjirates standing in front of the collapsing ruins of the Valde Cruz castle along with the massive, hideous beast that was the Belarus Rex, otherwise known as the Malum King. The massive Malum was rivaling the size of the castle as its massive chest and tentacles floated over it, imposingly frozen in time. Balast noted its horrible features, from the living black worms writhing around its neck and hollow chest to the hundreds of large obsidian pillars protruding out of its back and arms.

It is large but not as large as our creation… Balast thought as he grew sad as he looked in the other direction to see that on the Intervallum sea was a ship larger than the castle itself, interwoven trees making its hull mast almost breach the atmosphere. It was time.

"Balast!" Balast heard a voice come from above, and he saw a large form of a man with hair spilling all over. Balast looked up in disgust and waved his hand. His wand raised up and shot towards the man, cutting all of his excess hair off.

As the hair fell to the ground, the man yelled out, "No!"

Then the hair fell, revealing Inferneous with a nice mustache, flame armor still ignited under the pound of hair he had grown.

"My masterpiece of a beard! How could you, Balast!" Inferneous said, flopping to the ground.

"That was my longest streak of fifty years without cutting it!" Balast chuckled.

"You look better now. Plus, it's time." He stood up and placed his hands on his hips, facing toward the Malum King. "It's time to send them off."

Inferneous stood, pulling the excess hair off of him, and sighed as he stepped next to Balast, but instead of looking toward the Malum King, he looked at the Ninjirates at the foot of the castle. He breathed in deep, and fire blew out of his nose as he exhaled.

"I think, I think there is a lot more we could have done with them, but at the same time I think we taught them all that was really possible with the time we had." Inferneous looked at Balast, and he smiled softly as he saw Balast was holding his hand over his eyes, trying to hide his obvious tears. Inferneous put a hand on his shoulder and stood in silence as Balast cried freely.

"Ok, I'm ready," Balast said, sniffing and wiping his tears away. He turned toward Inferneous and said, "I agree with you. I just wanted to say that I think in every vision I have glimpsed in, you have always been there. Either dealing with my emotional inequities or really just stopping me from delving into the worst depths. I can't begin to apologize to you for everything I've done." He choked up a bit at the last part but stopped himself.

Inferneous nodded and responded, "It was never just you. I don't remember it ever being just me, either. We have both made mistakes." He turned to look at the Ninjirates one more time, seeing each face.

"Jayce, Zack, Rhinda, Holdren, Erica, and Drathni. Those people are going to create a lasting legacy that I can't even imagine." Inferneous looked to Balast, and forcing a smile, he said, "Even if it was just us after Diadus and Parquen died, I don't think that's what it was supposed to be. I think, in truth, we have been afraid to create something to support us because that would be an admission of something."

"What would that be?" Balast asked.

Inferneous stayed silent as he and Balast looked towards the Ninjirates and said, "Well, I still don't think I'm quite ready to admit it." They both chuckled lightly.

"I forgive you, and I hope you will forgive me," Balast said, standing up and embracing Inferneous one last time.

"Same here," Infereneous said as they turned back towards the castle.

They stood there looking at the picture frozen in time of the Ninjirates waiting to face Belarus Rex and enjoyed it for a few more minutes. Balast then let go of Inferneous and snapped his fingers. The Ninjirates disappeared, and they both covered their ears as a large boom sounded behind them. They turned around to see the massive ship grow large golden magical sails and leave the planet, rocketing into the sky with unparalleled speed. As they looked back, they saw the Malum King slowly move back into motion. It immediately looked down at both of them and let out a paralyzing scream. Ingenious flames grew larger, and magical lightning curled around Balast as they dashed forward, jumped, and flew toward the Malum King.

"Remember Inferneous! Let it destroy the castle first, then wait for my signal!"

Inferneous nodded and laughed as a large worm lunged at them and then split off into different directions. Belarus Rex writhed around, letting the worm leap from its neck, descend onto the castle and destroy the towers and base of it. The spiked pillars spun vigorously as the Malum King swiped at Inferneous, who was blasting large balls of fire at it. Balast, on the other hand, rolled his sleeves up and activated the glowing purple runes etched into his arms. He turned invisible and flew around Belarus Rex started searching for something on its body. He ducked and dodged stray tentacles and Malum worms as he did, but when he reached the back of the Malum, he saw what he was looking for. A ring of white obsidian pillars sticking out of the back of the Malum King with a statue in the center. He quickly flew down toward it and landed on one of the pillars, pulling out of his pocket a small smithing hammer. He struggled as the Malum moved; every time it took a swipe at Inferneous, he was almost flung off the obsidian pillar. He managed to get his footing and started to walk toward the statue, and just as he reached the flesh of the Malum, it swung again, knocking him off the pillar. He managed to bring out his wand and stab it into the obsidian, causing cracks to splinter into the obsidian. As he climbed back up, he reached the statue. He stretched to try and reach the top of the statue, almost slipping from the until the hammer floated to where it was when they found it, right above the statue's hand. As relief flooded into Balast, the pillar shattered, and Balast started to fall to the ground. He spiraled in the air, trying to regain his balance, when he collided with another person. When he got his breath back, he realized Inferneous had caught him.

"Hey! Get yourself together; we can't fail this time!" Balast nodded and smiled as Inferneous set him down on a nearby building.

Balast then jumped and began to fly again. This time, he followed Inferneous as they started to leave the Malum King's reach. As they reached the beach, they watched as the Malum King started to fly after them. As it reached the edge of the castle, though, a golden light exploded from its back, and it was pulled back over the castle. It tried to claw at its back, but a golden shield blocked the ring of white obsidian from being destroyed. The Malum King roared out again, then descended into the castle. As the castle crumbled beneath it, there was a faint purple glow as it started to tear through the bedrock of the tower.

"Here it comes," Balast muttered under his breath as he and Inferneous watched.

The Malum tore through the bedrock with a few swipes, and after a fourth swipe, it stopped as the ground crumbled, revealing thousands of purple flowers glowing with a sick radiance. Thousands of corpses were scattered around the flowers, but the roses hid most of them with their roots. The Malum grabbed the sides of the castle, raised up, and slammed its tentacles into the flowers, burying its bottom half in the ground. It roared again as it started to glow a dark purple and grow, and grow, until it started to block out the sun of Valde Cruz.

Balast looked to Inferneous, and Inferneous looked back as Balast said, "I'm glad we are friends again."

"We never stopped being friends," Inferneous said, summoning a large ball of flame. "Let's finish this!"

They both started to fly straight towards the Malum King, summoning all their magic to one point. Inferneous outstretched his right hand, and Balast outstretched his left as they flew together toward the Malum king. The Malum king swiped at them, but its massive claws burned off as they collided with Balast and Inferneous. They both summoned large orbs of magic, Inferneous wreathing himself in orange flames as a crown of flames encircled his head and Balast summoning an orb of teal blue lightning, thundering in his hand. As the Belarus Rex opened its mouth to swallow them whole, their magic intertwined, turning golden. As they descended into the Malum, they looked at each other and smiled. As the Malum closed its mouth, a sun formed between its jaws, exploding everything around it and disintegrating through the Malum King. The explosion reverberated through the ground into the mass of Lifeweed under the castle. The second explosion decimated the bedrock, sending massive cracks across the planet, and consuming everything in their paths. Oceans and storms raged as everything came to an end. Volcanoes erupted, and oceans boiled as the planet erupted into pieces. All that was left was shards of a planet and a red wizard's hat surrounded by golden flecks of ashes into the Aether of lights.

About the Author

Tarrence Bryant Jr. is an eighteen-year-old who lives with his mother, father, and little brother in Torrance, California. He loves listening to and sometimes creating music, drawing, and especially writing fiction and science fiction. Ever since he was nine years old, he has had a universe of stories developing and growing in his head, waiting to be written down someday. He has won the most creative writing award at his online school and created a creative writing club at El Camino College in Torrance, CA from scratch that is still running today. He plans to write multiple books and hopes to move out and buy a cat as soon as he can.